If only s

Elevator Girl

KIM HRUBA

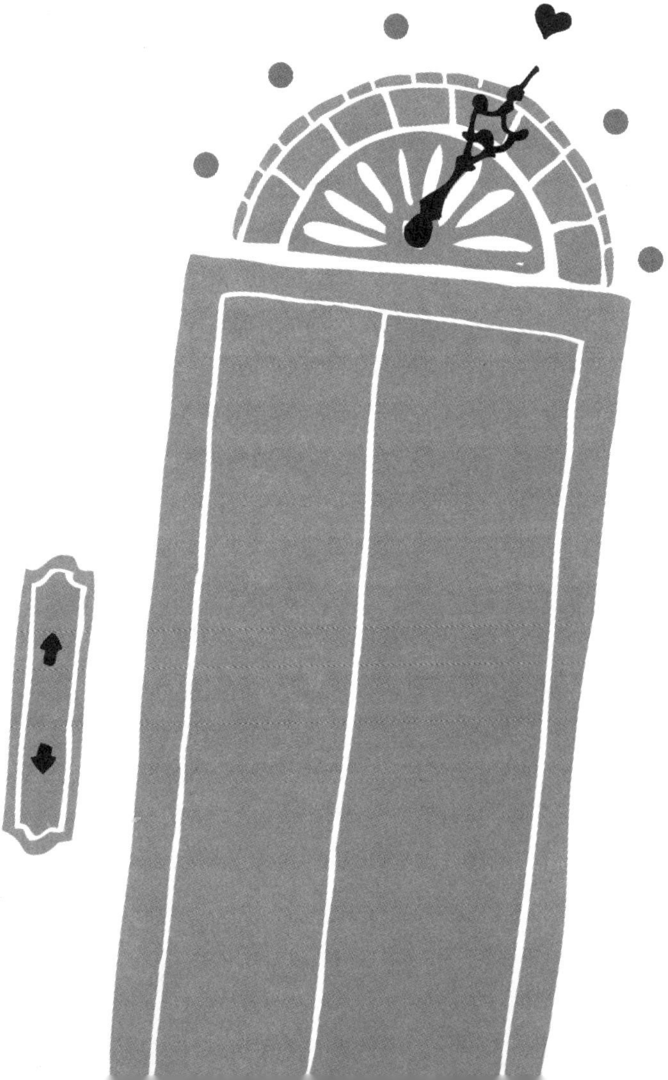

Elevator Girl

KIM HRUBA

Kim Hruba

ISBN 13: 978-1-940014-21-0
LCCN: 2014939700

Printed in the United States of America

First Printing: 2014

17 16 15 14 13 5 4 3 2 1

Cover design by Jessie Sayward Bright
Interior design by Tiffany Laschinger

WISE Ink
CREATIVE ★ PUBLISHING

Wise Ink, Inc.
53 Oliver Ave S.
Minneapolis, MN 55405
www.wiseinkpub.com

Reseller discounts available.

To the memory of my father, Jerry Koster, who would have been proud of this book, even if it's not about race cars.

Chapter 1

If she had known that she would see Jake Hanson in the elevator this morning on her way to work, she would have taken the stairs. All twenty-four flights.

She ducked behind her brown Flying Moose travel mug. *Please don't notice me, please don't notice me,* she thought, while memories of her teen years flashed before her eyes. A quick shoe count revealed five people in the elevator, leaving only three individuals as human foliage for Lisa Johnston to hide behind—or rather in front of.

Just seconds earlier, after hustling to the elevator then settling into the front spot—leading the pack, so to speak—she'd been musing about how great her life was. She had even splurged on a skinny latte from the Green Bean as a small way of celebrating all of the reasons she had to be happy. While enjoying the milky warmth of her latte, she'd gotten that sixth-sense feeling that a good-looking masculine specimen was in the vicinity. She'd scanned the mirrored interior of the elevator, covertly verifying her hunch. And she hadn't been wrong. Her eyes landed on the reflection of a man standing in the back, to the left of a woman wearing glasses with lime green frames. He was indisputably gorgeous. And for a few seconds at least, that's all he was.

His light blue eyes glinted like crystals and smoldered with coolness under his dark eyebrows. His brown hair was cropped short and his sideburns accentuated his angular face perfectly. She could see the trace of a dimple, ready to dazzle when he smiled. She wondered if modeling was his day job.

As her eyes had lingered on his smooth lips, another sixth-sense feeling crept under her skin. The face seemed ... familiar. She couldn't remember having met him recently. She was generally good with names and faces, and wouldn't have forgotten a face as striking as that. Had he been in a Calvin Klein ad? A Target flyer? Maybe he'd been on television.

Then—*Oh ... my ... God.*

Lisa had dropped her eyes, her heart had spasmed, and the elevator's interior had shrunk to claustrophobic proportions. It was not only a face she recognized, but one she had hoped to never see again—*ever.*

And now, here she was, hiding behind a moose on a cup.

Hefting her purse farther onto her shoulder, she took a deep breath. A heady bouquet of something floral consumed the already too small space, adding to the pressing anxiety rapidly filling her chest. Keeping her eyes pinned to her cabernet toenails showing through her favorite sandals, she resisted the urge to check if the man indeed was who she thought he was. She could recall with uncomfortable clarity just how good-looking *that* guy had been; that when he smiled those blue eyes crinkled cutely and a dimple *did* form in his right cheek. Did the man behind her really have a dimple or was it a scar?

She could sense, even three people deep, that the man was probably in great shape, like the person she had known. Any curiosity about how big his muscles were wasn't enough to make her want to peek, not because she couldn't appreciate a fine-looking man when she saw one, but because if it was Jake Hanson, *that* changed everything.

Behind her moose cup, she shook her head. It couldn't be him. *No way.* Sure, she'd thought about him once or twice over the years; even imagined meeting him. But in an elevator? Where she worked? With no escape? Even she couldn't have made up such a scenario. Her mind had to be playing tricks. The brain could do funny things, like match a familiar face to a stranger's; she'd read about it.

What if they got off at the same floor? The thought made her shudder. If that happened they were bound to make eye contact, because that's how it was when you got off the elevator with someone else at the same time. You locked eyes as if to say, "Please, go ahead. No, you go; I insist. Very well, thank you." Maybe she'd get lucky and they'd do the eyes-down shoulder shove. Or what if she got off first and he glanced up, because that was another law of elevator riding—*always look to see who got off first.*

She heard the high-pitched ding of the elevator bell as the door opened to the thirteenth floor. She cringed, trying to remain calm while bracing for the inevitable. The two men standing behind her, both wearing shiny black loafers with tassels, opted for the shoulder tactic. Their momentum pushed her to the far right corner, causing her purse to bump with wrecking ball force into the button panel. *So much for remaining incognito.*

Her cheeks hot, she glimpsed back into the mirrored reflection and saw that the guy she thought she recognized hadn't moved an inch. Their eyes met and the right side of his mouth perked up a tiny bit, denting his cheek with what definitely was not a scar. She pretended not to notice and glared at the backs of the exiting men, throwing invisible chains around their necks. The slight puff of cool air that sneaked in as the elevator closed provided no comfort against the sweat that had sprung up on her skin.

Freaking out was unwarranted, she reasoned, even if he was who she thought he was. Just because she recognized him didn't mean he would recognize her. Regardless, she willed herself to melt into the wall. The muscles in her neck wailed their protest as she turned her head as far to the right as possible. Her hands were sticky as she tightened her grip on the leather strap of her purse. She took another sip of her celebratory latte, which now tasted lukewarm and less cheery.

Then a chilly sensation tickled the back of her neck. She had an urge to brush the hair out of her eyes—which was ridiculous, because she had no hair in her eyes. While pushing away the bothersome, nonexistent hair, she felt a shift in the elevator and heard a baritone voice say, "Looks like it'll be nice today."

She glanced over ever so slightly, noticing that the void left by the black loafers had been filled by brown, expensive-looking Italian leather shoes tied neatly with slim, chocolate laces. Her eyes followed the shoes along the creases of a pair of crisp tan dress pants, to a brown belt with a muted gold buckle, and up a modestly striped powder-blue tie to his face. Sure enough, although older and with a bit more ruddiness in his cheeks, the very person Lisa had been hoping to avoid looked directly at her with a lopsided, hey-baby grin and that trademark dimple. He was *exactly* who she thought he was. Her mind blanked. The elevator bell dinged again and this time opened to her floor. She mumbled some form of agreement to his weather forecast then leapt from the elevator like a lion released from a cage.

. . . . .

The first time Jake had seen the woman, he'd been on his way to his first day at the new job.

Standing off to the side in the lobby of his new office building, he'd been checking his watch—not wanting to arrive too early—when, like a linebacker, she'd barreled through the revolving doors. A coffee in one hand, her eyes glued to a magazine in the other, she hadn't even bothered looking to see if anyone was coming and narrowly missed a head-on collision with a guy equally intent on texting. The guy looked up at the last moment and swerved out of her way, clutching his cell phone like a wide receiver. While most women would have yelped, this woman had only regarded the man coolly and continued on her way, unfazed. Jake had been amused and wondered if the woman was also employed with the law firm of Smith, Hakkula, and Schuler, or as he and his colleagues called it between themselves, "Smacker."

She hadn't shown up at his forty-third-floor office, which at the time he thought was probably just as well. His opportunity with Smacker had been his big break—his first opportunity to run with the big dogs—and he wanted to make a good impression. After law school, Jake had taken a job with a small firm in the Twin Cities suburbs. It was a good place to work, but he had spent most of his time drafting wills and divorce decrees. He hadn't become a lawyer to be a paper pusher; he'd become a lawyer to defend justice. He wanted a piece of the action. Smacker was a much bigger, high-profile firm in downtown Minneapolis and, so far, had proven to be the perfect boost for his career. The paperwork hadn't gone away. In fact, in less than two months, it had already tripled in size. But he got to go to court, the cases were more interesting, and he'd finally be able to afford that Audi he had his eye on.

Since that first day, he'd spied the woman twice more: once again in the morning, and once during a lunch break, plowing unwittingly through the lobby like an errant bull, her eyes fixed on her reading material. What kind of woman did that? Either she had some kind of internal GPS or trusted people to clear a path, because she seemed to have this thing about reading and walking at the same time.

Nevertheless, she'd caught his attention and he couldn't shake it.

So this morning, when she blew through the doors, he knew he would talk to her. Already standing by the elevators, he gauged the timing of her arrival with that of the elevator's. Surprisingly, today she only had a travel mug of some sort in her hand. Looking straight ahead, she locked in her trajectory toward his elevator. The doors opened and he stepped in with several other people, taking a spot in the back, confident she would arrive. As predicted, the woman squeezed between the doors just before they closed, and she turned to face forward.

Despite the two men in front of him, both with graying hair and matching bald spots and who partially blocked his view, Jake studied the woman as best he could. She wasn't unusually tall, so that didn't explain why people parted for her. Short people could be all elbows when they wanted to assert power, but she wasn't unusually short, either. He guessed she was about five feet five.

Jake followed the contours of what he could see of her body, confirming what he could make out in the reflection of the mirrors, and filling in the gaps with his imagination. He scanned her legs and found well-defined calves below the hem of a navy blue skirt that landed straight and sensibly just above the knob of her knee. She appeared to be slender but not skinny, and he wondered if she worked out. He craned his neck a bit to the left, but couldn't see enough of her front to make any kind of determination.

But his senses nagged him, insisting there was something about her; what, exactly, he didn't know. His skin tingled with the curiosity of just how powerful she was. What did she do for a living? Did she work in the building, too? Why wasn't she reading today and why was she holding her coffee cup so close to her face that it looked like she was trying to rest her head on it?

The older lady standing next to Jake bumped into his right elbow as she fiddled with a large quilted handbag. Her green glasses matched her outfit and she smelled like lavender and talc, reminding him of his grandmother. She beamed a smile of bright red lipstick, raised her eyebrows, and shrugged an apology. The lady rummaged through her bag a few seconds more, then snapped the clasps together before swaying back to her own spot. He subtly exhaled, clearing his nose of her overpowering scent and powder.

He heard a bell and the elevator slowed to a stop. The two men in front of him moved forward, simultaneously crowding the woman he'd been watching as they shouldered their way out. The woman scowled and readjusted her purse on her shoulder. She was leaning so close to the far wall—into the mirror, really—that her body looked like it had two heads. Her face had a natural look about it, which meant she probably didn't wear a lot of makeup. Then her eyes flickered and their gazes briefly met in the elevator's reflection. Her eyes were blue. He gave her a small smile. She darted her eyes to another corner of the elevator, and brushed her hand along the side of her face. Her hair was up, honey-colored strands neatly twisted into a bun that was playful, yet professional enough for the office. After the doors closed, he sidled into the vacant spot next to her. Closer, he could smell a hint of a whimsical fragrance. Her face looked a little red. Was it hot in here? He didn't think so.

"Looks like it'll be nice today."

As soon as he said it, he knew it really was as stupid as it sounded. Talking about the weather; what a dumb ass. Before he could think of a new topic, the elevator stopped again, the woman said something he didn't quite catch, and then she stepped out.

In the reflection, the green-glasses grandma was still smiling.

Chapter 2

Lisa made a beeline for her cubicle, hung her jacket in its designated spot, and flung her purse under the desk before grabbing her laptop and folder of handouts. Her heart palpitated in time with her steps as she walked briskly down the short length of hall to her first meeting of the day. When she approached the glass-encased conference room, she saw her boss, Susan, arranging a silver-colored plastic tray with some packets of creamer and sugar and several mugs bearing the foundation's logo. A pleasant aroma of coffee floated through the room and Lisa inhaled deeply as she set her own limp latte on the long black table and took a seat.

She flipped open her laptop and watched it go through the start-up motions. *Jake Hanson. Wow.* Her heart, although considerably calmer, continued to flutter as she replayed the last two minutes of her life.

What *were* the odds of seeing him again? While she'd *hoped* she would never run into him again, it wasn't realistic to expect she'd *never* see him again—especially if they were both living in the Twin Cities. It was statistically bound to happen. What that exact statistic was she didn't know, but seemed to recall some hazy data on the subject in *Shape* magazine. Even if there hadn't been a study, just last week she'd bumped into her old babysitter at First Avenue, so she had enough evidence right there to convince her that running into Jake in an elevator shouldn't be surprising at all.

But "Nice day, isn't it?"—What was that all about?

Lisa's coworker, Ingrid, entered the conference room. She poured herself a cup of steaming coffee, placing her own armload of paperwork on the table as she settled into the black leather chair next to Lisa. She felt Ingrid sizing her up as she stared at the paradise-beach landscapes rotating on her screensaver.

"Were you just running?" Ingrid asked.

"No. Why?"

"Your face is flushed."

Lisa could still feel a slight remnant of heat warming her face from her encounter with Jake. Taking one more breath, she clicked on a folder icon. "No. Nothing like that."

Ingrid sorted through her own handouts, laying them out neatly in five small stacks. "But there is something."

Should she get into it? Should she not get into it? Was it worth getting into? Lisa said, "I just saw someone."

Ingrid stopped straightening papers and turned toward her. "Oh?" And it wasn't that kind of *Oh?* that implied, *Okay, you can stop talking now.* It was the kind of *Oh?* with that rising inflection that begged her to tell more.

Before Lisa could respond, Susan stepped between them, placing a small assortment of muffins on the conference table, and asked, "Are you ready for the meeting?"

"Yes," Ingrid answered for both of them, while Lisa pulled up her PowerPoint presentation. Lisa shook her head, determined to rid her thoughts of Jake. Susan looked at Lisa, smiling politely, yet quizzically. It was Susan's Minnesota-nice way of shouting, "What? How can you not be ready?"

"We're ready," said Lisa, switching from shaking to nodding her head. "Everything's right here."

The worry lines across Susan's forehead smoothed out and she patted Lisa on the shoulder.

Lisa loved her job. It was one of the things she had been celebrating this morning before seeing Jake in the elevator. She worked for the Little Flower Foundation, a nonprofit organization whose primary mission was to improve the lives of children. One of the foundation's current projects, which Ingrid and Lisa had been assigned to, was the building of a park in the heart of the Nicollet neighborhood in Minneapolis.

Up until a half-century ago, this area of the city had been home to up-and-comers and the affluent. Anyone who had been anybody important had an affiliation with this neighborhood. Over time, with the aid of urban sprawl, the families there had packed up and moved to the suburbs. The beautiful homes left in Nicollet had been converted to cheap housing and the businesses, which had once thrived on the wealthy, had either dried up or relocated with their customers.

Today, the community struggled with the usual inner-city issues and was desperately in need of some positive growth and renewal.

The "vision" of this park was monumental in size and involved converting four city blocks into a safe community space for children and families. Whenever she talked about the project, she put the word "vision" in quotation marks, since it was one thing to have an idea and an entirely different thing to make it a reality.

The conceiver and chief financial backer of the "vision" was Grant Hollow, a lawyer and senior partner from the firm Smith, Hakkula, and Schuler up on the forty-third floor of the building in which she worked. His professional success came from a career in corporate litigation, but he was known for having a sizeable portfolio of familial wealth as well. Lisa's boss, Susan, was a personal acquaintance of Mr. Hollow and when he decided he wanted to make a philanthropic gesture for the community in which he grew up, he'd contacted Little Flower to execute his vision. Sometimes, though, Lisa couldn't help but question his motivation. As much as she was all for improving Nicollet, she wasn't fully convinced that this magnanimous offering didn't have anything to do with some kind of covert personal-identity crisis.

On cue, Mr. Hollow and another man entered the conference room. Susan welcomed them each with a handshake and greeting. As usual, Mr. Hollow planted himself at the head of the conference table. Susan shifted her pile of paperwork over to the seat on Mr. Hollow's left. Lisa was annoyed that he took such liberties with someone else's conference room. None of their other clients did that.

Mr. Hollow had a weathered exterior like chewed-up rawhide that reminded Lisa of Clint Eastwood from his cowboy movies. "Good morning, ladies," he said.

The rasp of his voice made the Clint imagery immediately take shape. Lisa mentally dressed him in the standard cowboy issue consisting of boots outfitted with silver spurs, some leather chaps, a Stetson hat, and a red paisley bandana.

"I'd like you to meet one of our junior partners," he said, indicating his guest. "This is Mark Schoenfelder. He and another one of my guys are going to be overseeing the rest of the park project for me. He's got my complete trust and confidence. Mark, this is Susan Karowitz, president of the foundation, and these two gals are Ingrid White and Lisa Johnson."

Mark smiled then said hello as he reached across the table, extending his hand first to Ingrid and then to Lisa. He was way younger than Mr. Hollow, with absolutely no cowboy aura whatsoever. He looked to be around thirty and was a few inches taller than Lisa, with short sandy hair, a slightly receding hairline, and brown eyes as dark as coffee beans. From his looks, Mark was probably the kind of guy she usually thought of as "the son of my parents' best friends" type.

Although she hated to break eye contact with the handsome newcomer, she turned and looked directly at Mr. Hollow so he would know that she was talking to him. "It's John*ston*," she said, clearly aspirating the *t* in her name. She smiled, hoping it would make her correction sound less like an admonition.

"Excuse me?" Mr. Hollow asked, as he flashed back a grin of impressive pearly white dentures. His teeth gleamed, producing a light of their own. She bet that if the sunlight hit them just right, they would sparkle.

"My last name is Johnston. With a *t*."

"Oh, right. Mark, you'll be working with these girls." Mr. Hollow picked up the first sheet from his stack of handouts. "Now, let's see what you've got for us today."

The man hardly skipped a beat.

It drove her crazy how frequently people got her name wrong. Her name was Lisa Johnston—not Lisa Johnson. Arguably, her last name was as common as Erickson, Hanson, or Smith, and yet unfortunately had been consistently trumped by Johnson. That *t* between the *s* and *o* clearly stood out next to its smaller neighbors, who stopped short of the dashed blue midline, and was the single distinguishing trait that separated her from the masses named Johnson.

Lisa had spent many hours of her childhood speculating on how the name Johnston came to be. Maybe it referred to John's Ton, and told the tale of a man named John who had great wealth or strength. Or perhaps there had been a naming trend in which people made common names more unique by adding, deleting, or changing one letter. Thus, Erickson became Ericsson, Smith became Smyth, and Johnson became Johnston. Or maybe it had been a nickname for a certain part of old John. No wait. That would be Johnson—*again*, but in this case, she didn't mind not being associated with that kind of moniker.

But if the Johnsons had thought that adding a *t* to their name would give them more distinction or inflate their social standing, they were mistaken, because she knew with absolute certainty that it had done the exact opposite. Anyone named Johnston would be repeatedly referred to as Johnson and this innocent mistake made over and over would eventually erode one's identity until one became what one really wasn't: Lisa Johnson.

High school had taught her this lesson well. With fifteen hundred students in her school, she'd had the misfortune of being cast into a class where there were ten other girls named Lisa, one of whom was named Lisa Johnson. Not only students, but teachers, too, confused them. Class schedules, test scores, notes from their parents; all of these things got mixed up from the time they were freshmen, all the way through their senior year. She wouldn't have minded so much except for two critical differences. First, she was white and the other Lisa was black. Not that she cared at all about skin color, but how could anyone confuse that? Secondly, the other Lisa was a six-foot basketball star and she was a scrawny mouse who categorically shied away from sports. Her parents about fell over from shock when they got a call from a recruiter offering her a scholarship and a spot with the Ohio State Buckeyes. Lisa Johnson's parents were similarly stumped when they received a letter stating that their daughter had achieved highest honors at band camp and invited them to attend the end-of-summer farewell banquet.

To twist the knife further into the ongoing misnomer situation, there was a Lisa Johnson in the grade ahead of her and one in the grade behind her, so that, even in her senior year, she could enjoy no notoriety. She was the only Lisa Johnston in the whole damn school, drowning in a sea of Lisa Johnsons. It was somewhere between getting called into the nurse's office for a pregnancy test and basketball star Lisa Johnson getting *her* letter of recommendation from their English teacher when she decided to defend her name and correct anyone who got in her way.

Chapter 3

Jake eyed the gigantic clock bolted to the concrete wall above the security desk, wondering if he'd see her again. If he did, he'd be sure not to talk about the weather. Just as he arrived at the bank of elevators, he saw the woman from the day before push her way through the revolving doors. He pressed his thumb firmly into the up-arrow button while watching her out of the corner of his eye. She walked about fifteen feet into the lobby, then stopped and turned back to retrieve a magazine from a square glass coffee table. Jake recognized the cell phone perched on a mountainous pile of landfill as the cover photo of the very same edition of *Time* he'd been paging through at the grocery store.

He heard the mechanical whir of the elevator's arrival, then the soft metallic click and slide as the doors opened. People pressed around him to get in while he remained standing just outside the doors. Intently focused, the woman lingered by the coffee table, her finger pointing to a spot in the magazine, her lips pressed tightly together.

If the magazine interested her that much, she should just take it. He didn't think there'd be a strong case for criminal prosecution as long as she returned it. He could argue that if she worked here, borrowing a magazine from the lobby of her own office building was kind of like borrowing from an extended collection of company resources. If the article she was reading pertained to her job, then this furthered the odds in her favor.

Jake heard the elevators threaten to close and placed his hand across the doors.

From inside the elevator came polite coughs. He looked in and saw an older woman checking her watch, while others fidgeted or shifted in place, all eyes fixed on imaginary locations. Then a forty-something guy, outfitted with white earbuds and a white cord that snaked into the front of his gray sport coat, looked directly at Jake and jacked his thumb upward. Jake delayed a few seconds longer until he was sure he'd gone past the point of good manners and got in. As the doors began closing, he glimpsed a woman's gold watch loosely fitted on a slender wrist. His hand darted out and smacked the button panel. The doors shuddered to a jerky halt before reversing their course.

The woman stopped just short of the doors as she and Jake made full-frontal eye contact. The black outlining on her lids and the mascara, coupled with a shimmery smudge of eye shadow a shade darker than her fair skin, enhanced the watery blue of her irises.

They were so vivid Jake could follow the faint lines radiating from her pupils. He remembered that he'd promised to go kite surfing with his friend Scott before it got too cold. Her hair was down today and he noted the blond and gold highlights, like light through honey. Her lipstick was a dark pink, something bolder than yesterday's lighter look. Jake smiled generously, offering her space next to him.

The woman swayed on the threshold as two more people squeezed past her and murmured thanks.

"Going up?" Jake asked, ignoring the restlessness of the other passengers.

"Uh ..." She looked over his shoulder, to the left and then to the right. She stepped back. "No." After a pause, she added, "Thank you." It sounded like a question.

The doors bullied Jake's hand, insistently pressing against his palm, while he processed her answer. Usually a person was grateful when someone held an elevator for them. The woman's look resembled that of a deer caught in the headlights. Maybe it wasn't him she was responding to; maybe there were too many people in the elevator.

"Okay." Jake removed his hand, smiled again, and kept his eyes on her until the doors closed. He sensed a collective sigh of relief as the elevator ascended. He didn't mind the dirty sideways glances or the knowing looks exchanged between the strangers around him. What really bothered him was he didn't normally get that kind of reaction from a woman.

. . . . .

As the elevator closed on his smug face, Lisa reeled from the shock of seeing Jake Hanson two days in a row. In nearly ten years, their paths had never crossed, and now it had happened *two days in a row.* Her mouth felt dry and she realized it was hanging open.

She heard another elevator descend and the doors opened on an elevator two down from where she stood. A lone man in a black fall trench coat with a matching briefcase exited. Lisa turned and treaded carefully the short distance, then peered cautiously into the elevator's vast, shiny emptiness. It stood gaping, beckoning her. For once, there wasn't anyone elbowing her for space. Lisa looked over at the door labeled EXIT with a picture of a stick man running up three steps.

She shook her head. It would be ridiculous, not to mention neurotic, to walk up twenty-four flights of stairs. A normal person would take the elevator and consider the benefit of getting to work on time. She was a normal person. She watched the empty elevator close on itself and waited for the next elevator—just to be safe.

When she got to her floor, she stepped out, half-expecting Jake to jump out and yell, "*Boo!*" It was silly, but she couldn't restrain herself from peering into each rectangle of window as she made her way to the office.

She marched straightaway to Ingrid's cubicle and said, "Okay, it's official. He exists and he is here. In the building." The way Ingrid winced made Lisa think that maybe she had shouted.

"Who?"

"The guy I saw yesterday."

"What guy? You mean Mr. Hollow's guy?"

"Yesterday I told you I saw someone. I just saw him again. In the elevator." Lisa jabbed her index finger toward the general direction of the accused apparatus, as if it was the elevator's fault.

"In the elevator?"

"Yes. And this time he held it for me."

"That sounds nice."

"It's not nice. It's annoying. Ingrid; that's two days in a row. What am I going to do? What if he works here?"

Ingrid came closer and placed her hands on Lisa's arms. Her brows furrowed with concern. "Calm down. Now, who is this guy?"

"Jake Hanson," Lisa said, enunciating slowly. His name felt rubbery in her mouth. Saying it out loud was weird, like she had violated a sacred pact by voicing the secret password.

Ingrid leaned in, with face clouded and her blue-green eyes narrowed. "Did he hurt you? Like—physically?"

"No. I just—can't stand him." She'd almost said hate, but heard her mother's nagging voice in her head, *Don't hate*. And anyway, she hated brussels sprouts, which made her gag; Jake made her see red. "I *loathe* him."

Ingrid loosened her hold on Lisa. "But he did do something, right?"

Her mind spun through her Rolodex of memories. How could Lisa sum up all of the citations she'd counted against Jake? It would not only sound childish, it would minimize the significance of all that Jake had done if she began with an explanation that was reminiscent of, *This one time? At band camp?*

Before she could answer, a woman from human resources passed by them and said good morning. Lisa looked around the office space the foundation shared with other nonprofits. It had an open floor plan filled with cubicles so small she and Ingrid called them cubbies. Sometimes she could hear others breathing. She was sure the receptionist was eavesdropping because, although her desk was at least ten feet away, the young woman seemed unusually quiet as she meticulously unpacked a small box of paperclips and set the clips individually in a holder shaped like a goldfish. The more urgently she wished for privacy, the louder the smattering of click-clacking on keyboards across the cramped sea of cubicles sounded.

Lisa lowered her voice. "I can't explain it now. The point is: what am I going to do if I start seeing him every day on the way to work?" *Hi, Jake; sucks to see you* didn't seem appropriate or adequate. Just then the receptionist was upon them, a white plastic pitcher in hand, watering the thriving spider plant closest to Ingrid's cubby.

Ingrid drummed her fingers lightly on her lips "Okay, based on what you told me, I think you're overthinking this. If you see him again, just ignore him. That's what I do."

"But what if he talks to me?"

"Just ignore him."

"And if he persists?"

"*Fake* it. It's probably just a coincidence, anyway."

"But it's been two days. In a *row*."

"Maybe he's somebody's client. Which reminds me; we have another meeting with that Mark tomorrow. It's first thing, so don't be late."

Lisa's anxiety eased down a notch. "Maybe he's somebody's client?"

"Yeah."

"Which would make his visits temporary."

"Or sporadic," Ingrid added. "It's not a big deal. Now try not to have any more meltdowns before noon."

At that moment, Susan stepped out of her office, one of the few reserved for executives that outlined the perimeter of the cubbie corral, with a door and windows facing the outside world. Ingrid dropped into her chair and turned to her computer while Lisa settled into her own cubicle.

That was what she loved about her friend. Ingrid could take a crisis and smack it down with one irreverent swat.

After a few hours of answering emails and making phone calls, Lisa opened a tab for Google on her Internet browser to search for any new funding sources or deadlines she didn't already know about. She sat for a moment meditating on the search box. On the other side of the partitioned wall, she heard Ingrid step away from her desk. The intern on her other side was out sick. Her fingers flew over the keys. *Click.*

The first hit was for the fictional character from the popular '90s television drama series *Melrose Place*. The next was for a Jake Hanson in California. She skimmed through the list. There were thousands of Jake Hansons mentioned in every conceivable forum. She typed in "and Minneapolis" after his name. Just as she was about to tap the mouse, Ingrid returned and said, "Hey, how about a lunch break?"

Lisa nearly jumped out of her seat. *Yep, no big deal.*

Skipping her jog, Lisa headed straight home after work. She sat on the couch petting her five-year-old tortoiseshell cat, Leroy, as her eyes roamed the living room. With the exception of two small paintings and a family picture, books lined nearly every inch of wall space. She rationalized that if she wanted to see some culture, she could visit a museum. This logic, however, did not apply to books. To say she had a love of books was an understatement. It was an obsessive love affair of the mind. There were some stories she had found so moving that she wished she could eat them, so as to forever carry them inside of her.

She'd lucked out when she had found this apartment, which was on the ground floor of a renovated Victorian house. The building was at least a hundred years old and had a screened-in porch with a large, white porch glider where she liked to read. It was located right in the heart of the artsy, eclectic part of Minneapolis's Uptown neighborhood. To be near Uptown was so unbelievably cool that her actually living there made her feel cool by association. The apartment was also only three blocks from Lake Calhoun, where she liked to run. She had a roommate whose parents paid half of the rent while their daughter was in the Peace Corps in Botswana. The place was all hers.

She stood, letting the cat hop to the floor, and went over to a shelf next to the narrow hallway leading to the kitchen. She walked her fingers over the bindings, stopped, and slid a tall book from the bottom shelf. It felt weighty and purposeful—a book with many stories. The binding was tight, the white and blue leather clean, the bear emblazoned on the cover still in good shape. She thumbed through it, letting the pages fall open at random.

The freshman class. The golf team. The football team. The choir. The cast of *Pride and Prejudice*. She recalled seeing a classmate of hers who'd been in the play on a reality TV show called something seductive like *Love in Paradise*.

Jazz band. The lunch ladies. The senior class. The senior class president. The senior class vice president. The treasurer. The secretary. Her eyes went back to the senior class president.

This was a time when having a cell phone created a clear distinction between the haves and have-nots. Reality shows like *American Idol, Survivor,* and *The Bachelor* were the entertainment equivalent of three square meals and Disney movies weren't just for little kids anymore. It was cool to listen to '80s music because it made the youth seem retro and wise. Never mind about Ronald Reagan or Margaret Thatcher, that the Berlin Wall had fallen, or that Sandra Day O'Connor had become the first woman appointed to the U.S. Supreme Court. All they really cared about was the big hair, Duran Duran, Cyndi Lauper, Pac Man, and movies like *Goonies, Top Gun,* and *Pretty in Pink*.

That year they had won the state hockey tournament and the volleyball team had switched from wearing bun huggers, those underwear-like "shorts," to the still-too-short but more respectable spandex bike shorts. Their principal, Mr. Wicker, had announced that he was taking a sabbatical abroad to partake in a special research project in Italy. This was code for: *I'm cracking up because of you kids, my marriage is on the brink, and I need a break. See you next year.* Lisa watched it all from the fourth chair in the clarinet section of pep band. *Go Bears! Grrrr!*

Lisa thought of the famous Dickens line: *It was the best of times, it was the worst of times.* Almost ten years ago, she had been a senior at Big Bear High School in the Twin Cities suburb of Big Bear. As cliché as it sounded, it definitely had not been the best of times and had certainly been the worst of times. She had been a nobody. A well-liked nobody, but a nobody nevertheless. How could someone be a well-liked nobody?

Aside from the whole name situation, she had been a plain Jane with dull brown hair, boring blue eyes, and no remarkable features. That wasn't to say she'd been ugly; her mother said so and her father verified it. Maybe she was gullible to believe her parents, but hey, she took what she could get.

Her hair was long and always pulled back in a ponytail. Within the safe confines of her pink bathroom she would experiment with all sorts of hairstyles. She tried the sultry look, parting her hair so it angled coquettishly across her face. Sometimes she created sassy tendrils. Occasionally she had pigtails or plaits to express her inner child. Yet when she went to school, she always yanked it back into a conventional ponytail—not even a spiky ponytail or a messy bun. Just a plain, straight, pulled-back ponytail. And her eyes were blue. Not a sparkly blue or an icy blue, or aquamarine, or even a murky, could-they-be-violet blue. Just blue.

She had no jutting cheekbones or pouty lips, no quizzical eyebrows or seductive smile—not even a mole that could be classified as a beauty mark. Her one saving grace had been the absence of bad acne. She had felt sincere sympathy for her peers who had faces reminding her of acupuncture gone seriously wrong. She might have been unremarkable, but she thanked God that she had been spared pimples.

She had especially liked English class, survived calculus, and loved dissecting the cat that she and her lab partner had affectionately named Meow Zedong. She went to football games like everyone else. She went to dances and the prom in her junior *and* senior years—even if it was with girlfriends. She cheered at the pep rallies and painted her cheeks with little blue and white stripes. She even went to Costa Rica on a summer trip organized by her Spanish teacher. She had not been some social leper skulking about in Gothic wardrobe bemoaning and soliloquizing about the horrible injustices of high school. She, at least, had worn regular clothes.

People had known who she was, more or less, and had been friendly for the most part. She suspected that no one was ever quite sure if she was a Johnson or a Johnston. But everyone knew her first name, so in this way she had at least registered as a blip on the social radar.

In junior high, she had been opinionated and vocal about her views. Had she stuck to it, perhaps she would've earned a spot on the speech and debate team. However, the eye rolling and mutterings she observed during class discussions in the early days of high school had taught her that her time there would be better spent retreating into books. Call it a coping strategy, but it had been easier to build relationships with girls like Anne Shirley, Elizabeth Bennett, Nancy

Drew—heck, even the gang from Sweet Valley High—than it had been to interact with her peers.

For example, somewhere around the ninth grade the girls had gotten all weird and gaga over the boys. As breast size increased, brain size decreased. The girls, even the smart ones, didn't know the answers to even easy schoolwork anymore. The same was true of boys who didn't know what to do about the inexorable blossoming of their former teammates. But there had been a small group of boys who'd been able to hold it together—to be charming and graceful in the face of all this adolescent strife. They were adored, revered, and idolized by all. In a phrase: they were *loved*. And the leader of this coveted clique was their senior class president, Jake Hanson.

Jake. What could she say about Jake? That he was considered perfect? He did it all: played three sports, got top grades, and was superinvolved in all kinds of activities. But it was his way with people that made him extraspecial. Their senior year, he convinced nearly every student in their class to volunteer ten hours at a drop-in center for street kids. Not a single teacher or administrator had to coax anybody; everyone had gladly done it because *Jake* had asked. Except for Lisa. She'd done it for the drop-in kids, not for Jake. When Jake hosted Senior Skip Day, he came out unscathed. That's how much people loved him. The teachers even let him play hooky.

Of course he'd also been one of the cutest guys in their class. "Beefcake Jake" and "Handsome Hanson" were two of his many nicknames. Jake had played Mr. Darcy in the school play. In his white neckerchief and black top hat, he had a confidence about him that made girls lose all coherence. While holding curtains and placing props backstage, Lisa had overheard countless Jane Austenesque fantasies of fairytale romance involving their own Mr. Darcy, complete with acts of chivalry and horseback riding into the sunset; an extension of every girl's secret belief that Ken would finally marry Barbie and they would live happily ever after in Barbie's pink castle. The drama teacher once commented how pleased she was that so many students had taken such a strong interest in *Pride and Prejudice* that year. Either she'd been brilliant casting Jake or incredibly oblivious.

The last time Lisa had seen Jake had been at their high school graduation. While everyone else wore a normal black graduation gown, Jake had been festooned with gold tassels and a large bronze medal with the school's crest around his neck. He was the first kid ever in the history of Big Bear to be bestowed such an honor usually reserved for adults. He had been class president, homecoming king, and a featured graduation speaker. And she hated him.

Well, no. She had loved him, too—initially. But there came a time when consternation tipped the scales, outweighing any respect she'd had for his otherwise goodness.

Chapter 4

"Jake."

"Jake," Scott said again, punching him hard enough to get his attention.

"What?"

"I said those two girls sitting at the other end of the bar are checking us out. Do you want to join them?"

Jake glanced over and spotted two young Asian women—one with long, shiny black hair and the other a tiger-striped blonde—both giggling over their foo-foo drinks. The tiger blonde chewed on her straw while the other one tapped on her smart phone with a viciously pointed black fingernail.

"Nah, I'll pass."

His other friend, Amir, turned away from the sports highlights broadcasted on the television above the bar. "What did you say?"

"I'm just not in the mood." Jake took a long drink, enjoying the different degrees of bitterness in his lager. The bar was already selling Octoberfest, a sure sign that summer was behind them. He pointed his Sam Adams bottle toward Scott. "But feel free to go over there if you want to."

Scott said, "Not in the *mood?* Are you sick or something?" He set his beer on the table, laced his fingers together, and leaned forward. "All right, what's up? It's not like you to pass up chicks."

Jake lightly twirled his bottle, watching a bead of condensation trickle down to the saturated green coaster advertising Heineken. He looked over at Amir who was no longer following the football scores. "It's nothing."

His friends drilled him with expectant eyes.

"I met a woman at work," he said. "In the elevator, actually."

"Oh yeah; I like where this is going," Scott said, nodding. "You did her, didn't you? Right in the elevator. Yeah, man; high five." He put his hand up to slap Jake's.

Jake ignored him. "Yesterday I tried talking to her and said something lame about the weather."

Scott and Amir both cringed, affirming his stupidity. "Today I held the elevator for her and she said no. Who does that? I almost find her more attractive because she blew me off. Is that weird, or what?"

Amir scoffed. "*That's* your problem?" He shook his head and turned his attention back to an interview with three players from the Baltimore Ravens.

Scott said, "Why do you care when there're girls sitting right over there, sending us a vibe?" Jake looked at the women again and watched as they turned their backs on a young guy wearing baggy jeans and a sideways-twisted baseball cap. The girls bent over their drinks and both eyed him while sucking their straws.

Because there was something about her, he wanted to say. He might have said it to Amir, but not to Scott. Despite having gone to a different high school, Amir had been Jake's best friend since kindergarten. And, although Scott was a fun guy and Jake liked having him as a roommate, these days he was too much of a man-whore to take anything other than sex with a woman seriously.

"Yeah, I know," he said instead. Lately, Jake felt like the most beautiful woman in the history of beautiful women could approach him and he wouldn't be interested. He'd had to call it quits after only two weeks with the last three girls he'd dated. If it had only been one woman, he wouldn't have been worried. But three? Clearly there was something wrong. He looked to Amir hoping he'd say something sensible. Instead, Amir flagged down a server and ordered a plate of hot wings and another round of beers.

After the server left, Scott said, "Let me tell you something: dating a girl from the office puts you on a whole other level. It suggests relationships. This," he said, indicating the bar, "is the best place to meet women."

"How do you figure?" Jake asked.

"Because it's neutral ground. You can have fun without it messing up the rest of your life, and if you decide to ditch the chick, there's no drama, because you can leave."

"Maybe I'm looking for something"—he knew he'd sound like a girl if he said it, but it came out anyway—" ... more."

Amir smirked while Scott groaned and put his face in his hands. Scott said, "Oh, man. Are you getting all grown-up on me?"

Jake laughed. "What's wrong with that?"

"It's depressing. Aren't we grown up enough as it is? We did the college thing, then *you* went to law school—which was hell, if you recall—and now we have to work to pay for grown-up shit like insurance and taxes. We're in the prime of our youth, Jake. I just want to have fun and enjoy life a little bit—which, at the moment, includes those two hotties over there." Scott glimpsed over Jake's shoulder and winked at the girls, who responded accordingly with more giggles.

Jake could appreciate his friend's sentiment, but, since starting the new job at Smacker, something in him had changed. Jake *had* become a grown-up. For the first time since high school Jake felt like a real adult, and the women he usually found attractive just didn't seem—*serious* enough.

At his new law firm, everyone was serious. His former employer had been serious, too, but that atmosphere had been different; more laid-back. There Jake could clock in, do the work, then clock out, knowing he'd put in a solid effort, and his boss would be pleased. In those days, Jake had been more interested in developing his social life than anything else, which included perfecting the science of picking up women. Scott often joked that they should offer a class because they were both so good at it.

But at Smacker, being a lawyer wasn't a job, it was a vocation. Everyone was expected to work overtime and his coworkers tackled each case with a purpose and tenacity that he admired and tried to emulate. The energy in the office was intense and fast paced, like any moment could be a game changer; and when that moment came, you were expected to seize it and play it to the client's or the firm's advantage. And the only thing he'd been able to figure out about his boss was that he had high expectations and only talked to newbies like Jake when he wanted something or when you screwed up.

The consequence of this recent shift in Jake's perspective was that he had started reacting differently toward women. The girls sitting at the bar, for example, looked likeable and definitely hot enough, but they seemed too young. Not jailbait young, just too immature; not serious enough.

Maybe that was why the elevator girl had caught his attention. On a scale of one to ten, her serious score was probably an eight or nine. Not quite a ten, because she drank out of a cup with a moose on it. There had to be some wiggle room there for either a sense of humor or adventure. Or irony.

Jake gestured to the bar and said, "Knock yourself out, buddy."

Scott was already standing when the server returned with their beers and food. He picked up one of the bottles and swigged it. "Preparing to launch," he said, hitching his belt. Scott continued to smile at the ladies and out of the side of his mouth asked, "Hey, sure you don't want in on it?"

"They're all yours," Jake said, picking up a hot wing.

It took less than thirty seconds for Scott to land, order another round of drinks for the girls, and engage them in conversation. He was so smooth it didn't even look cheesy.

Or maybe all this emphasis on being serious was a sign that wedding bells were starting to get to him. In the last year, he'd seen an influx in wedding invitations, as his friends, one by one, were tying the knot. He'd been asked to be *in* so many weddings he'd finally broken down and purchased a tuxedo. While Scott saw the abundance of bridesmaids as an opportunity, Jake, who was usually up for a good party, had had enough of the wedding circuit. He had one last car to decorate and a final dance with someone's grandma before the matrimonial season could be put to rest until next spring.

After a few bites of the spicy chicken, Jake asked, "What about you, Amir? What would you do if you wanted to get to know a woman?"

"I wouldn't," he said, holding up his left hand and wagging his slim brown ring finger, which sported a wide gold wedding band. Amir had married the very first woman he'd met at college, which had been the girl working the front desk for admissions. He was far from being an expert, but then again, he *was* happily married.

"I meant hypothetically."

"I might invite her for coffee or to hang out or something." Amir dipped a wing first in the buffalo sauce then into the blue cheese, and shook it. Greasy orange drops splatted onto the plate before he took a bite. "I'd probably do that typical stuff like dinner and a movie," he said while chewing.

Jake gave him a look over his chicken.

Amir shrugged. "I don't know. Take her to a comedy club? When Ani fixes her friends up on dates, she always suggests comedy clubs. She says you can learn a lot about a person by what makes them laugh."

Amir swallowed his food then took a pull of his beer before continuing. "Okay, seriously? Like in your situation? If I were really interested in finding out more about a woman, I might google her."

"*Google* her? You do not google a woman."

"Think of it as data collection. You know, find out if she plays volleyball or has a blog; if she's ever been arrested. Or you could try Facebook. Ani says you can learn a lot about a person from their Facebook page." Amir pulled out his phone. "What's her name?"

"I don't know."

Amir raised his eyebrows and laughed. "Okay. What *do* you know about her?"

"I think she works in my office building."

"You think?"

"I only saw her in the elevator."

"Okay. So what's the name of your building?"

"Perkin—West."

Amir flicked through some screens and entered the name. "Maybe there's an online pictorial directory."

This was beginning to sound like stalking and Jake was in no way desperate; more like curious. "You know what? Thanks for the suggestion, but I'll figure it out."

"Look here," he said, showing Jake his phone. "There's a section on craigslist called Missed Connections. You could put a message there. Or maybe she already posted one for you. Here's one for the downtown Minneapolis skyway. Where did you meet her again?"

The thought chafed against his entire sense of masculine integrity. "Would *you* put an ad on craigslist?"

"No, that stuff's chick-flick fodder."

"Good," Jake said, relieved, "because that idea sounds really creepy." He heard Scott's deep voice rise and fall as he joked with the girls. The three of them laughed loud enough to turn heads. Those girls were starting to look better.

Amir continued scrolling on his phone. "Anyway, this one in the skyway happened yesterday, but it's a man seeking a man."

Jake laughed and clapped his friend on the shoulder. "I'll figure it out."

"I've got another idea."

"What's that?"

Amir placed his phone back in his jacket pocket. "When you see her, you could try talking to her again."

Smart man, that Amir.

. . . . .

"What happened to you?" Ingrid asked when she saw Lisa fly into the office.

"I took the bus."

"Oh. It must have been your first time."

"How could you tell?"

"You've got that what-the-hell-was-I-thinking look stamped on your face."

"No kidding. I thought all I had to do was hop on any bus going in the general downtown direction and the next thing I know,

I'm headed for St. Paul. Here's a tip: the bus labeled Express does not mean a faster bus to downtown Minneapolis."

"You didn't know that?"

"You did?" Lisa challenged.

Ingrid shrugged. "Well, I knew it in theory."

Lisa threw off her coat and grabbed everything on her desk. "What time is it?"

"Eight thirty-five, and Mr. Hollow's guys are already here."

Over the short distance to the conference room, Lisa quickly ran her fingers through her hair then tugged repeatedly at her blouse, trying to circulate cool air under her arms and on her chest, where some light perspiration had accumulated. Every morning during her snail-like commute to the heart of the city, Lisa questioned the value of driving to work. Arguably, it was convenient to come and go as she pleased, but that was only a perceived freedom. Now that she lived in Uptown, the car insurance, as well as the cost of gas, was threatening to exceed her budget. The downtown parking ramps were consistently cramped and overcrowded, and when winter came, driving would be like dragging a ball and chain through a foot of slush. Plus, she'd read enough articles to convince her that excessive levels of exhaust fumes weren't all that great for the environment. So that morning, feeling particularly environmentally peeved, she'd decided to finally take the bus.

One look through the glass wall of the conference room made her stop in her tracks. She pulled Ingrid back until they were both behind the normal, non-see-through wall. "Um, Ingrid? Would you mind if I stepped into the bathroom for a second?" She wiped her brow and said, "Whew. I'm just so hot and with the whole bus debacle—I just need a minute to freshen up."

"Okay. But hurry up."

Peeking around the corner, Lisa spied the two men sitting at the large table, heads bent over some papers. When Ingrid entered the room, Lisa saw them glance up, then rise. She leaned out of view then scurried back down the hallway and out the door to the women's restroom next to the elevator. She set her things on the counter then checked the stalls, making sure they were empty. When she was sure that she was alone, she turned to the mirror and inhaled then exhaled so deeply it felt like she'd done an abdominal crunch.

Her reflection seemed that of an entirely separate being. Her boring blue eyes stared back at her with irreverence as the reality of the situation sank in. Apparently, not even taking the bus could prevent her from running into Jake Hanson for the third time in a week. Seeing him the first time had been disconcerting; the second time startling, but now—when he was sitting in the conference room? She didn't know what to feel.

So Jake must be the new guy, the guy who'd be working with the other new guy on Mr. Hollow's project with Ingrid and her. This meant she'd be seeing a whole lot more of him, and not just in the elevator. A troupe of high school cheerleaders dressed in blue and white sweaters and pleated skirts somersaulted through her head. The white bear mascot in a matching outfit came next, followed by Jake riding on the shoulders of the entire football team. Her stomach clenched with a powerful sense of annoyance mingled with dread.

Why was this happening to her? She was a good girl. No, she was more than that. She was a responsible citizen. She donated to good causes, volunteered for social justice issues, worked at a non-profit, recycled ... *she even went to church, for God's sake*. Surely, she had earned an exemption from situations like this.

The left side of her brain rattled through all the possibilities for escape, which her right side promptly rejected. It was too late to hide, feign illness, or concoct a family emergency and she wasn't sure she could fake it either, as Ingrid had suggested.

There was simply no getting out of it. When she stepped out there, it would be the moment of truth. What would he say? How would he react when he realized who she was? That they knew each other? What would *she* say? How would she be able to function? To do her *job?*

Her adult self mentally slapped her. Who did she think she was? She wasn't a clumsy, awkward girl who cowered behind books or in bathrooms. She was a strong, confident woman who worked hard, had built a respectable career, was considered a professional, and liked cats. That's what had been written about her in the foundation's newsletter and she believed it.

Her eyes sparked and reflected determination back at her. So what if she had to work with Jake? She couldn't afford to have a mini breakdown because she was about to come face-to-face with her high school nemesis. This was her job, and if Jake was the new guy that Mr. Hollow referred to at their last meeting, then so be it. She would go out there, look him in the eye, and discuss project planning as if he were any other person.

Taking deep, even breaths, she splashed some cool water on her face. She grabbed the tail of a brown paper towel and blotted her face, careful not to do any more damage to her makeup. She patted down her hair and gently ran her hands over her cheeks. Looking at her reflection, she squared her shoulders, set her chin, and muttered, "*Grow up.*"

Chapter 5

"Jake Hanson, this is Lisa Johnston," the other woman at the meeting said.

He immediately stood and extended his hand. He couldn't believe his luck. Lisa. The elevator girl's name was *Lisa*. And she worked here after all—in his office building. He thought she had looked familiar and now he knew why. He'd seen her picture on the foundation's website when he first learned that he might be assigned to Grant's project. He chuckled to himself. Apparently, Amir hadn't been too far off the mark with his suggestion. "Nice to meet you."

She glanced down at his hand, then back up at his face before shifting her load of a laptop and a few folders to one arm. Looking directly into his eyes, she accepted his hand and pumped it. Her grip was firm, just as he thought it would be. He noted again the watery quality of her eyes and in them sensed a challenge. For what, he wasn't sure, but he was game.

"You, too," she said, as she released his hand. Before he could say any more, she averted her eyes, opened a folder, and asked, "Where are we on the agenda?"

As they sat, Jake couldn't help but grin again. This morning he'd gotten to work a few minutes earlier in the hope of catching her at the elevator again. Unfortunately, the only person who showed up had been the iPod guy from the day he'd held the elevator. Apparently the guy recognized him, too, because when he saw Jake, he veered to the right to join a small cluster of people waiting at the far end.

"We were just discussing the timeline," the dark haired woman said, whose name he remembered was Ingrid. She pointed to a legal-sized sheet of paper centered on the table between him and his colleague and friend, Mark, and her and her colleague. She tapped a spot highlighted in yellow. Turning to elevator girl, or rather Lisa, Ingrid said, "They're suggesting we change the date of the golf tournament."

"What? Why?" Lisa's eyes widened as she looked at her co-worker and then over at Mark. She didn't look at him.

Before Mark could open his mouth, Jake jumped in. "We noticed that you have the golf tournament scheduled for the end of March. The golf course won't be open."

Lisa plucked a few sheets of paper from one of her folders, spread them across the table in front of her, and frowned. He liked how her eyebrows came together as if she were puzzling over a Sudoku instead of a calendar. She said, "But they were open in March this year."

Ingrid said, "I know, but they were explaining that this year was unusual."

"When was the last time we had snow at the end of March in the Twin Cities?"

"Last year, for one. And the year before that there was a blizzard mid-April," Jake said. He directed his next question to Mark. "And do you remember that year we got fifteen inches at Easter? When was that?"

"Five years ago," he said.

Jake snapped his fingers. "That's right. We went skiing." He thought he would get a small laugh or smile from them. Instead the women turned to each other and exchanged a few words while pointing to some other boxes on their papers. Lisa's brow furrowed more. Mark had his poker face on as he waited for the women to hash it out.

"Look," Jake pressed on, trying a different angle, "all anecdotes aside, the data suggests there's a high likelihood of snow still being on the ground in March. So, despite the good weather this year, golf courses likely won't open until the end of April. Maybe mid-April if we're lucky."

Mark took that as his cue and slid a printout of weather patterns Jake had prepared across the table as evidence for his claim. Ingrid took the papers and placed them between Lisa and her. Jake watched as Lisa tucked a strand of hair behind her ear. She wore silver earrings that held a small stack of green stones and dangled below her lobe. When she bent her head, the columns swayed slightly. To

Ingrid, Lisa said, "We could possibly reschedule for the last Saturday in April."

Ingrid looked up and asked the men, "Would that suit you?"

Mark nodded and Jake answered, "That should work."

When he glanced at Lisa again, this time she started then quickly looked away. He'd caught her staring at him.

Ingrid asked, "What else?"

Mark coughed quietly into his hand. "There's also a concern with the block party."

Jake took the silent hand-off from Mark and pointed to another box on the calendar between them. "The dance is scheduled for May, correct?"

"Yes," Ingrid answered, "Memorial Day weekend."

"I think you'll have a better turnout if you have it the Saturday after the Memorial weekend, or even later in June."

"We were thinking to incorporate a tribute to veterans," Ingrid said.

He smiled at her. "That sounds really nice, but the fact is, people typically go out of the city that weekend." Besides, Mr. Hollow was already planning a party with the senior partners at his cabin. He and Mark wouldn't be invited, of course.

"Which people?" Lisa asked. It was the first time she'd spoken directly to him. She crossed her arms across her chest. The top button of her white blouse was undone and a chunky necklace, with flecks of green, filled the triangular space of exposed flesh.

She continued, "I'm not sure if you're aware, but most of the residents living in the Nicollet neighborhood can't exactly afford to get out of the city for the weekend." Jake liked the tone of her voice. Not nasally like that of the last woman he'd dated, but a reasonable voice that sounded smart.

Lisa addressed Ingrid. "I think we could get really high attendance if we hosted it over Memorial Day weekend. People might leave the city, but people will be coming to the city, too. They'll be looking for things to do. This is the perfect family event and it'll be free. The crowd will be *huge*." The intensity and volume of her voice pulled his eyes away from her cleavage just as she looked at him again. "And no one's going to notice if a few *certain* people aren't there."

Jake shrugged. "That may be true, but if you want Mr. Hollow to be there, you should move the date."

Ingrid said, "We definitely need him there, so I think we should move it. Mark, can you guys ask Mr. Hollow what dates would work best for him?"

Mark nodded and jotted a note on his legal pad.

Jake heard Lisa exhale a short puff of breath. Her eyes were full of suspect, far more hostile than he thought necessary for a simple date change. All they had done was state the obvious. To recover some lost yardage and show he meant no harm, he smiled earnestly at her. She held his gaze for an instant before rolling her eyes slightly and returning to her papers.

Game on.

. . . . .

Somebody please pinch me now.

They'd been discussing the project for nearly twenty minutes and Lisa still could not believe she was sitting across from Jake in a real-life meeting at her real-life job. The encounter had progressed from unnerving to just plain annoying.

When she'd walked into the conference room, Jake's eyes had lit up with recognition, yet somehow they had managed to jump straight into calendar talk without any chitchat. She'd done her best to stay focused on the business and her eyes on her papers. She'd figured that if she ignored him as much as was politely possible, the meeting would finish faster and she could duck out before he had the chance to remind her of their shared connection. But when he'd started messing with their plan, she'd had no choice but to engage the enemy.

It was typical Jake to have no qualms about taking over at the last minute. Ingrid and Lisa had already spent months working on this project. These guys were on it less than a week and wanted to change things around? Mark leaned back in his chair, tapping a pen on his armrest, while Jake talked for the two of them. Ingrid sat next to her unaware. Lisa looked around the conference room, eyeing corners and cracks for telltale signs of hidden cameras; it was the only logical explanation.

"By the way," Ingrid said, "I have a call in to Spinach, asking if they'd be interested in being on the main stage for the block party."

"Spinach?" Mark asked.

"It's that funky hip-hop group that just went national," she said.

Jake said, "You know, 'Because It's Good For You'?"

Mark shook his head. "Sorry. These days if it's not 'Itsy Bitsy Spider,' I haven't got a clue."

"They're originally from Minneapolis. Because their fame is only recent, we might have a chance. They have a huge local following and we're hoping they'll be affordable," Ingrid said.

"Is the dance a fundraiser?" Jake asked.

Was this guy even listening? Lisa had already told him the block party was going to be free. She tensed her crossed arms and pulled her shoulders back. "Our goal is to raise enough capital so we don't have to charge admission. The dance is supposed to be a celebration of the neighborhood and its future with Grant Park."

"That's your goal? You don't have all the money raised yet?"

His insinuation made her nostrils flare. "No, but that's normal. You can see the projections I've put together."

Jake flipped through the pages of her finance report while Mark looked over his shoulder. In high school, Jake's hair had been short in the back with a mop of light brown floppy bangs in the front that made the girls swoon every time he ran his hand through them. Now his hair was darker and he wore it very short and clean cut all the way. He had a crease in his forehead that she didn't remember and it rumpled as he studied the document. He looked up and made eye contact with her again. Every time it happened, she felt her cheeks burn and her skin tingle. "If I'm reading this right, it looks like you might fall short of your goal by about 20 percent."

What was he talking about? She grabbed her own copy of the budget and scanned over the collection of tables. She had double checked her numbers—gone over them tediously—then reviewed them with Susan and Mr. Hollow. She knew exactly what she had to do to bring the money in.

"We've already received written confirmation of financial support from twelve companies, and verbal confirmation from another thirty-seven in support of Grant Park," Lisa said. "Mr. Hollow wants to have a hundred corporate sponsors by our next fundraising event, which is Grant's Gala. From that event alone we're looking at $1.5 million in projected revenue, which puts us ahead of our timeline." Jake smiled at her and she smiled back, pleased she'd managed to maintain her professionalism while taking him down a notch at the same time.

"I could help you look for more sponsors," Jake said.

Lisa's heart stopped. Her mind went black except for a single phrase that flashed like a neon sign: No way. No way. *No frickin' way.* "Oh no; that's okay. I can handle it."

Ingrid said, "I like the idea. Before you came in Jake was telling us about his fundraising experience in his previous job."

"I'm sure he's knowledgeable, but really, I've got it under control. I'm sure there are other aspects of the project that will need Jake's legal expertise, like securing the rights on the Brown buildings."

"Actually, it's the main reason why I asked Mr. Hollow to bring Jake in on the project," Mark said. "We were thinking that he could help with the financial campaign and I've got the acquisition of the Brown buildings almost tied up."

Great. Now Mark decided to speak up.

"Okay, then. Jake, you'll be working with Lisa," Ingrid said.

And just like that—high school was back.

Chapter 6

"That wasn't awkward," Lisa said.

Perched on high bar stools at a little bistro in Uptown, Ingrid and Lisa sipped apple martinis and assessed the progress on the park project. The bistro gleamed with chrome edging that balanced the gray concrete floor and the black matte bar and walls, giving the space an industrial yet modern look. Lisa took a big swallow of her drink, enjoying its blend of sophistication and girliness.

"No, not at all," Ingrid agreed. "I think Jake will be a good addition to the team."

"Do you remember that guy from the elevator that I was telling you about?"

"Yes," she said, sipping her cocktail. Then her eyes got large. "That's him? He's cute."

"Every time I looked at him, all I could think of was Jake throwing the winning touchdown. Jake being crowned homecoming king. Jake giving a speech about recycling."

"So you know him from high school?"

"Yeah." Lisa sighed. High school. A time and place she was glad to have behind her.

"He seemed nice."

"'Seemed' being the operative word. Can you believe the way those guys came in and completely changed our plans? Mr. Hollow looked at it three days ago and everything was fine. Why didn't he say anything?" Lisa leaned into the high back of her bar stool. "Jake Hanson—a lawyer. I suppose that fits. I always imagined him becoming an athlete or a politician."

"So," Ingrid said, her eyes twinkling, "do you think he recognized you?"

"I'm sure he did."

"He didn't really act like he knew you, though. But he did seem kind of anxious to work with you."

"Oh, he knew." Lisa had recognized Jake the moment she'd seen him in the elevator. Surely, he'd had the same reaction. And now that she was going to have to work with him, it was sure to come up. It would probably be the first thing out of his mouth the next time he saw her. "But what I'm really worried about is this gala thing."

"You don't think you'll be able to meet the financial goal?" Ingrid asked.

"No, it's not that," she said, waving off Ingrid's question. "It's the social part of it; how to behave properly at societal functions. I get an anxiety rash just thinking about it."

Ingrid glanced over her martini glass. "Don't you mean social functions?"

"No, I mean societal functions." She swiveled her stool to face Ingrid. "You see, a social function is a generic gathering, for anybody to celebrate something—a birthday, a graduation, an anniversary. A *societal* function is all about who comes to do the celebrating and how much money they'll spend doing it."

Lisa picked through their shared bowl of nuts until she found a broken cashew. "Anyway, you know me; I have no social grace. Thanks to you, I can at least figure out which fork to use and which wine glass goes with what. But it's the small talk that kills me. I blame it on my parents. They were far too into gender equality to bother teaching me any social etiquette."

The other looming problem was who to bring as her date. Ingrid would be bringing her husband, John. They had gotten married over the summer and still glowed with the giddiness of all things new. It wasn't that she begrudged them their happiness, but the brightness of their marital bliss shone a light on her being single. On the other hand, why was she assuming she'd be noticed amongst all of the glitz and glam of the local rich and famous, anyway? Nevertheless, despite her liberal upbringing, even she acknowledged it would be nice to go with someone.

"Are you going to invite anyone?" Ingrid asked as if she could read Lisa's mind.

"I don't know. Chad, maybe?"

"No, don't bring him. Brothers hardly count as a date."

"How about Tim?" Lisa suggested.

"He's got a girlfriend now. I don't think it would be wise to borrow him, even if you are friends." Ingrid paused. "Whatever happened to that guy you were dating?"

That was a good question. What *had* happened? "You mean Tony? I don't know. Everything seemed to be going well. The next thing I know, it's like he fell off the face of the earth."

Ingrid lifted her eyebrows. "When was that?"

"Let's see." Lisa touched her thumb to the tips of her fingers counting the time passed. "About a month or two ago? I lost count after four weeks."

"And you didn't say anything to me?"

"I don't tell you everything. Besides, it just sort of happened. I didn't hear from him for a few days, which turned into a week, and then weeks."

"Did you try calling him?"

Of course she had. She'd emailed him, texted him, left phone messages. Any more effort on her part would have made her a stalker. "Yes, but he never called back."

"Not ever?"

"As far as I know." Lisa slammed back the rest of her drink.

"But I thought you and Tony had really hit it off."

"So did I. But then again, we hadn't known each other that long, and it's not like we were dating each other exclusively. For all I know, he just wasn't interested."

Ingrid set her martini down forcefully, causing a bit of liquid to splash over the glass's edge. "What is it about men and getting spooked? You're not that scary to me. Look at you. You are a successful, beautiful, intelligent woman. What more could a man want?"

"That's how women think. We believe those are good qualities. Most guys like women to be beautiful and they'll tolerate success and intelligence to a certain point, but in the end, they want to feel like they have the upper hand; that they're either smarter or more successful than the woman—preferably both. Besides, we don't know that Tony got spooked. Maybe he died."

Ingrid laughed. "That's morbid."

"You're morbid," Lisa countered. "I'm not the one laughing." But she had been smiling.

"Anyway, not all men are how you described. John's not that way at all."

"That's why I included that little qualifier 'most.' Of course not all men are like that. Some are worse and some are better. But I will argue that all men *do* fall somewhere along the continuum of that line of thinking. Besides, as a newlywed you're too biased to see the cruddy side of your husband. Just wait, though." Lisa shook a finger at her friend and winked to let her know she was teasing.

They sat quietly listening to the sounds of mellow jazz coming out of nowhere. The tune sounded vaguely familiar, like something her grandfather would've liked. Ingrid's phone vibrated. She picked it up and glanced briefly at an incoming text. Setting her phone back on the bar, she asked, "What did you think of Mark? He looked nice and I didn't see a ring on his finger."

"Even if he had been wearing a ring, that wouldn't necessarily signify *unavailability*. But the reference to 'Itsy Bitsy Spider' was clue enough."

"Maybe he's a single dad."

"How about if I hired an escort?"

Ingrid shook her head. "No way. No brothers, no other girls' boyfriends, and no escorts. You have two months to figure it out."

"If the escort is hot, I could learn to like him," Lisa said.

"Come on. Isn't there anyone? At all? Someone just waiting for you to show them a speck of interest?"

The suggestion reminded her of Jake. Conjuring up Jake Hanson in a romantic association was like asking a dentist to do an unnecessary root canal.

"I need another drink," she said.

. . . . .

"I'm here to see Lisa Johnston."

His smooth, easy-going voice floated across the cubbies. Lisa glanced at the St. Anthony prayer card pinned to the gray fabric wall of her space before picking up her purse. Throwing a last look toward Ingrid, she tried to remember if Jake had been in choir, band, or both.

"Good luck," Ingrid whispered.

She saw him first, standing with one leg crossed over the other, a hand in one pocket, and his elbow resting on the receptionist's counter. Lisa could tell the poor girl was blushing as Jake chatted with her. Clearly his self-confidence hadn't diminished over the years. As she neared, he caught sight of her, turned, and took a step away from the counter. His broad smile pierced his cheek with the dimple that also hadn't diminished over the years.

"Hi. Are you ready?" he asked.

She was in no way ready, but nodded anyway.

They walked to the elevator, and when the doors opened, he ushered her in ladies-first style. Lisa moved to the far left, leaving plenty of space between them while he stood comfortably in the center. She glimpsed her reflection and a singular thought bounced back: *Why me?*

Jake said, "I thought we could go to this little sandwich shop around the corner."

"Fine," she said, keeping her eyes focused on the number one with a star indicating the lobby and, thus, freedom. His cologne reminded her of an ad she'd seen recently of a couple on a sailboat. The woman stood behind the man, her arms wrapped around his waist, while he held the boat steady at the helm. The woman had thick, auburn hair that was pulled back by the wind and the man wore a khaki-green skipper's hat with a gold anchor pinned to the brim. Their mouths were open wide with, she guessed, laughter. She wondered if Jake could smell her, too.

"Have you been there before?" he asked

"What?"

"The sandwich shop. Have you been there before?"

"Oh. Yeah."

She had no idea which place he was referring to. And why was she only capable of one-word answers?

Jake had wasted no time leaving a voicemail message for her the very next day requesting a lunch meeting. She'd called him back right away before overanalyzing it. Since then, she'd been prepping herself. They didn't need to have lunch to discuss business. She suspected it was a ruse; that Jake would out her at lunch. If that was the case, she much preferred having the conversation outside of the office.

The sandwich shop turned out to be a short walk from their office building and was a place she knew well. The host seated them at a tiny table that barely accommodated two people. She was glad she'd only brought a single manila folder that was slightly bent from her clutch and damp from her tight grip. When the host returned with water, Lisa gratefully gulped it. The server, right on the heels of the host, took their order and was on to the next table before Lisa could ask for an extra napkin.

She could feel that, regardless of gender, all eyes around her drew to Jake like iron filings to a magnet. He'd been in great shape and gorgeous in high school, but now, his boyhood lankiness had been filled out by manhood. His muscular arms and broad chest bullied the white fabric of his dress shirt. And she hated to say it, but he exuded an undeniable sexiness. No gut pooled above his belt. Knowing Jake, it was probably all washboard under there. He sat ramrod straight, and seemed at ease, despite the cramped space.

"I updated the budget," she said, handing him some papers. At this point, her strategy was to stick to business, eat her food, and react calmly if the conversation turned personal.

While Jake perused the information on the project, Lisa tried looking at anything but him. Unfortunately, her eyes, too, kept coming back to him. In between predictions of what he would say this time about her revised budget, she continued to compare his features with those of his younger self; laying the floppy hair over the new cut, seeing the promise of stubble on a smooth, sixteen-year-old cheek. Even his hands looked like they had grown up, as she noticed the curls of fine hairs sprinkled across his knuckles. His fingers were tan and he wasn't wearing any rings. And she liked his tie.

Jake looked up from the papers. "So, what exactly do you do at the foundation?"

She felt her cheeks heating up, like they had when she was a child and got caught sneaking cookies. She sat up straighter in her chair. "I'm the assistant development coordinator and corporate liaison responsible for the financial development of projects."

"And Ingrid is the project manager for Grant Park?"

"Yes."

"Have you done a project like this before?"

The question brought all of her focus back to the topic at hand. Her body tensed, prepared to battle if he started insinuating again that she couldn't do her job. Jake had railroaded her once before; she would have to be extra vigilant not to let it happen again—especially because this was about her job.

"Yes, I have done projects like this before."

"It says here that the estimated cost is at $20 million. How do you plan to raise that much?"

"If you turn to the third page, you'll see I've broken projected revenues down into categories." When he got to the requested page, Lisa pointed to one specific line. "Mr. Hollow has promised $10 million of his personal estate."

Jake whistled lowly. "Wow. Now there's a man worth admiring."

Lisa balked. One of the stipulations of building the park was naming every inch of it with some variation of Mr. Hollow's name. The entire park project had already been baptized "Grant Park." The community café would be "The Hollow" and the community center, which would include a small museum, would be something like "The Grant Educational Center and Hollow Museum for Young Bright Minds of the Future," and they had yet to come up with a name for the playground. If ego could be liquidated into dollars, they'd have enough money to build one park like this in every state with funds left over. She knew she shouldn't complain, because it *was* quite generous for one person to provide half of the funding for a project, and it made her job easier.

Lisa settled on saying, "He certainly is a character."

Since the project went public, Mr. Hollow's firm had received a huge influx of press and, consequently, business. This was why she couldn't help but be wary that the park would end up being nothing more than a publicity stunt. It wouldn't be the first time someone with money and status touted his intentions to do a humanitarian project, only to let the project slip into neutral and remain incomplete once the reporters walked away. But she wasn't about to tell Jake that.

He asked, "How much do you hope to get from grants and government?"

"As much as we can get."

He smiled at her joke. "And do you really think this—what's it called—gala?—and golf tournament are going to be enough to draw the interest and the money you need?"

"Yes, I do. They're both high profile and Ingrid really knows how to organize an event well." Because of her personal connection with Mr. Hollow, her boss was also exerting extra effort to ensure the success of this particular project by making calls of her own. Jake didn't need to know that, either.

By the time the server returned with their sandwiches, her stomach had wound into a tight fist. She'd regretted only eating a yogurt and banana for breakfast, promptly whipped her napkin across her lap, and bit into her sandwich. The effect was immediate, as the flavors of her turkey on rye with fresh spinach, tomato, and feta released their magic, relaxing her body. She had to remember that she was the expert in this conversation.

"You mentioned that you have experience fundraising?" she asked, taking another generous bite of her sandwich, feeling her power coming back.

"That's right. At my old firm, my boss was very big into Jerry's Kids. Personally, I think he was more motivated by the nostalgia of his youth, but he was a nice enough guy and it's a good cause. When Jerry was in town, they'd always meet for drinks."

Was she supposed to be impressed?

"Anyway, because I'd just gotten out of law school, I got the gopher job of going to local businesses to support Jerry's Kids."

She stopped chewing. It was her full-time *job* to go to businesses for good causes. She chalked up the infraction and continued. "Was this part of your job, or on your own time?"

"Both. But I didn't mind because in college and high school I did a lot of community service."

At the mention of high school, she felt the hairs prickle on the back of her neck. She was already halfway through her sandwich and Jake had hardly taken two bites of his. Lisa imagined the teen Jake bagging leaves for some old lady.

"And what about you?" he asked.

"Me?" She picked up her water glass and took another long drink, trying to find the right footing in her answer. The pause was long enough that Jake finally picked up his sandwich and took a bite. A small sprig of alfalfa dropped to the plate. Jake eating alfalfa. She almost giggled. What was happening to her? They weren't even having drinks. She picked up her napkin and carefully wiped her mouth.

"How did you get started in this line of work?" he asked.

She braced herself and kept her eyes locked on his steady gaze. It was time to face Jake and she would do so with all of the maturity she could muster. *She was in control.*

"Well, I guess I've always felt that those who can't speak for themselves need a voice. I like to think of it as doing my civic duty—especially for kids. These days, children are being dumbed down by reality TV, numbed by the constant exposure to violence, and lulled into blind consumerism between the cell phones, video games, shoes, bubble gum, fruit snacks—whatever the product may be. The sad irony of it is that this generation of kids is up on the latest technology, but couldn't tell you the first thing about the Depression or World War II—or the Vietnam War for that matter. Vietnam has been reduced to something that their *grandparents* fought in way back when.

"They hardly know what Desert Storm is—the first or the second. They're vaguely aware of Iraq and Iran and why it's important to know about them, but can't tell you which is which or where they are. They're not sure if the United States is made up of forty-eight or fifty-two states. And I bet if you set these urban kids in a park in their own neighborhood, they wouldn't be able to identify a single tree or flower unless it'd been featured on some rapper's album. And I ask you, whose fault is this? Who's responsible for this generation? For their future? For *our* future?"

Her speech left her breathless. Her fists curled; she was practically leaning over the table, ready to yank him down by his tie. Where had that come from? She was passionate about her work, but of course, not all kids were like that.

Jake said, "Well, the rant aside, I think what you do is very admirable."

"That wasn't a rant."

"Yes, that was a rant." His eyes twinkled.

"A rant is an emotional tirade. I was offering an explanation about why my work is important to me."

"With strong emotional undertones. I think that qualifies as a rant. Don't worry; I agree with you." Jake folded his arms across his chest and laughed. "I bet you were one of those kids who had Greenpeace stickers plastered everywhere."

This was it. Jake was finally going to drop the I-know-who-you-are bomb. She studied his face and waited for it.

And waited.

She searched his expression for some hidden meaning, knowledge, or innuendo, but apart from joviality, his eyes only held earnestness. At that moment she knew exactly how she would handle Jake Hanson.

Fake it. That's what Ingrid had advised and that's what she would do. She was one Lisa Johnston swimming in a pool of Lisa Johnsons. He wouldn't know the difference and if it ever came up, she would deny knowing him. It was the only way she'd be able to work with him and behave like a halfway normal human being.

"No, more like—quietly opinionated." She drained the water from her glass and calmly set it on the table. She inhaled deeply, feeling power course through her body with renewed energy.

"Quiet? I find that hard to believe."

To test drive the muscle of her most recent decision, she was tempted to ask him what he'd been like in high school. Instead she asked, "What else do you want to know about the project?"

The rest of the conversation was effortless. Lisa answered all of Jake's questions and discussed the Grant Park project like the professional woman she knew herself to be. She had even laughed at his jokes.

By the time he tucked her business card into his inner coat pocket and said goodbye from the elevator, she felt victorious. Almost.

Below the surface of her shiny confidence hung a small dust cloud of doubt. Was it really possible that he didn't remember who she was? Not a single mention of high school or anything outside of the project had come up again during the lunch. But could he *really* not know who she was?

When she returned to her cubicle and saw her image in the glow of her computer screen, it clicked.

Chapter 7

When Lisa went to college, she'd been fortunate enough to fall in with a roommate who had enough pity, social grace, and fashion sense to save her from herself. They called her the Fourth-Floor Fairy Godmother and it was as if God had sent down his own Cosmo angel. As things would have it, her name was Angela. She had soft, curly blond hair, the kind that you only saw in the movies, which in the normal world would take an army of veteran hairstylists to create. She was kind to everyone and wise like Heloise, dispensing sensible, respectable advice.

If there was one thing Lisa had learned from high school, it was that being obscure hadn't served her well. So her freshman year, she took the offensive and chopped off her ponytail, dying what was left of her hair red. She'd been going for pixy and ended up with punk. She was in college, she reasoned; it was a time for experimenting. But try as she might, she had difficulty embracing the new, bolder look.

One night, when her drab light brown roots were starting to show and the cut was growing out of bold and into blah, she'd finally admitted her regret to her roommate. Angela never admonished her for what she'd done, or questioned her about it. Instead, she knit a plum and gray striped beanie for Lisa and judiciously set the course for not only a new physical look, but also a new outlook on life.

Lisa's transformation this time around was slow, but painless. While they waited for her hair to grow out, the two girls walked often and everywhere—to class, to the library, to the coffee shop, along the river, to parties, and back to the dorm. Angela was a fast walker. Lisa felt breathless trying to keep up with her, but soon her body acquiesced to the pace.

Then Angela suggested they take a kickboxing class two nights a week. Lisa thought she was insane, but she liked Angela, so went and loved it. She felt strong and powerful and, consequently, more confident. She had no doubt that she could kick ass should she be called upon to do so.

Their sophomore year the pair decided that it would be "fun" to do a marathon. Lisa had never run a nonobligatory mile in her life, but under Angela's guidance, was swayed by the belief that anything was possible. They joined a training group for university faculty and students. For two semesters, they hauled their butts out of bed at five thirty in the morning, five days a week, including every other Saturday, to either run, strength train, or both. In June, they ran the Chicago Marathon. It was exulting and painful, absolutely crazy, and absolutely wonderful, all at the same time.

Throughout all of this, her body had morphed from its usual plank shape into that of a woman. Her hormones had done their final duty and, in a surge of pubescence, she'd gotten some feminine curves. She felt like a Venus de Milo. A headless Venus because from the neck up, she was still Miss Plain Jane.

Angela coached her on the proper application of makeup with the arrival of every monthly issue of *Fitness* magazine, and they maintained fit bodies with that month's suggested workouts. She washed her face with a special facewash, moisturized, applied the eyeliners and shadows, dabbed the lip gloss, lightly brushed the apples of her cheeks—all according to the magazine's expert instructions—and—*Voila!*—discovered an honest-to-goodness beauty. To this day, Lisa still subscribed to *Fitness*.

But her hair had still been a problem. Since it had grown back, it had resumed its natural ponytailed state. Angela insisted that Lisa had a lovely heart-shaped face that rounded into a cute pointy chin, and sought the advice of a hair stylist on Lisa's behalf. This time she got the cut right, with layers and bangs and some blond highlights thrown in.

The last thing to go was the glasses. Lisa had had contacts, which she wore occasionally. However, because she never liked the feeling of having something in her eyes and couldn't understand the logic of sticking something in them, she tended to favor her glasses. In her senior year, her fate was sealed and changed forever with one word: Lasik.

She'd been persuaded by claims that the simple surgery would free her eyes forever from contacts *and* glasses. Well, it didn't turn out to be so simple. It had hurt like hell and she nearly bucked off the table as her abhorrence of sticking things in her eyes resurfaced. She rationalized that it was all worth it in the name of convenience and beauty. And then the glasses were gone, too.

Lisa closed her eyes, feeling her body follow the rhythm of the Madagascan music, which was a fascinating Euro-African blend with an energetic beat.

She couldn't be happier. Angela was in town for the weekend, which meant lots of BFF adventures, like pedicures and shopping, going out all night, and talking until just before the sun came up, like they had done as roommates. Angela lived in San Diego now. When they graduated from college, they had promised to take turns visiting each other every year. Lisa thought it less than idyllic to visit Minnesota in October—especially coming from sunny San Diego—but her friend insisted that she enjoyed the change of scenery and the fall colors. *Whatever.*

Last year, Angela had taken Lisa to an Uzbekistani restaurant and a tattoo parlor that doubled as a bar, where guests could enjoy a drink while watching people experience the entire emotional gamut of getting a tattoo. It was quite entertaining. This year, Lisa was going to wow her friend with the best that Minneapolis had to offer by taking her to a Lebanese restaurant in North Minneapolis that had the best baba ganoush she'd ever tasted, followed by a nudist play.

The Lebanese food was delicious; the nudist play a bust. It was not a hilarious romp through a nudists' colony, as she had expected.

Instead the play had been a depressing series of soliloquies in which the cast referred to themselves in the third person and said things like, "Jane is afraid. Jane covers herself to hide her fear. Jane has come to the colony to face her fear. Jane will shed, layer by layer, until she is free. Run, Jane, run! Be free from the clothes in which society dresses you! Run!" The cast also wore flesh-colored bodysuits. That was the Midwest for you.

Fortunately, she'd salvaged the night by taking Angela to her favorite club near Loring Park. It was a trendy place that didn't judge girls for looking like *Sex in the City* wannabes. Every Saturday night they featured bands that came from exotic locations and played only original music. Arguably, it was quite cultural.

Angela elbowed Lisa. "There's a guy over there watching you."

She opened her eyes and looked out across the dance floor, then froze in midsway. "That's Tony."

"Tony? The guy who disappeared?"

"Yeah."

With a nod of his head, Tony acknowledged her, excused himself from a group of people, and crossed the room. As he navigated between sweaty bodies, Lisa considered her options. Was it too late to bolt? Could she push Angela through to the other side of the crowd? Pretend she didn't know him?

"Hey, Lisa, how's it going?" he asked.

She felt her pulse quicken, her chest squeeze, and her dinner mix uncomfortably with the two drinks she'd already consumed. He sounded like he'd just seen her yesterday. Which he hadn't.

"Great!" She plastered on her biggest smile, hoping it wasn't too fake, and pulled Angela in for moral support. "This is my friend Angela."

After the introduction, Angela said, "I need a break. Do you want anything from the bar?" *So much for moral support.* Lisa shook her head and watched her friend snake through the crowd, wishing she'd said that she needed a break, as well. She usually prided herself on being honest, but had to admit that bending the truth every once in a while—like when meeting a sort-of boyfriend who had sort of dumped her then showed up unexpectedly while she was getting her Madagascan groove on—would be useful.

Thankfully the band filled the empty verbal space between them with the steady pulse of drumbeats and shakers, while they stood side by side, watching the musicians. A list of things that she needed to do—pay the rent, ask her dad to change the oil in her car, bake cookies for the office potluck—marched through her mind like a singular line of ants on a mission.

As the three guitarists took turns doing solos, she snuck sideways peeks of the man with whom she'd spent a part of her summer. He was a whole head and some inches taller than she was and had a way of standing with a slight, casual slouch—a quality that she'd always liked about him. A royal blue soccer jersey hung loose on his frame and on his wrist hung a bracelet made of a single black leather cord and three round black balls. His forearms were muscled and tan. His streaked blond hair was damp and slicked back. It had gotten longer since she had seen him last. He smelled sexy.

She remembered the day they'd met. She'd been stretching by the beach house at Lake Calhoun after a run when he'd approached her. He'd asked about her shoes and she'd inquired about his interests in return. The weather had been good that day: warm and sunny—cheerful. So when he'd invited her to go for coffee, she'd thought, *Why not?* It had been innocent between them; hanging out mostly. He'd taught her how to paddleboard. She'd recognized right away that he was an aloof kind of guy—that being noncommittal was his style—so she hadn't anticipated anything more to develop than a friendship. Besides, she hadn't been necessarily looking to be in a relationship either, which is why she'd been surprised when he kissed her.

They'd been waterskiing with his friends. Tony had been the driver and she'd stayed in the boat with him to be the spotter. While his friends were getting the next skier ready, he'd leaned over and suddenly kissed her. Chills coursed her body despite the heat, and she'd spent the rest of the day with his arm settled comfortably across her shoulder, kissing her whenever the spirit moved him. It was shortly after things had begun to heat up between them that he'd disappeared. She'd never expected anything, but still, when a guy kissed a girl, that usually meant something, didn't it?

Lisa looked toward the bar and around the smattering of tables, not seeing Angela anywhere. Tony hadn't said another word or taken another glance at her—that she knew of—but he'd obviously made the effort to get her attention. Maybe if she focused on keeping hers on the riffs, he'd have the opportunity to sneak peeks at her as well.

She leaned nearer to him, and as she did, he bent, lowering his ear to her mouth. Inwardly, she smiled, pleased to see that even if he hadn't been looking at her, he'd been aware of her. She asked, "So, what about you?"

"Good. Busy." His breath felt warm and tickled her ear. A tingle ran down her spine. "I've been playing soccer in Germany. I just got back a few days ago."

That explained the shirt. "I thought you were in sales."

"Yeah, I was. But when I got this offer, I decided to go for it."

She'd seen him play but had no idea he was that good. "So, is it a professional team?"

"Not exactly. More like semiprofessional."

"Wow, Europe. So that's where you've been hiding."

He looked down at his feet, sort of sheepishly kicking them around, as if he wished he had a soccer ball between his legs. "Ah, yeah ... sorry about that. It all sort of came together at the last minute."

"Are you back permanently?"

"Actually, I leave tomorrow. But I'll be home for Christmas." He looked out over the crowd of dancers and rubbed his hand on his neck before bending back down. "It's good to see you."

"Oh?" she asked, trying to make light of it, despite parts of her body cheering him on.

"Yeah." He stepped closer, his shirtsleeves brushing her bare arms. "I am sorry, you know. Do you think I can make it up to you when I get back?"

"Well, you'll have a lot of making up to do."

"I think I can do that." When he spoke, his lips lightly touched her ear, sending more sensations racing down her spine like a fire truck on a run. The temperature shot up ten degrees, she was sure of it. Then Tony slung his arm around her waist. When Angela returned, she arched her eyebrow at Lisa, but said nothing.

The band was halfway through the next song when her phone vibrated and she saw she had a text from her brother. Turning away from Tony, she said into Angela's ear, "Chad sent me a text asking if we're joining them, or what."

Angela eyed Tony, then looked at Lisa. "What do you want to do?"

"Let's go," Lisa said. "Everyone's looking forward to seeing you."

"Do you want him to come with us?" she asked, slightly nodding toward Tony.

She glanced at him and her stomach flipped. She did and she didn't. While it was nice seeing him, she wasn't needy. If they hadn't bumped into each other, would he have even called her? Besides, this was her time with Angela.

She pulled him down to her level again. "Angela and I have to go."

He cocked his head to look at her. His green eyes told her he wanted her to stay. But instead he said, "Okay. When I get back to Germany, I'll email you." He kissed her once on each cheek, then planted a light kiss on her lips. She couldn't help but lean in and kiss him back. Thank God for Angela, who helped her stick to the plan by towing her through the crowd and toward the exit. When she turned back to catch one last glance, Tony signaled and mouthed, "I'll call you." She played it cool, but inside she was jelly.

Tim was agonizing over his current relationship. Whining was more like it, when Angela and Lisa met up with Ingrid and John; Lisa's brother, Chad; and their friend Tim.

"The thing is," Tim said, "I like her, but at this point, I'm pretty much only in it for the sex."

"How long have you guys been going out?" John asked.

"About three months."

"Ah, the three-month mark," Chad said. "This is the point in the relationship where you pretty much know if you like her or not. And if the sex is good and you don't like her so much, you'll drag it out for another couple of months or so."

The women glanced disapprovingly at each other. Lisa couldn't deny the claim because she knew first hand that it was true. However, she didn't like hearing about it, and especially from her own brother.

Chad added, "And Christmas is coming, so then you're doubly screwed."

"How do you figure?" Tim asked.

"Because once you're introduced to the family, you're stuck with her for an obligatory three more months. You'll look like a jerk if you get everyone's hopes up and then dump her right after Christmas."

Tim wailed, "She's not *that* bad. She's just insecure sometimes. Plus she's so hot."

This time the women collectively groaned and Lisa swatted her brother's arm. "Listen to you guys and the way you're talking about women. It's disgusting."

Chad set his beer down and raised his hand to stop her protests. "No, listen. When you consider the price Tim will have to pay, the sex isn't worth it." He turned to his friend. "Think about it; you'll have to buy her a Christmas gift, sit through her family's Christmas—and possibly yours, if she makes you invite her—knowing full well that you don't want a relationship."

"Plus girls get weird around the holidays," John said, which got him a dirty look from his wife.

"Right," said Chad. "If a girl has a boyfriend, even just a new one, she thinks the guy's going to buy her a diamond ring or something."

"I got a diamond ring," offered Ingrid.

John put his arm around her. "Yes, but that's because I loved you and we'd been dating for three years."

Chad's eyes lit up and he pointed to his sister. "This one time, Lisa thought her boyfriend was getting her a pair of diamond earrings and she got a floor lamp instead."

Lisa rolled her eyes, but had to laugh with him.

"How about telling her you need some space and letting her go gently?" Angela suggested. They *all* groaned at that one.

Lisa said, "Telling a woman he needs space is man-speak for 'I don't want to date you anymore.' When they're done, they're done. No second chances."

"Yeah, Lisa, like that guy who dissed you this summer." Chad said.

"Okay, that's enough reminiscing out of you. Or should I tell them about the time you grew a mustache to impress an older woman?"

"There's nothing wrong with that," he said.

"You were fifteen."

"A very mature fifteen."

"Oh, please," she said. "By the way, that guy? His name is *Tony* and I just saw him. It turns out he didn't need any *space*. He got a once-in-a-lifetime opportunity to play soccer semiprofessionally in Europe. He's been in Germany." She loved it when she could prove her brother wrong.

"He dumped you for soccer?"

"For your information, he didn't dump me—as you so eloquently put it. He got the offer at the last minute and had to go right away."

Tim smirked. "He plays *soccer*? That's not a man's sport."

"Just because he doesn't play *football* like you two doesn't mean he's not a man. Look at David Beckham. He's like the British epitome of masculinity."

"Who?"

Before Lisa could defend the validity of soccer as a sport, Chad poked her in the arm. "Don't we know that guy?"

She looked across the bar and saw Jake and Mark sitting with two women. Her heart leapt into her throat. She swallowed it back down with a sip of her Moscato. *Great*. Nothing for ten years and now Jake was not only showing up at her job, he was making an appearance outside of the office. "No, I don't think so."

"Sure we do. He was in your class. What's his name?" Chad snapped his fingers, trying to jog his memory. After three snaps, he shouted, "Jake! Jake Hanson. That's it! Come on, let's go over and say hi."

The suggestion made her stomach turn and she felt her wine threaten to rise back up her esophagus. Evidently, her body hadn't caught up with her mental resolve about how to handle Jake. "I'd rather not."

"Fine; I'll go by myself." Chad picked up his beer glass and began moving away from their group.

Lisa gripped his arm, stopping him. "Don't talk about me."

"Okay."

She squeezed his arm tighter and gave him her best older-sister glare. "I mean it. Not a word."

"All right. *Geez*."

Finally letting go, she disguised herself with a shaded hand and followed the bob of his brown-haired head through the crowd, perturbed by the fact that her fate was potentially in the hands of her loving yet not-always-loyal brother. He was the happy-go-lucky type. Chad would shake hands and talk to a dog if it could speak, and she didn't need him blabbing to Jake about her. She could only hope that her brother would remember all of the good things she'd done for him, instead of all the bad things she had done to him.

Chad was two years younger than she was and had played sports with Jake in high school. He'd been good, but not as good as Jake, but with that self-confidence and easygoing attitude, he had definitely been a well-liked somebody. When Chad approached the men and began gesturing, it was easy to imagine the dialogue.

Jake, hi! It's me, Chad Johnston.

Chad who?

Johnston. We played football together at Big Bear. You graduated with my sister.

(Omit that last line.)

Oh, right. Chad! Now I remember.

Yadda, yadda, yadda.

When the men got to the backslapping part and she heard that loud, "Ha! Ha!" followed by her brother's annoying yuk-yuk of a laugh, she knew she was in the clear.

Through her fingers she surveyed the women with Jake and Mark. They were gorgeous, that much was a given. The woman by Mark was quiet, her head tilted to the side listening to the conversation, while she sipped a white wine. At first glance, there didn't seem anything particularly unlikable about her, while the woman sitting by Jake was slowly oozing onto him. Initially she stood next to him from a respectable distance. Then she flicked her hair and leaned across him to reach her drink. With each flick and sip, she strategically closed the gap between them until her body pressed into his.

The woman flung her head back, made a raucous bray that Lisa guessed passed as a laugh, then adroitly, yet nonchalantly, draped her arm across his shoulders. He reflexively responded by putting his hand on the small of her back. She wasn't sure who to be more repulsed by: the woman for being so aggressive or Jake for being so easily sucked in; the woman for being gullible enough to fall for Jake's charm, or Jake for being so unapologetically male. In any case, together they'd staked out their territory, and what did she care, anyway?

Chapter 8

Mark owed him big time. Here Jake was, having drinks at this bar catering to the middle-aged with Mark and his wife, Cynthia, when he could've been at the club packed with hot twenty-somethings five blocks down with Scott. He'd known better than to say yes, but Cynthia had this cousin in town for the weekend and asked if he'd mind going out with them for the evening. The cousin's name was Tiffany and she turned out to be annoying as hell. What had started out as innocent swats on the shoulder had turned into an outright onslaught. The girl—or rather woman pushing forty—was blatantly throwing herself at him. He found it really unattractive—not to mention embarrassing—for both of them, even if Cynthia had insisted that her cousin was a very nice person, "nice" being code for some flaw that female friends like Cynthia didn't have the heart to tell a guy about.

He felt his cell phone buzz in his pocket. It was Scott texting, *WTF?! Where are you?* As much as he wanted to go, he couldn't see how he could remove himself from the situation and not lose credibility points. Mark was a good friend, but Jake had to remember that, at the firm, Mark had more clout than he did. Being the new guy, Jake had to be careful not to take their friendship for granted. On the other hand, if he pussyfooted too much around Mark, he feared looking like a suck-up. He wanted to make a good impression and earn respect based on his own hard work.

He didn't like Tiffany pawing him, but figured there was no harm in playing along a little. Otherwise, Tiffany might take his leaving the wrong way, feel rejected, then get all weepy and ruin everyone's weekend. No matter from what angle he thought he might be able to spin it, he was stuck.

So Jake would have to sit it out and, at the end of the night, give Tiffany a friendly hug and send her on her way, with her dignity intact. Tomorrow she would be hung over but glad nothing had happened, and Jake would still be able to go to Mark's and watch football with a clear conscience.

At least one good thing to come out of his years of dating experience was a skill for letting women down on good terms. It didn't benefit him to be a jerk. Knowing how women gossiped, he couldn't afford to acquire that kind of reputation. His grandfather used to say, "Hell hath no fury like a woman scorned." After having three wives, he should know.

"Sorry for interrupting, but aren't you Jake Hanson?"

Jake regarded the man and hesitated. "Yes."

"It's me, Chad Johnston. We went to Big Bear High School together. How are you?"

The man clasped his hand and pumped it. Jake rifled through the contents of his mind, searching for a memory that went with the guy's face. When he'd played college hockey, he'd gotten used to fans approaching him, but that hadn't happened in a while. High school was even further back. After a moment, Jake was finally able to make a connection.

"I'm good. Sorry. I didn't recognize you with the, ah ... ," he said, motioning to Chad's face.

"The goatee," Chad finished for him.

"Yeah." Jake put his hand on Chad's shoulder. "Everybody, this is Chad. We played football together. In fact, now that I think about it, you were the up-and-coming running back."

"But you, Jake—you were the quarterback." Chad turned to the group, "Jake here was an *icon*."

"Oh no, that's not true," he protested.

"I think you're being modest," crooned Tiffany as she bopped another inch closer to him. He placed his hand on the small of her back, putting enough pressure there to keep her at bay. Mark was so going to owe him.

Chad said, "He *is* modest. That's what made him so great. He played football, hockey, and baseball, was captain of all three teams, and he never got cocky."

"Technically, I was a co-captain," Jake murmured.

"I rest my case."

Mark asked, "So you play football? Jake, don't we need another guy for our team?"

"Yeah, we do. Would you be interested? It's just a small, informal league."

"Yeah, sure." Chad was already reaching into his pocket for his phone.

They traded numbers and Jake put his phone away before Tiffany could get too nosy or offer her number.

"We have a practice tomorrow and a game on Wednesday."

"Awesome."

Jake tossed the ball to Mark. The wind caught it, carrying it out of Mark's reach. They were midseason and their team wasn't doing too well. Jake was somewhat embarrassed because, as one of the founding members of the league, he couldn't help but feel that he should be winning, too.

Five years earlier, Jake and some friends had decided to create an informal football league. That first year, there were only two teams and whichever one won received a subscription to *Sports Illustrated*—courtesy of the losers. The league got popular and now there were twelve teams and official referees. Along the way, someone managed to get a lifelike resin replica of a pink pig and created a traveling trophy. The pig stood over two feet tall, was four feet long, and wore a red and white football jersey with the number nine and a white helmet, so dinged and scratched that a test dummy wouldn't have worn it. Epoxied to its back was Cheerleader Barbie, holding one pom-pommed hand in the air. To give it proper credence as a trophy, it was mounted on a four-by-six sheet of plywood with a brass placard screwed to the front with the inscription: *In the end, there can be only one.*

Jake spotted Chad walking across the field. "Did you see who Chad was with last night?"

Mark shook his head and threw the ball back to Jake. "Who?"

"That Lisa from the foundation working on Grant's park." Just as Tiffany had been testing her bravery by putting her hand on his thigh, he'd noticed Lisa, and then Ingrid, across the bar. Her back faced him, but he was sure it had been her. Then *Chad* had joined her and they'd left. Together. Jake had wasted no time encouraging Chad to come to practice.

"So?"

"So, she's pretty cool, don't you think?" Jake chucked the ball back.

Mark caught it easily and hurled it back. "She's a little—intense, but … I guess."

"No," Jake said, throwing the ball a little high this time. "That's confidence. She's got balls."

"That's one way to put it." Mark jumped and caught the ball, then walked over to Jake, offering it to him. "Listen, at our law firm, they expect work to come first and always before women. Seriously, Jake; don't even think about it, and especially not while we're working on this project. You're still the new guy, and believe me, Grant will notice."

Jake opened his mouth to protest, but closed it as Chad neared. It was through this league that Jake had met Mark. And it was through Mark that Jake had gotten hired at Smacker. So he said, "Thanks for the advice."

When Chad got close enough, Jake tossed the ball and shouted, "Catch!"

From what he saw and recalled, Chad didn't play too badly. He was fast, agile, and when he got a great grip on the ball, he didn't let go. Maybe they'd see a turnaround yet.

During a break, Jake found himself standing with Chad apart from the group.

"So, Chad," he started. "Last night—that woman you were talking to—was that Lisa Johnston?"

"Yeah. You recognized her?"

"We're working on a project together."

"Really? What project is that?"

"It's a park in the Nicollet neighborhood. My boss is building it and her foundation is overseeing the project."

"Cool. That sounds like her."

"Why's that?"

"You know, being the change you want to see in the world and all that Gandhi stuff. But be careful what you say to her, because if it gets too political, she'll go on a rant."

"I've already had the pleasure. What else is she like?"

"I don't know. She likes to read. She runs. She's pretty boring."

His answer confused Jake. "So, you're not seeing each other?"

Chad spewed his water across the grass. "Are you kidding me?"

"Sorry," Jake said, putting his hands up in self-defense. "I guess I assumed."

"Are you *serious?*" Chad sort of shook his head and muttered, "Oh, brother ..."

Jake took it as a sign to shut up and focus on football.

Chapter 9

Cozying up on a sofa at a coffee shop after Mass, Angela asked, "Lisa, are you really serious about this Tony guy?"

"Sure," she answered, perusing her new literary treasures from the used bookstore next door. Tony had already shown promise by texting her a selfie from the airport before boarding.

Angela wrapped her hands around her Mona Lisa mug. "Don't you think it's strange that he went to Europe without even saying goodbye?"

"He said it happened fast and had to leave right away." When she heard herself, she sounded like a parrot regurgitating his explanation.

"Okay, but seriously? He couldn't take ... what, two seconds to call you when he left the first time? Really, what do you see in this guy?"

Lisa had to think about it for a minute.

"If you can't think of anything, then maybe that's a sign."

"I've thought of plenty of things. I'm just putting them in order." She stacked and restacked the three books in her hands. "Okay. He's spontaneous, adventurous, fun—an athlete," she said, ticking off each quality with a finger. "He's very cute."

"Yes, *that* I agree with. But how do you *feel* about him?"

She sighed, feeling too lazy to explain what she herself didn't know yet. "I'm ... curious. We had a lot of fun when we were together."

"Just be careful that he's not looking for a booty call. For all you know, he's got some girl over there in Germany. I know I only met him last night, and who am I to judge, but if he was crazy about you, he'd go the extra mile to make you feel special."

"Is that what Julian does? Go the extra mile?"

Angela blushed. "And then some. I know it probably sounds corny, but I really feel like I've found my soul mate."

"It doesn't sound corny. It's what we all want." Lisa relaxed into the sofa. Julian was the guy Angela had been seriously dating for over a year. Lisa had met him on her last visit to California. She'd seen how he was kind, like Angela, and recalled his many small yet considerate gestures. He opened doors for her, offered her the first bite of his entrée, poured her the first glass of wine, waiting for her first sip and approval before drinking his own.

"What's it like, having what you two have?" Lisa asked.

"First off, there are no games," she began. "I mean, a relationship is work, I know that, but this work feels effortless and worth it. If we disagree about something, I want to resolve it; and not necessarily by demanding that it has to be my way. And when we fight, I don't feel like I'm going to lose him. Like the argument is just that—an argument; it's not a reflection of our relationship as a whole. The relationship feels solid."

"Remember the guys we dated in college?"

"Oh God," Angela said, covering her face. "Like the one I was totally infatuated with, who decided to become a priest?"

"Or the poli-sci major who danced badly and only listened to public radio?" Lisa added. "How about that Egyptian guy you were dating?"

"The one who casually introduced me to his newly imported *wife* at the International Club's Christmas party?" Angela asked. "That was lovely."

On a sadder note, Lisa said, "The guy who slept with me because he wanted to use my lecture notes, then dumped me after the final."

"The guy I put my heart and soul into for two years only to have him join the Peace Corps."

Lisa reached for her friend. "He wasn't a bad guy, Ang. He just had different dreams; that's all."

"I know, but that didn't make it hurt any less."

"I don't think any of the men I dated were really in love with me. Not even my first love. Not like what you have."

Angela clasped Lisa's hand. "They weren't good enough for you. Consider them practice and have faith that when the real thing comes along, you'll know."

"Right." Lisa squeezed her eyes shut and said, "I do believe in love, I do believe in love, I do, I do, I do." And she did. She wanted to anyway. She was too young to be cynical. Maybe she should make better use of her being Catholic and start praying to St. Jude, the patron saint of hopeless causes, because clearly, she needed some intercession.

Then Angela asked, "Why were you acting so weird when Chad went over to talk to that guy?"

"That was Jake."

"*The* Jake? The infamous from-high-school Jake?" Lisa had been texting Angela regular updates each time she had a Jake encounter. It was what helped her stay on track when working with him.

"Horrible, isn't he? Did you see how he acted with that woman he was with?"

"I can't really say, since I was too busy watching *your* reaction."

Lisa's face heated up. She alternately fiddled with the creased corner of one of her new purchases and smoothed her thumb over it. "I just needed to make sure Chad wasn't going to blow it for me."

"Come on. Once Chad spotted him, you were like a different person. You kept hiding behind your hands and peeking through your fingers."

Lisa scoffed. "I couldn't care less about Jake."

"So, are you going to tell me what happened or what?"

"I've told you everything."

"I mean about what happened in high school."

Lisa clutched her own Leonardo da Vinci coffee cup, swirling the coffee as she thought about Jake. Emotions tussled in her chest, a big ball of congealed yuck trying to claim ownership of her heart.

The first memories to float to the surface were the embarrassing ones.

Like in Spanish class, when Jake's friends had had a running joke about her being flat chested. Why they cared about this, she had no idea. Usually boys focused on the girls who were ample, not meager. When they got to the unit about housing and had to describe Señora Gomez's apartment, Jake and his friends would look her way and say, "Ella no tiene un balcon. Ella necessita las ventanas grandes." *She doesn't have a balcony. She needs big windows.* Hardy-har-har. She'd watched them laugh, then resumed conjugating verbs, more annoyed than hurt.

Another time, she'd sneezed during an oral report comparing the book *A Room with a View* with its film version. A sneeze can be a very innocent thing, except that she'd had a very bad cold. Two big globs of bright green snot exploded from her nostrils and lurched out at the class before settling on her upper lip. She had no tissue in her pocket and the Kleenex box on the teacher's desk was an empty carcass. Looking around the classroom, her eyes begged someone for a tissue. Jake just sat there with a stupid grin on his face. He folded his arms across his chest and extended his legs, resting his right foot on his left. Because he wouldn't budge, no one was going to. Lisa had to walk to the girl's bathroom at the other end of the hall, holding her head back with her hand over her nose, trying to prevent the snot from sliding any farther down her face.

And the crown jewel of the most embarrassing things she'd experienced during high school, all of which for some rash of dumb luck had Jake as a witness, had happened in AP human geography. One day, while taking a test, Lisa's stomach began to gurgle. She could feel bubbles forming in her guts, lining up, and threatening to push their way through the nearest exit. She squirmed in her seat, regretting the taco salad she'd consumed at lunch. She tensed her body and spied the clock, hoping she could hold it in until the end of the period. The long hand hovered between the seven and eight, which meant she had either another twenty-one or twenty-three minutes left before the bell rang, depending on the angle at which she viewed the clock.

She knew not to bother her teacher, who never showed any mercy and was too suspicious of kids faking bowel issues during test time. Her heart sank as she felt another bubble take shape. She took as deep a breath as her body allowed and went back to tackling the essay question about the global impact of agricultural practices of the United States.

She scribbled a few more words then stopped. Then a few more and paused again. She couldn't think straight. The pressure was building.

She looked around, considering her options. All heads were bent. One kid who'd already finished the test was slumped over his desk, resting his head on his crossed arms. She would have to try her best to discreetly ease them out.

She relaxed just enough until a few bubbles slowly slipped out, each one providing a small release to the squeeze she felt on her abdomen. Relief flooded her as she discovered they didn't smell. Thank God.

Other than pencils scratching on papers and an occasional cough, all was quiet. She bent back over her papers, ready to resume the logic of the course she'd taken on the agriculture question. Lisa shifted forward in her seat and suddenly—*KABOOM!* She lit one so loud the room vibrated. This wasn't any innocuous toot—it had been a full-blown blast of gas.

Everyone in the room—and it had been *every single person*—sat upright like puppets yanked up by their puppeteers. In that moment, she clearly understood the phrase "stunned silence." Then one of the boys dared to speak what was on everyone's mind.

"Whoa."

That one word unleashed a steady stream of commentary. Lisa sat, still as a statue, too terrified to laugh, for fear that if she ha-ha'ed with the rest of them, she'd let out a series of blasts this time. Just as she was debating between accepting the embarrassment of what had happened or blaming it on the boy behind her, Jake whipped around in his seat, his eyes wide, and looked directly at her.

She was hoping against hope he wasn't looking at her, but couldn't break away from his gaze. A huge Cheshire cat grin spread across his face. He didn't say a word—just wore an enormous, idiotic grin. His laughter burbled, then erupted, and when he really started to howl, the rest of the class joined in. He turned red from the effort and tears came to his eyes.

The teacher was dumbstruck. As the regrettable stench wafted through the room, he came to his senses and said something authoritatively lame like, "All right everybody, that's enough. Get back to work." The class quieted down for a few seconds and then broke out into laughter again. These little convulsions resumed for the rest of the period. When the bell rang, Lisa slunk out of the room, ready to crawl into her locker and stay there until someone discovered her rotting corpse.

Jake had known it was her. She saw the recognition in his face. And he had laughed. He had laughed so hard she thought he might pop a blood vessel.

But these embarrassing things were the more trivial of her memories. They had been humiliations on a sophomoric level, and she'd gotten over them long ago. What bugged her—scraped at her conscience—was that Jake had had an uncanny knack for outshining people.

Her friend Yumiko had been one such casualty. Even in high school, Yumiko had been a brilliant photographer. Every year she painstakingly prepared her submissions for the regional arts competition and did well. Despite Yumiko's previous wins and talent, their junior year, Jake, not Yumiko, won regionals and placed at state, with a candid photo of a hockey player on an outdoor rink shooting a puck into a net. The shot had been captured by sheer luck. The art teacher had framed Jake's winning submission and hung it outside of her classroom. But Yumiko? She had photo portfolios full of perfection and the teacher had only ever tacked up a few in the classroom or referenced Yumiko's work in her slide presentations.

On the surface, it had made sense when Jake received awards or recognition. He'd been good at everything. But when Yumiko got one-upped by Jake, Lisa started paying closer attention. In the classroom, she noticed the small things, that—when tallied up—turned into quite a pile of significance. Teachers liked to call on Jake, knowing that if he participated, others would follow. It didn't matter how much she or others raised their hands. She'd nearly pulled a ligament once, trying to get the teacher's attention for the sake of testing her hypothesis. In fact, the teachers enlisted Jake's support in managing the classroom by offering him duties such as handing out papers, organizing groups, and running errands for them. In nearly every class he was teacher's pet and he gladly played the part. Despite what people thought about teenagers, some of her classmates would've liked to have been chosen at least once.

No one had been immune from Jake's trumping talent. Not even someone as unimportant as her.

Her senior year, Lisa realized she needed some more extracurricular activities to put on her college applications, so she joined theater, helping backstage, and got involved with Key Club.

Key Club was the catchall club for the miscellaneous kids who didn't fit into arts or sports. When the time came for officer elections, she decided to run for president. And why not? No one wanted the job. When the advisor had asked for volunteers, everyone ducked their heads, knowing that if they made eye contact, they'd get nominated. So she had raised her hand and offered to be president. The announcement was enough to lift heads and she liked to think that she'd even seen a spark of admiration for her bold move.

There was a brief campaigning period of one week during which she was expected to "run" for office, so she slapped up some green flyers around school that read, "Lisa for (Key Club) President!" The day of the election, Jake entered the ninth-grade science classroom with a large constituency of his friends. She'd never seen him at a Key Club meeting—not ever. He explained that he had some community service ideas he wanted to get the school involved in, and if it wasn't too late, would like to put his bid in for president.

He hadn't needed to run for Key Club president. He was already class president, captain of all his sports, and in the top 10 percent of their class. Wasn't that enough to impress college admissions counselors? However, since high school was a democracy, at least among the students, and Jake *was* the most popular kid in the school—something noticed even by the advisor of the obsequious Key Club—Jake's request was granted. There probably hadn't been that much action in Key Club since the 1970s.

Jake won in a landslide election. The vote had been by secret ballot, but she could tell by how quickly the teacher counted his way through the slips of recycled paper—Jake, Jake, Jake—who the winner would be.

After everyone left the room, the advisor awkwardly glanced at Lisa and offered her the vice president position. She politely deferred. By that time, she couldn't stand Jake Hanson, much less wish to volunteer with him. Instead she took a position with the Humane Society, where Jake had absolutely zero affiliation—and put that on her college application. She also had excellent SAT and ACT scores and was a qualifying Merit Scholarship finalist. It would have to do.

When Jake received a little-known scholarship from the Lions Club, all she could do was shake her head. He'd already gotten an athletic scholarship to the University of Minnesota; he didn't need the money, whereas one of her friends, Nate, had been counting on it. According to Nate, it was only supposed to go to young men with a Lions affiliation. The only Hanson involved with the Lions Club was a retired bachelor named Norm.

But that wasn't all. Jake's ultimate coup de grace had been positively artful.

Their senior year, Mrs. Nelson, who taught civics class, tried to excite students about government and the democratic process by making them debate various social and political topics. Lisa took these debates very seriously for two reasons. First, at the end of the year, one student from each of the civics classes would get an all-expenses-paid trip to Washington, D.C. to spend a week with the state's legislators. Secondly, she discovered that she genuinely found the subject interesting and whatever her college major would be, wanted it to be something along these lines.

It was the last debate of the year and she'd been assigned to a workgroup that included Jake. They had been asked to debate whether education should be publicly or privately operated and funded and what role, if any, the government should have in it. They would defend the privatization of education.

The four group members could never seem to organize themselves to meet and divvy up the labor. Collaborating via email hadn't produced any results, except to litter Lisa's email box with empty promises followed by weak excuses for the lack of follow-through, then apologies punctuated with sad-faced graphics. She was so close to winning, she wasn't leaving anything to chance and had prepared for the debate herself.

The day of the debate, it was no surprise that two of their four members were missing. Her teacher was well aware of how much time she'd spent researching and preparing for these debates. If Lisa was on the team, it was a pretty safe bet that the group would win. All year, Lisa had racked up wins. The unspoken consensus of her classmates was that she was a shoo-in.

So when Jake volunteered to be the group's spokesperson, Lisa had handed over her note cards. At the time, she considered it a fair trade. She was best doing the behind-the-scenes work and despite her dislike of him, couldn't deny that Jake's strong suit was appealing to an audience. Besides, she reasoned, it would look far better for her if she came off as a team player instead of an opportunist—or worse, a martyr. Who liked a "woe is me attitude" when "woo-hoo" was far more peppy?

Jake had taken her dense stack of note cards, spent a few seconds on each one, then turned them over to glance at the back before placing them at the bottom of the pile. While he looked at the cards, the first group presented their arguments for keeping education public. Three of their four members stood in a scraggly line at the front of the class. They had no note cards and said um a lot and things like, "Public education should be free because, um, we pay taxes and that's what they're for. So, um, yeah."

If Jake ever had a calling, it would have been as a magician. When it was their group's turn, he confidently stepped to the front of the room and coaxed the crowd with the arguments Lisa had created. He didn't just lay out bullet points, he crafted a tale that had made her feel that the privatization of education was not only necessary, but critical, vital, and *urgent*. She felt spurred to contact her senator as soon as possible and share the brilliance that they—*she*—had created. He finished his speech to thunderous applause, hoots, and whistles. Mrs. Nelson held one hand over her heart and fanned herself with the other.

They won the debate.

A week later, during civics class, when the secretary announced the winners of the Washington, D.C. trip, Lisa sat up tall in her desk, preparing to hear her name over the loudspeaker. Caught between the indecision to display an expression of surprise or of modesty—or better yet, *knowing* modesty—she heard, "And the last winner of the Meet the Movers & Shakers of Our Nation Contest is Jake Hanson."

Lisa looked over at Jake, up to Mrs. Nelson, back to Jake, and then again at her teacher. Jake took all of the congratulatory whacks in stride. Doing a cheesy impersonation of a crooked politician, he said, "Thank you. Thank you very much." He winked and shot imaginary bullets from his finger pistols to his constituents, then blew the smoke off before reholstering.

And Mrs. Nelson … well, Mrs. Nelson kept her eyes fixed on Jake. Lisa tried to pry her teacher's gaze away from him by staring her down until her own eyes burned and her vision blurred. Mrs. Nelson beamed and offered Jake her congratulations. How could this have happened? She had *known* how much Lisa wanted to go to

Washington. Never once during this little celebration did either of them acknowledge Lisa or her efforts. Lisa was more than mad—she was livid.

Despite her label as a quiet, good girl, she immediately confronted Mrs. Nelson after class. "What happened?"

Mrs. Nelson was startled, like she'd just been asked to take on a new student at the end of the school year. She stepped behind her desk, creating distance between the two of them. Crossing her arms, Mrs. Nelson leaned against her chalkboard. "Well, Lisa, he put forth a very convincing argument. The committee was very impressed with him."

"But I put together that argument."

"Well then, Jake has very persuasive speaking skills."

"That's because I told him what to say." *And she had done all the work*, she wanted to add.

"Then maybe you should've done the talking." Mrs. Nelson threw up her hands and started to furiously erase the board, which Lisa interpreted to mean: *The boy spins magic; what am I supposed to do?*

Lisa's ears had burned as she stood there, stunned. "But I've been on nearly every winning team." *I deserve it* hung implicitly between them.

Mrs. Nelson squirmed under Lisa's glower. "Well, maybe next year we'll try a different kind of rating system."

Jake swooping in and taking Washington at the last minute was unforgivable. Clearly, he'd wanted the trip enough to woo their teacher in the final hour. Or maybe he hadn't. In any case, he'd wowed her, casting a magic spell long enough to get him through. Jake wasn't as nice as everyone thought. Behind that cute smile, letter jacket, and jock strap, he was as all-American as moldy apple pie.

"That explains a lot," said Angela when Lisa finished her story.

"What do you mean?"

"Aside from the hair incident, you were like a racehorse coming out of the gate in college, joining every club that would take you. Now I see you were just overcompensating."

"I had to make up for lost time. It took three years before I got to Washington."

"You could've gone on vacation."

"That's not the same thing. I wanted to meet legislators and lobbyists; learn how the system works from the inside out." Lisa sipped her coffee. "I know it sounds stupid, and I thought I was over it. But seeing Jake again brings all that stuff back. It drives me crazy."

"It's not his fault he was chosen to go to Washington."

"Don't take his side."

"Lisa, you don't know *his* side. For all you know, he worked just as hard as you did in all of the other groups and that was the one time he may have done a little less. At least he showed up for the class and offered to do the talking. He could have left it *all* to you."

"Apparently he should have. The *least* he could've done was given me some credit."

"High school sucks for everybody. That's why we say dumb things like, 'This is the best time of our lives.' How are we supposed to know? We *think* we know everything, but we don't know anything. Everyone has a high school horror story. I bet even Jake has one."

"Oh yeah? What's yours?"

"Umm ... well ... okay. I can't think of one, right now ... oh, wait. I do have one. You know I grew up in a small town, right? I had big poof hair and the wall of bangs to go with it."

"That is so not the same thing. You were popular. If you had the Wall, most likely all of the girls did."

"True, but my pain was self-inflicted."

"You didn't look like that when you went to college."

"That's because my older sister took me to Chicago and enrolled me in a summer beauty-school seminar."

"I would've never known."

"Exactly. It's what you do with yourself after high school that matters. Jake may very well be a perfectly nice grown-up. Like you."

"The logical side of me wants to agree with you, but I just read an article that talked about gender bias in the classroom and how teachers *do* call on boys more—the alpha males especially. So I know I'm not making that up. There's research behind it. The stereotypical injustice of it all makes me so mad." Lisa kicked her legs out, bumping the coffee table in front of them.

Angela argued, "Again, that's not his fault. He'd be a fool to turn down opportunities presented to him. And who's going to say no to a teacher? Like, 'No, ma'am; I can't answer your questions because according to research you call on me too much.'"

"I agree, but with Jake it was different. He won this Outstanding Student Award totally based on his popularity. The award was supposed to go to a student with stellar academic, athletic, *and* artistic achievements and who did community service. There were other kids who had better grades and were far more artistic than Jake who also had athletic accomplishments and volunteered. And all of his charity work? He probably only did it because it would look good on his college applications. Do you know what I mean?" Lisa searched Angela's eyes for some kind of comprehension.

Angela sighed. "I'm sorry for what you went through, but I can't relate."

"Of course not," Lisa mumbled, imagining how popular Angela must have been in high school.

"Maybe he's just one of those people who gets lucky all the time. I have a cousin like that."

Lisa countered, asking, "Did I tell you that he just started at his firm? I bet he'd do anything to make a good impression on his boss. I'm telling you, the guy is a glory hound."

Angela took another sip of tea and tucked a leg under her as she resettled into the couch. "Maybe he's changed."

Lisa shook her head. "I just saw him do it too many times. Believe me, I want to be mature about this, but I can't help but be guarded. I've got to be ready and anticipate how he might screw me over."

"Does he even remember you?"

"It hasn't come up, but if he doesn't, then I'm considering it my advantage."

"If you need therapy, let me know and I'll get you some for your birthday," Angela said, lightening the mood.

Lisa couldn't help but laugh. "What, you're not qualified?"

"Not for this kind of emotional trauma," she teased.

Lisa couldn't deny it; unearthing those memories had brought back odds and ends of anger and resentment that knocked on her heart, beckoning her like small children to play with them. "Did you see him last night the way he was pawing that girl? I heard that his high school girlfriend dumped him right after graduation. I bet *she* knew what he was really like."

"I think you sound a little jealous," Angela said, winking at her.

"All I'm saying is, based on my experience, Jake may not be the wonder boy people think he is."

"So, here's a questions for you: If what happened in high school was so upsetting, why didn't you tell me about it in college?"

"Because I wasn't about to let it plague me. Gosh, I'm not that emotionally scarred. Besides, what good would it have done to keep churning the dirt? It wouldn't have changed what happened."

"And yet here we are, having this conversation anyway. Maybe I should order those sessions now."

Chapter 10

"How's the capital campaign coming along?" Lisa's boss, Susan, asked. Jake heard the question and shifted his eyes toward Lisa. Today she was wearing a gray sweater with a thick collar that swallowed her neck.

They had been working on Grant Park for nearly two months and, so far, he'd hardly gained an inch of social ground. He knew he shouldn't, given Mark's comments about the priority of work over women, but that didn't stop him from wanting to. They'd exchanged emails and phone calls, and they'd had one more meeting in his office, but he was making no headway with her personally. When Lisa talked to him, it was all budgets, charts, and projections. He wouldn't call her friendly, like women usually were with him, but rather polite at best. He was determined to figure out how to crack her shell.

Lisa said, "So far we've raised about $2.3 million. I've been phoning, emailing, and meeting with everyone who's on our list. So far, we've secured eighty-eight corporate cosponsors for the gala."

"We need at least a hundred names on the program by the night of the gala," Susan said.

"I know and I'm sure we can do it," said Lisa. "Even at this late date, I've found a few new grants we can apply for. Here are drafts of the applications for you to look over."

Lisa handed her boss the papers. Jake didn't need copies because he'd already seen them and she had done good work. She said, "We've been having an ongoing discussion with the city and the Nicollet neighborhood for some financial support. I have a meeting with the mayor of Minneapolis next Thursday at two o'clock. Do you think you'd be able to join us?"

Susan looked at her planner. "I can fit that in."

Jake knew she would say yes. Not only was Mr. Hollow an acquaintance of Susan's, so was the mayor. He'd already heard a couple stories around the office about Susan's ability to push projects through to their ends because of her connections. Mark told Jake how Grant had commented once that Susan was the kind of woman who was good to have in your corner, but not in your bed.

Watching Susan, Jake saw her look up at Lisa and then to him. "Did we meet our fundraising goal for this month?"

"Yes, we did. Actually, we made it above our goal," Lisa said. He eyed Lisa discreetly as she exhaled and handed over another set of papers to Susan. It made him wonder what it would have looked like if they hadn't reached their goal.

Susan raised her eyebrows. "Really? By how much?"

"About 2 percent," Lisa answered. "But with the current state of the economy, it's been harder to convince people to commit financially, and if they do, the contribution has been less than what we'd hoped for. I'm trying everything I can to personalize the donation experience."

Jake kept his face straight, but smiled on the inside. He was pretty confident it was because of his efforts that they'd squeaked over their monthly goal. He'd been hitting the streets hard for this project, despite his caseload.

Susan said, "Okay. Give me the list of everyone you've contacted and the progress with each one, and I'll see what I can do."

Ingrid added, "We've also been brainstorming unique gift ideas for donors. You know, really trying to think outside the box, beyond recognition opportunities like plaques and room dedications."

"I can look through our lists of top philanthropists and business people in the area, or originally from the area, again, to see if anyone has ties to the Nicollet neighborhood," said Lisa. "There has to be somebody besides Mr. Hollow."

"Haven't we already booked that band from Minneapolis for the block party?" Susan asked.

Ingrid said, "Yes. I confirmed it with their manager last week. Spinach will provide great publicity, but they're on tour right now and I don't think we'll be able to get much more from them until spring. It would be nice to get someone now who would appeal to the public."

"It would give the project such a boost if we could get a big name—like someone really famous. And have them be from that neighborhood? That would be even better," said Lisa.

"If we could get a celebrity ... think of the PR we could do with that," said Ingrid.

The request dangled between them like bait on a hook, and Jake took it. "David Cibulka is from that neighborhood."

All eyes zeroed in on him. He could feel the surprise coming from Ingrid.

"The hockey player?" she asked.

He felt a small sting of disappointment that it had been Ingrid and not Lisa who'd recognized Dave. Jake explained. "He plays for the San Jose Sharks. Last year they won the Stanley Cup and Dave was voted Stanley Cup Finals MVP."

"Do you know him?" Susan asked.

"We played college hockey together." Jake sat up straighter in his chair, watching the women's reactions.

Lisa said, "Do you *know him* know him, or did you just share a locker room together?"

Jake laughed. "No, Lisa, I *know him* know him. We're actually pretty good friends. When we graduated, he went on to the NHL and I went to law school, but we've still kept in touch."

Susan said, "Run the idea by Grant and see what he thinks. If he says yes, would you be able to contact your friend?"

"Yes I would."

Jake took in her gaze as Susan regarded him. Then she said, "Thank you, Jake."

He glanced over at Lisa, who was sitting back in her chair looking indifferent. Her game face sure made it hard to read her. But he liked her; he was certain of that. She was complex, which wasn't the same as complicated. And smart. It would just take a little more time and patience to peel back her layers to see her softer side.

After the meeting, he consulted Mark right away, and Mark agreed that Jake should email Grant directly about Dave Cibulka. Both of them were sure Grant would go for it, and he confirmed it after lunch in a one-word email: YES. Jake immediately wrote up a contract and an outline of what needed to happen next. When he was finished, he printed a copy of both documents and headed to the elevator to deliver his work in person. He couldn't wait to see the look on her face.

When he arrived at her desk, he saw that Ingrid was gone and Lisa was shutting down her computer. "Everyone at the firm likes the idea of Dave being the park's poster child," he said, interrupting her.

Her eyes lit up as he proudly handed her his papers. She said, "That's great. Do Susan and Ingrid know yet?"

"Not yet," he answered, as Lisa put on her coat and picked up a messenger bag with the Little Flower logo on it. "Where are you going?"

"I have a meeting." She started walking toward the exit, then turned and motioned for him to walk with her. He was next to her in two steps. "So what happens next?"

"Look over the conditions outlined in the contract, make any changes you need, and then once Grant approves it, I'll fax it over to Dave's lawyers." When they reached the elevator, he pushed the down button for her.

"That was fast." She sounded impressed. "We'd like him to do at least one public-service announcement. Or two?" she asked as if to herself. "Yes, two. Can you get two?"

"I think so. Yeah." The elevator arrived and the doors opened but she made no move.

Instead she asked, "Or how about up to five? Is that too many? We wouldn't necessarily need five. Just in case. Can you include that in the contract?"

"I'll check."

When the doors started closing, Jake stopped them with his hand. She hopped in and beckoned him to join her. When the doors closed, she said, "And be sure it's for free."

He smiled. "I'll try my best."

She suddenly placed her hand on his arm. "And invite him to the gala. And the golf tournament." At the end of her request, she removed her hand; it was a mannerism his mom had, too, when she wanted to remind his dad of something.

"Lisa, he's a professional athlete. He probably won't be able to make it."

"I didn't say *require* him to be there; just invite him."

"He doesn't have much time now. The Sharks have a game against the Wild in December, though. Maybe we could arrange a meeting then."

She put her hands in her pockets. "We'll take whatever we can get."

He still felt the imprint of her brief touch and grinned. Ever the negotiator; he enjoyed the fervor she had for her job.

Under her breath she said, "Oh my gosh, this is so awesome."

Her eyes shined with excitement. Three positive reactions. He'd hit the emotional jackpot. Even if her enthusiasm wasn't for him, he'd made progress.

Suddenly her bag started playing music. She threw open the flap and pulled out her cell phone. Her eyes lit up for the second time and a small smile raised the corner of her mouth.

"Something important?" he asked.

"Huh? Oh. Yeah."

He could tell that whatever was happening on her phone threatened him to lose ground. "Dave told me to give you his email address. If you have any questions, contact him directly."

She was still glued to her phone, her thumbs gliding like rain over the smooth screen as she connected letters to make words. "Okay."

When the elevator slowed, she stepped closer to him. He felt the wooly thickness of her jacket next to his dress shirt. She was oblivious to anything except her phone.

The elevator stopped. She finished what she was doing and slipped her phone into her pocket. As she stepped out, she turned, held up her fist, and gave it a small shake, like she was considering giving him a high five then changed her mind. "Thanks."

He replied with his own corny victory fist. He'd finally done something right. And all it had taken was one hockey player.

. . . . .

Whenever her phone played "Let's Hear It for the Boy," she knew it was Tony. What could she say, except that she'd recently caught the last half of *Footloose* on cable.

Without hesitation, she switched on her video chat and clicked on tony_soccer_germany, watching his handle line up with hers, Lisa_runs_usa; another little joke between them. After a few moments, Tony's face bopped up next to hers, pairing them like a couple. The delight of seeing his adorable face pop up on the screen made her laugh. It was so good to see him again. If things progressed as they had online, she envisioned them becoming that real-life version of their little chat heads.

She still got tingly sensations remembering his first text she'd received once he'd landed. *Back in Germany. Cold and rainy. How are you?* She'd texted back, pleased with her own quip. *In U.S. Cold and windy. I'm fine. You?*

"Hi," he said. "How are you?" She loved the deep register of his voice. He sounded just like his personality: casual and unhurried.

"I have huge news for you. David Cibulka is now our official spokesperson for Grant Park. Can you believe it? *David Cibulka.* The hockey player! Famous—from Minneapolis—working with *us*."

"No way. That's cool!"

"His first PSA brought in $500,000 alone. I have so many people inquiring about the project, I can barely keep up. Plus, with the national coverage we've gotten, we've solidified the support we were looking to get out of Grant's Gala."

He smiled broadly and gave her a thumbs-up in the camera. "Nice."

"Unfortunately he won't be able to attend the gala, but hopefully he'll come to our golf tournament in April. If you're here, you could meet him."

He smiled again. "Very cool."

She prattled on. "From this day on, I vow to become a devoted follower of hockey. I mean, *David Cibulka.*" She loved saying his whole name, like that. David Cibulka. It sounded so exotic. "He's the perfect spokesman for what we want to accomplish. And the fact that he comes from the neighborhood that we're building in? People personally identify with a guy like that."

Tony's eyes were no longer focused on the camera, but moving about the screen. It took five seconds of silence before he brought his attention back to her. "That's great. I'm happy for you."

"So what about you?" she asked.

"Good. Playing a lot."

"Where did you go this time?"

"Berlin."

"What's it like? Did you see the wall?"

"No, we only had time for our game."

"How did it go?"

"Good. We won."

"Give me the highlights."

He replayed the game, giving her a few detailed accounts of the best moments. She didn't understand all of it, but enjoyed his exuberance for the sport. He was most animated when he talked about soccer and she liked seeing him happy.

"You're so lucky," she said. "Since college, I've only done a camping trip on the Canadian side of Lake Superior and a day trip with Angela to Tijuana."

"Well you'll have to come visit me then." His green eyes danced with the promise of fun. Glee squeezed her heart at the prospect of seeing Tony again and having an adventure with him.

"Where else have you been?"

"Uh, let's see, Hamburg, Frankfurt, Stuttgart, Moonkin."

Moonkin? She couldn't remember seeing that on the map. "You mean Munich?"

"Yeah, Munich. In German it sounds like Moonkin. Oh, and we played an exhibition match in Paris, and one in Prague, too."

He was drifting again, his eyes flicking from one spot to another across the screen. A black man entered in the background. It was Kwami from Ghana.

"So what's the culture like?" she asked. "Have you been to any museums?"

"Yeah, Kwami and I have been to a few." When Kwami heard his name, he raised his hand in the background and shouted, "Hi, Lisa."

She waved and returned the greeting. "Did you ever get to Notre Dame when you were in Paris?"

"Isn't that in the U.S.?"

"That Notre Dame is a college. I meant the big cathedral in Paris."

He looked over at Kwami, who nodded. "Oh. Yeah, we saw it."

"What was it like?" She shifted in her chair, resting her chin on her hand, ready to soak up the details of the City of Light.

He scratched his head. "Um, old? I don't know. It's got this, like, European feeling, you know? It was cool."

That was it? Couldn't he come up with anything else? He was living in *Europe*, for crying out loud.

"What's your favorite part about being in Europe?"

"Oh man, the beer. Definitely the beer."

"Are you homesick?" she asked. What she really meant was did he miss her, but didn't want to embarrass him in front of his friend.

"A little," he admitted. "I don't mind when we're practicing or we've got a game. But otherwise, it can get a little boring."

"When you get back, we'll have to have lots of fun."

That got his attention. He leaned into his computer, his eyes full of mischief. In a low voice he said, "I'm counting on it."

Chapter 11

Lisa stood in her tiny bathroom, cursing the color black. Tonight was the gala and she'd managed to smear a conspicuous white band of deodorant across the front of her dress. She was dabbing, blotting, scrubbing—doing whatever she could—to get it off, when the phone rang. She softly booted Leroy out of the way.

"I'm not going to be able to make it tonight." It was Ingrid.

"What happened?"

"I just don't feel well. I think I might be getting sick."

"What kind of sick?"

"Pukey sick. I feel nauseous. I don't know what happened. I was feeling kind of crummy at work and now I feel worse. I wonder if it's something I ate."

"I hope not. As I recall, we had the same thing for lunch." Which happened to be egg salad sandwiches and a spinach salad. Oh no. The thought made her queasy.

"I'm really sorry," Ingrid said.

"It's okay. Well—it *is* inconvenient, but …" Then she got an idea. "What were you planning on wearing?"

"My long black dress with the spaghetti straps."

Lisa pictured the dress, knowing instantly which one she meant. She adored it. "Do you mind if I borrow it? I managed to muck mine up with pit stick."

"No problem."

"And one more thing?"

"Yeah?"

"Could I borrow John?"

"Borrow John? Ahem. Well. He was just about to undo his bow tie. Oh. Now he's on his knees praying. Oh wait, no, he's mouthing *no, no, no* and begging me to stay home."

"Please? *Pretty please?* It would make things so much easier if I had at least one person there for emotional support."

"Just a sec." Lisa heard Ingrid cover the receiver and could only make out muffled voices. "Lisa? He'll be there in twenty minutes."

The hall felt warm and intimate despite its vastness. Large golden orbs suspended soft light over the dance floor. Dark centerpieces arranged with a striking combination of ivory lilies, butterscotch and scarlet Leonidas roses, and rust mums graced the tables. Votive candles paired with fall foliage completed the setting. Behind the podium, an inconspicuous orchestra played a slowed rendition of the Viennese Waltz. Lisa lightly drummed the bum-bum-bum rhythm of the waltz against the linen paper program in her hands.

She thanked Ingrid's ailing tummy for the good fortune of not having to come alone after all.

Clint Eastwood sauntered through Lisa's mind as she watched Mr. Hollow shift on his feet behind the podium and gesticulate to a small, captive audience across the room. Instead of wearing the requisite bow tie with his tuxedo, he sported a large turquoise stone and silver bola. She'd bought a smaller one for her father when her parents joined her grandparents' square dancing troupe. She must have had too many predinner gin and tonics, because she swore she heard *Rawhide* ringing in her ears. The champagne, too, was working its lovely magic.

She watched Jake as he listened to Mr. Hollow. He was tracing his forefinger along his own jawline, a habit she noticed he did when he was concentrating. Shadows played across his cheeks, giving his face a sculpted look. Jake looked undeniably handsome. When Mr. Hollow stopped speaking, Jake spotted Lisa, smiled, and raised his hand. She recalled that first working lunch with him. She'd been so fidgety, anticipating him to drop the bomb. But their past hadn't come up, and the more they worked together, the less it was an issue. She raised her glass in return and took an appreciative drink, enjoying the bubbles tickling her throat as she swallowed.

Her working relationship with Jake had upgraded from impossible to tolerable, which both pleased and irritated her. To her chagrin, a tiny part of her liked working with him. She tempered this with a healthy cynicism that ultimately his motivation was linked to his own career advancement.

He'd had some good ideas about how to appeal to corporations. His enthusiasm appeared genuine, making it all the more contagious. He knew how to connect people personally to the larger picture. But while she had a growing appreciation for him, watching him work his magic also reminded her now and then of their debate all those years ago. He'd finessed and perfected his woo, making it more difficult to determine if he was sincere or all smoke and mirrors. She was still guarded, yet happy to see the park benefit from his effort. Mr. Hollow had asked her to find at least one hundred cosponsors for the gala and they'd gotten 125. And of course, they had David Cibulka.

Over the years she'd wondered on occasion what she would say to Jake if they ever met again. It usually involved telling him how fabulous her life was. For example, she had a fabulous job running her own company with her fabulous golf-pro hubby and business partner. Business required them to travel often. *Oh, sorry, Jake; gotta run. My flight for Paris leaves in a few hours. So lovely to see you.* Kiss-kiss, like they did in France. Or she was off to be a guest on a syndicated talk show to discuss her work saving the lives of children in Africa. *Oh, sorry, Jake; gotta run. I have a meeting with Oprah.* Whatever the scenario, the ending was always the same. He would be left hanging to the wispy threads of her last words, amazed by all she had become.

And yet here they were in so very different circumstances. She didn't think she would've minded too much if Jake's efforts on the project had failed. However, they'd been a success—which everyone benefited from—so she was willing to give him a little credit.

. . . . .

That night they had two objectives: to thank each individual for his or her financial support for the park and to coax those who'd given only the minimum to give more. Jake, Mark, and Lisa had been on the prowl all evening. As Jake made his rounds, he'd watched Lisa do the same. He liked how she had a tendency to raise her chin when she listened. She held her back straight with a slight overarch, like a dancer. The thin straps of her black dress complimented her bare shoulders, the dress itself conforming nicely to her shape. An ivory shawl of delicate lace hung loosely across her arms. Her smooth back—her hair up—stirred in him a desire to touch her.

She was the girl-next-door type, a woman he wouldn't have noticed if he'd been out with Scott. He'd always thought her pretty, but hardly glamorous. But tonight she'd glammed up beautifully. She glowed with passion for her work and had an aura of authority and authenticity that took his breath away.

Satisfied with his efforts securing a few more financial commitments, he wanted to follow through on his one personal objective as well. He walked over to Lisa's table. He'd been surprised that she'd come with a date. But as Chad had only been a friend, he wasn't going to make any assumptions about this guy either. He asked, "May I have this dance?"

Lisa looked over to the man sitting with her. The guy said, "Go on. It's okay."

She stood, draped her shawl on the back of her chair, and walked ahead of him. When they reached the dance floor, she turned and stepped into his readied arms. He listened for the music's beat and they stepped at the same time. She needed no leading.

"Good work tonight," Jake said.

"Thank you. You, too."

She looked steadily over his shoulder, holding her arms taut, keeping space between them as they waltzed. He circled them around the dance floor, taking in her scent. She smelled sweet, like pears. It was subtle and didn't make him sneeze like the pungent musk Susan wore. "Did you notice we're the only couple under the age of thirty to be waltzing?"

"I was just thinking that. I expected to have to lead you."

"My grandmother was a dance instructor." He spun her, then pulled her quickly through the next three steps, slowing down only after coaxing a smile out of her. "This place looks great."

She took in her surroundings with a large sweep of her head, while he admired her neck. "Ingrid did an amazing job with this place. It's like being in a fairytale."

"If this were a fairytale, which one would you choose?"

She thought for a moment. "I think it would be Cinderella."

"Why's that?"

"Because this is how I always imagined a ball to be; it's magical." Then she added, "And at the stroke of midnight, it all ends and goes back to reality."

"But in the end, the prince also finds his true love and he and Cinderella live happily ever after."

"And that's why it's called a fairytale." Her eyes sparkled with humor.

He pulled her closer, noting she didn't resist, and nodded toward the man watching them dance. "It was very generous of your date to let me dance with you."

"He's not my date. He's Ingrid's husband."

"Ah. An affair then."

"Only the proper kind. Ingrid wasn't feeling well and let me borrow him."

"Ménage à trois. Yes, that is a proper kind." Her eyes got big. When she saw he was only kidding, she relaxed, and he took another step closer to her. He liked how their bodies fit together and sensed her chest rising as she breathed.

"Where's your date?" she asked.

"I didn't bring one."

"Why not?"

Jake leaned in and whispered, "I'm looking for my Cinderella."

"Have you had any luck?" she asked, looking around.

"I think I might have."

"Don't let me keep you, then. It's almost midnight," she said, and made to pull away.

He steeled his arms, gently keeping her in his embrace. "Then I better keep dancing with her before she runs away."

Her head whipped, her eyes meeting his, looking as large as the lights hanging from the ceiling. It reminded him of their second meeting in the elevator. His gut tightened as he waited for her reaction.

It was *not* good.

He thought she might blush or laugh; instead, she stopped dancing, dropped his hands, and said, "I have to go."

Before he could pull her back, she was already to her table, gathering her purse, her shawl, and Ingrid's husband. Jake stood there wordlessly. He couldn't call her back; that would make him look weak, not to mention unprofessional. Still rooted to the spot, Mark came over and asked, "Are you okay?"

"Yeah," he said, his answer barely audible.

But Mark knew him better than that. "Not the reaction you were expecting?"

"Something like that."

. . . . .

The next morning, Lisa trapped her brother into doing a postmortem by inviting him over for breakfast.

Jake's intimation had stunned her. When John pulled out of the guest-only parking last night, the clock on the dashboard had glowed 11:58. Not even midnight, and she'd already transformed. What was Jake trying to do? He seriously couldn't be interested in her, could he? It wasn't scientifically, logically, or humanly possible.

"Do you remember that night when Angela was here and we saw Jake Hanson at that bar?"

"I knew there was a reason you were buttering me up with pancakes and eggs," Chad said and slapped two more pancakes on his plate, dowsing them with maple syrup.

She ignored his comment and launched into her attack. "The truth is, the last few months we've been working on a project together."

"Yeah, I know."

"How could you know that?" she asked, and Chad filled her in on the football league. "You mean to tell me that he saw us together and you've been playing football with him ever since?"

"Yeah," he said, grinning. "It's awesome. He's still pretty good."

"How come you never said anything?"

"I don't know. Why would you care?"

"You didn't rat me out, did you?"

"No. But I was tempted. What's the big deal, anyway?"

"The big deal is that last night we were working at this fund-raiser and he asked me to dance and then he laid this Cinderella analogy on me. Like I'm Cinderella and he's supposed to be the prince."

Chad covered his ears and said, "La la la. I can't hear you."

"Seriously, Chad," she said, pulling his hands away. "The weird thing is that—I don't think he remembers me."

"Lisa, the dude totally doesn't remember you."

"How do you know that?"

"I figured as much when he asked if we were dating."

"He did?"

"Yeah, but I told him you were too much of a snob to go out with me."

"You did not," she said, socking him in the arm. She picked up her coffee mug, assessing the situation. "So you already knew that Jake was interested in me?"

"Basically. Why are you even telling me this?"

Right. Why *was* she grilling her brother instead of processing with her girlfriends? Because Angela was in Vegas and Ingrid was recovering from stomach flu. "Because you know Jake. You know what he's like."

Chad scoffed.

It was bad enough he didn't remember her, but to be attracted to her as well? It was ridiculous. "Do you think you could do me a favor?" she started. "I—"

"You know what?" Chad interrupted. "I don't think it's in my best interest to be having this conversation with you. I hang out with Jake and—you're my sister. I don't want to know the details."

"But could you—"

"Ah—," he cut her off, slicing his knife through the air. He stabbed his eggs and stuffed a forkful in his mouth.

She watched him a moment. "At least—"

"No," he said firmly through a mouthful of eggs. "Keep me out of it."

They eyed each other in a standoff, Lisa over the rim of her mug and Chad with a fork in one hand and a knife in the other, ready for battle.

"Then keep your mouth shut," she said, grabbing the pan from the stove. "Do you want some more eggs?"

"Yes, please," he growled.

. . . . .

"All I did was hint at my interest and she locked down," Jake told Amir the following week. He was building a tower out of large pink and purple blocks for Amir's two-year-old daughter while Amir tried to figure out the recording function on his new television.

"That's unusual for you."

No kidding. The twinkling lights of the Christmas tree reflected off little Mirijana's earrings, making them glint as she marched her plastic ponies over a bridge Jake had constructed. Jake loved coming to Amir's. Lately he'd felt envious of the comfort of Amir's home and the life he'd created with Ani. Jake and Scott's place was a typical bachelor pad. Couches lined the perimeter of their sparse living room while the walls held the largest flat screen TV on the market, a kick-ass sound system, and posters of chicks on motorcycles. Last week he'd taken down the posters and replaced them with a gigantic autographed poster of the Rolling Stones. Scott disliked the décor change and hung the girlie posters in his own room.

"Everything was going great," Jake continued. "We were putting in a ton of hours on my boss's project. We'd strategize, then argue, and just when I thought she was about to strangle me, we'd get Chinese takeout. We're such a great team." He shook his head, just not comprehending his situation as he restacked blocks that Mirijana removed from his tower. "She'd make an excellent litigator. She's tough, smart, has an opinion about everything ..."

"Maybe you came off a little strong," Amir said, fighting with his flicker.

"I don't see how. All this time, I haven't done anything out of line. I haven't even flirted with her. I made one small comment and she—freaked out—like I'd asked her to marry me."

"Are you sure she's not seeing someone?"

"I'm pretty sure."

"Do you know?"

"No, not exactly. But that's never been a problem before." Ani came out of the kitchen and placed a stack of dishes on the glass dinner table. Jake got off the floor and began arranging the plates and silverware around the table.

Amir asked, "What are you going to do?"

"I have no idea." This was totally uncharted territory for Jake. He thought getting Dave on the project would be enough to win Lisa over. She'd been pleased, but hadn't given him much more than that. "What do you think?"

Ani set a platter of hamburgers, a bowl each of peas, and a large salad on the table while Amir abandoned the remote control, scooped Mirijana up, and placed her in the high chair. "The way I see it, you have two choices. Give her some space; see how she responds. You may have caught her off guard. If it turns out she does like you, she'll make the next move."

"What if she doesn't make the next move?"

"Oh, she will. Women these days are pretty assertive. If they feel they've missed an opportunity, they don't waste time waiting for us to offer a second chance." Ani approached Amir and wrapped her arms around his middle. "Right, honey?"

"Oh, yes, of course," she said, laughing as Amir put a bib around Mirijana's neck.

Jake took his seat. "And the other choice?"

"Give it up now before you get stomped on. Like before."

"No, no, no." Jake shook his head adamantly, placing his napkin in his lap. "There will be no *like before*."

Amir was referring to Anna Garcia.

Anna had been Jake's girlfriend all through high school and the only girl he'd ever loved. Compared to other girls, Anna had been exotic. Her family was from Mexico. Anna's grandparents had lived with the family, taking care of the younger siblings while her parents worked, her father as a roofer, her mother as a housecleaner. Jake had never been sure of their legal immigrant status, but had figured that they worked hard to make a living for their five kids and it was better not to ask.

Anna had been the queen bee of the Spanish-speaking clique at their high school. Jake fell for her because she was strong, beautiful, and complicated. She didn't care how popular he was, or that others thought he was; she treated him like an equal and expected him to do the same. She knew exactly what her worth was and never let anyone make her feel any less.

She had started out—and had remained—an enigma, a puzzle he could never quite figure out. She could be sweet yet ruthless, compassionate yet harsh. Her actions were decisive and passionate, black and white. She had told him many times that she loved him, but sometimes the relationship was too turbulent to tell. Just when

Jake thought things were going well, she'd pull away. One moment she insisted she didn't need him, the next she would grasp his neck and declare she couldn't live without him. He rode out the highs and lows because he thought they had a mature relationship—something special that was more profound than what high school dating usually looked like. He had thought it must be love.

She dumped him promptly after graduation. Amir was there for the breakup. *Literally.* He was standing right there. They'd been shooting hoops when Anna approached them and said that she and Jake needed to talk. Guys know that when a girl says, "We need to talk," it's not good. But Jake thought he was immune to such language. After all, he and Anna had been together four years. In high school, that was like the equivalent of thirty years of marriage.

Feeling secure, he continued dribbling the ball. "What's up?"

She folded her arms and announced, "Jake, high school is over now and I think we should see other people."

Her speech caught him in midswish. The ball bounced off the backboard and fell to the ground, bouncing a few more times—an unceremonious thump, thump, thump—before rolling away. Even Amir didn't go for the rebound.

She said, "Don't get me wrong; you've been really good to me, and I do love you, but I realized that I love you more like a friend—a really good friend, like, close to my heart—but not like a boyfriend."

When he heard her say it, he could tell by her tone and word choice that this was a prepared speech. She'd obviously spent a lot of time composing it, including the part where she crossed her hands like butterfly wings of perfectly manicured nails of seashell pink, across her heart and patted it. Nevertheless, Jake said, "Don't you think we should talk about this?"

She shook her head and played with the pendant on a necklace he didn't recognize. Her fingers were smooth and fleshy with youth, nothing like her mother's calloused, cracked hands. He pictured Anna stroking his face as she shot him down.

She said, "No. I've made up my mind and I think it's for the best."

Then she kissed him on the cheek and offered him the mother of all insults. "You're a great guy, Jake, and I wish you all the best."

She partied her way through the summer and right into college. He never saw her again. The benefit, he supposed, was that he got to experience getting his heart ripped out at the onset of adulthood. The lesson had served him well. He'd come close to being in love since then, several times, but whenever it veered toward messy or too complicated, he had the foresight to break it off. It was ironic, but in the end, he was actually thankful to Anna, at least, for that.

As he munched on his burger and watched little Mirijana line up her peas, he felt confident that Lisa was nothing like Anna.

Chapter 12

People ebbed and flowed through the Xcel Energy Center as they found their seats and waited for the game to start. Lisa was hardly a hockey fan, but even she felt charged with mounting anticipation. The Sharks were in town, playing against the Wild, and David Cibulka had offered everyone free tickets. Jake had managed to score a face-to-face meeting with him after the game. She was finally going to meet the man behind all of the emails, posters, and public-service announcements.

Their seats were a few rows behind San Jose's bench. In Tony's absence, Lisa had invited Chad, and they sat next to Ingrid and John. Jake was on the other side with a guy she'd never seen before. She immediately disliked him as his eyes crawled over her body, trying to survey her through her bulky coat.

"Hey, Chad, who's your friend?" Jake's friend asked. His voice sounded cheap and scratchy, like polyester being passed off as silk.

"This is Lisa," Jake answered. "And she works with me."

Scott gave her another smarmy look, before following the ass of a woman who was making her way up the stands.

Lisa whispered to Chad, "How do you know him?"

"From football. He's Jake's roommate."

Lisa had accepted the fact that her brother fraternized with the enemy, but this guy? He was low grade, even for Chad. Mark showed up next with his wife, Cynthia, whom Lisa had met at the gala. Nudging Ingrid, Lisa said, "I told you being ringless didn't mean anything."

Other than knowing the basic objective of the game—get the puck into the opponent's net—she was unfamiliar with the finer points of hockey. So as not to appear too ignorant, when the game started, she followed the crowd, mimicking the growls and groans, the critiquing shouts and victorious cheers. She knew enough to cheer sincerely when the Wild scored, and had enough heart to wince when players got smashed into the sideboards. Chad instructed her through the rest, offering bits of information that suddenly gave the game more sense. She stayed glued to number nineteen, following his every move. He glided over the ice, skating with a speed and power that looked effortless. He was focused and never took his eye off the puck. Even if he was on the opposing team, she hoped that he would do well personally. When the buzzer sounded ending the first period, the score was tied one-one.

Suddenly, David turned toward the audience and faced their section. Lisa jumped up. "There he is! Hi! David! HI! *DAVID!*" She waved her arm. She thought she saw him wink. Chad pulled her down and said through clenched teeth, "You're embarrassing me."

"I thought he could see us."

"He can't."

Oh.

During the second period, the teams turned on the fury as each one scored two more goals. Lisa was sucked in now, because even she understood that sitting at three-three after the second period made for a great game. Tony would've loved this.

When not in the throes of spectator theatrics, Lisa occasionally glanced at Jake. He seemed just as involved in the game as she was. She'd worried that it would be awkward between them after the gala. But he'd shown no animosity toward her and it hadn't been strange between them at all. He hadn't brought it up, so neither would she.

While waiting for the third period to start, Jake said, "Chad. Lisa. I just realized you both have the same last name. Are you related, by any chance?"

Lisa was horrified; Chad, fearless. He said, "No. It's how we became friends, though. Lisa sat behind me in a class in college."

Say what? College students didn't sit alphabetically. She watched Jake's face.

"Huh," was all he said as he turned to watch the players skate back onto the ice. In that moment, Lisa loved her brother as much as a sister possibly could.

The game ended with a four-three victory for the Wild.

Afterward, John and Ingrid headed home while the rest of them waited for David. Once he had cleaned up, he emerged from the locker room like a god. On the ice, he appeared taller than the other players but not larger. In person, however, David Cibulka towered over Jake, who wasn't a small guy by any means, with six inches of additional height. His broad shoulders reminded her of the wingspan of eagles. It was all she could do not to gawk as he handed out passes to an exclusive, members-only club off of Grand Avenue. His demeanor was low-key and an ironic contrast to his size.

Wow, she thought, as her eyes adjusted to the seductive darkness of the club. She considered her usual pseudo-Sex-in-the-City club sophisticated, but this place made that one look like a teen hangout. She sensed a code of conduct—a certain savoir faire. Sit in small discreet huddles. Maintain a subdued attitude. No finger pointing or arm waving when spotting a celebrity. She guessed yelling across the bar was out, too.

Everyone ordered a drink. Lisa could only imagine what kind of booze they had. She was too afraid to order anything in case she mistakenly got a five-hundred-dollar snifter of brandy. She settled for water, joking with the server that someone had to be the designated driver. Ha-ha. Ahem. Yeah, right. But she was glad she did. That water cost her seven bucks.

They settled into some very soft, very smooth black leather couches around a small black table. The men relaxed, immediately getting into their element. Even Cynthia seemed cool. Lisa was in awe of the whole scene, paranoid she'd make a serious faux pas, thus barring her from future visits. Not that she'd ever be invited again, anyway. Hell would have to freeze over before she got here on her own merit.

She smoothed her knit Fair Isle skirt, which went well with her gray tights and urban mukluks, and jiggled her foot, trying to shake off her nervous energy. Even though she stared intently at David's face, she barely caught a word of what he was saying.

"Nicollet was a tough neighborhood, but once you got to know the people, it wasn't so bad," David was telling the group. "Sometimes life makes people hard, but they're mostly good on the inside."

That she heard, and her heart swelled with appreciation. Here was a man who understood her mission. Who would have thought that a hockey player, of all people, would get it?

Cynthia asked, "What was it like living there?"

"We lived in a quadruplex that operated more like a commune than an apartment building. My parents were artists, which meant we were broke most of the time. But we got by. When the art wasn't selling, my dad did carpentry work and my mom was a waitress. My two older brothers had paper routes. I was the youngest and spent most of my time at the outdoor rink across the street. The neighborhood wasn't as dangerous as I hear it is today, but still, you had to be careful. There were some old guys, though, who looked out for me, showed me some moves on the ice. I owe them a lot."

After hearing this, Lisa blushed, feeling guilty about stereotyping David. If roles had been reversed, she would've been incensed by her shallow judgments. But still, when was the last time she'd heard a man like him talk like that? Never. Maybe they existed—but she suspected they were rare. *But that's not fair either,* she scolded herself. Maybe lots of athletes were like David. She didn't hang out with them. What did she know?

"What Dave isn't telling you is that he not only had natural talent, but a good, solid work ethic on that ice rink," added Jake. "That's what got him noticed early on. When his parents realized that he had talent, they did whatever they could to get him every opportunity possible. That's how he got on the University of Minnesota hockey team." Jake looked to David, who nodded.

Perched on the edge of the couch, Lisa remained quiet, sipping her water, waging the internal social-versus-societal debate. While trying to place the genre of the music echoing throughout the club, her brain registered a lull in voices. It occurred to her that maybe she was being included in a conversation after all. When she glanced over, she saw that all eyes from their little party were on her.

"I'm sorry?" she asked.

"What did you think of the game?" David was addressing *her*.

"Oh, the game. Yeah, it was great. I was sorry to see you lose on your home turf and all, but I was happy for us. Go Wild!" She raised her fist in a little rah-rah cheer. *Pathetic*. Where was her composure? Chad rubbed his hands over his eyes, shaking his head.

But the little cheer seemed to have had its desired effect, because David laughed and said, "Well, you win some, you lose some."

"Is that what your coach said after you lost?"

"Ah, no. He took a different line of thinking."

"Do you ever feel guilty, like you're not doing your job, when you lose?" she asked.

"Yeah, sure. I mean, we're getting paid and we're getting paid to win, so mistakes aren't allowed. All you can really do, though, is play your hardest and if the best team wins and it's not you—so be it."

A philosophical hockey player. She loved it. "I don't think I could take the pressure. Aside from not being much of an athlete anyway, I think I'd feel too guilty getting paid as much as you guys do—win or lose. I wouldn't be able to stop thinking about the starving children in Africa or something along those lines." She cringed. David had likely been a little like one of those kids.

"You mean the children our parents told us would suffer if we didn't eat all of our vegetables?" David asked with a smile.

That was when she relaxed and noticed his uncomplicated brown eyes as they chuckled at their small joke.

Chad chimed in, "Lisa, you're an athlete." The eyebrows went up all around. "She runs marathons."

Cursory glances, especially from Scott, pelted her body, no doubt seeking out a runner's physique. Jake studying her, David looking at her—she hadn't felt this self-conscious since, well, probably high school. She started swinging her foot again. "That's a bit of an exaggeration."

"But you did a half-marathon last summer, didn't you? And you do those fun runs," Chad persisted.

"Yeah, once in a while." She racked her brain for another topic. World peace?

Chad started laughing and said, "Remember when we did the Shithouse 5k?"

"No way," said David. "For real?"

"Really," Chad said. "It's a race in La Crosse, Wisconsin. The course runs along the Mississippi River near the sewage treatment plant. It finishes at what they call The Shithouse Flame."

"It stinks so bad, but the race is so much fun," Lisa added.

"Yeah and then we got these T-shirts that said 'I just ran the shittiest race in the world.'"

"And you've got to love a postrace party that serves beer," Lisa said, "in the morning."

"I think you guys are full of shit," said Scott, pointing his drink at Chad and Lisa.

"You can find it on the Internet," Chad insisted. "They have it in the spring because that's when the ice starts to melt and the sewage flows." Chad turned to David. "The next time you're in town, we'll show you our shirts. How about that?"

"When do you think that will be?" David was asking her, not her brother.

"The next time you'll be in town? I think that depends on you."

"I'll email you," he said and winked over his drink. It was definitely a wink. She was sure.

. . . . .

Jake couldn't stand watching one of his best friends make a play on Lisa any longer. Not that he had a claim on her, but still he couldn't resist throwing in a grenade and blowing it to pieces.

"Dave, remember some of the shit-related stuff we did?" He turned to the rest of their group. "Once we went out to this horse farm and collected all of the manure we could find. When we got back to campus, we put a big piece of dung in each locker of every rookie player. Oh man, that reeked for weeks."

"No, I don't remember that," said Dave, hiding his amusement with mock embarrassment.

"Or that semester we spent peeing our names into the lawns of that sorority house across the street?"

"Nope, wasn't there." Dave covered his eyes, trying to suppress his laughter.

Scott said, "Why wasn't I a part of that? I don't remember that. Was I there?"

Then Dave uncovered his eyes. "Although I do remember the time you passed gas next to this pretty girl and blamed it on her. The poor girl kept insisting she didn't do it, but no one believed her."

Very soberly, Jake said, "And I stand by that to this day. I didn't do it." And really, he hadn't. "Is there a law that says pretty girls can't break wind?"

"Yeah," interjected Scott. "Biological ones. God did not intend for beautiful women to fart. It goes against their feminine nature."

"Are you suggesting that farts are only for ugly people?" Mark challenged.

"Well, not necessarily. Men can fart; that's a given. But, yeah, I suppose ugly girls can, too. Especially ugly, fat girls."

The guys groaned while the women looked at each other. Neither was laughing. Cynthia looked at her watch and then at Mark. He could see the wheels and cogs grinding in Lisa's brain as she processed Scott's crass remark. She was going to blow if he didn't fix it first.

Jake said, "Please, not in front of the ladies."

"What?" Scott asked.

"You can't say stuff like that, man. Especially in the twenty-first century and especially not in front of women," he explained.

"I didn't mean *them*," Scott said, pointing to Cynthia and Lisa.

Jake felt Lisa's eyes pierce him. If she stared any harder, she'd set him on fire. Their fun evening was going down in flames. Cynthia had already slipped on her coat and Mark was chugging his whiskey as best he could. Jake cleared his throat. "You shouldn't mean anybody."

"Come on." Scott looked around at the group and saw no one laughing. "Okay. Let me amend my statement. I would be more inclined to accept flatulence from a less attractive female."

Lisa was pushing up the sleeves of her sweater, her universal sign she was prepping to launch into a rant. Lisa giving Scott a lecture he should've gotten from his parents would be wasted breath. All Scott would hear was the Charlie Brown, "Wah-wah, wah-wah," while he calculated her cup size. This was Jake's fault. He had to act, do something dramatic to really shake Scott up and come out on top.

Jake stood up. "You know what? I need to go. Dave, thanks for the game. Mark, see you tomorrow. Chad, ladies, have a good night." On his way past Scott, he muttered, "You're an asshole."

Behind him, he heard Scott say, "What? I was just expressing an *opinion*."

Jake kept walking with a confident stride toward the lobby. He wasn't sure if walking away had been the best choice, but he had to appear strong and wouldn't look back. Scott would know that Jake had been the one to have the last word. Aside from being personally offended, Jake was mostly embarrassed. It was bad enough that Scott talked that way in general, but to do it in front of Lisa? And *Dave?* If it hadn't been Amir and Ani's date night, he would've brought Amir instead.

All he could do was hope he'd been able to do some kind of damage control. Lisa would probably think he was a wuss for leaving instead of arguing, but at least he was a wuss with standards. That had to count for something. As he reached the lobby, cramming on his stocking cap and zipping his jacket, he heard, "Jake, wait." He looked back and saw Lisa.

When she got closer, he said, "I'm sorry for what he said. He's a prick and I can't believe I actually hang out with a guy like that." He flexed his fingers, working out the nerves that had bunched up in his fingertips.

"Well, if that's true, then maybe what he said shouldn't surprise you." He'd expected a reprimand—a thorough telling off—but her tone was gentle.

"I don't want you to think that I'm like that, because I'm not." There was a piece of hair out of place next to her ear. He wanted very badly to touch her.

At first she didn't say anything then looked away. "Jake—"

Before she could finish, he said, "It's all right. You don't have to say anything." Honestly, he had no idea what she was going to say, but whatever it was, he didn't want to hear it. He'd already had large doses of two emotions he hadn't experienced in a long time: jealousy and fear of rejection.

Chapter 13

When the elevator opened, the sweaty steam of the room hit them. This party was literally *hot*. Energy pulsed through the room as the music thumped and bounced off the walls. Right away Ingrid and Lisa took to the packed dance floor while the men stationed themselves by the bar.

"What's with the guys tonight?" Ingrid asked after they'd danced a couple of tracks. "They're huddled around a napkin writing stuff."

"Tim broke up with that girl just before Christmas, so he and Chad have a specific directive for tonight: to find a girl to kiss by midnight. And it can't be just any girl. She must be single, reasonably attractive, and within the age limits: i.e., no kids or grandmas."

She rolled her eyes. "I'm so glad I'm married."

Lisa said, "All I can say is watch out; the testosterone is flying tonight. We may become unsuspecting casualties." They watched the men shake hands, then disperse through the crowded room; Tony and John headed their way.

Tony slid his hands around her waist and began dancing. Enjoying his strong grip, she moved closer. He was so lithe and sexy when he moved; he couldn't help but draw attention to himself. Lisa was more than happy to accommodate the stares. Tony was already leaving tomorrow—on New Year's Day. There was still so much to say, so much to decide.

Neither one of them had used the L-word, not even saying, "I like you." She admitted she was sucked in, but not so much that she'd lost her senses. Yes, he was good looking, a great dancer, and an awesome kisser. And of course she liked him. *A lot.* But reuniting with him hadn't been exactly what she expected. It bothered her that he'd been back over a week and, still, they didn't quite seem to have that bobble-head chemistry like they'd had online. Conversation felt—stilted. Asking him questions was like an inquisition and his answers disappointingly short. If she heard him say "cool" one more time, she thought she'd smack him. Just when she started reconsidering her attraction to him, Tony would redeem himself by taking her to a Eurotechno club she'd never heard of or to a *capoeira* demonstration. Maybe he was verbally challenged, but the guy was adventurous.

She also hadn't forgotten about the abrupt way he'd upped and left the country with no notice. Given him the benefit of the doubt, yes—but not completely forgiven. That's why she hadn't slept with him yet.

Besides, women who slept with men too quickly lost first their credibility, and then their self-respect. Especially if there was a falling out. Lisa had learned that lesson in college. In the sexual arena, the playing field was not level. Men got notches in their belts for sexual conquests; women got points knocked off for being those sexual conquests.

Furthermore, when a woman slept with a man at the onset of a budding relationship—unless she was tainted by too many one-night stands to give a damn—she was signaling that she was willing to fall in love with him. She didn't actually come out and say the words, "I'm falling in love with you," in case the man didn't plan to return the sentiment; but that's what a woman meant. Angela thought Lisa watched too much *Dr. Phil*.

In any case, she wasn't ready to go there. *Yet.*

. . . . .

To celebrate his liberation, Jake headed over to St. Paul with Scott to meet up with some guys from their football team to ring in the New Year. Amir and Mark had couples' plans. Chad and Tim were going out with a group that included Lisa. As much as he liked hanging out with them, he wasn't too interested in spending New Year's Eve around her.

A new year meant new beginnings, starting fresh with new plans and promises for a better year. Lisa had made it very clear, in more ways than one, that she wasn't interested. It was already unusual for him to spend this much time pursuing one particular woman. He'd seen something in her that appealed to him; something different, but maybe he'd been wrong. It had been an experiment with change that hadn't worked; a small investment which hadn't yielded any gains. Because he hadn't gotten too deeply involved, it was okay, though. He had his career and broomball started in January. Going out tonight would be a symbolic act of moving on.

He and Scott went all out and rented Prom King pale-blue polyester tuxes with ruffled shirts that exuded the 1970s spirit. Jake found an awesome vest studded with silver diamond sequins. Scott wore orange sneakers. They both opted for the fedoras.

Everything was cool between Scott and him, but not without a price. No one offered Scott a ride that night after the hockey game. Jake hoped that either the walk home or the pain-in-the-ass search for a taxi had given him time to ponder what had occurred. Scott had thought about it all right. Two days later, Jake found a Summer's Eve feminine douche and an issue of *Martha Stewart Living* on his bed. For payback, Jake signed him up for a month's worth of etiquette lessons and recruited Scott's boss—who was an ex-girlfriend of Jake's—to attend with him.

Sitting at the bar, Jake held up his whiskey and announced, "I intend to get fully inebriated throughout the course of this evening. Due to said inebriation, I am further exempt from any responsibility pertaining to my behavior."

"That's fancy lawyer talk for 'I'm gonna get piss drunk and you better watch out,'" Scott translated.

Jake wasn't really going to get hammered. He'd said it only to embrace the spirit of the holiday. If anyone was going to get drunk, it was going to be Scott.

"I think we should celebrate," said Scott, handing Jake a second whiskey.

"Okay. What are we celebrating?"

"For one, this is the first time in weeks you've been out. Secondly, I predict that this night will include some very fine women. That, my friend, is always worth celebrating."

Jake, feeling gregarious, lifted his glass and joined Scott's toast. "I did it all for you, Scott."

"And I appreciate that, Jake. For a while there, I was getting a little worried. You've been so serious lately—I was starting to wonder what had happened to my friend."

"It's all under control now." Jake watched as couples and groups of girls convened on the dance floor.

Scott said, "What we need to do tonight, boys, is get Jake laid. It's been more than six months since he's been with a woman."

"How do you know?" Jake asked.

"I'm your roommate; I would know. And the celibacy is killing you."

"It's not as bad as you would think."

"Don't kid yourself. It's killing you." Scott nodded toward a pair of women he'd chatted with earlier. "What do you think of them?"

Scott wasn't one to settle for less than gorgeous and the women looked like they came straight out of Photoshop—airbrushed to perfection. Jake said, "You know how to pick them, that's for sure. What do they do again?"

"The redhead is a personal trainer. Her friend's a nurse. Or was it a dental assistant? I don't care. Which one do you want?"

"You know what, how about if I be your wingman tonight?"

"Cool. In that case, I'll take Red. I like a woman who takes care of herself. Besides, I don't like sick people much."

Scott set down his drink and stood. "It's time we put these monkey suits to good use. Let's go, men."

Before Jake could convince him not to, Scott was already shimmying and jiving into the crowd. He took one hand from each woman and led them onto the dance floor. Jake followed Scott to make sure he stayed out of trouble while the others held down base camp at the bar.

Scott had his groove on and, before Jake knew it, they were breaking out all the moves. He hadn't had this kind of fun since before starting at Smacker. Usually he stuck to the man-shuffle, but the festive mood was encouraging. A group formed around them and cheered. Scott's hair was plastered to his forehead, he was so sweaty, and Jake guessed he didn't look any better. Then the deejay spun "Stayin' Alive" by the Bee Gees. The crowd went berserk. The circle around them disbanded and they were practically trampled by people swarming to the dance floor. It was *awesome.*

. . . . .

"I'm pregnant," Ingrid announced in the restroom as they were freshening their makeup.

Lisa nearly dropped her lipstick. "You are?"

"Remember the night of the gala when I had to cancel because I felt so sick? The nausea wasn't going away and I hadn't been sleeping well. I was afraid I had cancer or something, so I went to the doctor and found out I was pregnant."

"Congratulations! I'm so happy for you." Lisa hugged her. Ingrid looked doubtful. "Are you happy for you?"

"Well, yeah," Ingrid said, tossing her gloss into her clutch and snapping it. "It's a baby, right? But it's kind of scary, too. I mean, we want to have kids; we just didn't think it would happen this soon. We haven't even been married a year." She stuck out her belly and asked, "Do I look fat?"

Ingrid had a small bump that was hardly noticeable through her dark purple party dress. "No, you look amazing. How far along are you?"

"Fourteen weeks. We finally told our parents over Christmas."

She hugged Ingrid again. "I'm really happy for you."

As they exited the powder room and made their way back to their group, Lisa linked arms with Ingrid. "So, if you're pregnant, who am I going to have after-work cocktails with?"

"Me, of course. Instead of martinis, I'll have Shirley Temples."

"With the little umbrellas?"

At the bar, Ingrid released Lisa to sit next to John. She asked, "How goes the hunt?"

"The night is young, my squaw," he said, planting a kiss on her cheek.

Lisa asked, "Is there any money involved in this juvenile bet?"

"No," said Chad. "The potential loss of manhood is far more threatening than the loss of any sum of money."

John asked, "How about rules regarding appropriate levels of drunkenness?"

"That's a good point!" Tim said. He pulled out a wad of napkins and added, "Must be sober enough to choose to engage in aforementioned New Year's Eve kiss. If girl vomits, she ceases to be a qualified candidate. If she vomits afterward, kiss becomes null and void."

Tony guffawed and high-fived Tim, while Lisa looked away, embarrassed. She eyeballed her brother who shrugged and returned the look with his own that said, *Hey, we're guys. What do you expect?* Why did they associate with such Neanderthals? She wasn't about to be a mood killer, but she'd explain to Tony later why female intoxication was no laughing matter. She already had a pamphlet or two on the subject that could easily be tucked into some materials she'd put together about the Little Flower Foundation and Grant Park.

Ingrid looked over Tim's shoulder. "This is written like a contract. Look, they all signed their names."

"In blood, my dear," said John as he wrapped his arm around Ingrid and kissed her cheek.

"John!" Ingrid admonished with a slap on the wrist.

"I may be married, but I can appreciate a good hunt." John squeezed Ingrid around the waist.

Lisa said, "You see, Ingrid. What did I tell you? You're the first casualty of war for the night. Even being married doesn't protect you."

Tony had a smoldering smirk. He leaned into Lisa and whispered, "Watch out. You're next."

. . . . .

Sometime after "Stayin' Alive," Jake got entwined in the arms of a woman with frizzy, dark brown curly hair and a cocktail dress that didn't hold her in well enough. He was dancing alongside Scott, minding his own business, when she just appeared. She was a lawyer, too. Keeping his eyes averted, they talked shop and played a couple rounds of "Do You Know So and So?" The woman liked camping and rock climbing and *loved* to cook, especially Italian. She'd met her last boyfriend while backpacking through Italy, and unfortunately they had to break up because he couldn't get a job over here, and as much as she loved Italy, couldn't possibly imagine living there. He knew all of this because from the moment she'd latched on to him, she hadn't stopped talking. On a night like New Year's Eve, when time pushed relentlessly, unfeelingly forward—no matter how much a person wanted to stand still, clinging to their jar of collected memories—and began anew, he could understand her missing her ex.

Jake removed himself from her clutches by excusing himself to go to the men's room. He lingered in the back awhile, checking his messages, then called his parents to wish them a Happy New Year. When he looked out to the dance floor, he discovered his new lawyer friend had found another guy who seemed only too glad to have a woman cry on his shoulder. He returned to the bar and found his other friends chatting with a group of women, who seemed to be exceptionally knowledgeable about hockey, enough, maybe, to be recruited for their broomball team. Jake looked out to the dance floor, making sure Scott was still standing. He'd locked in on the personal trainer redhead and both looked all right. His watch told him it was two minutes shy of midnight.

The deejay quieted the music and turned everyone's attention to the jumbo TV mounted on the wall. Ryan Seacrest, in a charcoal pea coat, stood at the ready, with microphone in his gloved hand, preparing for the final countdown of the year.

Ten ... Nine ... Eight ... Seven ... Six ... Five ... Four ... Three ... Two ... One ... Happy New Year! Partygoers tooted horns and streamers unfurled across the bar. Jake generously gave man-hugs to the men and kisses on the cheek to the women. Scott and Red were in a liplock that looked like it was going to last awhile. Jake sighed contentedly and watched the confetti flutter. It was going to be a good year.

Chapter 14

It had been the best New Year's Eve party since the one in Times Square with Angela four years earlier. On the cheer of *Happy New Year!*, Tony pulled Lisa into a hug, lifting her off her feet, then gave her the most unhurried, luscious New Year's kiss she'd ever had. After the kiss, he set her down and said, "Let's get out of here."

"The night was fun, even if we didn't score, right buddy?" Chad said, as he ambled over to the couples on the dance floor, his arm slung around Tim's neck. Despite the men's sincere prowling efforts, Tim and Chad ended up by the bar at midnight, forlorn, yet happy to be in each other's company, at least. They hugged with lots of masculine backslapping and belted out "Auld Lang Syne."

Tim said, "Totally. Let's go find an after-party and then have breakfast."

"Thanks for the invite, guys, but we should be heading home," John said, patting Ingrid's belly. "Mama can't party like she used to."

"We're going to call it a night, too," Tony answered for both of them. Her heart swelled with relief that her affections had not been for nothing. Tony was usually more inclined to transition to the next party than to call it a night.

On the taxi ride to Lisa's apartment, Tony held her close, her hand in his. Lisa was *deliriously* happy. Her eyes closed, she cozied into his body. She still couldn't believe he was here again. One minute in another country, the next—present. Right next to her. All she could think about was freezing this exact moment and staying like this forever. She would ignore the math that told her Tony would be gone in seventeen hours.

Twenty minutes later, the taxi reached her place and deposited them on the sidewalk. She led Tony toward the house, her fingers loosely clasped in his. Her heart raced. She wasn't really sure where all of this was going. They'd had plenty of fun, but he hadn't given her any indication of where he thought this might be headed. She didn't want to make the first move, but still wanted him to know she was open.

When they reached the stoop he solved her dilemma by pulling her to him. His kiss was deep and ravenous, with a sense of urgency that she hadn't felt from him before. She smelled the remnant of sweat on his skin and tasted a hint of champagne in his mouth.

Before making it from the porch through the front door, they were already tearing off jackets, kicking off shoes, and cursing winter, all the while kissing each other wildly. Landing on the couch, she wanted to rip off his button-down oxford like they did in the movies, but the practical side of her didn't want to ruin a perfectly nice shirt.

She deftly slid her fingers over the buttons instead. In return, Tony bypassed the zipper of her dress and slid his hands under the fabric and over her skin. His hands felt cool and slightly rough against her warm thighs. Although she thought the word that flitted through her mind sounded hysterical, the sensation was *titillating.*

Lisa pushed his shirt open and kissed his smooth chest and ripped abs. He laid back and lifted his hips as she worked her way down to his belt. He moaned and pushed her head lightly against his crotch. She hovered. What would all of this mean tomorrow?

Tomorrow? She didn't want to think about tomorrow. She unbelted his jeans, which were her absolute favorite, but left it at that. She kissed her way back up to his face and aligned her body with his. Tony pressed himself against her, leaving no space for doubt.

They made out for a while until the hot fire he'd stoked within her had waned to embers. Random thoughts ran through her mind. If Tony spent the night, which it looked like he would, what would they have for breakfast? And did she have enough milk? She admired how soft her skin was against his, priding herself on the purchase of the outrageously expensive razor that had produced ideal results, and reminded herself to call Angela tomorrow. She noticed a slim crack in the wall and wondered how it had happened, how long it had been there, and if her landlord would want her to pay for the repairs.

She pulled back from the action and looked at Tony. She loved his face. He had a chiseled, square jaw and a few hairs of stubble poked through his otherwise smooth chin. Despite it being winter, Tony's skin tone had a healthy surfer-dude glow. His wavy blond hair completed the look. She noted that his eyes weren't just green—they were green-gold, dotted with specks that reminded her of freckles.

He smiled. "What are you thinking?"

"You don't want to know," she kidded—which wasn't so far from the truth.

He grasped a lock of her hair and twisted it gently around his finger. "You are so beautiful."

His comment sounded an alarm instead of pleasing her. In all the time they'd been together, he'd never declared she was beautiful. She'd sort of hoped and assumed he thought she was, and now that he'd said it, it sounded like the sort of thing a man said when he wanted to sleep with a woman. Which Tony, by the size of his erection, clearly did.

Instead of sharing what she was really thinking, she said, "Thanks. You're not so bad yourself."

He released her hair and combed through the strands. She liked the affection, but noted the air was very dry and hoped he'd stop before it crackled with static electricity and gave them a shock. Tony said, "It's going to be really hard leaving tomorrow."

She held her breath. Was this his way of saying that he was in love with her? Was he going to say it? Were they going to take that next step? She *knew* it had been worth it to wait on having sex. Now it was not only going to be worth it, it was going to be beautiful and meaningful. She played it conservatively, not wanting to appear too eager. "You'll only be gone a few months, right?"

"I should be able to come back for Easter." He hugged her to his chest. She reveled in his arms and waited for him to say more. Then he whispered in her hair, "Should we go to your bedroom?" and gently kissed the top of her head.

Instead of feeling relief that there was indeed some kind of emotional connection that could lead to a possible relationship, her body tensed up. She didn't tense up—her *body* tensed up. Her shoulders crept up to her neck and remained there, rigid and cold. She commanded her body to relax and enjoy his warm embrace, but it refused to obey.

How do you know it's not a booty call? For all you know, he's got some girl back in Germany. She could picture Angela standing over her with crossed arms and an arched eyebrow.

"Are you okay?" he asked.

"Yeah, I'm fine. Just a little cold," she lied.

"I can think of a way to warm you up," he said and slid his hands under her panties.

Her hormonal center screamed *YES!* while the rest of her body shivered, she suspected more likely out of fear than with anticipation. She kissed him again. Having sex with Tony would be the perfect stamp of approval. To get herself back in the mood, she recalled all of their romantic moments since they'd met. But it was no use. The logical side of her brain had engaged, the heat already dissipating from her hoo-ha, no matter how much she'd been looking forward to the prospect of a good orgasm. She couldn't deny the sinking feeling that if Tony spent the night, it wouldn't signify anything.

"Lisa?" He was waiting for her answer.

"I think maybe we should wait."

His fingers stopped.

"Because you're leaving," she explained. "I really want to be with you, but it's already going to be hard enough as it is saying goodbye."

He studied her face, gauging her seriousness. Or perhaps he was wondering if she was drunk enough to be persuaded into the act. Her uncharitable thought made her cheeks burn.

"You'll be back in a few months," she said. "If we still feel the same way, then we can pick up where we left off."

"I thought this is what you wanted, too."

"I do. Believe me, *I do*. I just want to do it right." His gaze shifted from her face to the wall past her shoulder. Instead of an embrace, he rubbed her arm with one hand and stroked her head with the other, which made her wonder where the cat was and if she'd neglected to feed him before going out. She felt compelled to say more, but willed herself to stop before it turned into an emotional gush that would really cause him to question her worth.

Tony stopped petting her and gently pushed her up to a sitting position. "So, I guess I should be going."

He looked like a boy who'd been told he couldn't have the puppy after all.

"You could still spend the night," she said. The offer sounded hollow and her immediate thought after was *What's the point?*

He swung his feet to the floor, stood, and buttoned his shirt. "Do you mind if I use your bathroom?"

When he came out, she was waiting for him by the door. He pushed his feet into his shoes, not bothering to tie the laces. She handed him his coat. To lighten the mood she said, "Have you finished packing—for your flight?"

"What? Oh ... I have a few things left."

"Do you still want me to bring you to the airport?"

"Yeah." He moved a little closer to her and offered a half-smile, which lifted her spirits.

"Okay," she said. "So, I'll see you later today then."

She closed the gap between them, placed her hands on his face, and pulled him to her for the most serious and sensual kiss she could lay on him, given the circumstances. During the kiss, she half-considered reneging on her refusal and saying to hell with integrity and love.

Tony pulled away first, said a quiet goodbye, and left.

Closing the door, Lisa turned and leaned against it, dazed, her hand still on the knob. *What the hell had just happened?* How could she turn him down? He was only *the* guy she had been brooding about for months. Finally he wanted her and she'd said no. At last he was ready to take their relationship to the next level and she'd decided to develop a conscience. What an idiot.

Leroy came out of hiding and rubbed against her legs, purring his greeting of animal devotion. Lisa grabbed a glass from the kitchen and filled it with water. Taking it and the cat into the living room, she placed her phone in its dock station and selected her "For a Rainy Day" playlist. This was her go-to when she wanted to wallow in self-loathing or grieve romantic loss. Tonight she could do both. An electric guitar strummed chords that paired perfectly with her regret.

She lay on the couch—the very spot she had just been with Tony—and sipped her water. She could still feel the warmth left over from their bodies and smell his cologne on the pillow.

Maybe she should call him, apologize for being so stupid, and ask him to come back. Would that fix everything? Would that make it all right between them? Why hadn't she accepted his compliment gracefully when he'd said she was beautiful? Why did she question his sincerity? Why had he chosen *that* particular moment to say it? It had sounded like *a line*. But maybe it wasn't. Why couldn't he just tell her how he felt? And why, *why* couldn't she be one of those girls who could just *do it?*

The lyrics of the song playing answered her question for her.

She would go to her own sweet bed tonight—not just because of her integrity, but because of her insecurities. She didn't want to get hurt and couldn't deny that or wish it away. She just couldn't make herself vulnerable—no matter how physically attracted she was to Tony. But like the singer said, in the moment it *was* too hard to explain, that everyone had something inside of themselves—that *something* that needed more than a feel-good moment, but rather consideration for another person's heart. Kindness.

Then, Jake, of all people, came to mind. She groaned and turned on her side, covering her head with the pillow.

Despite falling asleep on the couch in the early morning hours of New Year's Day, Lisa awoke at her usual weekend time, a few minutes before eight o'clock. The cat was wrapped in a warm, furry ball on her belly and her mouth had that parched, cottony taste.

Sliding Leroy aside, she got up to brush her teeth, shower, and get dressed. Feeling semihuman again, she headed to the kitchen for her morning coffee.

From the moment her eyes opened, her mind looped over and over her decision. Instead of feeling better, she felt guilty. Her insides twisted with worry as she wondered if Tony would call. She decided to go for a run, even if it was freezing outside.

The air was cold, yet the sensation felt invigorating against her warmed body. She loved how peaceful the city could be sometimes, catching her off guard and thrilling her with newness. For the first time since she woke up, her mind was able to settle itself and pay heed only to her breathing and immediate surroundings. She saw a pair of women in their early fifties walking at a brisk pace. She passed a man walking his dog. Frost clung to the bare trees. When she got back to her apartment she took a second shower, thrilling in the contrast of the outside cold and the hot water.

The rest of the morning, she waited shamelessly by the phone, catching up on some reading. Tony called after lunch. She drove to his parents' house, and when she arrived, he was already outside.

He barely looked at her as he hoisted his luggage into the backseat.

"Is there anything else you want to do before you leave?" That didn't come out right.

"Nope."

Neither one of them spoke about the incident at her apartment, but it was at the very forefront of *her* mind and defined her every action. At the airport, she helped wheel his luggage. She filled out his baggage handling tags, all the while maintaining constant physical contact by touching his arm, linking arms, or holding hands. She fussed over him like a mother with her baby. She combed down his hair with her fingers and picked the lint off his jacket. She was one spit away from wiping a speck of imaginary dirt from his cheek. It was critical he know that she hadn't said no to him as a person and—for what it was worth—she could, or would, be a good, reliable girlfriend.

Lisa opened the purple suede handbag she'd gotten for Christmas. "I got a few things for you for the flight."

She'd prepared a farewell package that included a spy novel, an iTunes card, a pack of gum, some snacks, and a cute little Hallmark card. She wasn't sure how to sign the card, so she settled for ambiguity and drew a single heart followed by a comma and then her name.

His face harbored that look of disenchantment again—like she'd given him underwear when what he really wanted was a BB gun—but he accepted her offering with no complaint. "Thank you. You didn't have to do that."

"I wanted to." And there were so many more things she wanted. She wanted a chance to do that night all over again. She wanted him to stay here with her.

"I have to go."

Tears threatened to ruin her composure. She bucked up, determined to be strong, and said with a slightly dramatic tone, "I'll be eagerly awaiting your return."

"I hope so," he said, as he pulled her head into his chest and hugged her hard. "Thanks for hanging out with me." His voice sounded croaky.

This was her very last moment to bare all and make things right. Taking a deep breath, she said, "I'm really sorry about last night."

"It's all right. I understand." His sad green eyes spoke the rest for him. Finally, he gave her the kiss she'd been yearning for since she'd picked him up. She eagerly accepted it and went so far as to give him a few encouraging gropes around his middle—promises of things to come when he returned. He gave her one last kiss, then let her go.

In that moment, Lisa felt like she loved him. He got in line at the security checkpoint, then turned and grinned. "I'll be back before you know it."

With that, he gave her a half-hearted wave and crossed through security without looking back.

Chapter 15

"Mr. Hollow wants a full reception after the golf tournament," Jake said. He raised his hands, ready to stop her protests. "I know we originally talked about a simple luncheon and then people leaving when they pleased, but now he wants to draw it out and dole out the recognition. If we really put the spotlight on everyone who attends and make it be about them, they'll be more likely to increase their contribution than skip out. Also, since this is costing us so much, let's make the most of it and make them stay for the entire day."

"Okay," Lisa said, offering no resistance. "What do you think of giving out awards? We could do the usual ones like Best Individual, Best Team, and then some funny ones like Best Sand Trap."

"That could be interesting, but make sure you run the list by us before you go ahead with it. We have to be careful not to offend anyone."

Of course she would be careful not to offend anyone. She knew how to do her job. She ignored the annoyance brought on by his remarks, simply because pointing it out took too much energy, and moved to the next bullet on her agenda. "If Mr. Hollow wants, Ingrid can get the series footage from Channel Nine and play that during the reception. I need to know if he wants to personally foot the bill, pass it on to the firm, or have it come out of the fundraising budget. I'm assuming it's still invite only."

"Yes, although attendees are allowed to invite a guest."

"Are all of these people actually going to golf?"

"Sure, they'll go in rounds. If not, there's always mini golf," he teased. "Some of these guys will be bringing their wives. Some of them golf, but they're more likely to go shopping."

Lisa looked Jake square in the eye. "Oh yes. And the husbands of the female executives will probably head over to Best Buy until it's time for lunch."

"That wasn't a sexist remark and you know it. We've both done enough of these things to know that more often than not the wives *do* go shopping. Saying it doesn't make me a sexist if it's true."

"Whatever," she mumbled. Where was her gumption these days? Even the opportunity to spar with Jake hadn't perked her up. "Anyway, let's aim for a balance between the number of celebrities and executives attending. About a third of the celebrities we've invited are involved with some kind of foundation or organization whose mission is in line with ours. That's a good thing, but we have to be careful not to let them promote their own causes too much. We want them to stay focused on ours."

"Where are we with the fundraising so far?"

Lisa glanced at her spreadsheet. "Last fall we raised $5 million from the gala and the initial interest in the park. There was a spike after David's ad aired, which held steady through the holidays. If the finances allow it, I suggest we run a second public-service announcement around tournament time. I've also been talking to Rose Chang."

"Chang? As in the Chang Chinese restaurants?"

"Yes. Her husband died four years ago and she's been running the enterprise ever since. She recently put out her own line of frozen Chinese foods. She's very nice and has strong ties to the Nicollet community. She's interested and wants to hear more. There's one condition. She wants to be on the park board *and* she wants to add her creative two cents to the concept."

"How much are we talking about?"

"It's hard to say with Mrs. Chang, but I'm guessing at least a million, maybe two. It's a lot from a private donor."

"What, they don't all give $10 million?"

"Not exactly. I have a meeting with her February fifteenth."

"Can I come?" he asked.

"Sure. If you want."

"Will we take her out for Chinese?"

His humor was lousy today. She continued, "We got that grant for inner-city development, and one for urban park revitalization. That brings us to an amount just shy of $8 million."

Jake scribbled the numbers down. "Is the construction coming along as planned?"

"It is. Despite sub-zero temperatures, we're only a couple weeks off our timeline. Mark or Ingrid can give you the details."

Lisa looked over the invitees and saw David's name. "Is David bringing someone to the tournament?"

Jake's eyebrows went up.

"I'm not inquiring for personal reasons."

"It's funny you should ask, because he was wondering the same thing about you."

Oh, geez. Give me a break. Just to spite Jake she said, "I have a *boyfriend.*" It was almost true.

"Ah. And he'll be your date?"

"He won't be able to make it. He's in Europe."

A look of realization dawned on Jake's face. "Lisa, if you don't like Dave, just say so."

"I didn't make him up, Jake. He plays soccer and he's on tour in Germany."

"Uh-huh. Now if you'll excuse me, I have to call my girlfriend before it gets too late in France."

He was incorrigible.

When Lisa returned to her desk, the first thing she did was check her messages. Nothing. No email, no video chat messages, no texts, nothing anywhere online. *Nothing.* Her shoulders sagged. It wasn't a good sign. She clicked open her Internet browser and stared blankly at a list of just-released grants.

It had taken him two days to text her. She understood. Bruised egos needed time to heal and she'd given him quite the unexpected kick. In the meantime, the buoyancy of her romantic fantasies kept her spirits afloat. Her mind occupied itself with dreamy fairytales of Tony showing up unannounced at her doorstep for a surprise weekend. Or Tony sending her a plane ticket and a note saying, *Hope you've got a passport ...* She'd dug out her passport and saw she had two more years before it expired and watched ESPN on the off chance she'd catch a news clip on European soccer and thus a glimpse of her beloved.

The emails and texts didn't come as often as she liked, but when they did, each one was like an oasis, replenishing her hopes. They'd had a couple of video chats; their bobble heads, oblivious to their small setback, still looked as adorable as ever. Now they were in a dry spell and she hadn't heard anything from him. Her happy bubble was expelling its stale air, causing her to question if they'd had anything at all.

On top of it, her best friend was getting married.

Angela had called the night Tony left while Lisa was folding laundry and wallowing. She'd asked her right away to be her maid of honor and Lisa had committed by circling the date on her new Thomas Kinkade calendar. Then they'd simultaneously watched *Bridezillas* and discussed dresses, venues, and wedding planners. She was happy for Angela, although a little sad for herself. Here she was getting married and Lisa could barely qualify the man in her life as a boyfriend.

After the news sunk in, she wondered how her relationship with Angela would change. She'd already seen what marriage did to friends. Dating couples and singles managed to coexist fine, then marriage came and *whack!*—the ax fell, and suddenly the singles were being excluded because they lacked a pair. What was she? A lost sock?

Ingrid took one look at Lisa, sullenly slouching in her chair, and asked, "Haven't heard from Tony?"

"No. He has a game in Milan."

"Milan. That sounds nice."

She imagined Tony meeting a beautiful Italian woman. Tim and Chad explained to her that European women were hot, had cute accents, and knew how to take care of a man. She could barely stomach her jealousy.

"I googled Minnesota weather patterns," Lisa said, changing the subject. "Jake was right; March in Minnesota has been known for being prime blizzard weather. You can have a balmy Wednesday followed by three feet of snow." She pointed to a new picture pinned next to St. Anthony on her wall. "I've added St. Clare of Assisi, patron saint of good weather, to my list of intercessors." Another benefit of postponing the tournament was that David would be able to attend. He would also be back in March to play against the Wild again. He asked if she'd be free after the game. As if she'd say no.

Ingrid could see right through her. "After work, you're going baby shopping with me."

Fortunately "after work" was in twenty minutes. She complied only because Ingrid was resolute and not going would have been rude. Looking at baby stuff was always a gamble. It either sucked you in, or left you feeling bitter—brooding about the meaning of life and if you were even meant to have children. Ingrid was all baby talk now, devouring every book on pregnancy, childbearing, child rearing, prenatal care, postnatal care, breastfeeding, baby psychology, blah, blah, blah. She often quizzed Lisa during their lunch breaks. Ingrid had enough of those books to build the kid a dollhouse. A duplex dollhouse—with a tower.

She slapped shut her Grant Park folder, chucked her pen into her desk drawer, and decided to call it a day. She hadn't gotten anything done anyway. Her computer pinged, and she eagerly clicked on the email flag. Her shoulders drooped again. It was only from Jake.

"Remind me again why standing outside freezing my butt off is supposed to be fun?" Lisa asked Tim.

"It's all in the spirit of broomball. And I promised I would buy you a drink."

"Drinks, yes. That was the motivation." Mark passed the ball to Chad, who got around one of the other team's defenders.

"Why aren't you out there playing?"

"GO CHAD!" he shouted. Chad scored. "My role is moral support."

"You play that badly, huh?"

"I'm afraid so."

"Isn't this Jake's team?"

"Uh-huh."

"I don't see him."

"He had to work late."

Lisa stomped her feet and wiggled her numb toes, trying to coax some warmth back into them. "Is Chad wearing his Shithouse T-shirt?"

"Never leaves home without it. Why couldn't you have invited me to the game? I love hockey, too."

"You'll be next, I promise." The mention of the game brought her back to that night. Since the gala, she'd transmitted a consistent signal that Jake's apparent interest in her was unrequited. And she was pretty sure he'd gotten the message. His emails became less frequent; he no longer dropped by unannounced, offering to pick up lunch. Today had been their first meeting since the game.

But despite all this, Jake kept popping into her mind uninvited anyway. She'd never seen him get so worked up as he had that night. He was always so confident and laid back. Gearing up to ream Scott, as soon as Jake had walked away, she'd realized Scott wasn't worth the effort. What surprised her more, though, was she'd felt genuinely concerned about Jake. What kind of guy just up and left his friend? Regardless of their history, he'd been upset and she'd actually cared—which was definitely *not* part of the master plan to ignore Jake.

Jake's goalie slipped on the ice, creating an opening for the other team to score. "You mean to tell me you're worse than that guy?" she asked, pointing to the goalie.

"Jake said Dave's got another game in March. Are you going?" Tim asked. Either he wasn't listening or didn't want to answer.

"I haven't decided yet."

"He also said you and Dave have a date."

"I would call it a meeting after the game and I thought men didn't gossip." Mark regained control of the orange rubber ball on the ice.

"Only about you," he said. "GO MARK! PASS! PASS! PASS!"

The guys talked about her? Lisa saw an opportunity. "What else do you gossip about?"

"That soccer guy."

"Tony? I thought you guys didn't like soccer." A player from the other team stole the ball away from Mark and passed it to his teammate.

"You're seriously not back together with that guy, are you?" He shouted at the rink, "I TOLD YOU TO *PASS*!"

She turned away from the game to look at him. Tim didn't usually give her opinions on the men she dated.

"Maybe. Why?"

"Well, other than the soccer thing and he still lives with his parents, the guy's a tool."

"Playing soccer is his job. So what if he stays at his parents' house when he's in town; he spends half of the year abroad."

"Exactly, he's in another country. As in not here."

"Plenty of couples have successful long-distance relationships."

"But how many of them last?"

"I don't know, but that doesn't mean we shouldn't try. With that kind of attitude, athletes would never be in relationships." Her comment made her think of David, instead of Tony. "I think your issue is with the soccer and not with Tony. If I'd said I *did* have a date with David, what would your reaction have been?"

"I would've said, at least he lives in the U.S. Look, soccer or no soccer, all I'm saying is that I don't think Tony's the right guy for you."

"You didn't seem to mind him at New Year's." She put her eyes back on the game. Some other Joe Schmo had the ball and frankly, she hoped he'd fall on his ass. "Do you all feel this way?"

"Pretty much."

"Chad?" He nodded. "*Mark?*"

"Yep."

And she figured, what the hell, if Mark had an opinion … "Even Jake?"

"Especially Jake."

. . . . .

Scott walked into the kitchen and asked, "What? No date?"

"No. You?"

"No way. A real bachelor never dates on Valentine's Day and I've got the perfect way to celebrate." He opened a brown paper bag and dramatically pulled each item out, one by one. "Beer, *The Expendables 2*, and—viewer discretion advised—*Tasmanian She-Devils*. And the pizza's on its way. Happy Valentine's Day, honey!"

Jake grabbed the remote control and took the movies. "I love you, baby."

"I love you too, dear."

Jake put in the action movie. Scott said, "I see the old Jake is back."

"How's that?" he asked as they both settled into their respective couches.

"You're not so moody anymore."

Jake skipped the ads and selected "play" on the main menu. He was looking forward to all of his action heroes being in one flick.

Scott asked, "So, what's changed?"

"Nothing much. I decided to stop pursuing that woman from the office I told you about."

"Amen to that. Anyone else in the works?"

"Nah, not really." Jake's cell phone rang. It was an old high school friend. "Hey, Brando. How's it going?"

"Good. Guess what we're doing this summer?"

"Road trip?"

The summer after high school graduation, Brandon and Jake had ridden their motorcycles, the first they'd ever owned, cross-country to California. For four weeks they camped and hiked everywhere: Yellowstone, Glacier, Grand Teton, Grand Canyon, Bryce Canyon, Yosemite. When they reached the Pacific, Jake sprinted like a maniac into the ocean. It was insanely spiritual and one of the coolest things he'd ever done. He wondered if Brandon would be up for the same kind of adventure.

"Our reunion."

"Our reunion? Already?"

Scott looked over. "High school?"

"Yeah, ten years. Can you believe it?" Brandon said.

"Man, that was fast," Jake said. "Aren't people supposed to be married and have kids and stuff when they go to reunions?"

"Probably," Scott interjected.

Brandon said, "I got an email from Megan Phommachan. She said we have to plan it because we're officers."

Jake vaguely remembered seeing an email from a Megan, but he'd thought it'd been spam. Megan apparently was now Megan Clark. "What about the rest of student council?"

"She contacted everybody but wants you to get us together. So, when do you want to start planning this thing?"

"Couldn't we form a reunion committee and let them do it?"

"We could, but you still have to oversee it."

"Fine, I can do that."

"Great, and Megan's already created a website."

"Thanks. Hey, don't forget we play broomball Thursday nights. Come if you can."

"I'll have to see what's going on with the kids."

"You have kids?"

"Yeah. Twins. Can you believe it?"

No, he couldn't.

Chapter 16

She braced herself for Jake's chitchat while they waited for Mrs. Chang. Instead, he read the newspaper. So many mornings she wished Jake would just shut up and now he finally did. She thought she'd feel relief, but it actually felt amiss.

Valentine's Day had sucked. After six weeks, she was still drifting through that nebulous zone between "just a friend" and girlfriend. Lisa spent hours looking for an e-card that expressed the exact sentiment of a girl stuck in this ambiguous region. It was a tricky thing to say "I love you" in camouflage. She settled on an animated one that had a teddy bear climbing a ladder to a full moon. The bear painted it in until all that remained was a U. Then stars twinkled into the words "I MISS," followed by the U-shaped moon. Below the sky it said, "Every day ... and especially today ... on Valentine's Day!" She sent it two days early.

His response: *Thanks for the card. I liked the bear. Sorry I've been so busy. We've advanced in our division and have matches lined up in Italy, Slovenia, Spain, Portugal ... Gotta run ... more practice. Happy V-day, Tony.* No lovey goo from him, either.

Tim and Chad hadn't had dates either, so they'd taken the masculine route and gone to a bar to watch hockey. Hanging out with her brother on supposedly the most romantic day of the year sounded gross and desperate. With everyone else coupled up, she'd spent another exciting night in. So, take a crappy Valentine's Day, add it to how she felt right now, and no wonder she was twice as crabby as usual.

"Lisa. So good to see you." Mrs. Chang said as she welcomed Lisa and Jake into her office. Standing in Mrs. Chang's office, which was all whites and glass with vibrant green plants, made Lisa forget it was dreary outside. On her walls hung two tapestries framed in cobalt blue. At first glance, they looked like a busy collection of designs. But on further inspection, Lisa saw that they were complex depictions of villages—small buildings separated by thousands of minute stitches of blooming trees and flowers, small figures on black silk paths to waters flowing silver, storks standing sentinel. On the window ledge sat a procession of family pictures, neatly angled, from a small, aged sepia photo of an unsmiling couple in their twenties, all the way through the generations to the last LCD picture frame that rotated through digital images of Mrs. Chang's family and friends.

"I'd like to introduce you to Jake Hanson. He works for Mr. Hollow and is helping us with the park," Lisa said. After sitting, she added, "Thank you for meeting with us, Mrs. Chang. I'm a big fan of your volunteer work."

"Thank you. Tell me more about your project."

Lisa held up her computer. "May I?" Mrs. Chang nodded and Lisa placed it on the desk and opened her presentation.

She clicked to her first slide. "The Nicollet neighborhood originally started out as a hodgepodge collection of ethnic European immigrants. A few of these neighbors were successful businessmen or academics in the Old World. It was a unique pocket of Minneapolis that quickly established a reputation for innovation."

She regretted her opening immediately. Why had she started with the beginning of time? It would take forever for her to make her point. She clicked through the next five slides and came to her first charts and graphs. "As you know, Mrs. Chang, today Nicollet has a large Asian population and here's a chart with the breakdown by nationality. I know there's a lot of diversity among these groups, but what's interesting is that the Asian demographic as a whole makes up over half of the Nicollet population, at 52 percent. Having a person like you on the park board will help guarantee that these people aren't unintentionally alienated."

Why had she used that word—"alienate"? It sounded like she was implying these people were weird or illegal. Not citizens. What was wrong with her brain today?

Switching gears, she skipped ahead to the part about the finances. She brought up projections, charts, and graphs of every shape and color, laying out the bare bones of the costs they'd incurred and anticipated, how much money they'd already received and would receive, and the amount they were still looking to get. "As you know, the construction and building renovations and updates are just about taken care of. Your investment would be providing the long-term support for the actual programming happening in Grant Park. A sustaining private donor can provide that long-term financial sustainability that nonprofits and parks like this only ever dream of having."

As she continued through her slides, she picked up speed, the confidence coming back into her voice. Numbers was what she did best. Throughout her presentation, Mrs. Chang remained quiet. When Lisa finished, though, Mrs. Chang remained silent, while Lisa's stomach sank to her feet. This was what having a shitty love life had done to her—turned her into mush. She'd wasted precious energy pining for a man who'd been reduced to a chat head, instead of concentrating on her job.

Then Jake spoke. "What Lisa has illustrated, Mrs. Chang, is the legacy you would be creating by joining Mr. Hollow in revitalizing this community. You're known in this community for bringing people together, for celebrating diversity, for honoring the uniqueness of all of our cultures. You're our very own ambassador of goodwill in a real-life festival of nations." He smiled big and even Lisa thought his dimple was too cute to ignore.

"With this park, you would be bringing all of your efforts together under one platform, in one place. You wouldn't just be providing dollars today; you'd be investing in the long-term sustainability of a healthy community for future generations."

He orated further, but all Lisa heard were harps strumming in her head. She watched in amazement as he spun his magic, just as she'd witnessed in high school.

"Right, Lisa?" Jake asked, inviting her back into the conversation.

"Yes," she answered. "The economic benefit to the revitalization of inner-city parks is staggering. Case studies on urban parks, like the Discovery Green in Houston and the Millennium Park in Chicago, say that these cities have had up to $2 billion in new development since the rejuvenation of those parks."

"They not only provide a pleasant, relaxing place to hang out in the city, but they also improve health and quality of life, crime goes down in these areas—it's a place you could take your family, Mrs. Chang," Jake gestured toward the photographs, "for a picnic."

Lisa added, "Mr. Hollow has been most generous to jump start the creation of this space—but the real change happens in how that space gets used."

Jake said, "Mr. Hollow had the vision, but you would be executing it."

As they progressed through their pitch, Mrs. Chang's eyes filled with sparks of hope. She asked questions, which she and Jake batted back and forth between them like a shuttlecock. Mrs. Chang's silky gray hair brushed her jawline as her head moved between each of them as they spoke.

If there's one thing she could say about Jake that hadn't changed since high school, it was his alluring optimism. He looked at the glass as being half-full, which grated on her glass-half-empty nerves. But she couldn't begrudge him this time. He'd taken her funk and given it focus. She felt—*grateful*. She twisted in her chair. Grateful to Jake. That was a new one.

Hell had reopened and she was invited. Amidst the junk and bills shoved haphazardly in the mail slot, that night Lisa uncovered a suspicious piece of mail from an address she didn't recognize. She skeptically ripped open the packet and riffled through the contents. She found a questionnaire with the heading *Tell us a little about yourself!*

She skimmed the questions. *What is your best high school memory? What were you like then? Now? What were you best known for?* What could she say? Boogers and farts? And her favorite: *Who do you hope to see at the reunion?* That one made her want to throw up.

It was an invitation to her ten-year high school reunion. It was so cheery she could already narrow the list down to five girls from her class who would be perky enough to draft such a horrid document. If there'd been i's dotted with hearts she could've narrowed it down further.

Jake would be there for sure. He'd probably emcee the gig. Any curiosity or interest in seeing her classmates was cancelled out by that one fact. She imagined the look on his face if she went. "Hi Jake. Boy, I bet you're surprised to see me. Um … surprise?"

No way. She was past this chapter of life. The day she graduated from high school, she'd chucked all of that crap into a dark corner in her parents' basement and gone off to college to make her mark. Going to her reunion would be a regression and she only wanted to move forward.

Along with the invitation and questionnaire was a black-and-white photocopy of the entire senior class sitting on bleachers. Jake was seated front and center, flexing his muscles in a row of similarly muscle-flexed friends. Lisa was the blurry spot about two-thirds of the way back. There was a blue and white bumper sticker cheering, *Go Bears! Grrr!* A demographics sheet grilled—Are you married or single? If single, are you in a serious relationship or really single? Do you have children? Are they bastards? Please list postsecondary education; those who never made it through college, please go to Question #17. A poll copied on neon green wanted people to vote for the most popular, the funniest, the cutest, etc. A survey asked for opinions on the format of the class reunion. *One day or two? Classmates only or spouses allowed? Would you like a family picnic? How about a bonfire?* How about a poke in the eye? A pink half-slip requested a most recent photo with easy how-to instructions for uploading to the reunion website.

But wait. There was one last thin strip of yellow pastel paper. This little gem asked her to cough up eighty bucks to cover the cost of all of the fun. Wonderful. She would get to pay for her torture. She pitched the whole heap into the recycling and went to bed with the cat and a book.

She was dancing with Kevin Bacon when she realized it wasn't just a dream; her phone was ringing. Her hand self-navigated across the nightstand.

"Lisa?"

"Tony?"

"Yeah. Did I catch you at a bad time?"

"No." She glanced at the clock. It was three o'clock in the morning. "I was just sleeping. How are you?"

"Good. You?"

"Sleepy." She rubbed her eyes. "What's up?"

"I was just calling to say hi."

"Oh." At three in the morning? "Okay. Um, hi."

She settled back into her pillows and pulled the blankets up to her chin, glad to hear from him, even if he wasn't Kevin Bacon. "Um, how'd your last game go?"

"Great."

"Where are you now?"

"Back in Hanover."

"How long are you there for?"

"Um, that's why I called. The coaches are pretty happy with me and they've offered me a year-long contract."

Whoa. Hold on. When she'd asked how long he was going to be in Hanover, she meant how long before he traveled for another game. "Oh. Are you going to take it?"

"Well, yeah. It's a great opportunity for me."

"That's great," she heard herself say. "I'm happy for you." What she really wanted to ask was where she fit into this bright future of his.

"Thanks. I'm pretty psyched about it."

"I can imagine you would be. You've worked hard and now you're living your dream."

"Yeah. I'm pretty lucky."

She gulped, then asked, "So, does this mean you'll be staying in Germany?"

"Uh … yeah. The tour keeps us really busy and after that we start the regular season. The earliest I'll be able to come home is Christmas."

"Christmas! That's the end of the year!"

"I know; I'm sorry. But this is important."

And their coupledom wasn't? "Couldn't you take some time off?"

"Um, you can't really ask for time off—especially during the season."

So now the soccer season appeared to be year-round. "I understand. You need to do what's best for your career."

"Are you sure you're okay with it?"

"Yeah, of course," she lied. "If I were in your shoes, I'd do the same thing." If she were in his shoes, she'd discuss it with him first and figure out how to include him. But, hey, that was just her.

"Great. Listen, I gotta go. Our bus leaves in twenty minutes."

She pictured him looking over his shoulder at a dirty purple and white coach bus, fumes spewing from the exhaust pipe, while another player or two finished up a smoke. They wore green and purple nylon tracksuits, which on Tony was probably sexy.

"Okay. Bye." She tried to add sarcasm, but it came out as disappointment.

"Bye." Click.

I love you, she thought to herself. She tossed her phone onto the floor.

Tim's disappointment of her failed promise vanished as soon as she handed him her free ticket. The Sharks were back in town, and instead of going to the game, she'd have David over afterward for dinner. It wasn't like a date, but she was looking forward to the distraction. She made spaghetti, which wasn't very exciting but was something she knew how to cook. A five-buck bouquet of carnations and daisies she'd bought on impulse at the checkout sat between the two place settings on her small formica table. She chose a California Chianti instead of an Italian one as symbolic protest against Tony's decision to stay in Europe.

After a run, a good rant to Angela about the reunion invite and the Tony update, followed by a cereal dinner in front of the TV, she was mostly back to normal. Mostly, because whenever she saw Jake, it was like pushing play on her mental DVD player. *Who was the most popular boy? Who did you have a crush on? Who has the prettiest eyes?* She couldn't help but get snappy. Just when she thought she'd gotten it out of her system and could be civil to the poor guy, the questions played *again* like movie credits through her mind and it began all over. She sensed he'd begun avoiding her. After two weeks of this, she went for a massage, gave herself a good attitude adjustment, and decided to throw herself back into her work. And now she was feeling pretty good.

At ten minutes to eleven, she heard a knock and opened the door. "Hey, you made it."

"Thanks for having me over," David said.

"No problem. I'm happy to do it." She took David's coat and they went into the kitchen.

"It's nice to be in a real home instead of a hotel."

Lisa pulled out a chair for him. "Sit down. Would you like some wine?"

"Sure."

She poured him a glass of Chianti and handed it to him. "Good game tonight."

"Thanks."

"If you'd gotten a hat trick, it would have been even better." She'd curled her fingers in air quotes as she said "hat trick."

"Wow, I see you've been doing your homework."

"Well, a little google never hurt anybody. I looked at the Sharks' website and saw the Sharks' Foundation has a wine tasting event coming up."

"Yeah, it's on Saturday."

"Are you a wine connoisseur?"

"Not really. The only difference I can tell is if they're red or white."

"I have beer, too, if you want," she said, moving toward the refrigerator.

"No, no it's okay. I like wine; I just don't know anything about it."

"Are you supposed to?"

"No. Our job is just to be there."

"Well, maybe next time you guys can hold a beer-tasting event."

"Now *that* I would know something about. Jake and I tried making beer once."

"How did that go?"

"Not so good. Let's see, how would Stephen King put it? It had the sickly sweet aroma of a putrid corpse and tasted like rotten syrup-water."

"Mmm ... yum," she said, laughing. She appreciated his literary reference. "Well, hopefully *this* food will be a little tastier than rotting corpses."

David smiled. "I'm optimistic."

Over dinner, they talked about what the Sharks' Foundation was doing, about Grant Park and the Little Flower Foundation. David told funny stories about Jake and him and Lisa dug up a few about her and Angela. While David helped her wash the dishes, she no longer felt starstruck. Despite the fame, he was pretty much a nice, normal guy.

After everything was put away, she asked, "Would you like anything else? Or do you need to get going?"

"No, I can stay a little longer. I'm still on California time, so for me it's only ten-thirty."

"Okay. Do you want to watch TV?"

"Sure."

She led him to the living room and picked up the remote control. "What do you want to watch?"

"Whatever is fine," he said, yawning.

She chose a talk show she found funny and informative while he settled onto the couch. "Would you like a brandy?"

"Yes, please."

Then Leroy sauntered in and meowed. David called, "Here kitty, kitty." Her cat approached, sniffed him, and leapt into David's lap. "Well, hello there." He scratched Leroy behind the ears. "What's his name?"

"Leroy," she answered, preparing to explain why she thought Leroy was a perfectly good name for a male cat.

But all David said was, "Hello there, bad, bad Leroy Brown," and hummed a few bars from the song. Leroy purred and circled himself into a ball on David's lap.

She returned to the kitchen. Raising her voice, she said, "Thank you again for being a part of our project."

"I'm glad to do it," he said, yawning again. "I've wanted to do something like this for a while, but there are so many good organizations; it's hard to decide."

Pouring the brandies, she wondered what David would be like as a boyfriend. He was all manners and it wasn't an act because he had no reason to impress her. It was just how he was. If Tony weren't in the picture, how would *she* have acted toward him?

Holding a brandy in each hand, she walked back to the living room. "You know, Chad is so obsessed with proving that the

Shithouse race exists, he's worn his T-shirt every day since. You should see—"

David's chin was resting on his chest, his hand deep in Leroy's fur. Lisa moved the cat and draped a blanket over him. Then she turned out the light and went to her room to read.

Chapter 17

Peeking into the living room, she saw David was still there, covered by the blanket, sprawled out on the couch. Not up on the proper protocol for when a celebrity accidentally falls asleep at her house, she went about her usual morning routine.

Once the coffee was brewing he shuffled into the kitchen. His bed head made him look like a ploughed-out mouse. He rubbed his eyes and yawned.

"Good morning, Sleeping Beauty," Lisa said. "You woke up and I didn't even have to kiss you. Want some coffee?"

"Thanks." He blew on it before taking a gulp. "I didn't mean to fall asleep like that."

"It's all right. Did you sleep okay?"

"Yeah. I woke up in the middle of the night and for a second, forgot where I was. When I realized I was here, I felt so bad. I considered leaving, but then thought it would be rude to leave in the middle of the night."

"Well, it would've been a little weird, although I probably wouldn't have minded either way."

He looked at his watch. "Are you going to work now?"

"I am." She wondered which option, driving or taking the bus, would allow her a few extra minutes before she really needed to leave.

"Okay, I'll head out with you."

"If you need to stay longer, that's okay. You know, take a shower, eat something, whatever."

"That's really nice of you, but I should be going. Do you need a ride?"

"Sure."

While David drove his rental car, they listened to the morning news and drank their coffee. Innocent fantasies of cruising Main Street with a famous squeeze—someone like David—played in her brain. Tony was in Europe; a little daydreaming never hurt anybody. When David pulled up to the curb, he said, "Thanks for dinner and for letting me crash at your place. I had a great time."

She blushed from the compliments. "You're welcome."

"You know, Lisa, it's not often that I get treated like a regular guy anymore. Thank you for that, too."

"Well, I'm glad I could be of service." She felt a little squeeze around her heart, noticing how warm his brown eyes made her feel, and that made her blush even more. "Thanks for the ride. I'll be in touch."

Lisa stepped out of the car and bent to wave goodbye as he pulled away. Yes, definitely a very nice guy. She traipsed into work, feeling cheerful and springy. Bouncing into her chair, she turned on the computer and saw she had five new emails. One was from Tony. As she scanned the first few lines, her chirpiness was sucked out of her in one breath. It was a "Dear John" email.

Dear Lisa,

Hi. How are you? How's the weather? Is it warm yet? My mom says it's been pretty nice. That's cool. I wanted you to know that I met someone here in Germany. Her name is Eva and she is a medical student. I never meant for it to happen, but it did. I think it's the real deal. I'm sorry things didn't work out between us. If you're ever in Germany, let me know. I'd love to see you again. Take care and say hi to the guys from me.

Tony

She immediately texted Angela, *What are you doing this weekend?*

Saturday was hysterical as they spent the day in search of a wedding gown for Angela and a dress for Lisa. Right away, Lisa found a long, fitted, sleeveless gown that shimmered a pale gold. Angela's dress was another story.

There were puffy ones and frilly ones. Lacy ones and bejeweled ones. Some were whimsical and wispy, others were skintight. Some covered her up to the neck and the one she had on now squeezed her boobs together so tightly, her cleavage was nearly up to her chin.

"How would that dress look in a Catholic wedding?" Lisa teased.

"No kidding. I'm supposed to look virginal. In this thing, I look like a born-again ho."

"Don't knock Mary Magdalene. She turned out to be a very respectable woman."

"No disrespect intended." Angela dropped the fabric from her hands. "I can't wear this thing. The priest wouldn't be able to perform the ceremony." She went back into the changing room to extricate herself from the dress.

"He'd probably say something like, 'We are gathered here today in the bosom of St. Mary.'"

"That's blasphemy," Angela hollered from the changing room.

"Right. So pick a dress that's comfortable so we can get out of here."

A few hours and fifty dresses later, Angela found "the one." It was an off-the-shoulder number that accented her lovely neck and collarbones without overemphasizing her breasts. The bodice was a simple fitted cut of sheer white satin. The skirt flowed into a train. It was the most ordinary looking of all the dresses they had seen. Yet on Angela, it looked elegant, classic, almost regal.

"You look beautiful, Ang."

"You think so?" Angela looked in the mirror, lightly swishing her dress back and forth. It reminded Lisa of the time when, as little girls, she and her cousin dressed up as princesses. The pink ball-gowns, their mothers' high heels, and plastic tiaras with the peeling silver—all symbols of their hopes and dreams. And now, here was Angela, all grown up about to marry.

"Come on," Lisa said, "let's get out of here. Prince Charming awaits."

Before meeting Julian, Angela and Lisa headed down to the beach to catch the sunset. The dichotomy of the Pacific's vastness and gentle nature always surprised and allured her. It was the largest ocean in the world and yet its waves kissed the shore with such loving tenderness. Lisa relished being barefoot and exhaled. Gathering her thoughts, she asked, "Are you sure you want to marry Julian?"

Angela raised her eyebrows. "Of course, I'm sure."

"You really, really *know* that you love him?"

"Yes, I do. Is this some kind of intervention?"

"Apparently, Tony *needed some space.*"

"Ah," was all Angela said, putting her arm around Lisa.

"With this new girl, he called it the real deal? What does that mean? That he loves her?"

"I don't know, Lisa. It is what it is."

"I thought he was falling in love with *me.*"

"Did he tell you that?"

"No, but I thought I was in love with him."

"Did you tell him that?"

"I wanted him to say it first. I was afraid I'd scare him away like the first time."

"Not to get too technical, but were you two actually dating?"

"I thought we were. We never had the official conversation, but it seemed like it when we were together. Then he wanted to have sex on New Year's and I couldn't do it. I *wanted* to, or at least felt like I *should* want to, but I couldn't."

"That's a good thing. If you had slept with him, you'd be feeling a million times worse right now."

"Sure, but if I *had* done it, maybe he wouldn't have strayed."

"And how long would that have lasted? He's on the other side of the world. Relationships have to be based on mutual love, truth, and respect—not on memories of one-night stands and half-filled hopes."

"Do you think I pushed him too hard? The first time around?"

"No. I think he hopped on a plane and went to Europe. That wasn't about you."

"I've been thinking about what you said about how you know when you love someone? That there are no games? Honestly, with Tony, I kept trying to think of the right thing to say. I *did* feel like I had to hold back in case he didn't feel the same way."

"At least you're able to be honest about it."

"I want a soul mate, too—like you. I want to be in love. I want to *be* loved."

"This may sound lame now, but trust me: When the 'real deal' comes along, you'll know it. Being with that person will be the easiest decision you ever made. Being with *you* will be the easiest decision he ever made."

"Yeah, I suppose." She sighed and dug her toes into the sand, which had long lost its warmth. Life felt so free on the beach, here, with Angela. Maybe she could figure out a way to telecommute and move to San Diego. "I wish it wasn't so complicated with men. I don't mean to complain, but here I am, twenty-eight and still single, while everyone around me is either in love, getting married, or having babies. This was never a problem before and suddenly it's my ten-year reunion and I feel like the only person who doesn't have her act together is me."

"What are you talking about? Millions of people are single and thriving."

"Tell me, who's single? That we know? Hmm? Who?"

Angela thought for a second. "Tim broke up with that girlfriend, right? That makes one."

"Not anymore. He already found a new one, on Valentine's Day while watching hockey at a bar with Chad."

"Your brother! That makes two."

"Great, so now it's a genetic problem."

"You're *fine*. A little neurotic maybe, but hopefully that will sort itself out." Angela hugged Lisa.

"Are you really, really, *really* sure you know what you're talking about, or is this all motivational mumbo jumbo?"

Angela laughed. "There's my doubting Thomas. Have faith."

"Do you think I judge men too harshly?"

Angela didn't answer immediately, which Lisa recognized as a silent form of agreement. "I'm not that bad, am I? I have lots of guy friends. One of my closest friends is my brother, for crying out loud. How many women have that kind of sibling relationship? And if I didn't like men, I wouldn't be doing crazy things like flying all the way to San Diego to mourn the loss of a man I never had in the first place!"

"Let's just say you can be a tad cynical sometimes," she said, softening the blow.

"That is not cynicism. That is experience. Men do not have to follow the same rules as women. I'm not being a cynic for being aware of it; I'm being a realist."

"Okay, fair enough. Be a realist, but let yourself be open to love."

Lisa raked the sand with her fingertips. She thought she *was* open. She saw herself as two people. The first was, okay, maybe opinionated, but strong with an unwavering set of values that served her and others well. The other was what she wanted to be: a carefree woman who danced through meadows of daisies in golden sunlight wearing a peasant blouse and flouncy skirt, like the lady in the erectile dysfunction commercial.

"Why do we women waste so much time on this subject?" Lisa asked, throwing sand. "I haven't found the right guy yet. So what? It shouldn't bother me because—when I don't analyze it—I have a *great* life. My marital status shouldn't be the primary factor defining who I am, and yet as I get older, it could. I'm not any less of a woman because I don't have a man in my life. And if I did have one, I wouldn't want to be solely defined by being with him, either."

"So what do you want? If you're single you feel sad and lonely and if you have a man you feel ... What? ... Categorized? We're all subjected to judgments. Live your life, Lisa, and stop worrying about how others see you. I guarantee you that people are more worried about their own troubles than they are about yours." Angela squeezed her lightly around the shoulders. "I hate to break it to ya, kid, but you're not the center of the world."

"Clichés always do make me feel better," Lisa said, putting her arm around her best friend's neck. "How about this one: To the world you are someone; to someone, you are the world."

"That's a good one."

The sun dropped below the horizon, covering the ocean with a pink blanket. They collected their shoes and started back to the parking lot, pushing their feet through the soft sand. Angela asked, "Speaking of someones, how's it going with Jake?"

"You know, it's actually okay."

"Let me ask you something. If you didn't have this history with Jake, what would you think of him?"

Lisa tried erasing the chalkboard of her mind, looking at Jake not as a teenager, but as a man. "He works hard. He's conscientious. He tries to be funny. He loves sports." She shrugged. "I guess he's okay."

"If that's the case, why can't you let bygones be bygones and give him a chance?"

"Because I don't want to." It fell off her tongue faster than she could think. "I just don't see Jake in that way. Besides, we work together. It would only complicate things."

"I see," she said. "And your reunion? Are you going to go?"

"Are *you* going to *yours?*"

"I'm from a small town. When our class gets together it's like a family reunion."

"My class wasn't like that and I am *not* going. Did you know there were kids who walked across the stage on graduation day whom I didn't even recognize? Believe me, I don't think I'll be missed."

"Aren't you curious though to see what's become of your classmates?"

"That's what Facebook's for."

"Won't Jake notice?"

"No."

Angela eyed Lisa suspiciously. "Don't tell me you still haven't said anything."

"Okay. I won't."

"Lisa!"

"What?" Angela was really eyeballing her now. "Look, there's no point, all right? It's not like we're even friends. We're hardly coworkers."

"But what if you *do* become friends? You said yourself that he was a good guy. It's not entirely inconceivable."

She remembered how Jake had helped her recover from her uncouth cultural gaffe with Mrs. Chang. There was no animosity between them, just a good working relationship.

"Fine. In the most unlikely yet possible of chances that Jake and I become friends, I'll cross the bridge when I come to it. Deal?"

Angela watched her face then shook her head. "Okay."

She didn't sound convinced or happy about the arrangement, but at least the interrogation was over for now. Lisa saw two men standing at the edge of the parking lot, both dressed in khakis and light dress shirts that glowed against their brown skin. Angela waved to them.

"Come on," she said, picking up the pace, "Julian made reservations for us at a great place."

At first, Lisa was wary of the friend, suspecting it was a blind date set-up. But as the night progressed, she was glad for his company. She couldn't remember his name exactly, Alberto, Roberto … Abierto … He had a loud, infectious laugh that made dinner entertaining. He was Peruvian like Julian and had a soft, almost imperceptible Spanish lilt in his speech. He was quite animated, speaking with big gestures, telling stories about Julian and Angela—especially about Julian.

Alberto/Roberto was also a very good dancer, and after dinner, he taught Lisa how to loosen her hips so she could dance salsa, samba, and merengue—something she'd always wanted to learn. He was a respectful partner, with no wandering hands, and he didn't ask any questions too personal. She relaxed in his presence once she understood the evening was nothing more than an innocent soiree. She grasped to the relief that she could, in fact, behave normally and enjoy the company of a man without analyzing it. And she was glad to have a steady dance partner. At the moment, she didn't think she could handle the testosterone of more than one man.

She couldn't help but watch Angela and Julian. When they looked at each other, she saw pure love and complete devotion flow between them. He deferred to her, but she always asked his opinion. He stayed close to her, but gave her space. He was considerate, intelligent, and didn't draw attention to himself, preferring to let Alberto/Roberto do the talking. Lisa blinked back the threat of tears. She saw what Angela meant about a man going the extra mile for a woman.

Sunday came all too quickly as Angela, Julian, and Lisa stood in a tight circle at the airport saying their goodbyes. After they hugged each other for the tenth time, Angela looked directly into Lisa's eyes. "Do me a favor, will you?"

"What's that?"

"Be nice to Jake. Maybe being nice to him will help you let go of the past."

"I'll try. Turn over a new leaf, right?"

"Kill two birds with one stone?"

"How does that fit?"

"I don't know, but it sounded good."

Julian stood apart from them, but she saw him smile at their banter. Lisa said. "Take care of my girl, all right?"

"Okay, but I will eventually require some financial compensation for the trouble," he joked.

"Put it on my tab."

"Cash only," he said, with a straight face.

She hugged her friend one last time. "Bye, guys. See you in July."

When she got back to Minneapolis it was only six in the evening. Feeling restless, but not ready to go home—wanting to be alone, but still among people—Lisa headed to her favorite coffee shop, the Serene Bean. She liked it because of its name, its atmosphere, and what it did to her. When she went there, which hadn't been often enough lately, she slowed down. The coffee wasn't that great, but otherwise, it was worth it.

She walked in with a pensive mood and ordered a cappuccino and a chocolate cookie. She found a small, battered-but-loved secondhand table near the window and placed her luggage on the opposite chair. Pulling out a book, she settled in for some undisturbed reading.

After an hour, she stood, stretched her legs, and went to use the restroom. On her journey back, she saw Jake standing by the counter. Immediately Angela's advice sprung to mind. *Be nice.* She couldn't shake that sixth-sense feeling—that it wasn't happenstance that their Sunday evenings had collided. Gathering her courage, she walked up behind him and stopped. A few seconds passed and he still hadn't noticed her. She tipped up on her toes, then rolled back down to her heels.

"Hi, Jake."

He turned at her voice then smiled. "Hi."

"So, what are you doing?" What a stupid question. What did she think he was doing in a coffee shop, looking for furniture?

"Nothing much." He raised his to-go cup. "Just grabbing some coffee."

There was a standing silence as they surveyed the room, waiting for the other to say something. *Be nice to him.* Angela's voice echoed through her brain again.

"Would ... you ... like to sit down?" she asked, hooking a thumb toward her table.

He glanced at his watch. "Uh ... sure. I could do that."

They walked over to the table, and while she moved her luggage from the chair to the window ledge, he asked, "Are you going somewhere?"

"No. I just got back. From San Diego."

"What were you doing there?"

"Visiting a friend of mine."

"Really. How long were you there?"

"Just for the weekend."

"Oh. That was short."

"Yeah. I needed to get away." She didn't need to say that. Before he could ask why she needed to get away, she asked, "What did you do this weekend?"

"Not much. Did some work, watched a movie, went for a run."

"You run? I didn't know that."

"I haven't regularly since college, but when you and Chad told us about that race in Wisconsin, I thought it would be fun and Scott wanted to do it for the T-shirt."

"When is it?"

"Last Saturday, actually. I thought you might be there."

"Sorry." She was surprised because she really did feel sorry. "Was it smelly enough for you?"

"Oh yeah, but it was worth it. And you were right—good after-party."

"I'll have to let Chad know."

"He was with us." Of course he was.

"Will you do any more races?" she asked.

"Yeah, I think so." He took a sip of his coffee and crossed his leg. He wore a black boot of good-quality leather and solid stitching. She liked that Jake had good taste in shoes.

"Are you still running?"

She looked up from his shoes. "I am—not religiously—but trying to get out a few times a week."

Another pause hung between them, but this one less strained. "Have you seen the progress on the construction lately?"

Jake nodded. "I was at the site last week. It's really moving along. You and Ingrid have done a fantastic job." For a split second Lisa questioned his sincerity, but his face showed he meant it.

"Well you were part of it, too," she conceded.

And there it was. She had taken her first step toward befriending Jake.

Jake grinned. "Thanks."

Chapter 18
an Interlude

Her phone rang.

"Hey, are you sleeping?"

"No. I'm putting my shoes on. Where are you?"

"Standing in front of your house."

Lisa pulled the curtain back and saw Jake, cell phone at his ear, standing on the sidewalk, waving. He was wearing a maroon Gophers hockey hoodie and black sweatpants.

She slipped on her running shoes, grabbed her phone and earbuds, then put them back. She wouldn't need them today.

Jake and Lisa were at Buca di Beppo sharing a huge plate of ravioli, a bowl of Caesar salad, a half-loaf of garlic bread, and a carafe of red table wine. Lisa was packing it away as much as he was. He wiped his mouth on a red cloth napkin and took a sip of the wine, sensing it evaporate and permeate his nose before he swallowed. He said, "I love a girl who eats."

"Me, too." She raised her fork. "Bon appétit!"

"Why do girls think it's attractive to eat like birds?"

"I don't know." She stabbed a large romaine leaf and held it on her fork. "I suppose it has something to do with the messages we're bombarded with. If you eat less than a man, somehow you're more feminine." Then she pushed the entire leaf into her mouth.

"When I'm hungry I want to eat, and I want someone to eat with me, not shuffle their salad around and sip a Diet Coke."

"Maybe she wants to show you she's not an expensive date."

"Nah, that's not it. I've found that how much salad a woman picks at is inversely proportionate to how much she shops."

"In that case, pass me the ravioli, please."

"Okay," Jake said, pointing out to the ice at the indoor rink. "Do you see that black thing over there?"

"Where?"

"Over there between those two players."

She squinted. "I think so."

"That's called a puck."

She poked a finger into his thick jacket to get at his ribs. "Even *I* know that."

"Okay, good. Number two: They hit the puck with a stick."

She locked his head under her arm. "I'll hit *you* with a stick."

He wrestled against her grip, exaggerating his imprisonment. "Let me go!"

"Never! Mwah-ha-ha-ha," she cackled.

He stopped struggling. "You smell nice."

Lisa gave him a final squeeze around the head before releasing him. "Thanks. Deodorant works wonders."

Jake was venturing into the truly unknown. Lisa had invited him to an artsy movie. Fortunately, it wasn't as lame as he thought it would be. He wouldn't mind seeing a little action, maybe a car chase or some kung fu, but it wasn't bad. He whispered, "What's going on?"

"Dimitri is sculpting the meaning of life out of the vegetables, but he's struggling because the vegetables are decomposing too quickly."

"What does that have to do with the Asian guy?"

"He symbolizes Dimitri's conscience."

Jake sat back and pondered this insight, then leaned over again. "I don't get it."

"Dimitri is trying to decide if he should try another material or accept the decomposition as a metaphor."

"Oh." He still didn't get it. "That's deep." Jake retracted his earlier opinion; this movie was totally lame.

"What do you think?" Lisa asked.

"It's … interesting."

"Isn't it, though?"

"Jake, did you ever have a shot at the NHL?"

"I had some prospects."

"Why didn't you do it?"

"It wasn't for me. I love hockey, don't get me wrong. I just ... I don't know ... I wanted to do something more, if that makes any sense." He hoped it didn't sound too banal or too self-righteous.

He continued, "Hockey's great, but a career in professional sports has a shelf life. I'd get to play for—what—ten years at the most? That's assuming that I don't get too banged up and have to hang up the jersey before that. The average age of retirement is twenty-eight. I'm already twenty-nine. Then what would I do with myself? I thought I'd save myself the extra step and physical pain." After a pause, he added, "And I don't think I could've handled the lifestyle."

"How does David do it?"

"He doesn't let the fame go to his head. He works hard, stays focused, and off the ice he pretty much minds his own business."

"Why did he choose to play?"

"I think for him, it *was* his dream."

"So, why did you choose law?"

"Do you want the canned or the corny answer?"

"Both."

"The canned answer is: for the money. The corny answer is: because I want to help people. People don't believe me when I say the second reason, so I usually make a joke about the first."

Lisa said, "I believe you."

A woman's voice crooned from Lisa's stereo. *Will I wait for you to say I love you? One time I thought not, until the moment came when I realized, I love you ...*

"What *is* this?" he asked.

"What?"

"This music. It's so depressing." Jake picked up the cracked and scratched jewel case. It fell apart when he opened it.

"It is not. It's tragically romantic."

"Why do girls listen to this stuff?" When she didn't answer right away, the silence made him look up. Lisa was fiddling with another battered CD case.

"It helps us to recover from loves lost," she said. Then she looked, not at him, but toward the window. "And restores hope for future romance."

"What stage are you in? Recovery or hope?"

Then she looked at him. "Both."

He felt a pang in his chest.

"Jake, look at this article," Lisa said, handing him her magazine. "It's about a teen center built in Cincinnati."

They were both so engrossed in the article that neither registered the *ding* of the elevator's bell until it reached Jake's floor.

He said, "You missed your floor again."

"Yeah, yeah," she said, waving his comment away. "Look what it says here about their funding."

"Got a hot date tonight with your imaginary boyfriend?" Jake asked.

"He wasn't imaginary." Lisa pulled a photo from the kitchen drawer and tossed it to him. The picture showed Lisa with a tall blond guy. He was wearing a soccer jersey. She wore yoga pants and a T-shirt, both of which clung to her in all the right places. "And for your information, we're not dating anymore."

"Oh." He wasn't sorry to hear it.

"Yes, apparently German medical students named Eva are more appealing than American nonprofit girls named Lisa. Chad told me I had no chance against those European chicks."

"I bet he was just saying that so he could win you over."

"Believe me, I'm not Chad's type."

"Just think, if you two got married, you wouldn't have to change your last name. That would be convenient."

"That would be a little too close for comfort. Want a beer?" Lisa opened the refrigerator, bending to reach for two bottles. He couldn't help but admire her curves. She straightened up, twisted off the bottle caps, and handed him a bottle. When he took it, their fingers touched. Jake was conscious of holding his there for a second more before taking the bottle from her hand.

They sat on her porch glider reading, Jake absentmindedly rocking them with one foot. He belched. "Excuse me."

"You're excused," Lisa said, then giggled.

He looked up from his book. "What?"

She put her nose back in her own book. "Nothing."

She leaned her leg lightly against his. He didn't move away.

"What are you doing tonight?" she asked. Lisa was at her place. Jake was at his.

"I don't know."

"Aren't you going cruising for chicks with the guys?"

"Nah."

"Come on. It'll be fun."

"How do you know? Are you switching sides?"

"Ha-ha. I don't know for a *fact*; it's all hearsay."

"I'd rather stay home and watch a movie."

"You sound old." She raised her voice. "Hey, old man, watch out! Before you know it, sitting in the bathroom with a *National Geographic* is going to be considered a night out."

He pulled the phone away from his ear then put it back. "For a girl, you're pretty gross. The sad part is I know exactly what you mean."

"So come out with us."

"You're going, too?"

"Yeah. I wouldn't want to miss the fun of watching you all humiliate yourselves."

"Well, if you're going ..."

Chapter 19

She leapt to the window like a kid on Christmas morning, hoping for green grass and blue skies for the tournament. Her prayers had been answered. *Thank you, St. Clare.* And Jake. At the end of March, there had still been a foot of snow on the ground, and that was after the blizzard that had come two days before their originally scheduled date.

Her phone rang. Assuming it was Ingrid, she answered and immediately said, "I know—pick up the programs, copies of our presentation, and the remaining goodie bags. I'm on my way."

"Good. Pick me up a seven-grain bagel while you're at it," Jake said. Her heart leapt. "I just wanted to call and wish you good luck."

"Thanks. You, too."

It was going to be a *great* day.

Ingrid was already at the country club when Lisa arrived. True to what they said about pregnant women, she was glowing. Ingrid's radiance made Lisa even happier—if that was possible.

"Did you bring the rest of the stuff?"

"Yeah, it's right here," Lisa said, lifting two totes of materials. "There's more in the car." She hauled in the remaining bags while Ingrid busied herself with laying out the last of the programs, arranging flowers, and overseeing the waitstaff. A large spread of beverages and snacks sprawled along a ten-foot-long table dressed in white linens.

Lisa asked, "Is John coming?"

"Yeah, he'll be here later. I told him he had to figure out how to assemble the crib before he could come out and play. His brother, Jim, was over at seven this morning, armed with his toolbox and belt."

"It's just a crib."

"That's what I said. I think there must be some male-bonding ritual associated with building stuff."

"Are Mr. Hollow and his people here yet?" She really wanted to know if Jake was there yet.

"No. They're coming later with the rest of the group."

"You know, Ingrid, I didn't invite anyone to the tournament, so if you want, Jim can have my guest ticket."

She brightened up. "That's a great idea. I'll call John right now."

While Ingrid went outside to phone John, Lisa turned on her laptop and reviewed some graphs in their presentation. A few minutes later, she heard a knock and looked up. It was David Cibulka, dressed in a polo shirt bearing the Sharks logo and light khakis. His biceps were round like grapefruits stacked on each arm. He leaned against the white door frame.

"Mind if I come in?"

"Not at all. If you're not too snooty, I'll give you a job."

He laughed. "I think I can handle some manual labor." She passed him a stack of yellow plastic bags and they worked side by side, assembling the last of the goodie bags.

"It's nice to see you again," he said.

"Thanks. That's pretty nice coming from you, although ... if you were a rock star, I'd give you more points."

"I appreciate your humor. Usually people only want to talk about hockey, if I have connections to get their kid into hockey, or if they can have my autograph."

"You already know how much I know about hockey, so that conversation would be pointless. I don't have any kids, and I don't need an autograph. I've got emails."

"What do you like?"

"Movie trivia and *Name That Tune*."

"I met Bruce Willis once. He's a Sharks fan. And he can't carry a tune."

"Well, well ... look who's name dropping now."

"What can I say—I'm just a guy trying to impress a girl."

She jabbed her elbow playfully into his side. "That's what they all say."

She was acutely aware of his physical presence. She'd always been impressed by how very tall he was, but after that comment he seemed to have grown into a giant. He stood close enough for her to feel an occasional breath of warm air on her head as he moved toward her to pick up a freebie, and then away from her to put it in a plastic bag. While she enjoyed the joking between them, she didn't think she should be encouraging him. "Jake told me you're going out tonight after the tournament."

"Ah-ha. That's who you're interested in, is it?"

"Please," she scoffed, "Jake?" She hoped she sounded convincing.

"Now that's a first. Even when I was first starting out in the NHL and people started to recognize me, Jake and I would go out and women practically gravitated toward him. I'd be lucky if one gave me the time of day."

"Maybe Jake is just more aggressive. You seem to be the sit-back-and-watch type." She thought that was a much more respectable way to pursue a woman, anyway. "Why would you want to look for your soul mate in a bar?"

She stopped, not wanting to offend him with her opinions about finding potential spouses. What did she know, anyway? "So are you guys meeting up later?"

"We're planning on it. Do you want to join us?"

"Thanks, but I can't. Ingrid and I have a lot more work to do when this whole thing is done." And it might be awkward, considering how she'd been feeling lately about Jake.

"Maybe next time." He took a step away from her.

"Okay, All-Star, your work here is done. Now go out there and make us some money."

"Right, coach," he said. His eyes twinkled with fun and he high-fived her before leaving.

If Ingrid and Lisa had been on *The Apprentice*, Donald Trump would have been proud. The weather cooperated beautifully, people golfed well, and those who didn't—well, they didn't mind. John and his brother arrived in time to play a round as well. Susan approached them, looking immaculate despite a tinge of sunburn across her cheeks. "Good job, ladies. Very well done."

Guests trickled in from the green and seated themselves around the banquet tables. Lisa saw Jake escorting Mrs. Chang to the head table and sat her between Mr. Hollow's wife and Susan. Jake took the place on Susan's other side. Mrs. Chang and Mrs. Hollow chatted at length and Lisa wondered if they attended the same bridge club. David sat next to Jake and Mark claimed the last spot. Jake caught her eye and winked.

Ingrid made the rounds, checking on guests, while Lisa took care of the golf awards, the laptop with their presentation, and the video footage from Channel Nine. Some reporters approached her and Lisa answered questions, while John and Jim sat at an inconspicuous table with a poor view of the podium.

After the guests ate, Susan approached the podium, thanking everyone again for coming. Together, Susan and Lisa handed out the golf awards, then Susan launched into the presentation Ingrid had prepared. She spoke enthusiastically about the fast pace in which the buildings were being renovated and the grounds completed. She announced the block party, which would celebrate the opening of the park the first Saturday in June. She updated them on the capital campaign, noting everyone's generosity, and urged them to participate in that final push to make the "vision" a reality. Susan was careful to mention every single company, contributor, and foundation present in that room. She was flawless. While Susan spoke, Lisa stood off to the side, her chest puffing from the pride she felt in their work. Maybe there'd be a promotion in her near future. Jake clapped loudly and beamed. At her.

When Susan finished, Mr. Hollow stood, met Susan at the podium, and gave her a friendly half-hug. He placed his hands on the podium, his arms stretched out, standing like a king surveying his subjects. Even slightly stooped because of his age, he looked tall, and Lisa admired how much of his silvery hair he still possessed.

"Thank you; thank you, Susan. Thank you everybody for coming out to join us for a glorious day of golf and for joining us in this grand and noble endeavor. As many of you know, as a boy, I grew up not far from where Grant Park stands today. In my day, this neighborhood flourished. You can imagine my sadness as time wore on and eventually all that was left were empty lots of weeds and broken glass for the boys to play baseball in. I told myself, 'Grant, one day you're going to go back there and turn it into something. Get rid of that junk and build those boys a real baseball field.' So that's what I set out to do. It took a lot of years of hard work, but I made it happen."

Inwardly, Lisa groaned at the display of egocentrism. *Yeah, Grant. You walked to school, in the winter, in ten-foot drifts, with no shoes, five miles, uphill, both ways.*

Impervious to the fidgeting and glazed-over stares, he proceeded to digress, launching into a long-winded and excruciatingly detailed account of his life's struggles. Didn't his firm have speechwriters?

"But enough about me," he said, eventually finishing his soliloquy. "I am an old man with many tales. I've seen successes and I've seen failures and this has been one of my brighter moments. Now I would like to take this opportunity to acknowledge those who have worked to make my boyhood dream a reality. From the Little Flower Foundation, I'd like to thank Susan Karowitz, president of the foundation and close family friend. Thank you, Susan, for your tireless energy and support for this project. And to her assistants, Ingrid White and Lisa Johnson. Thank you, ladies, for providing this delicious food."

By her side, she felt Susan stiffen. The food? Had she heard him correctly? Is that all he thought they'd done? Order the *food*? And did she have to be Lisa Johnson again? She swore that on Monday, she would go down to city hall and change her damn name. Then she really *would* be Lisa Johnson.

"From our law office, Smith, Hakkula, and Schuler, I'd like to thank Mark Schoenfelder and Jake Hanson for the countless hours they spent convincing you all to come here." *Chuckle, chuckle.*

Mr. Hollow continued. "While I certainly don't wish to discredit Mark here—he does a fine job for us and is an excellent lawyer—I'd like to take a few moments to talk about a certain ambitious young man, who seems to have the Midas touch."

Lisa's ears perked up.

"When I first hired Jake Hanson I thought to myself, 'This kid has spunk.' And so far, he hasn't proven me wrong. Jake has been a driving force in our capital campaign to complete the park and has pulled through for us in ways that have surprised even me. He whisked us all off our feet by bringing in his college hockey buddy, David Cibulka. David, please stand up. Give him a hand, folks." David stood just long enough to hold up a hand.

"But Jake didn't stop there," Mr. Hollow said. "No, this young man has got real fire in the belly. Stand up, Jake! Show them who you are!" Jake was up in one bounce and waved to the crowd, giving his best smile, as if he were the famous one.

Mr. Hollow continued, "A few months ago, Jake approached Mrs. Rose Chang, who we all know as an esteemed and highly respected woman and colleague, not only in the business world, but in the circles of philanthropy as well. He took the time to carefully detail every aspect of our cause with Mrs. Chang and to fully involve her in the implementation and execution of Grant Park. And on that note, I have the distinct pleasure of making a very, *very* special announcement. Mrs. Chang has decided to become not only a contributor but also a partner in this venture, and will be giving Grant Park *$5 million*. Mrs. Chang, will you please stand up?"

People rose in a standing ovation for Mrs. Chang. She smiled, acknowledging the recognition with a simple nod of her head. Mr. Hollow concluded, "Thanks, Jake, for a most excellent job well done."

Flabbergasted, Lisa couldn't remember what she was supposed to do next. She looked over to Susan, who met Mr. Hollow at the podium, pushed "play" on the video footage, and escorted Mr. Hollow to his seat. When he got to the table, he shook Jake's hand and gave him a hearty backslap. Jake was all smiles, accepting the accolades that came from around the table.

Lisa tried to catch his eye, but he was too engrossed with the praise to notice. She scurried back to the temporary office, closed the door, and exhaled. She had no reason to be mad. *No reason.* Mr. Hollow was being a windbag. That wasn't Jake's fault. Glancing through the door's window, she saw Jake watch the screen, his face calm.

When Ingrid joined her, Lisa said, "Can you believe that guy?"

"What? Mr. Hollow?"

"You know just as well as I do that *we* were the backbone of this project. We worked our butts off for those guys. All Mark and Jake did was what we told them to do and provide progress reports for their boss."

"That's not exactly true. They did their part," Ingrid reasoned. She ticked off their tasks on her fingers. "They did all of the legal verbiage for us. Mark oversaw all of the land and building acquisitions with me, plus he helped us when we got into a technicality skirmish regarding the abstract on one of the buildings. He's been there every step of the way in dealing with the construction and renovations. Jake helped you by getting more corporate sponsors. He *did* bring in David and yes, you were the one who introduced the project to Mrs. Chang, but Jake, apparently, is the one who got her to commit to more than double what we thought she would."

"I'm the one she's been working with for the last two months! Jake met her once and that was with me."

"Did you know about the $5 million?" she asked.

"Well … no." Mr. Hollow's remarks had been such a slap she hadn't even processed that news. And what *had* happened for her to double her contribution?

"Then it would seem that Jake deserves some credit, doesn't he?"

"Aren't you bothered at all—even the tiniest little bit—that we got the shaft?"

"It bothers me a little," Ingrid admitted, "but I wouldn't say we got the shaft. Lisa, this is our job. We help people like Mr. Hollow do good for society. And because they've got the money, they're going to take most of the credit. That's how it works. We have to consider the bigger picture. A great thing was done by building Grant Park. If that park has a positive impact on the life of just one kid, a kid like David Cibulka, then I'm willing to forego the recognition. I could care less if my name's on some plaque. Who's to say Jake will even be remembered a year from now? Two years? Ten years? The only names that are going to stick are Grant Park and The Hollow."

Her rationalization, although not fully appreciated in the moment, was just enough to assuage Lisa. Ingrid said, "Frankly, I don't think this is about getting recognition. I think this is about Jake. I don't know what's going on between you two and your friendship, if that's what it is, but as the project manager of this project and as your friend, I strongly advise you to set aside your personal feelings and stay focused on your work. You're good at what you do, Lisa. Be proud of that."

Ingrid's words stung, but rang true.

Still, Lisa couldn't shake the nauseous feeling she had each time she handed a guest a goodie bag and wished them well while thinking about the gender dynamics of the workplace. After the last bag had been passed out, Jake approached her. "What a day, huh?"

"Yep," she said, placing leftover programs in a box.

"Listen, we're leaving now. Are you sure you don't want to come with us?"

"I have work to do."

"Okay. I'll call you tomorrow."

She thought he might put a hand on her back—he'd done this a few times when saying goodbye—so she moved before he could. She folded the flaps of the box shut, picked it up, and walked out to her car.

She shivered with goose bumps when the gospel was about the two sisters Martha and Mary. Martha was all work, work, work, while Mary sat at Jesus's feet and chatted. When she asked Jesus if he was annoyed that Mary wasn't doing any of the work, Jesus basically said, "Chillax. Mary rocks."

That's not exactly how the priest said it, but that was how Lisa took it.

She fidgeted in the pew, regretting coming to the Saturday night English Mass at the Cathedral instead of the Spanish one at St. John Neumann. No one from the firm had helped them today. Sure, she and Ingrid functioned like parts in a well-oiled machine, and including those guys would've been like throwing a wrench into the cogs. But that didn't exempt Lisa from feeling that it was like the women slaving away all day in the kitchen while the men entertained. The only Mary out there had been Susan and Susan was still more of a Martha. Was that God's message for her? To be more like Mary? To be like *Jake?*

She had no *rational* reason to be mad, but her annoyance segued into irritation, which bubbled into frustration, which began roiling old emotion. It was Washington all over again.

When she got home, she parked the car in the alley, got out, slammed the door, stomped to the backdoor, wrenched it open, and crashed into the kitchen, muttering profanities on one side and mimicking parts of Mr. Hollow's speech on the other, like a two-headed monster. The cat cowered under the plant stand. Mass had been over hardly an hour and already she'd forgotten the penitential act, the Lord's Prayer, the Eucharistic prayers, and all the other prayers that had passed her lips.

She refused to believe that anything other than her hard work had gotten them to this point. *Their* hard work: Lisa's and Ingrid's. They'd put in countless hours implementing their ideas and building relationships. And Jake got the glory because he happened to know David Cibulka? Lisa was sure they could've gotten him without Jake.

And it hadn't mattered that she'd stacked a hundred facts like a neat row of dominoes for Mrs. Chang; Jake had the woo. All it took was one airy-fairy wave of his wand, a cute story, and—*abracadabra!*—$5 million appeared. In real money. Why hadn't she known about it? At what point had she ceased to be part of the negotiations? Facts shmacts. People liked woo.

Fool me once, shame on you. Fool me twice, shame on me. Fool me three times, shame on both of us. She was the fool. She'd become exactly what she'd feared: an adoring follower of the cult of Jake. It broke her heart to think he'd reeled her in with his charm, then screwed her over in the last minute. She was a sheep who hadn't seen the slaughter coming. Who did he think he was that he could step on people at will? How could she let him know how it felt to be strung along, and then have *his* chain jerked? Her mind clicked.

It was either a wonderfully terrible idea or a terribly wonderful idea.

She ran out to the back alley where the recycling sat in large bins and clawed through the stacks, looking for the invitation. Out of the corner of her eye, she caught the ripple of lace curtains from the house next door. She ripped every newspaper, magazine, and piece of junk mail out of that bin. It wasn't there.

When had she gotten that thing? She had to think hard, but guessed it was at least four pick-ups ago. She raced back to the apartment for her laptop. The site she wanted popped up, accented in gaudy gold and blue. She clicked on the registration form, paid her flippin' eighty bucks, and uploaded a most recent photo—the best one she had from the gala. It was the perfect revenge. She would show that cocky bastard, once and for all, who was Miss Thang now.

Chapter 20

"I think we should go coed this year." Jake was at Amir's, putting together the roster for the year's softball team.

"Do you know any girls who are good enough to play?" Amir asked.

"Chad knows this girl named Erica. Maybe she'll know somebody. And Lisa."

"Does Lisa even know how to play?"

"I don't know. But she's a runner. And she's competitive. We can teach her how to bat and put her out in right field. It'll be fine."

"Okay," Amir said, adding her name to the list. "Are you two dating now?"

"I'm not sure." From his side, he wasn't spending time with any women other than Lisa and he saw her as much as he could. "But I will tell you I can't remember the last time I had so much fun hanging out with a woman."

"Yeah?"

"Yeah. She's really cool. It's like I can have a real conversation with her. She doesn't try to figure out what I want to hear; she tells me what she really thinks. We get into these debates and she gets so fired up. Sometimes I egg her on just because she looks so cute when she's angry."

"So fighting with her is hot," joked Amir.

"A little, but seriously, it's more than that." How could he explain it? Amir and Ani had clicked from the get go. For Jake, it had been one mismatch after another. "It's like, usually when I meet a woman and I tell her I'm a lawyer, she immediately assumes that I'm somehow better than she is, or that I know more than she does. If I ask what she thinks about current events, she says, 'I don't know.' Lisa actually has opinions about war, politics, social issues—everything. Once I asked her every kind of opinion question I could think of, just to see how long it would take for her to say, 'I don't know.' When she finally did, it was because I asked what time it was."

"Okay. So what's holding you back?"

"Two things. First, we've been working on this project together."

"Why should that make a difference? People have office romances all the time."

"This is different. It's my boss's project. It's his legacy; he treats it like a baby. Plus, I haven't even been at the firm a year. I have a lot to prove and I don't want to mess that up."

"And the other reason?"

"The other reason is that I don't want to scare her off. Last fall I only *hinted* at my interest and she ran away. She said she had this boyfriend, but I don't think it was just that. Then about a month ago, I saw her at this coffee shop and she was really nice to me. Since then, it's been great." There'd been a couple moments when he'd wanted to grab her and kiss her, not caring about the consequences. But he could tell something was holding her back, too, so he'd resisted the temptation and stayed just inside the friend zone.

"What happened to the boyfriend?"

"I don't know. He's in Germany." He didn't want to know the details of her being with another guy.

"You're sure she's not dating anyone?"

"Yeah, I'm sure." Jake had become the newest member of Lisa's social circle, replacing Ingrid, who was more inclined to stay home these days.

"So what makes you think she's interested in you?"

"Because we're always together. She's always there." His face got hot and he knew he was turning red. He just felt it; that was his reason.

"I'm not trying to give you a hard time, I'm just saying be careful. I *saw* what Anna did to you."

"It's not like I'm in high school anymore."

"I know. Just be sure she doesn't jerk you around."

"Lisa's not like that."

"Listen to us," Amir said, laughing. "Me, giving you dating advice. Talk about role reversal. And since we're talking about Anna, I thought you might like to know she hasn't RSVP'd for the reunion yet."

"How's that going?" In exchange for some babysitting, Jake had recruited Amir to help with some of his reunion committee duties. He had great memories of high school—some of the best—but didn't necessarily agree that the responsibility of party planning should fall to him by default.

Amir opened a spreadsheet on his computer. "So far only forty-seven people have registered."

"That's it?"

"That's not bad. June is still a ways off. You'll probably see the numbers pick up the second half of May. A guy from my office, whose ten-year reunion was last year, said most people don't commit until the last minute."

"Thanks for doing this, man."

"No problem. Just don't forget to be here at six o'clock sharp on Friday. Ani and I have dinner reservations and Mirijana can't wait to play with Uncle Jake."

. . . . .

"Okay, ladies, how'd we do?"

Lisa spoke first. "Extremely well, Mr. Hollow. The final numbers surpassed our goals." She looked over at Jake, who was reading her report, then back to Mr. Hollow. Since the tournament, she'd hung out with Jake, but only with their group and with much less exuberance. He'd hardly seemed to notice. "First, I'd like to say that I thought you gave a wonderful speech, sir. I found it really touching and inspirational."

"Well, thank you." Mr. Hollow gave her his best denture gleam.

"You're welcome." Her voice sounded controlled but had an edge, like a sharp blade, that gave her confidence. "Anyway, as you mentioned so eloquently, Mr. Hollow, thanks to *Jake*, we've exceeded our fundraising goal by $3.8 million." Jake's head snapped up when she said his name. Hopefully it was her subtle sarcasm that got his attention. "Between your moving speech and Mrs. Chang's generosity, many of the guests increased *their* financial support. This is superb news, because since our last meeting, we also received four rejection letters for grants we applied for."

Susan nodded, as did Mr. Hollow, who was following the columns of numbers on his handout. Ingrid said, "Because the finances have fallen into place, the block party can be free."

Lisa said, "Yes, and I bet Jake has some excellent ideas for the party. Mrs. Chang has already emailed me some concepts. Perhaps Jake could work with Mrs. Chang and figure something out?"

Ingrid shot her a warning glance. "We were successful in getting the band Spinach for the main stage, and I've got a list of bands to contact who can play throughout the day on the smaller stages; we're giving priority to those from the community."

"And it would be *very good* to have David Cibulka there since he *has* been the project's face from the beginning. Jake, do you think you can arrange his visit?" Lisa said irascibly.

True to his nature, Mr. Hollow plowed on, unaware. "Excellent. Jake, you follow up with Mrs. Chang and Dave, and help the girls in any way you can to plan this party."

Ingrid was firing eye darts at her, and she didn't know how Jake was taking it, because she refused to look at him. They spent the next fifty minutes discussing details and final financial strategy while Lisa dug into Jake every chance she got.

Jake had been holding out on her; she could see that clearly now. Playing the David Cibulka card, and then swooping in on Mrs. Chang when she wasn't looking, was like playing the queen of spades in her game of hearts. He'd taken all her tricks. She scolded herself for being surprised. She'd known all along what she was up against. Unfortunately, she'd been too caught up in her online romance with Tony to notice what Jake was doing. He'd done it so gracefully; it had looked heroic, a magnanimous gesture in the eyes of everyone, while Lisa was left like a shredded earthworm still wriggling, but forgotten, on his hook. The tension in the room had ratcheted up a notch—Lisa could sense that Ingrid felt it, too—but she was like an emotional drunk; she couldn't stop, feeling far too emboldened to feel guilty for her recklessness.

Then Mr. Hollow looked at his watch and announced they were done. As soon as the men walked out, Ingrid said, "Let it go and do your job," then hauled her pregnant girth up from the chair and left.

Only Susan remained. She stood, calmly closed the door, then took Ingrid's vacant chair next to Lisa. Her grave gaze made Lisa uneasy. "Is there something I need to know about?"

Lisa's heart lurched into her throat and her mouth went dry. She gulped. "No, I don't think so."

Susan watched Lisa for a moment, then slowly metered out her words. "Mr. Hollow is a *very* respected person in this city. I don't think I have to explain the importance of what we're trying to achieve here and how it will reflect on the foundation."

Lisa was too terrified to speak.

"I assume that I can rely on you to continue doing your utmost to see that this project is executed in a most respectable and professional manner."

"Absolutely," Lisa said eagerly.

"Good. That's all I wanted to hear."

Susan collected her belongings and left. Lisa stayed in the conference room recovering from Susan's verbal warning. The peaceful frame of mind she'd worked so hard to Scotch Tape back together since the tournament had come undone. Her work, which normally inspired her, had the opposite effect. Every time she saw Jake's name, or David's, or Mrs. Chang's—heck, even the numbers themselves—she got stoked like a too-hot furnace all over again. The whole project incensed her, even if it was for a good cause. She couldn't even convince herself to focus on all the people benefiting from Grant Park.

Her body felt stiff from all the tension that she'd been bottling up. She'd never had a conversation like that with Susan. When Susan started to speak, Lisa feared her boss would fire her right there. If she were a smoker, Lisa would've needed a cigarette about now.

When she returned to her cubicle, Jake was standing next to it.

"Can I help you with something?" she asked, trying to regain a professional semblance of sorts.

Jake asked, "May I speak with you, please?"

She spied Susan's door standing open. In the spirit of her promise to play nice, she acquiesced and led him out of the office space and into the hallway. As soon as the door clicked shut and they were by the elevator, Jake turned on her with an expression of such seriousness that she hardly recognized his face.

"What's going on?" he asked.

"Excuse me?"

"Grant Hollow is my boss, Lisa. I didn't appreciate or deserve what just went on in there."

"I'm sure he took my comments as an extension of his praise for you."

"No, I don't think he did." He folded his arms across his chest. "Is this about Mrs. Chang? Is that why you've been avoiding me?"

"It's about you throwing me under the bus. You *knew* I was working with her. How could you go behind my back like that?"

"I didn't go behind your back."

"Did you know about the money?"

"Yes, but only because I was her golf partner. I wanted to tell you, but I couldn't get away. I didn't know Grant was going to announce it right then and there."

"The way he talked about you, it was like you were the frickin' goose laying golden eggs right into his bank account."

"I didn't do anything. Except for a few emails, I only met her that one time."

"Well, then it must have been quite a golf game for her to pony up a few extra million."

"She was telling me about her family and her granddaughter's piano recital. We didn't even talk about the project."

"I've seen you in action, Jake. I know what a schmoozer you are. Then your boss says all that—*shit*—and you just let him."

"I was just as shocked as you," he insisted.

"*Shocked?* You were lapping up the praise."

Jake threw his hands up in frustration. "Look, I'm sorry about what Grant said, but I didn't ask him to go up there and give me all the credit."

She gave him a steely glare. "Cut the golden-boy act. When he was saying how great you were, I think you *loved* the attention. I think you love *being* the center of attention. That's how you are. You flash your smile and the whole world swoons for you. I'm not buying it, so don't think that blowing me a little sunshine is going to make it all right, because it won't."

"What was I supposed to do? Walk up there and take the microphone out of his hand?"

"You know what, Jake? A greater man would have." Red spots danced through her field of vision and she began moving away from him.

"Lisa, it's not as simple as that."

"It *is* simple," she said, turning and coming back to him. "The truth is always simple. And it's not just about Mrs. Chang or your boss; it's the whole way you operate. Like the way you brought David in? That wasn't only clever; it was—strategically *brilliant*."

"I wasn't trying to be strategic. Ingrid said 'celebrity' and it just popped into my head."

"Seriously? We'd been talking about rich people for weeks and it didn't click?"

"We'd been talking about philanthropists and business people and Dave isn't either one of those. He grew up poor and that's how I knew him. Maybe he's rich now, but not like bling rich, like 'check out my crib, yo, yo' rich. He's a regular guy."

She didn't respond. She wasn't going to give him an ounce of sympathy.

"I've already apologized to you. What more do you want? I've worked hard on this project—aside from my caseload—and if memory serves me correctly, I *have* made a significant contribution, even before Mrs. Chang. I know you're mad, but don't try to discredit me professionally."

"You are a manipulating opportunist," she hissed, pointing a finger at him.

He shook his head then pushed the button for the elevator. He didn't look angry; he looked sad. "I really don't get you, Lisa. I thought we were friends."

"I guess you were wrong."

"So that's your opinion of me. Honestly?"

"Yes." Lisa fixed her unwavering eyes on him. She didn't want him to have any doubt about it.

. . . . .

Jake shook his head again and looked down at his shoes before looking her in the eye. "You don't know me at all."

"Believe me," she retorted, "*you* don't know *me*." He'd seen her angry before, but this was different. There was a troubling darkness in her blue eyes.

"That's the first thing you've said that I actually agree with." After that, he didn't have anything more to say to her. He banged his way to the stairwell, forgetting about the elevator, and took the stairs two at a time. No self-respecting man—no *person*—should have to listen to that kind of garbage. Especially when he knew he was right.

So Grant had said a few nice things about him. So what? It wasn't enough to warrant Lisa's reaction. She was being way over-the-top. He hadn't used her. He'd only ever cooperated with her, done whatever she'd asked of him. So what if his boss made some harmless remarks about him? Grant had just been building up to his big announcement. He doubted his boss actually thought those things about him. What mattered was the objective had been achieved: they'd gotten the money needed to complete the park and open it according to Grant's specifications. Couldn't she see that was far more important than anything else?

But she'd called him an opportunist. And that hurt. He'd only ever been honest. Maybe aggressive when he'd seen an opportunity, but hardly an opportunist. And hardly manipulative.

Jake got back to the firm, sweaty under his shirt, his blood pumping from his nineteen-floor detour. As he passed Grant's office, he heard his boss call his name. Jake stopped and looked in. "Yes?"

Grant motioned toward the chair opposite his desk. "Have a seat."

Jake entered and sat. Grant's desk was dark mahogany and mammoth in size, exuding power. Jake tried to look casual but felt sweat trickle into the small of his back and stick to his shirt. He could count on one hand the number of times Grant had invited him into a personal conversation.

Grant leaned back in his matching leather chair and swiveled around, just enough to look out the tinted window. Jake could make out a blue sky with a few voluminous clouds in the distance. With his eyes on the window, Grant asked, "Do you like working here, Jake?"

"Yes, sir."

"And the work? Does it interest you? Does it challenge you?"

"Yes, sir."

"I'm not going to lie to you, Jake; I like you. I think you're a good man and you work hard. You're ambitious and you've got great potential. You remind me of myself at your age."

"Thank you, sir." Jake sat still, maintaining his stalwart composure.

"I have no doubt that you could go far with our firm and build yourself a great career. You could go on to politics, maybe become attorney general, should you so desire."

Grant swiveled back toward Jake and fixed his hazel eyes on him with the intensity of a hawk on a field mouse. "Because I like you, Jake, I'm going to give you some advice. When at the office, keep your pecker in your pants—and you'll do all right."

Jake held his face in the exact same position, despite the bile rising in his throat. "Yes, sir."

Then Grant smiled broadly, clapped his hands, and said, "And that's it. You can go now."

"Thank you, sir."

When Jake made it to his own office, he shut the door and released his bated breath.

Chapter 21

At four thirty, Lisa slinked out of the office and headed straight to the lake for a run. In the fresh air, she realized just how dry and wrung out she was. Her legs on autopilot, she concentrated only on the path. But in the sobering sunshine, even she saw how audacious, not to mention stupid, it had been to put her personal opinions of Jake into the middle of everyone else's business.

But why had he done it? They weren't coworkers. They weren't vying for the same job. They didn't even work in the same field. Why would he do this to her? Because he could, was all she could come up with. It was the classic white-male advantage Jake had known his whole life. He'd worked the situation to his advantage *just because he could.*

But when she'd confronted him, he'd seemed genuinely surprised by her accusations. His explanation was plausible and he seemed sincere. And the way he looked at her. His sparkling eyes had dulled with—sadness. It had poked a small hole in her shield of anger. Was it possible that Jake just didn't know the power he had over people?

To be fair, she agreed that Jake had contributed to their success. He'd provided them with a whole new list of potential financial supporters from his Jerry's Kids days. The night of the gala, he'd worked the room just as much as the rest of them, if not more so. Had she forgotten how he'd spent countless hours helping her research companies and their philanthropic mission statements, trying to find a match? In some ways it seemed that Jake was better at her job than she was. Where would the project be now if it *hadn't* been for him?

And why was she so willing to hinge her success on someone else's praise, especially someone like Mr. Hollow? He was a chauvinist who was tolerated only because this park had such important long-term ramifications for the entire city. She'd read enough studies about self-promotion and women to know that getting her accomplishments noticed was *her* job. Traditionally, people didn't appreciate women stepping out of the box of modesty that had been defined for them. But this was a new age, a time when women were outperforming men and taking on more executive roles, spurring on the creation of stay-at-home dads and house husbands. Men like Mr. Hollow were approaching extinction.

So what was all this pent up angst really about? That Jake got credit? That people were naturally drawn to him? That she had trusted him? That she was possibly falling in love with him? That's when she felt the pang. She ran another half mile, trying to shut down her mind, but was pulled back to what her heart was saying.

That's what it was. She'd gone from loathing him to being crazy about him and it was only their professional boundary that had held her back. She loved hanging out with Jake. He was the first thing she thought of when she woke up, wondering what they would do that day, what article she'd find to share with him, what topics they would discuss—if it would be politics, religion, or something lighter, like if pineapple was on sale, or if there was a new play or art exhibit they both wanted to see.

Furthermore, in the midst of this evolving friendship—she'd called it that, oblivious as she had been to her evolving feelings—Lisa had grown comfortable with one very important, omitted fact: Jake still had no idea who she was. He wasn't treating her based on any previous knowledge he had of her. But she had done that to him—immensely and intensely, without a jury or proper trial. She hadn't given him the benefit of the doubt, because she'd doubted his credibility from day one.

Her hypocrisy slowed her from a run to a walk, the anger circulating through her body dwindling to a weak pulse. It shamed her to think that, because of one speech by a pompous blowhard, she'd been ready to throw *him* under the bus.

. . . . .

He spotted her car first. Taking some practice swings, Jake watched her walk to the dugout and place her backpack on the bench. Her hair was in a ponytail under a Little Flower baseball cap. She pulled out her glove and set it on the bench. Ani and Mirijana approached her. Mirijana raised her arms and Lisa picked her up and twirled her. The little girl squealed as Lisa hugged and tickled her before setting her down.

Jake turned away. After their argument, he hadn't been sure she'd show up for practice. Part of him hoped she wouldn't. He was a mess, still trying to sort out which parts of what she'd said to him were true and which ones were bullshit.

He felt her approach but kept his back to her.

"Hi," she said.

"Hi."

"How are you?"

"I've been better." He didn't have anything to hide and hadn't done anything wrong—he'd figured out that much so far.

"I'm sure you have," she said. He looked at her incredulously. "I'm sorry; that was a stupid thing to say."

He kept his back to her. Amir watched them from the pitcher's mound.

"Let me try that again." She took a deep breath. "Um, I want to apologize for what I said. You know, after the meeting. It wasn't fair or entirely true. You *have* worked hard on this project."

From the corner of his eye, he saw Amir throw a practice ball to Chad on first base, who hurled it to Tim on second before bringing it back to Amir.

"But Jake," she began. "I need to explain something to you. You see, you have this way with people. And the way they respond to you—like Mr. Hollow—that's not normal."

He finally turned to face her. "What are you talking about?"

"Most people don't get that. Most people have to work really hard and they still don't get noticed. It might take them years, and you—you get it every time, the first time."

"I don't care about that stuff."

"Of course you don't, because you don't see it. You're so used to it that you don't even realize it's not normal."

She paused, then made her hands into a triangle. "This is you," she said, indicating the apex. Then she nodded to the bottom part of the triangle. "And this is the rest of us. Do you understand what kind of power comes with that?" Her eyes searched his for some understanding.

"You don't know anything about me," he answered reflexively.

"I know enough."

He gritted his teeth, bucking against what she was saying. "I work hard, too, Lisa."

"I know you do. What I'm trying to say is, you're special. I know I can't blame you for how others treat you. It's who you are."

She had really pissed him off, but now she looked genuinely sorry. He wasn't sure if he agreed with her, but *she* believed it, and right now all he wanted to do was pull her into his arms and tell her how sorry *he* was. He'd taken the praise so casually, but it had meant something to her, and that reason alone was good enough for him to take it more seriously than he had. But he didn't pull her to him. They were standing at a softball practice that should have started five minutes ago.

When he didn't respond, she looked down and kicked the toe of her tennis shoe in the dirt and said, "Anyway, I just wanted to say I'm sorry."

"Forget about it."

She lifted her eyes and met his. "That's it?"

"What else is there? I accept your apology."

"You're not mad?"

"No," he said, sighing, "but this *thing* between us—I've been doing some thinking and—I think that it would probably be best to—"

"—just stay friends?" she finished for him.

"Yeah." He exhaled. "Don't get me wrong, it's been great. But—I need to focus on my career right now. Grant's already doubled my caseload."

"I understand."

Jake could tell she was disappointed, but he *did* have to think about his career. Grant was watching and if Jake made a single mistake, he would know about it. It would be easier to work together without the emotional tension, and after the street dance, the project would be finished.

"So, we're cool?" he asked.

"Like, dude, totally."

He laughed. "Go join the lineup, then."

Jake walked over to home plate where Scott was getting his catcher's gear on.

"What was that all about?" Scott asked.

"Ah, nothing."

"You dumped her, didn't you?"

"We weren't even dating."

"'I need to focus on my career right now?' What's up with that?"

"How do you know I said that?"

"I can read lips."

"I have a great opportunity with Smacker and I can't afford to screw it up because I happen to be attracted to a woman I'm working with."

"That's too bad. There's nothing like office sex."

"Well, there's going to have to be, because my boss specifically told me to—and I quote—keep my pecker in my pants."

Scott looked at him disbelievingly. "Man, that's harsh."

"Tell me about it." And it was, only not in the way Scott meant.

Since the verbal warning, he'd kept his head down, working his hardest to regain lost ground. But many times, especially during those late nights at the office, Jake recalled his time with Lisa. Remembering her laugh and her smile; the way they teased each other. Either he was a glutton for punishment or he had discovered a new way of being with a woman. In either case, he couldn't help but be drawn to her.

"Why are you making us do this?" Jake asked, tying a blindfold on Lisa.

"Because it's fun!" said Kirsten, Ingrid's older sister.

"Coed baby showers are not fun. Jell-O shot? Blue or pink?" John asked. Since when did they serve shots at a baby shower? Lisa heard one clink and two slurps and guessed either they'd each had one or Jake had accepted one of each.

Ingrid said, "Neither is leaving your pregnant wife home two weeks before she's about to give birth."

"No way," Lisa said, adjusting her blindfold.

"Yes way," said Ingrid. "For his brother's bachelor party. They're going fishing up north. Can you believe it? I'd rather they go to a strip club in town."

"Come on, baby, he's my only brother."

"And you're *his* only brother. He should change the date."

"It was the only time that worked for him. Besides, the doctor said you're doing great and you're only 50 percent effaced. Did he say if you were dilating yet?"

One of John's friends said, "That's not bad. You'll be fine."

"Okay let's get on with it," Lisa said, sensing Jake's discomfort.

Kirsten said, "The object of the game is to dress the baby the fastest. As you can see, I've placed some items in front of each team. You must get all the items on the baby."

"Hey, I didn't get to see them," Ingrid said.

"That's the point," Kirsten said. "Only the women can dress the baby. Now guys, it's your job to tell the ladies how to dress the baby and you are *not* allowed to touch it."

Lisa edged a finger in front of her, bumping into a small foot.

"No cheating!" Kirsten snapped. Lisa snatched back her hand. "You have two minutes. On your mark, get set, go!"

On go, Lisa grabbed the baby, feeling its plastic nakedness in her warm hands, and patted around for the first item. This baby sure seemed small.

Jake said, "Okay, stick the hat on first."

"Aren't we supposed to put the diaper on first?"

"I don't know. Just put the hat on."

"Where is it?"

"To your left, next to the plug."

"The plug? What the hell is that?"

"You know, the thing the baby sucks on."

"A *pacifier?*"

"Yes! Hurry up!"

She felt around, noting the pacifier. He put his hand on hers and guided it until she felt thin cloth under her hand.

"No touching," Kirsten barked. Man, now Lisa understood where Ingrid got her bossiness from. Imagining a hot air balloon, Lisa placed the hat on the baby's head and made a bow under its chin.

Jake said, "Okay, now move your hand to the right until I say stop."

Lisa complied and when she did, she felt a shirt. "Which way does it go?"

"Who cares, just get it on the baby!"

Next to her she heard a baby klunk on the ceramic tile. Ingrid swore.

Kirsten said, "Come on, people. Consider this practice!"

With each item, Jake and Lisa found their rhythm. He told her which direction to move her hand and when he said stop, she dropped it and picked up whatever was there, slapping it on the kid any way that it would stay on.

"One minute!" Kirsten hollered.

"Okay, we're down to two blankets," Jake said.

"What about a diaper?"

"There isn't one."

"That's not possible."

"Maybe we're supposed to wrap it, like a towel?"

"No. Wait! It's a cloth diaper! Quick!" She peeled off the plastic pants and patted around until her hand brushed against a very soft fabric. She placed it under the baby's butt, folded the cloth around the middle, then pulled the little shorts back on.

"Thirty seconds!"

She located the last cloth, slapped the baby on top, and folded the bottom up and each side over, like she did with her sweaters. She and Jake shouted, "Done!"

She pulled off her blindfold. The white bonnet and shirt were on backwards, and the cloth diaper was actually a green polka-dotted blanket and they'd swaddled the baby in a white towel. But it didn't matter. They had *won*.

Kirsten handed them their prize rattles, one blue and one pink, and they shook them together. They pumped their fists, bumped them, then let them explode. They were one step away from a chest bump.

"I have to pee," announced Ingrid.

"I'll come with you," Lisa said. She pulled on Ingrid's arms and hoisted her up. Ingrid wasn't just pregnant; she was *huge*. Not that she was big in a bad way; she was perfectly healthy. What was scary was watching how her body had morphed into Michelin Man proportions all because of a baby. Lisa always pictured pregnancy as a more graceful process. She still couldn't believe there was a kid growing inside there. Marveling her middle, Lisa asked, "Doesn't your back hurt?"

"Sometimes. What I haven't gotten used to is my boobs. Did you notice how big they've gotten? They're like melons. They're like jugs. Melon-jugs."

"I had noticed, but I didn't think it would be polite to say, 'Hey Ingrid. Your boobs are melon-jugs.'"

"I'm so ready to get this baby out. Poor John. By the end of the day, I'm so crabby and uncomfortable. And I have to pee all the time," she said with a sigh as she stepped into the bathroom.

Lisa considered the magnitude of what it meant to have a baby while she waited outside the door. *A baby.* It wasn't like getting a new haircut. What would *she* be like as a mother? Or Jake as a father? She blushed. Such thoughts were premature and unlikely. With her, anyway.

After Ingrid came out, she showed Lisa the baby's room, freshly painted in a bright yellow. The crib was assembled and a mobile of baby zoo animals hung over it. A white glider sat in a corner between the changing station and an antique dresser that had been repainted white with little yellow bees buzzing across the drawers.

Ingrid said, "I still can't believe that this is happening to *me* and it's *my* body. But I've done as much reading as one can do and guess I'm as ready as I'll ever be. The scary part is the unknown."

While she spoke, Ingrid rubbed her belly like it was a crystal ball. "I've realized that no matter how much you prepare, you won't *know* what it's like until you go through it. I've heard so many birthing horror stories that some days I'm terrified. But then I remember that millions of women have babies and some do it more than once, so it can't be all bad." Her hands stopped and centered on one spot to the side. "Oh! The baby just moved. Do you want to feel it?"

They'd hugged hundreds of times, but touching her friend's belly? She kicked herself. It was just a baby. It wasn't like it was going to burst from her womb like in *Aliens*.

Ingrid took Lisa's hand and placed it on the right side, below the ribcage. At first there was nothing, and then she felt it. One big kick. Then Ingrid's entire stomach lurched. "That is so cool!"

Ingrid laughed. "I know. So, what's going on with you and Jake?"

"Nothing is going on." Her fear disappeared as she became enthralled with Ingrid's belly. She wanted to put her ear on it, hoping the baby would make some kind of gurgling sound.

"Nothing?"

"Well, not nothing. But not something, either. We just—are."

Ingrid smiled, accepting her philosophical answer. "Well, I for one am glad. It makes working with both of you so much easier. Can you believe the dance is only a week away?"

"And we get to meet Spinach—the best, most famous band ever."

"So, have you resolved the whole former identity issue?"

"Yes and no."

"Meaning?"

"Yes, in the sense it doesn't bother me anymore. And no because, as far as I can tell, Jake still hasn't made the connection."

"I don't see why you don't say something, especially if you're friends now."

"Maybe. We'll see."

Chapter 22

The streets were jam-packed, as a sea of bodies surged through the blocked-off corridor. The hip-hop reverberated off of them and the ground felt like it was vibrating. Seeing the crowd of people at the free concert with one of the hottest bands in the country, Lisa thought they should've charged a cover, just to keep the numbers down.

To Lisa, it felt like the biggest event ever in the history of Minneapolis. It was certainly true within the Nicollet neighborhood. There were information booths, food stands, first aid, merchandise, make-and-take craft stations, science stations for the kids, and rows and rows of artists selling their wares. They'd had so much interest from local bands that they'd set up three music locations on opposing corners of their four-square-block takeover, and could only offer them forty-five-minute slots. They cordoned off the playing fields adjoining the playground to prevent delirious Spinach fans from trampling them. The police were out in droves, along with every employee from the Little Flower Foundation and the law firm, as well as several crews of volunteers.

At nine o'clock the crowd turned its attention toward the community center's roof. High enough to keep the fans at bay and for everyone to see, but close enough so no one looked like a stick figure, all of the key players of Grant Park assembled: Mr. Hollow, Mrs. Chang, Susan, the mayor, and a few other local celebrities. Even David had been able to fly in for a quick appearance. Lisa beamed with pride.

Susan acted as the master of ceremonies and when she stepped up to the microphone, was a PR pro. She spoke so feelingly and in such detail about the park and its progress, you would've thought she had designed and built it with her own two hands.

The previous day they'd toured the facilities with the neighborhood leadership and the transformation was astounding. The original buildings had been dilapidated—run-down shadows of a yesteryear long since gone. The new buildings sparkled and shone with modernism and technology. Kids had chased each other around the new playgrounds while parents visited. The Minneapolis chief of police had commented that crime in the Nicollet area had already *decreased* since the park's completion.

Mr. Hollow commanded, as usual, quite a stage presence. Viewing him from afar, Lisa saw he was dressed in his best Clint Eastwood regalia, his bola glinting against the bright stage lights. After Susan's introduction, he gave a controlled yet moving speech about the work that had been done. It was vastly improved, with no sentimental meanders. This time he got her name right as he listed and thanked everyone who worked on the project. She'd been impressed for all of two seconds before she noticed the white note card tucked into his large palm. Then she let it go. Maybe Mr. Hollow's intentions for building the park hadn't been entirely altruistic, but they'd been good.

Their best asset had proven to be Mrs. Chang, who'd opted not to take a turn at the microphone. She'd been a cornucopia of ideas. She assisted Ingrid with many of the interior details of the buildings, gave her input on the educational programming, and suggested they offer multilingual brochures and services. Mrs. Chang had high expectations, but was very hands-on and practical. It made Lisa wonder what Mr. Chang might have been like.

Before Spinach came on stage, a five-minute film was projected onto the walls of the community center. The film was a montage depicting the before and after of the neighborhood, showing the project through its various stages of completion. Interspersed were pictures of kids and families from the Nicollet community. The music accompanying the film was a slow rock ballad that made Lisa misty. If she'd had a lighter, she would have lit it and let it shine old-school rock-concert style. Instead, she flipped open her illuminated cell and held it high above her head, feeling like the world in this exact moment was a perfect place.

Suddenly fireworks whistled into the sky, followed by a deafening, smoke-inducing clap of *kaboom*. Out of the rising haze appeared a lanky twenty-something youth, clad in torn jeans and iconic green T-shirt. Isaiah Keller, lead vocalist of Spinach, swaggered to the microphone, while the other band members sauntered to their instruments. Keller pushed his shaggy lock of bangs across his forehead and looked out over the audience. The bass player adjusted his sunglasses.

When they were in position, Keller gripped the mike and asked, "How's everybody doin' tonight?"

Everyone cheered wildly. He was the quintessence of übercool. Then he said, "Let's get this party started!"

The crowd erupted and Lisa screamed and jumped up and down with everyone else. Without thinking, she grabbed the nearest person around the shoulders and hugged him; the person turned out to be Jake.

In a more controlled environment, she probably would have looked first, but the energy of that very moment forgave her impulsiveness. Besides, they were basically back to their version of normal, having worked fervently this last couple of weeks together getting ready for the party. Jake wrapped an arm around her waist, hugging her back. All of their hard work had culminated to this point. Jake's arm stayed fixed around her middle. She enjoyed the solidness of his arm around her, and if things had been different, would have loved to stay in that position. Without appearing rude, she danced, slowly but surely, out of his grip. When she felt his arm fall away, she peeked at him, seeing he was as into the music as she was. Lisa was still very much attracted to him, but wasn't assuming anything. The dust of their drama had settled, and she was thankful to have at least their friendship back.

John, Chad, Tim, and Tim's new girlfriend appeared next to them.

"Hey, guys! This is awesome!" Chad said.

"What?" Lisa shouted.

He showed a thumbs-up sign and mouthed, "Good job."

Jake spoke directly into her ear, "I have to check on a few things, but I'll be back." He disappeared through the masses, the crowd filling his vacant spot like water. The suggestion of work reminded Lisa that she had a few things to take care of, too, before the concert ended. She pulled on Tim. "Hey! Listen. I have to get back to work, but let's all meet over at Stumpy's after the concert. Text me when you get there and I'll be over as soon as I can."

She headed over to the foundation's informational booths. Gathering a few flyers scattered around, she put them in a box and brought it to the merchandise table. A few shoppers milled about, while a group of volunteers boxed the remaining items for the park's gift shop. Next, she went to the first-aid station. An elderly man was talking with one of the paramedics, counting through his exhaustive list of ailments and prescribed medications, while a medic treated a girl with a small cigarette burn on her arm. Otherwise, the team assured her everything was under control. She bumped into one of the police officers and discussed traffic control. The officer did her radioing and in a few minutes, assigned officers were on their way to their designated intersections. Lisa spotted Ingrid, who agreed to oversee the volunteers and told her to invite them out to Stumpy's, too. With only thirty minutes of the concert left, most of the food vendors were sold out and already cleaning up. The artists had long since packed their wares, but the stands needed to be taken down, so Lisa assembled a few volunteers to work on those.

As they worked, they heard a huge never-ending wave of screaming and cheering, signaling the concert's end. Lisa double checked with a security officer, then put on a reflective neon-yellow vest to pitch in with the fleet of clean-up crews for the grossest task of all.

There were papers, food, bottles, and plenty of unidentifiable you-don't-want-to-know scraps everywhere. Nevertheless they were all in high spirits. Bravely donning rubber gloves and grabbing trash bags, brooms, and poker-stick thingies, they set about their business. An hour later, the people had dispersed, the traffic was almost back to normal, and the streets were clean. Susan took care of the rock stars and David had already left to catch his flight back to California. Lisa gave the doors of the community center one final tug and set off for Stumpy's.

It was nearly midnight when she got there. Everyone else and their brother must have had the same idea, because the place was packed. Good solid rock 'n' roll came out of the walls and Lisa felt like one welcomed among the many. She found her friends, including Ingrid and John, by the bar, and sat down. Her feet ached. Lisa beckoned the bartender, cupped her hand around her mouth, and shouted, "A shot of Crown Royal and an Amstel Light, please."

"That's an unusual choice for you, isn't it?" Tim asked.

"If there's ever been a time in my life when I've earned such a treat, this would be it."

"Why not just ask for a beer chaser?"

"Because tonight I want the best whiskey money can buy—or at least that I can afford—and still want to watch my calories."

Chad said, "Leave it to my sister to ruin a perfectly good drink by discussing calories."

"You guys did a great job. I'm really impressed," said Tim.

"Ah, you're just saying that." She nudged him, feeling her face heat up with embarrassment and pleasure.

"Seriously. Not only was the concert cool—I mean, that was amazing. How did you manage to get *those* guys?"

"That was all Ingrid's doing. She knew right away who she wanted, so she booked them last September."

"Cool," said Tim. "As I was saying, I checked out that skateboard park and it's one of the best I've ever seen. I used to skate, you know."

"No, I didn't. They're talking about starting a mentoring program. Maybe you could volunteer."

"Yeah, I totally would."

Chad balked. "This is the guy who would pay someone to sell raffle tickets for him. This is the guy who hides when kids come ringing the doorbell selling cookies and magazine subscriptions." Chad shook Tim. "Who are you and what have you done with my friend?"

Lisa felt Tim's forehead and inspected the inner lining of his lower eyelids. "Say ah."

"It's this new girl he's seeing," Chad said. He pointed over to her, drawing her into the conversation. "She's a veterinarian, and now Tim's gone all Boy Scout on us."

"I have not," he protested. He put his arm around his girl. "It just so happens I had a positive adult role model when I was a teenager and I've always had it in the back of my mind to be a mentor when I got older."

"That's sweet," said Tim's girlfriend.

Chad said, "Yes, I suppose there's some lost soul out there dying to learn the art of lighting farts."

"Chad, that's disgusting. Grow up," Lisa said. "Tim, I don't care if you are trying to suck up to your new girlfriend. I think you would make a fine mentor. And I would hope that you, Chad, would look to our friend here as an example and do some volunteering yourself."

"Yeah, okay, whatever," he mumbled.

"I'm married to a do-gooder. Does that count?" John asked.

"Volunteerism by association does not count."

"Okay you good-for-nothing do-gooder, thanks for making us feel guilty," Chad said.

"It's a tough job, but somebody's gotta do it." The bartender brought Lisa her drink.

Tim raised his beer glass. "I propose a toast. To Lisa and Ingrid on a job well done."

"Hear, hear."

Lisa added, "And to Mark and Jake, who aren't with us, but are equally deserving."

Ingrid added, "And to the future of Grant Park."

"Cheers."

She threw back her whiskey and felt the comforting burn down her throat. She looked at her cell phone and saw that Jake had called, but hadn't left a message. It was too late to call back. She would talk to him in the morning. She said, "Okay, guys. Last call and I'm buying."

. . . . .

After the concert, Jake couldn't find Lisa anywhere. He called her cell, but when it rolled over to voicemail, he hung up. He decided to drive by her place. If the light was on, he would knock.

He passed by the community center, went back, and ran up the steps, giving the doors a violent tug. When he was satisfied, he skipped down the steps, resuming the walk back to his brand new silver Audi. It was still in one piece. He pressed the unlock button on his key fob and the car tweeted. The streetlights shone a steady stream of light, store marquees glowed, and traffic lights blinked. Groups of people crowded the sidewalks as they moved from one club to another. The city felt alive.

Jake parked a few houses down from Lisa's apartment, in the only remaining space on the block. Her place looked dark. The dashboard clock told him it was just after one o'clock. He got out of the car and stood next to it, contemplating what to do next. The sky was clear and stars were actually visible, despite the orange glow of the city lights. The air was warm and felt comforting against his face. He inhaled deeply, then looked up in time to witness a shooting star. A few seconds later, another one burst quietly across the sky in a slim line that fell just short of the shadowy treetops. Jake ambled up the short walk to her front stoop and settled onto the top step. Hopefully the neighbors wouldn't think he was a burglar. All was dark over there, too.

He reclined and turned his head again upwards to look at the sky. When was the last time he'd done this—looked at the sky? When he'd gone camping with Amir? That had been before Mirijana was born. It was sad to think he hadn't *looked* at the sky for two years. He saw another shooting star. As his eyes grew accustomed to the dark, he recognized satellites, mere pinpricks of light whizzing steadily in a straight trajectory overhead.

Tonight he was going to tell her. He'd tried to hold his resolve to be friends, but he couldn't take it anymore. He was already in love with her and he was pretty sure she felt the same. If things turned out as he hoped, he would be sure to work doubly—triply—hard to ensure Grant's confidence in his abilities at work. He'd maintained a professional decorum, but just barely. Now the project was done, and he could no longer *not* be with her.

She drove him crazy, true; but she also did something else to him. She challenged him. She questioned him. She debated and argued with him. She showed him interesting stuff he'd never heard of. Never had Lisa tried to impress him, and that was what *had* impressed him. She was authentic and true to herself. Even when she'd wigged out over Grant's speech back in April, he could respect that she'd held fast to her values.

A pair of headlights illuminated the street and stopped in front of Lisa's apartment. He recognized the car as Chad's. Jake heard Lisa laugh and say goodnight as she got out, and other voices from inside the vehicle echoed her goodbye. Chad continued up the block as she made her way between the parked cars and onto the sidewalk. Jake stood, shook the tension from his hands, then crammed them into his coat pockets.

"Lisa," he called.

She looked up. Jake leapt lightly off the last step to meet her.

"Jake, wha—?" Before she could say another word, he pulled her into his arms and kissed her. Her lips were soft and initially cautious. He held her tight, speaking his feelings through kisses instead of words. He felt her hands touch his face then slide behind his neck as she wrapped her arms farther around him, bringing them closer together.

After their long kiss, Lisa tilted her head back to look at him. Even in the dark, he could detect bewilderment in her eyes.

"The project is done," he said. "We don't work together anymore."

Lisa smiled. "So much for being friends, huh?"

"I don't think I can just be your friend." His voice was shaky with emotion.

"I think that's okay."

She lifted her face to his again. This kiss was longer and he felt her melt into him. All it would take was one step backward, then another step, and another and one more, and they would be on the porch and in her apartment. The old Jake would have pressed his advantage and talked her out of her panties without a second thought. But that's not what he wanted. He wanted this to be different. He needed it to be different. This was more than the beginning of a new relationship; it was the beginning of a new way of relating. Reluctantly, he pulled back and said, "I should be going."

Lisa furrowed her brow. He would explain it to her later. But for now, he didn't want to ruin the moment. He trusted that she would understand. She loosened her grip on him. "Yeah, okay."

He took her chin in his thumb and forefinger and gave her a final kiss. "I'll call you in the morning."

"It is morning," she replied.

One small joke, and like that, they were back to that comfortable space—that perfect spot on the couch of the relationship that had been building between them. It was what he loved best about being with her. "Right," he answered, with a hat tip. "Go to church then meet me for breakfast."

He brought her hands together, squeezed them before letting go, and walked to his car before second-guessing his first sexually virtuous act ever. His body was sounding all kinds of alarms, the loudest one clanging, *Hey buddy, where the hell do you think you're going?* But on this one, he was going to go with his heart and it felt good. Weird. But good.

Chapter 23

She arrived at Green Eggs and Ham first. The waiting line leaked out onto the street and curved around the block. Lisa added her name to the list and perused the newspaper while standing on the sidewalk. On page three of the main section, she found a lengthy article about the Nicollet block party and the success of their project. Accompanying the article was a very nice photo of Mr. Hollow with Susan, Jake, and David Cibulka, and another one of Mrs. Chang standing with Spinach. Jake looked incredibly sexy in the picture. His broad smile and dimple made him as adorable as a beagle puppy.

Her face flushed as she luxuriated in the memory of that morning's kiss. It was so romantic—exactly the kind of first kiss a girl wanted. She'd been more than ready to bring him inside, but his decision to go home instead was so noble, so—*chivalrous*. What kind of guy did that anymore? She couldn't think of any, which made Jake even more special. After he left, she was so giddy she hadn't been able to fall asleep. Finally, she had tucked her extra pillow under her arm, pretending it was Jake.

The host called her name and seated her on the patio. Jake arrived a couple of minutes later, riding a large red and black motorcycle. She could already imagine sitting behind him, arms clasped around his waist. She watched him take off his helmet and run a hand through his hair. A prickle of joy rushed over her skin. When he saw her, he smiled.

"Hey. Sorry I'm late," he said, as he approached the table. He kissed the crown of her head and sat down. She flushed red again. He'd kissed her so naturally, like he'd done it a million times and here she was, blushing.

"Man, what a crowd," he said. "Did you have to wait long?"

She didn't know what to say first. Should she start by delving into what happened last night and what that meant for them? Or answer his immediate question?

"About fifteen minutes," she said. "Here, look at this article." They rehashed the block party and speculated about the future of Grant Park.

After they ordered their food, Jake laced his fingers into hers and asked, "Where did you guys go last night?"

She reddened again at his touch. How could he be so calm? She'd dreamt of this, but now that it was real, it felt so daring.

"Oh, right," she stammered. "Sorry about that. We met at this bar called Stumpy's. Do you know it?"

He nodded.

"I just assumed I'd see you again and then I got so busy with the cleanup, I forgot. When I did think of it, it was almost one o'clock and figured it was too late to call. But *apparently*, it wasn't." She gave him a knowing smile. "What happened with you?"

"I had to take care of a few things for work. I have to be in court early tomorrow and it's going to be a long day."

"You were doing *work* on a Saturday night during the best concert ever? Isn't that what Sunday is for?"

"No, Sunday is for rest. You're a Catholic, you should know that," he teased. "Seriously, though, it's an important case, and I like to be well prepared. I've never been good at cramming at the last minute."

"I've turned it into an art form. When I get down to the wire on something, I'm constantly calculating and recalculating how much time I have and where I can squeeze out a couple more hours in the day."

"I couldn't handle that. The stress would probably make my hair fall out."

"It's not stressful; it's exciting to see if I can beat the clock." Her eyes grew with the adrenaline from describing it. "When I was in college, I was on a perpetual high when it came down to finals week. I thrived on the crush of exams and papers due all at once."

"You're weird," he said, shaking his head. "What were you like in high school?"

On the word "high school," Lisa's shoulders tightened. "Oh, I don't know. Not as exciting as I was in college."

"I think I recall you saying once that you were quietly opinionated."

"Basically," she said, studying his face. He looked so happy. She had to tell him, but how? "What were *you* like in high school?" It was a legitimate question. How had Jake seen himself?

"I don't know, either," he said. "I was class president and homecoming king, if that counts for anything."

"In some people's minds, it does. For some, it defines who they are."

"Well, for me it didn't. High school was fun, don't get me wrong, but I also felt a lot of pressure; like I had to be perfect."

"Really?" Lisa was genuinely surprised. She'd always thought Jake was perfectly comfortable with being perfect. "Why is that?"

"When you're class president and stuff, people expect certain things from you. I was always worried that I wouldn't deliver. I didn't want to disappoint anyone."

"But you're so easygoing and self-confident. I can't imagine you being worried about what others think of you."

"Maybe I look like that, but I don't always feel like it. It's a hard image to keep up. Plus I was an honor student and played three sports. I felt like there was no room for me to fail."

"I'm sure your friends didn't judge you like that."

"We'll see. I haven't had much contact with them, except for Amir, who didn't even go to my high school—and Chad—so I don't know what they think of me."

Jake? Mr. Popular didn't keep in touch with his high school friends? That seemed to defy some kind of high school pledge. Lisa could understand why she hadn't bothered to keep in touch with anybody. But Jake?

The server placed plates of pancakes and eggs over easy with bacon and whole-wheat toast between them. Lisa, thankful for the interruption, set to her pancakes, slathering them with whipped butter.

"My high school reunion is coming up," he said, catching her between choosing the maple or the triple berry.

The reunion. *Their* reunion. Lisa marveled that Jake had stepped back into her life nine months earlier and still had no idea. How was it possible? He always paid attention to details.

"Oh really?" she asked, feigning ignorance. She poured on the syrup and dug into her pancakes. Maybe if she kept her mouth full, she wouldn't say anything stupid.

"Yeah. Ten years. Man, I can't believe it's already been *ten* years. I wonder what it'll be like."

"Where did you think you'd be in your life in ten years?" she asked, hoping to steer the conversation in a more philosophical direction.

Jake munched on his toast and took a bite of his eggs. Lisa didn't like runny eggs. They looked too goopy to be edible. He pushed them around with the toast and took another bite as he thought about her question. "I guess right where I am. I mean, it's not a bad life. I got to play college hockey. I have a job that I love."

She waited for him to say, "And a girl that I adore," or something romantic like that.

"Did you ever want to be married? Or have kids?"

This time he looked surprised and laughed. "Are you kidding? No. No way. Maybe someday." He pointed his fork at her. "What about you? Are you where you thought you would be?"

Where had she wanted to be? She'd wanted to go to Washington and become a page. But that hadn't happened, so she'd gone to college and found her niche in nonprofit. "I guess the same as you. Not ready for kids or marriage yet, either, but wanting to be on that path." She looked him directly in the eyes despite the burning sensation in her cheeks. It was true. Just because she was saying it to Jake, didn't mean that she expected him to become her husband and the father of her children.

"I was wondering if you'd like to go with me."

She nearly choked on her orange juice. "Um," she said, stalling for time while a deluge of high school memories flooded her brain. "Isn't that a little fast?"

"Why?"

"Jake, people bring spouses and significant others to reunions. Not—," she pointed at him and then herself, back and forth, trying to think of the right word, "Us. *This*—whatever this is between us."

He leaned over the table and took her hand. "Lisa, I love being with you. I don't expect that to change."

She squirmed in her seat, tethered to Jake's hand. In this small time frame, she watched the girl at the table next to them complain to her girlfriend, "I should have bought those shoes. What was I thinking? Do you think they'll still have them if I go back today?"

Then a thought slammed into her head. Shit. Oh, shit. Shit, shit, shit.

She had already registered for the reunion. Lisa watched the girl scroll through her phone, no doubt looking for information on the shoes. Lisa would gladly trade troubles. She'd wanted to hurt Jake, get her revenge, and now he was holding her hand, looking at her with those innocent blues, his eyes searching hers.

He still had no clue. *No goddamn clue.* How could a guy so smart still be so clueless?

Tell him now.

Tell him now.

Tell him now.

You have to tell him now.

She could hear every person she knew shouting inside her head.

Just ... say ... it.

"I just think you need more time to get to know me. Maybe you'll find out something about me that you won't like," Lisa said instead.

"What are you talking about? You're amazing and there is no one I'd be more honored to have with me than you."

Honored? God, that was laying it on thick. She extracted her hand from his and forked her pancakes, stacking small squares up the tines as she struggled to think straight. How could she create a reasonable refusal that wouldn't sound like long-term rejection? "But Jake—"

"Please. Will you please go with me?" He put his face next to hers and dotted a few kisses down the edge of the petal of her ear.

She felt her resolve weaken. She had to tell him. It would be wrong to go on like this and not say something.

She started again, "Jake, I have to tell you—" Then he kissed her neck. *Oh … ha … ahem.* She was sure her face was a fierce shade of red, and not because the sun was hot on her head. "You're quite persuasive."

"Please?" he asked, grinning like a naughty boy. She heard her resolve snap.

"When did you say it was again?"

"The fifteenth."

"Which month was that?"

"This one. *June.*" He thought she was teasing. She was terrified.

"Where is it?"

"In the suburbs. Big Bear. Do you know it?"

"Hmm. Is that on the north side?"

"Southwest."

She picked up her napkin and twisted it around her fingers. Jake picked up his coffee and sipped, his eyes never leaving her. The guy was patient, she had to credit him that. They could sit in silence for five more minutes and it wouldn't bother him. Suddenly, she thought of the perfect win-win. "Let me check my calendar and I'll get back to you. I think I'm free, but I need to check."

All she needed was more time. What harm was there in that? As soon as she could, she would either call Angela or visit her parish priest. It *had* been awhile since she'd been to confession. All deception was a sin, wasn't it? But maybe it didn't count if it was used for *good?*

He looked puzzled, but said, "Okay. Let me know."

She took up his hand again. "Hey, I have an idea. Let's go see that new Daniel Craig movie. My treat."

Jake finished his breakfast, while Lisa flipped to the movie section of the newspaper. There was a matinee a few blocks from her apartment, right in Uptown.

He parked his motorcycle in front of her place and they walked to the theater, holding hands along the way. He'd taken her hand first.

She and Jake relaxed in the cool, dark movie theater as content as well-fed cats. Lisa was sure the movie was just what Jake needed: a healthy affirmation of the masculine need to save the day. With his half-smirk and cheesy one-liners, Daniel Craig was as loveable as an action hero could get. Lisa enjoyed the cinematography while Jake wondered aloud if Daniel Craig did his own stunts or had stunt doubles.

After the movie, Jake invited her for a ride on his motorcycle. He patted his bike and said, "This is Cherry."

He even had a helmet for her.

They rode all around Minneapolis's chain of lakes admiring the palatial estates surrounding them: Tudor, Colonial revival, Georgian Colonial, Victorian, contemporary, and modern—there were so many styles to admire. She had just finished reading a book about Frank Lloyd Wright and wondered which of the houses he'd designed. Maybe she and Jake could take a tour sometime. They stopped by Lake Harriet to get ice cream cones and strolled around the lake, talking about every subject under the sun: philosophies, politics, art, science, pop culture, music, movies, and books.

But he kept coming back to the topic of high school. He told her about Anna and about his parents. He went into lengthy detail about the pressure he had felt as the only child—the only son—to be the best. His father had hoped Jake would become the third-generation doctor and he'd feared disappointing his dad when he majored in political science, and then chose law.

He even talked about Key Club. It turned out that Jake had met a guy in summer baseball who was living out of his car. Both his parents were in jail and the kid worked three part-time jobs trying to hold it all together. Baseball was the one thing that kept the kid connected to the sane life he'd once known. Jake had felt sorry for the guy and wanted to do something. But the kid said he was okay; he didn't need help, and then he'd told Jake about this drop-in center where there were kids worse off than him. Jake thought it would look corny if he came to school and just said, *Hey, let's do this,* so he used Key Club as a way to legitimize his intentions. He actually blushed when he spoke about it.

Jake, I know, had been on the tip of her tongue so many times. But she didn't know. Jake wasn't just offering a window into his life; he was opening a door. She didn't want to take that away from him, so she just listened.

Afterward she invited him to her place for a sandwich. Making her way to the porch, Lisa had an uncomfortable feeling of déjà vu. She didn't want this wonderful day to crash and burn in a similar fashion as New Year's had with Tony.

Lisa went into the kitchen while Jake stayed in the living room. "Do you mind if I take a look at your library?"

"Sure, go ahead."

While preparing a salad, she heard Jake say, "Hey! How come you have *this?*" Her head swiveled, horror-stricken by the possibility that he'd discovered her Big Bear yearbook. She tore into the living room, nearly tripping over the blue braided rug. Jake stood at a bookshelf on the opposite side of the room where she kept it. He held up a Louis L'Amour novel, *The Trail to Seven Pines*. "I thought you didn't like Westerns."

She wheezed a sigh of relief. "Oh, that. It was a Christmas present from my dad. He tried hard to convert me. It's not entirely true that I don't like Westerns. I just don't care for L'Amour's style."

"Really? I think he's great. My dad has every book he ever wrote. If you don't like him, why do you keep it?"

"Because some day I might. I have plenty of books like that."

"How long have you had this one?"

"That one … since I was sixteen, I guess."

"Ouch. That's some serious shame." He put the book up to his ear. "I think it feels depressed."

"I think I'm hungry. I promise I'll try reading it. If that doesn't work, then I promise to pick up some literary Prozac. Now, come on," she said pushing him toward the kitchen. "You can help me slice tomatoes."

He put the book back in its place and went to the kitchen. When Jake was out of sight, she grabbed her yearbook, raced to the bedroom, and shoved it under the bed. Taking a deep breath, she ran her hands over her hair and returned to the kitchen. "Jake! I said slice the tomatoes, not wedge them!"

As eight o'clock approached, Jake, putting his dishes into the sink, said, "I better head home. I still have some work to do."

Lisa got up too and walked him out to his motorcycle. "Thanks for today. It was fun."

"Yeah, it was." He wrapped her into his arms again.

Nestled next to him, she still couldn't believe it. They were a couple. Lisa placed her hands on his chest and looked up at him. "Jake, before we go any further, don't we need to talk about this some more?"

"What's there to talk about? I like you, I *think* you like me. Grant's park is built. It's pretty clear to me."

"Is it? Are you sure?"

"Of course I'm sure." He frowned. "Are you sure about me?"

The pressure of the impending responsibility of telling him the truth felt like a large stone in her stomach. But she smiled up at him anyway. "I am—Jake."

"You have this funny look on your face. What is it?"

"It's nothing. I'm just a little overwhelmed, that's all." She pushed all other thoughts from her mind and gave him an assuring smile. "But I'm glad you showed up last night."

He relaxed and kissed her.

Oh, boy.

Chapter 24

"WHAT? You haven't told him yet?! Why not?"

Lisa winced at Angela's reproach. Since it seemed silly to call her priest at ten thirty at night without a serious medical or family emergency, Lisa opted to call Angela, who was two hours behind at a very appropriate eight thirty.

"Because, I'm a wuss?" she suggested. "I tried to tell him today, but then he started kissing me and I caved. Please, Angela; I know I messed up, but now I really am worried that I might ruin what could possibly be the best relationship I've ever had. What am I going to do?"

"*Hell-o!* You tell him."

"I figured that much out. When do I tell him?"

"I think you should tell him as soon as possible."

"No. If I tell him too soon, he might really despise me."

"Maybe he won't despise you. Maybe he'll say, 'Lisa, I love you and I don't care.'"

It sounded nice, but Lisa wasn't ready to be Jake's date for the reunion either. She'd been a wallflower in high school. Going with Jake would be like ripping her off the wall and planting her smack in the middle of the football field. She would be too paranoid about people checking her out, analyzing how she, of all people, ended up with Mr. Class President–Homecoming King–Hockey MVP.

"All I know is the longer you put it off, the worse it's going to get," Angela said. "He's developed strong feelings for you. You could really hurt him."

"I know," she sighed. "That's what Ingrid's been telling me."

"Then what I'm telling you is nothing you haven't heard before."

"I've got it," Lisa yelled. "I could go to the reunion by myself and surprise him."

"And where would the logic be in that?"

"I think it would lessen the shock. You remember what happened at the golf tournament, right? I was so mad at Jake, I registered for the reunion just to spite him. But now I could go, and instead of being a revenge thing, it would be sort of like a funny surprise. Like, 'Ha-ha. Boy, aren't you surprised? Can you believe it's me?' Maybe surprising him at the reunion won't make it seem like such a bad thing that I haven't told him. If you think about it, it is rather a funny situation, isn't it?"

Angela started slowly. "Well, that is certainly a *creative* way to go about it. I'm not sure, Lisa. When is the reunion?"

"In two weeks. It'll be perfect," she continued, convincing herself more than Angela. "This new step in our relationship just happened, so if I tell him at the reunion we can have a good laugh, get it out of the way, and then focus on the future."

"Maybe he won't care and will think it's a funny coincidence?"

"*Exactly.* Telling him beforehand makes it seem much more serious than it really is." Lisa was starting to genuinely buy into her own scheme. "It's the perfect plan. The timing is impeccable."

Angela always knew how to solve a problem.

Monday went by, followed by Tuesday, and on Wednesday, she knew she had to give Jake an answer. Other than a few loose ends, the foundation was finished with Grant Park and no longer needed to work with the law office of Smith, Hakkula, and Schuler.

It was bad enough she hadn't given Jake an answer on Monday. Tuesday would have been considered fashionably late, but she had let that day slip by, too. If he didn't hear anything by today, he'd begin to wonder what's up. They had softball later that day, and he'd be sure to ask her about it then.

An email popped into Lisa's inbox. The subject header read, *We're looking forward to seeing you!* It was a confirmation of her attendance to the Big Bear High School Reunion and link to a map. *What had she done?* She groaned and put her head in her hands.

She couldn't call him. If she called, she'd find herself doggy paddling into the why or why not. An email would suffice. She spent twenty minutes composing and recomposing the perfect message, careful not to let any nuance be too obvious or subtle.

Dear Jake,

Hi! Sorry it's taken so long to get back to you about your reunion. I have a new assignment and have been swamped. I checked my calendar and I have something already scheduled for that weekend. But I look forward to hearing all the details. Maybe you'll get crowned Reunion King! Then you would not only be politically required to attend reunions for the rest of your life, but royally obligated as well.

Go Bears!

Lisa

P.S. See you at the game.

That had a nice, airy tone, didn't it? She wondered if the closing was too much. She could still back out of this ridiculous plan and take her medicine like a big girl. Angela's logic rang in her ears.

But Lisa knew him best.

In one decisive motion, she swished the mouse and clicked, setting her plan into irretrievable motion.

. . . . .

Jake wasn't going to say that he wasn't disappointed, because he was. Maybe she was right. Maybe taking Lisa to his reunion signaled something more than where they were at right now. Maybe she needed more time. Did he do something wrong? Should he have done something differently? Should he call Amir? He picked up his cell phone. What the hell was he doing? *Call Amir?* He was acting like a girl. He hit reply and wrote:

Hi,

That's okay. However, if I do become Reunion King, I hereby bound you to attend the next reunion. I'll call you when the festivities are over. In the meantime, see you after work.

Grrrr ...
Jake

. . . . .

Over the weekend, Chad and Lisa spent the night at their parents'. They had promised to help with yard work in return for grilled brats and burgers and expensive, high-quality imported beer. While sitting out on the deck enjoying the fruits of their labor, Chad turned to Lisa with an impish grin and said, "I'm going to your reunion."

"You can't go. Lower classmen aren't *allowed* to go."

"They can if they have a date," he said.

"Who'd be desperate enough to take *you?*"

"Jenny Peters."

"Jenny? You're kidding. How did you manage that?" Jenny had been an all-star athlete, good student, first-chair cellist, and all-around nice person. To say she had been ambitious would be an understatement. Lisa had heard that she'd gone on to study music.

"Do you remember Chad Blum, her high school sweetheart? Well, they broke up last week. Jenny and I have always been friends and stayed in touch off and on since we graduated. Anyway, she's really upset about the breakup but still wants to go to the reunion.

She thinks that if she doesn't go, people will think that *she* did something wrong."

"Did she?"

"I don't know. He doesn't want to get married and says it's because of her. Who knows. I try to stay out of it. The point is, she asked me to go to the reunion with her. And that, dear sister, is why I'm going." He took a long pull on his beer and relaxed into his chair. "Are you going?"

"I wasn't planning on it, but now I have to."

"What do you mean have to?"

Lisa explained the situation concerning Jake. Chad whistled. "Man, that's some messed-up stuff. Why didn't you just tell him?"

"It's a long story, one that I don't feel like getting into with *you*. Just do me a favor, all right? Please, *please* don't say anything. I'm going to the reunion to right things with him."

"I can't believe you've held out this long. He really doesn't have any idea?"

"Unless he's playing some kind of Jedi mind trick. Isn't that just ... weird? I mean, it is abnormal, isn't it?"

"I think so. You don't look so different to me. But then again, I see you all the time. Are you sure you had a class with him?"

"Yes," she said, rolling her eyes at him. "Several, actually. There's no way he could *not* know who I am—once he finds out, that is."

"Well, I think you're making a huge mistake and I only hope that it doesn't blow up in your face."

"Who asked your opinion?"

"Nobody, but you're going to hear it anyway." Chad set his beer down and angled his body toward her. "Do you know why everybody likes Jake? It's not just because he's nice or cute. He's got this sense of integrity that's really inspiring. I've never seen someone who works so hard and yet is so well rounded and easy-going. And don't take that lightly; it takes a lot for a guy to talk about another guy like that."

"I'm not taking it lightly, Chad. I care a lot about him."

"It doesn't seem like it. You should've been honest with him."

"I have been."

He eyed her with his give-me-a-break look.

She backpedaled. "I haven't lied. I just haven't mentioned this one tiny, insignificant detail about our past, that's all."

"Insignificant? Are you high? He's going to care."

"No he's not. He sees me for who I am now, and that's all that matters."

"Yeah. That's what you think. Believe me, he's going to care."

"We'll see."

"Yes we will," he said smugly.

"Chad?"

"Yeah?"

"What's he like when it's only the guys around? I mean ... before."

"You mean what was he like around other women?"

She hated it and loved it when he knew exactly what she meant. "Well, yeah."

"You have to understand that Jake is a really cool guy. He's fun and women like him."

"Well, did he respond to their … interest in him?"

"He was friendly. Sometimes he bought them a drink. But other than that, I don't think I ever saw him hook up with anybody."

"Huh." What had she expected him to say, that Jake was chaste? She hadn't been that way. She'd even gotten back together with Tony. It was a wonder that Jake was interested in her at all.

"He's a nice guy, Lisa, and I'm going to say it again: Don't screw it up. For some reason—which I can't imagine—he chose you. And if he still wants to be with you after the reunion, and you bring him home to meet Mom and Dad, let me know. That'll be a show I don't want to miss."

"Oh, shut up."

Chapter 25

It was the big day. She would go to the damn reunion, face Jake, and be done with it.

She was in pretty good spirits, considering. She imagined the reveal being like one of those gags from *Just for Laughs,* where actors played pranks on strangers. She was laughing already it was so funny. Wasn't it?

She didn't think Jake would be mad, despite what her brother thought. He might feel a little silly, but he wouldn't be mad. Jake was too compassionate to feel angry or resentful about something as relatively trivial as this. Since the block party, they'd spent some part of almost every day together. Last night his innocence had nearly killed her when he'd kissed her goodnight. Lisa would be so glad when this was over.

Lounging on the porch reading, Lisa reached for her phone when she heard it buzz.

"I think I'm in labor," Ingrid said. "Can you take me to the hospital?"

"Oh my God! Did your water break?"

"No. But I'm having contractions and I don't think they're the Braxton-Hicks type."

"You can't be in labor. You're not due for another two weeks!"

"Lisa, I think the baby's coming. Please, just get here as fast as you can. I'll be waiting outside."

Lisa grabbed her keys and purse, flew out of the house, and cleared her backyard in five bounds to the car. While driving, she tried remembering the stuff from the baby books that Ingrid had quizzed her on.

How many minutes apart were the contractions when you were in real labor? How many stages were there? How were you supposed to breathe? Was it hee-hee-hoo or hoo-hoo-hee? And where the hell was John? Lisa scanned through the radio stations looking for something calming and landed on Bonnie Tyler caught in the middle of a "Total Eclipse of the Heart" lyric. Lisa pounded the beat out on the steering wheel and sang at the top of her lungs.

She reached Ingrid's in a record seven minutes, and in this short interlude managed to get her wits about her; she was ready to do whatever she was asked. Lisa jumped from the car, sprinted around to the other side, and helped Ingrid in. She then threw Ingrid's bag into the backseat, raced to the driver's side, and got in.

"Where to?"

"Mercy Hospital. I called and they're expecting me."

"How do I get there?"

"Are you serious? How can you not—forget it. Go straight and I'll tell you when to turn."

Lisa pulled away from the curb without looking. She glanced in the rearview mirror and saw a white Tahoe right on her butt. "How are you feeling?"

"Okay when I'm not having contractions. But when one comes, it feels like my belly is being seized in a vice grip."

"How far apart are they?"

"That's the funny thing. Some are every five minutes, and then it'll be ten minutes before the next one, then two minutes, then eight, then five, then back to ten again. Turn left at the next light. This is so not textbook. At first I didn't know what to do. And John's not here, so I wasn't sure if I should wait for him or go by myself."

"He went on that trip?"

"Yes," she said, exasperated. "They're not supposed to be back until tomorrow. I've been trying to call his cell and there's no answer. Either it's dead or he doesn't have a signal. The cabin doesn't have a landline, either. Turn left up here. I needed to tell *somebody*, so I called his parents to let *them* know and called my parents in Michigan, too. I pray to God he gets my messages. What if the baby is born and he misses it?"

"He'll make it, don't worry," Lisa said. "Just ... try to relax; do that breathing stuff. You don't want to stress the baby out, or yourself for that matter. Come on, breathe with me."

"He's probably sitting in the middle of some lake," she grumbled. Ingrid's face was pinched with worry and tears brimmed her lids.

"Come on, through the nose," Lisa said and inhaled, "and out through the mouth." She exhaled. Ingrid followed and together they did this a couple more times.

"Turn right at the light. Oh no, not again," Ingrid said, and groaned.

"What is it?" Lisa asked, her voice rising.

"I'm having another contraction," Ingrid wailed. "It hurts!"

"Keep breathing through it. Close your eyes and exhale through the contraction," Lisa said, as bits of information from the baby books came back to her. She took Ingrid's hand. "Come on honey, you can do it."

Ingrid breathed in and out for a few more seconds, then her body released the tension and melted into the car seat.

"Are you okay?" Lisa asked.

"Yeah. Thanks. The hospital is just up ahead on the left side. They said you could pull right up to the front door."

When they got to the hospital, Lisa helped Ingrid to the reception area and a couple of nurses seated her in a wheelchair. Despite Lisa's sense of urgency, the nurses were calm and moved through the check-in duties as slowly as sloths climbing a tree.

"If you could fill these out," the nurse said, and handed Ingrid a stack of forms. "May I have your insurance card, please? Sign here. Then you need to go here." She handed Ingrid a map.

The nurse asked, "How are you feeling?" to which Ingrid replied, "Like I'm going to have a baby."

After this rigmarole, Ingrid was wheeled to the maternity ward and Lisa headed out to park the car.

. . . . .

His first job as class president was to serve drinks at the reunion picnic. Jake wished they were stiff ones, because that's what he could have used at the moment. But considering the picnic was family friendly, the most daring beverage was raspberry lemonade.

Seeking relief from the scorching sun and sweltering heat, groups of his classmates clustered under the large, shady maple trees, lounging on blankets and in lawn chairs. Babies sprawled on spread blankets, while toddlers chased Wiffle balls or wrapped themselves around their parents' limbs.

Jake was still in awe that these were actual families created by members of his class. Ten years had gone by and to Jake, it had only felt like two, four tops. Some of the kids playing catch with their parents looked to be about ten years old, or older. How did they find time to get married, have children, *and* pursue careers? What had Jake done that could account for ten years of living? He'd gone to college, played some hockey, went to law school, and now he worked. Had it really taken ten years just to do that? Being around all of these families, he felt a little guilty, like he hadn't used his time well.

"Jake! Is that you?" bellowed a man with a receding hairline and a paunch. Jake had five seconds to place the man who was strolling up to the tiki hut. Had he been in his chemistry class? Phy ed? Why was he so bad with names and faces?

When he arrived, Jake still didn't remember who he was. Baldy, paunchy guy stuck out his hand. "How ya doin', man?"

"Hey," Jake said, glancing down at the man's nametag, thankful that it was pinned to his orange T-shirt. "Jeff! Nice to see you. What can I get you?"

"Two bottles of Coke. Oh, and can you fill this, too?" Jeff handed him a sippy cup. "Water for that one," he added with a wink.

"Sure. Are you having fun?" Jake asked, fumbling with the child's cup. He'd never handled one of these before. Did it have a lock cap like a prescription bottle?

"You bet. Good weather, eh? What are you up to these days, Jake? Professional bartender?"

"Nah, a lawyer, actually. And you?" Jake handed him back the kiddie cup and then the Cokes.

"Graduate school. Working on my Ph.D."

"In what?"

"Economics." Jeff pointed over his shoulder. "That's my family over there."

Jake saw a woman, her red hair held back in a simple ponytail, playing catch with a little boy while feeding bits of food to what appeared to be a younger sister. The sight of the boy and his mom playing together gave Jake a small stab of envy in the ribs. They looked nice together, the mother and the child. "That's great, Jeff. How old are the kids?"

"Paxton is four years old and Jaimica is almost two."

"Wow. Interesting names there."

"Yeah, thanks. My wife and I wanted to come up with something original. *Paxton* sounded cool and we named our daughter

Jaimica because we couldn't decide if we should name her Jaimie or Jessica; so we compromised. Neat, eh?"

Jake still had no idea who the guy was.

Jeff grinned then looked around. "Where's your family?"

"Ho-ho," Jake laughed. "I don't have any kids yet."

"Oh. Are you married?"

"Nope, still single." No need to go into details.

"Well, cheers to that," Jeff said and raised his Coke on Jake's behalf before taking a long drink. "Still playing hockey?"

"Just for fun. And you?" Maybe they'd played hockey together?

"Ha! You always were funny, Jake!" Jeff offered him an opportunity to fist bump before heading back to his family.

This was the basic dialogue, with little variations here and there, which played itself over and over with every classmate who approached the beverage stand. Some folks Jake recognized, others remain lodged deep in his memory, refusing to reveal their identities. After a couple of hours, Jake felt like a domestic loser. He gladly handed over the duty to the next shift and rallied some of the men for a friendly game of football.. He wondered what Lisa would have to say about all of this and what kind of mother she would make.

. . . . .

Lisa found Ingrid set up in a room on the maternity ward wearing a hospital gown and a beltlike device strapped around her exposed belly. She was hooked up to a beeping machine that was spewing paper. A nurse picked up the long strip and studied it.

"How are you feeling, honey?" Lisa asked. She heard herself say honey for the second time that day. It was a term of endearment her mom used when Lisa needed comfort.

"Better now that I'm here. I've already dilated four centimeters. I knew it wasn't just Braxton Hicks."

"Is four centimeters a good thing?"

"So far." She pointed over to the beeping machine. "Right now they're checking the baby's heartbeat and tracking the frequency and intensity of my contractions."

"Do they know how long it will be before the baby's born?"

"It's hard to say. I have six more centimeters to go and it depends on how quickly I continue to dilate. It could be a few hours or it could take all night."

"Where's your cell phone? I'll try to call John." Lisa took Ingrid's phone and went out to the hall. When she dialed John's number, it went right to voicemail. She left a message with the updates. Ingrid was the toughest person Lisa knew. She would give birth without him if she had to, but Lisa had promised John would be there. Her friend deserved that. She decided to try John's parents.

"Hello?"

"Hello. May I speak to Mr. White, please?" Assuming there was a Mr. White and not a Mr. Brown or Mr. Smith in case Mr. and Mrs. White turned out to be divorced.

"Speaking."

Whew. "My name is Lisa Johnston. I'm a friend of Ingrid's."

"Oh! Hold on a second, please." Then Lisa heard a shout away from the receiver. "Milly! Get on the other line. It's a friend of

Ingrid's!" After a few seconds, Lisa heard the click of another phone being picked up and then a woman's voice. "Okay, honey. Go ahead."

"I wanted to call and let you know Ingrid's at Mercy Hospital. We just got here and she's doing fine. She's dilated to four centimeters, but at this point, we still can't speculate when the baby will be born. I tried calling John and all I got was his voicemail. Have you been able to get a hold of him?"

Mr. White said, "Not yet, and nothing from Jim, either."

"Do you know where they are exactly?"

"Well, the cabin is just a little thing up by Isabella off of Highway One. The boys brought the boat up and I'm guessing they'll be fishing somewhere near Dumbbell Lake."

Lisa had no clue where they were talking about. "How far is that from the Twin Cities?"

"Bert? How far you'd say it is to the cities?" asked Milly, who Lisa presumed to be Mrs. White.

"Well, let's see here. The cabin's about an hour and a half north of here and we're about three and a half, four hours north of the cities. Oh, I'd say about five hours or so."

Lisa looked at her watch. It was ten minutes after two o'clock and she only had six centimeters of time left. "Mr. White? Do you know where this cabin is?"

"Why, I sure do. My daddy built it when I was a boy—a first-generation Finnish-American, you know. His mother, my grandmother, came over from Finland with her parents when she was a little girl and settled near Ely. That was in about ... oh ... let's see here ..."

"Do you live in Ely now?" Lisa asked, sidestepping the informative yet untimely trip down memory lane.

"Oh, good heavens, no. We moved around quite a bit, didn't we Milly? No, no; now we live in Duluth."

"Do you know anyone in the area who might be able to contact John?"

"The only neighbor I know of is old Jack Schultz. But I haven't spoken to him or seen him in a couple of years. I heard he got cancer."

"This might sound crazy, but do you think you could drive up to the cabin and find John?" The suggestion was met with silent hesitation. Lisa pushed on with her campaign. "I know it's probably really inconvenient for you but Ingrid would really, *really* appreciate it. I would drive myself if I could, but I can't leave her alone."

More silence, then Milly asked, "What do you think, Bert?"

Another pause. "Milly, get your coat. We haven't got much time."

. . . . .

At four o'clock, Jake was ready to head home. He'd told the reunion committee that he'd be at the reception hall by six o'clock and he still needed to shower. Thanks to summer road construction, the drive took about forty minutes. At the apartment, he saw that Scott was gone. He peeled off his grimy, sweaty clothes and headed to the bathroom.

The water stung a bit on his sunburned face and shoulders, but overall he felt relief to get the summer heat and grit off his body. After drying off, he squeezed a glob of aloe vera gel—a useful gift from a past girlfriend—into his palm and rubbed it gingerly into his skin. In the mirror, he scrutinized his features. How much had he changed in ten years? He ran his fingers through his damp hair. Except for a sprig or two of gray hair, it was still brown. He pulled his bangs back and inspected his healthy hairline. He squinted. The skin around his eyes was still tight. Okay, maybe there was a trace—just a hint—of a few lines around his eyes. He stretched his lips over his teeth and pushed the tip of his nose up in search of any errant nose hairs. All was clear in that department. He grabbed a mirror and looked sideways for any hairs sprouting in his ears. His grandfather had hearty patches of wiry grays and his dad already had a few shoots coming out. But that looked good, too.

Jake smiled broadly. His smile lines looked a little deeper and that darn dimple was still there, probably making him look younger instead of mature. He frowned deeply. He looked serious. He wiggled his eyebrows. The creases in his forehead looked a little deeper, too. His skin was rougher and he needed to shave. He had a smooth speck of a brown mole in the hollow of his left cheek that he didn't remember seeing before.

Except for a different haircut, he looked more or less the same as he had ten years ago. He wrapped a towel around his waist, and proceeded to examine his torso. He contracted his chest muscles and slapped them. While flexing his biceps he heard a falsetto voice, "Oh, Jake; you're so *cute*!"

He looked over and saw that Scott was back. "Oh, yeah, baby; you know it," he said, and emphasized his masculinity by doing a Hulk impression.

"Going out?"

"My reunion." He took the cap off his cologne and gave himself a couple squirts here and there.

"Oh, right. You had that picnic thing today, didn't you? How'd that go?"

"It was pretty cool. Some of the girls turned out really hot. You wouldn't believe all the people who are married or have kids, though."

"Tell me about it. At my ten year I was, like, the only single guy."

"No kidding."

"Are you taking Lisa?"

"No. She couldn't make it."

Scott broke out into a huge grin. "The lady's man is goin' solo. How about a beer and a round of Xbox? I'm feeling the need to kick your butt."

. . . . .

Six o'clock, six centimeters. Where was John?

"Lisa, quit stalking the room like a caged cat. You're stressing me out."

"Sorry. How are you doing?"

"Okay," Ingrid said, sighing. "I've actually gotten used to the cycle of contractions. This experience is completely redefining my concept of pain. Like now? What I thought hurt like hell at noon has been reduced to pain level one."

"So what's pain level two like?"

"I have no idea, but I'll let you know when I get there."

Ingrid's comment was interesting. Was it possible that each new painful experience, physical or emotional, recalibrated the thresholds of pain tolerance? Was it possible that what she thought she couldn't endure was only relative to what she'd already endured? How much pain was manageable and how much was too much? She didn't know, but if what Ingrid had already experienced was level one, then Lisa was not having kids.

"What time is it?" Ingrid asked.

Lisa looked at her watch, disappointed. "Three minutes past six." Wasn't time supposed to fly during a crisis? This felt like slogging through goop.

"It's all right if you need to leave," Ingrid said. "Isn't your reunion tonight?"

She wavered, considering Ingrid's proposal. Ingrid's dark hair was flat and disheveled, partly held back in a half-ass ponytail, the remainder pushed behind her ears. Her face appeared worn out, despite a red flush in her cheeks. She looked stranded in that bed, hooked up with tubes and gadgets, like a beached whale subjected to a science experiment. What would Lisa want if she were in Ingrid's position? Well, that answer was obvious. There was no way she could handle *this* by herself. She would have to fix things with Jake later. At this point, it didn't matter if she surprised him with the truth today, tomorrow, or next week. Ingrid needed her now.

"Don't worry about that," Lisa said. "It's just a stupid party."

"Are you sure? Because really, it's okay. I'll be fine."

"Ingrid, you're about to give birth to your first child. That is much more exciting. I'm not going anywhere."

Ingrid leaned back into her pillow and exhaled. "I'm so glad you said that. I was just being nice. I don't want you to go either."

"I'm *choosing* to stay, if that's what you're worried about. Now, what do you need? Do you want some water? Orange juice? Cookies?"

Ingrid's cell phone rang. She grabbed it and nearly yelled, "John? Thank GOD! Where are you? What happened?" As she fired questions at him, she began to cry. The exposure of such raw emotion was almost more than Lisa could take. Misty eyed, she got up and went out to the hallway, intending to do a lap or two around the floor to calm down.

Ingrid was so brave. She would do this alone if it came to that. Lisa felt completely inadequate. She was supposed to be the strong one—the supportive one—in this situation. And yet, Ingrid was the one giving *her* strength and encouragement: to live, to love, to cut through the sarcasm, to release her inner cynic. To be vulnerable. When Lisa returned to the room, Ingrid was drying her eyes, the cell phone lying on the bed next to her side. "He's on his way. He's in Two Harbors right now, getting gas."

Lisa did some quick calculations. "So … that means he should get here around eleven?"

"I hope so. He promised he'd be here as soon as he could. Jim is driving with him to keep him company."

"Do you think you'll be able to hold out that long?"

"God willing. My contractions seem to have stabilized and I'm not dilating as rapidly as the nurses thought I would."

Lisa leaned over Ingrid's belly. "Hang on, little baby. Daddy's coming! You're not done cooking, so you have to stay in there!" That made Ingrid laugh. She squeezed Ingrid's hand. "You and the baby will be fine."

. . . . .

Eight o'clock and Jake was having a great time. According to the website, about two-thirds of the class showed up and according to Amir, that was a great turnout.

His chemistry lab partner now had her Ph.D. and was researching something that had to do with, well, chemistry. She explained it to him and it sounded cool and cutting edge. The class clown was married, had three daughters, and ran his own marketing firm. Jason, a hockey buddy, now owned four major ski resorts in Colorado. And the Goth girl? The one who had always worn black, listened to the Cure, and had body piercings? She traded in her black digs for a pantsuit and was now a member of the Oregon State Senate. Democrat, not Republican—which would be too far of a jump, even for Jake to believe. And the best discovery? Quiet little Shelly Newton, nicknamed "Turtle"—because of her name and her painfully shy demeanor—was on Broadway. Unbelievable.

The only somewhat uncomfortable aspect of this whole reunion was seeing his female classmates pregnant. Was it creepy to find another man's pregnant wife attractive? He'd watched Ingrid grow and that hadn't bothered him at all.

The reunion party reminded him of prom. They were at the exact same hall and the dinner was catered by the exact same caterer, Goldilock's Goods, and the exact same music they listened to in high school played. The disco ball twirled and the lights dimmed over the dance floor. The only differences really were the new hairstyles—or lack of hair—spouses, and permissible alcohol.

Chad Johnston was across the room. Why would he be here? Seeing Chad reminded him of Lisa and he scanned the room for her. He shook his head. Of course she wasn't here. Chad spotted Jake, raised his glass, and motioned him to his table. As Jake got closer, he saw that Chad was with Jenny Peters.

Whoa. That couldn't be right. Jenny was with Chad Blum. Wait a second; hadn't he just seen him? Jake gave the room a thorough once-over and saw Chad Blum sitting at a table with his buddies, a perky, attentive blonde perched next to him. *That* was definitely not Jenny Peters.

When Jake reached Chad, he did his best principal impersonation. "No underclassmen allowed, Mr. Johnston."

Chad laughed. "That's what my sis—uh—*Lisa* said."

"Really."

"Yeah, I, uh, mentioned it to her." Chad sipped his drink. "So, are we still on for softball this week?"

"Yeah."

"Cool. Hey, nice party by the way."

"Thanks."

"Jake, do you want to join us for dinner?" Jenny asked, as servers made rounds with trays of chicken and rice pilaf.

"I'd love to, but I have to sit up front at the officers' table. You know how it is."

"Sure, no problem."

"Take it easy," Chad said.

"You, too. Jenny, great seeing you."

"Thanks, Jake."

Chapter 26

Eight forty-five. Her hand was sore. Every time Ingrid had a contraction, she squeezed Lisa's hand so hard the blood stopped flowing. Lisa was convinced she was going to have permanent bruises in the shape of little finger silhouettes. This girl had a grip. They tried watching TV, but Ingrid complained it was too loud. They tried playing crazy eights, but had to put the cards away because Ingrid couldn't concentrate on the game. Now they just sat, her room shaded, waiting for each contraction to surge through her body.

To say Ingrid's sense of humor had dwindled was an understatement. It had vaporized. Being a woman, Lisa was all too familiar with the suffering of PMS. But this birthing stuff? They were wading into totally new waters here. Ingrid was way beyond sensitive, bloated, and moody. The room was too light and then it was too dark. The room was too cold, then the room was too hot. It was too noisy, then too quiet. The ice chips were too watery, yet couldn't quench her thirst. She shifted to her left side, only to switch back to her right. Any way she positioned herself, she was uncomfortable.

The nurses encouraged her to walk around and they did that for a while. A nurse brought in an exercise ball and suggested Ingrid roll on it or drape her upper body over it. She looked skeptical, so Lisa tried the ball out first. She lay on it, face up, stretching her back, and stared at the ceiling. The speckled tan tiles looked new. She counted across, then down, multiplied, then counted each one individually to confirm the correct number. Counting ceiling tiles relaxed her.

She did a few abdominal crunches and practiced balancing on the ball by tightening her core. The real fun came in bouncing on the ball. Lisa was so intently focused on improving her vertical bound, she hadn't noticed Ingrid's irritation until she barked, "Would you *please* stop doing that?" Yikes. And Lisa was starving.

A night-shift nurse, an ebony-skinned woman with high cheek bones, diamond earrings the size of peas, and thick, ropy dreadlocks held back by a wide red headband, came in and checked Ingrid's progress. Her presence was calming. Lisa looked down to see what kind of shoes the nurse was wearing. Turquoise crocs.

As much as Lisa enjoyed the nurse's aura, she was equally embarrassed being privy to Ingrid's cervical examination. Lisa wanted to ask if she should leave, more for her own sake than for Ingrid's, but the nurse was already en route. When the nurse did the exam, Ingrid winced and squeezed Lisa's fingers one more time. She needed a break.

The nurse snapped off the glove. "Eight centimeters. Getting close to nine. It won't be long now. Can I get you anything?"

"Could we have some juice please?" Ingrid asked.

"Sure. Grape or apple?"

"Grape. Thank you."

Lisa jumped in. "Is there a cafeteria or something in the hospital?"

"Yes. Go down to the first floor, through the lobby and it's at the other end of the hall. But you better hurry, because they close at nine o'clock."

"She seemed really nice," Lisa offered when the nurse left.

"Hmm," was all Ingrid said and closed her eyes.

"I'm going to go down to the cafeteria and grab something. Are you going to be all right?"

"I think so."

"Focus on happy thoughts and try to relax. The other nurse said you should rest in between the contractions." Lisa handed her an extra pillow. "Here, squeeze this in my absence. If you need anything, ring for the nurse. I'll be back as soon as I can."

Ingrid nodded, which Lisa took as permission granted.

She darted from the room, like a kid fleeing the classroom for recess, gratefully taking a few deep breaths to rid the fatigue that had collected in her body. It was terrible to say, but she was so glad she wasn't Ingrid right now. She much preferred being the bruised hand, instead of the big belly of painful contractions. Watching her friend, Lisa wondered at what point she would be ready to do something like this. She was nearing thirty. Shouldn't she have maternal instincts by now? Instead she felt the complete opposite. She wasn't sure she wanted to have sex—*ever*—if this is what it led to.

Lisa reached the cafeteria and made her way to the food counter. A few people sat scattered throughout the room, like small, isolated islands of quiet activity. An elderly Indian man read the newspaper while slowly turning a Styrofoam cup in his hand. A young black man was listening to an iPod and pushing buttons on his cell phone. A few figures in scrubs were munching their dinner, looking down at their food, not speaking. She welcomed the silence.

Lisa grabbed a tray and selected a turkey wrap with the least-wilted-looking lettuce, a very yellow banana, and a large cup of black coffee to go. She paid the attendant, a woman wearing a pink headscarf streaked with glittery threads and a long dark skirt, with the name Zaiida on her nametag. The woman's fingertips felt soft as they brushed Lisa's palm, laying the dollar bills and coins in her hand. Zaiida smiled warmly. Lisa bet Zaiida had the maternal instinct.

She set her tray down near a window, sat, said a brief mental prayer of thanks—for everything, she guessed—and took a satisfactory chomp out of her turkey wrap. She leaned back in her chair, feeling the food work its magic on her innards.

Who knew that waiting could be so exhausting? She shouldn't complain. Here she was eating a sandwich while Ingrid could only have fluids—and Ingrid was doing all the work. But Lisa was *so* hungry—she couldn't help but be a little forgiving of herself. While chewing her sandwich, she heard a little beep-beep. She remembered her cell phone in her pocket. It was a text message from Chad. *Where are you? You're missing the fun!* The second text was a photo of him, all thumbs up, with Jenny Peters. Lisa replied, *I'm at the hospital. Ingrid is having the baby!* She added a smiley face.

Finishing her sandwich and banana—her hunger somewhat appeased—she rested her chin in the cup of her hand and let her mind go to Jake. What had his day been like? Was he having fun? She hadn't seen him since Friday lunch and she missed him. Thoughts of Jake made her smile. She was ready to tell the truth and couldn't wait to move forward in earnestness. She should really go back to Ingrid, but instead, she closed her eyes. Just ... two more minutes ... of ... *peace.*

. . . . .

That was delicious. Jake stroked his satiated gut. If he were home now, he'd unbutton his pants. It was nine o'clock and time for the class slideshow. He walked over to Brandon, who was setting up his computer.

"Are we almost ready?" Jake asked.

"Yeah. Why don't you go ahead with your introduction? I should be done by then."

Jake moved to the head table, where he found a cordless microphone. He put it up to his lips and blew. Nothing. He examined its side and switched it to the ON position. He blew again and heard his breath amplified.

"Hello. Hello. Everybody. Hello!" He watched the crowd, giving them time to finish sentences and settle themselves. "Thank you, thank you. If you could all take your seats, please. First, I'd like to start out by saying thank you for coming. It has been an incredible day. It has been *awesome* seeing you all again, meeting your families, learning about your successes. I can say, sincerely, that I am proud to be the president of this class."

Thunderous clapping and whistling circulated around the room. In a wave of nostalgic school spirit, Jake raised his hand in a victorious fist and said, "Go Bears!" which was received with an even wilder applause.

"Tonight we have a special treat for you. If you remember, our class theme was 'It was the best of times—and only the beginning.' We're going to take a few moments and travel back to those memorable times and look at how far we've come. I'd like to thank Brandon and Megan and the rest of the reunion committee for organizing the reunion and assembling the show we have for you tonight. So grab a drink, sit back, and let us take you back to where it all began. After the show we'll be revealing the results of our *Who's who?* questionnaire. If you haven't voted yet, check with Megan back there at the table. Any questions?"

No questions, only cheers. Jake turned off the mic and set it on the head table.

The lights went down, followed by the kind of ooh-and-aah murmurs you hear at a fireworks display. Someone shouted, "Hands on the table!"

Everything was dark and still, the anticipation charged up to high voltage. Then "Monkey Wrench" by the Foo Fighters blasted from the speakers and the screen jumped alive with home movie clips. The pace of the slides matched the song's fast tempo.

Jake recognized photos from the original slideshow they had put together for graduation night. The first scenes depicted various classmates waking up, brushing their teeth, and making their way to school. For the reunion, Brandon had modified the show by interspersing recent photos of classmates—kind of like a "Guess who?" component mingled with the memories. Then the steady, energetic jamming of the Foo Fighters faded out and was picked up by an electronic, techno beat followed by the broody Oasis tune "D'You Know What I Mean."

The lyrics and style of each song complimented the snapshots and home movies in the show. Jake said, "This is amazing." Brandon smiled and tapped on his keyboard.

The first time Jake saw his own face up there, it was in a photo of him with three friends. They were wearing sunglasses and were parked in his dad's red Pontiac Bonneville SSE. Haddaway's "What Is Love" accompanied the shot, which got a big whoop from the crowd. The scene continued: the four friends standing around at a dance, doing the neck jive paired with the man shuffle and a few rapper-inspired hand gestures. They were so confident in their swagger. For Jake, looking at it ten years later was just plain torture—although admittedly funny.

Later in the slideshow, Jake watched himself get crowned homecoming king. There he was again, leading the student government—and the student pep rallies—*and* a leaf-raking procession for the elderly living around the school. Next, Jake was having lunch with friends in the cafeteria, at Burger King, then outside on the grass—even in his own house. He didn't remember ever seeing a video camera in his kitchen. There he was again: Jake wearing a big sombrero and a mustache; his mouth a big O, singing in the choir; looking all political during a debate in civics. He was kneeling down on the football field, apparently in a moment of silence. He was on the ice, holding the state hockey tournament trophy over his sweaty head. He was standing at bat. He was curled up in a sleeping bag, and in another photo he was holding a cup of coffee, looking into the morning campfire. Now, he was sitting in class, leaning over his textbook. Next Jake was talking to the principal.

Jake had been involved in school, very involved, but this was ridiculous. This looked practically iconic. There were more pictures of him than of anyone else in their class. What would be next? One of him picking his nose? Jake joked, "I guess I must have been pretty high profile back then."

"That's an understatement," Brandon said.

"Come on. Are you serious?"

"Yes." Brandon looked at Jake a little amused and astonished. "Didn't you know that?"

"I guess not."

"You were the most popular guy—no—*person* in our class. And you were in practically everything," he said then added with a grin, "Dumb ass."

"It's not like I saved some kid from getting hit by a bus. I don't think I even knew half the class that well."

"It doesn't matter. They knew you. And you *were* a do-gooder. You had our class do more volunteering in our senior year than any class ever in Big Bear High history. Megan looked it up. You just have a way with people."

"Is that what it was?"

Brandon said, "Classic."

Maybe there was some truth to what Lisa had said. Maybe he *was* a golden boy. He didn't feel that way, but looking up at the screen, he saw that was how he'd been treated.

While the music reel played on—a James Bond Medley, Smash Mouth's "Walkin' on the Sun", "Wannabe" by Spice Girls, "Good Riddance" by Green Day (now there was some irony), some Beethoven—for the first time Jake seriously analyzed what high school had meant for him. It sounded funny, but it was true. When he was elected class president, he hadn't expected to make a real difference, which is why he went for Key Club. Being crowned homecoming king had been kind of flattering, but mostly embarrassing. He'd felt like a Ken doll. Thinking back on it, he couldn't deny he had had a certain amount of status, but he'd hardly considered it privilege. Jake knew people liked him; he just never realized it was in such idolized proportions. Jake was the one who came up with the class motto about it being the best time of their lives and only the beginning, and he had really felt that way. After high school, he had essentially moved forward in his life without looking back.

The yearbook cover materialized on the screen, giving way to a photo of their entire class. The music faded then crescendoed into "I Believe I Can Fly" by R. Kelly. One by one, each classmate's graduation photo appeared, paired with a current photo of the person. The frame held for a few seconds before fading out and moving to the next one, reminding him of before-and-after photos in weight-loss advertisements.

The roll call of classmates prompted many memories. Some of them were vivid, like seeing Josh Branston and remembering their well-intentioned camping trip in the Boundary Waters. They had planned to be out in the wilderness for two weeks. It had rained and rained. Eventually, they were so soggy, they'd abandoned their canoe and spent the rest of the trip playing cribbage and reading in a one-room cabin at a backwoods mom-and-pop resort. He'd heard today that Josh had died in a car accident.

Other memories were murky puddles of recognition, like the one of the kid who had the door knocker piercing. Jake read the name *Christian Fletcher*. He'd only ever known his face.

Anna Garcia. There was no current photo, but her graduation photo still took Jake's breath away, her dark hair cascading down her back. She looked over her shoulder and into his eyes with a passion he thought had only been meant for him. She hadn't come to the reunion, and he couldn't say he was sorry. He would've been friendly, of course, but beyond that he wouldn't have known what to say or do. The brief survey she'd sent back only stated she was living in California and frankly, that was all he needed to know.

There he was again. Jacob Phillip Hanson. There were big cheers and applause from the audience again. He hammed it up and waved.

He couldn't believe how many Johnsons were in their class. Abigail, Carrie, Charles, Christine, Christopher, David, Duncan, Frances, Forest, Hilary, Hunter, Katherine, Lisa, Miles. The list of Johnsons was so long that R. Kelly's song finished before it did. Jake went to the bar and got another beer during the Johnson litany. "Barely Breathing" by Duncan Sheik started to play. The song was intensely out of place after hearing the inspirational R. Kelly number. It was one of *the* classic heartbreak songs of the '90s and one he'd listened to over and over after Anna dumped him. The mood of the crowd shifted from reminiscent to sullen. Jake remained at the bar, taking an occasional swig of his beer, watching Chad Blum with his perky blonde as his hand traveled up her thigh.

Suddenly, he glimpsed a familiar face. Not an old familiar face—a *recent* familiar face. Jake walked over to Brandon.

"Can you show me that girl again?"

"Which one?"

"Just go back."

Brandon opened a new screen on his laptop, playing a muted, mini version of the slideshow. He fast-forwarded it through the Johnsons. There she was.

"That one," Jake said. Brandon stopped the show. Jake read the name. *Lisa Claire Johnston.*

Jake felt his body go cold. He looked around for Chad and spotted him talking to a circle of friends, his back to the screen. In an instant, he got it.

Lisa was Chad's *sister.*

That's what he had meant to say earlier. "That's what my *sister* said." Jake looked at Brandon's computer, analyzing the two girls on the screen. The first was a mousy thing, scrawny with a ponytail and glasses, looking philosophical, barely even smiling. The other one, a woman, was beautiful and vivacious, grinning into the camera. It was from the gala. He recognized his own shoulder just within the shot.

The first girl—he had to really stretch his imagination to remember. The other girl, he couldn't stop thinking about. He could recall everything, in marked detail, that they had ever done together.

Brandon asked, "Are you okay?"

Jake was too stunned to answer. Betrayed. He felt *betrayed.* What the hell was going on? When Brandon asked his question a second time, Jake said stiffly, "I'm fine."

. . . . .

Since Lisa's small dinner, Ingrid's contractions had been coming on stronger and stronger. She'd gone from crabby and irritated to sobby and miserable. This was no time for jokes. The best thing to do was sit by Ingrid's side and be quiet. Lisa felt so bad for her—her suffering—and so helpless. John called to say they'd reached the Twin Cities and would be there as soon as possible. It was ten minutes after ten and Lisa didn't think she could hold down the fort much longer. Her stolid shell was on the verge of cracking.

Ingrid's hand lay in Lisa's and her eyes were closed. Lisa placed her face near her friend's, mentally tracing Ingrid's silhouette, noting the gently curving forehead, ski-slope nose, and round, jutting chin. Her eyebrows were thin dark lines, like the ones painted on ceramic dolls. She had a small pink mole on her temple. Lisa watched her nostrils flare as Ingrid inhaled and exhaled, her eyes closed in simultaneous concentration and rest. Ingrid sucked in a gulp of air and winced.

"Breathe through it, honey," Lisa said. "You can do it. Breathe. Breathe. There you go. Good job; keep it up. Good, good, good."

Her sound bite was the same, but like a mantra, seemed to have a soothing effect on Ingrid. Occasionally, Ingrid opened her eyes, turned them toward Lisa, and locked in. This was Lisa's cue to breathe with her. Lisa demonstrated the correct way to breathe at this stage of the labor—thankfully, the calming black nurse, whose name was Lateefa, had given her a crash course—and Ingrid mimicked her actions.

"I feel like I need to push."

"Hold on. You can make it. John is almost here."

"I don't want to hold on anymore. I need to push."

Lisa went out to the nurse's station and announced, "She's saying she needs to push." Lateefa came immediately.

"How are you feeling, Ingrid?" Lateefa asked, putting a hand on her arm, creating that same comforting effect on Ingrid she had on Lisa.

"Like I need to push. I don't think I can wait anymore."

Lateefa slipped her fingers into another rubber glove and checked her cervix. "Well, you're close, but not quite ten centimeters yet."

Ingrid closed her eyes and groaned. "I don't know how much more of this I can take." And then she growled through another contraction. "I just had another one. They're really close together now."

"You're almost fully dilated. Just a little bit longer and then you'll be able to push."

"I really feel like I have to push *now.*"

"I know and that's a good thing. But if you push before your body's ready, your cervix can swell or tear and then you can have more complications with the birth. Keep listening to your friend here, and I'll page the doctor."

Lateefa's confidence in Lisa gave Lisa a boost. Lisa was strong. She was able. She was *woman*. She could do this. When Lateefa walked out, Lisa said, "Isn't it exciting? You're about to have a *baby.*"

"I noticed," Ingrid responded. "I'm so tired. Can't I go to sleep and have the baby come out by itself?"

"I don't think so. Besides, you want to be sure you get the right kid." Lisa teased. "One of your books said that when you get to this point, you should think of all of the positives of having the baby."

"I don't want to think. The more I think the more tense I get."

"Okay, I'll go first." She thought for a moment. "You'll get to dress your baby up in really cute outfits. It'll be like playing with dolls, only this one will be *alive*. How cool is that? Your turn."

Ingrid turned her head away. "I don't want to play."

"Here's a practical one: You'll get a child tax credit."

"That's not making me feel any better."

"Okay. How about you get to experience the miracle of life? Pretty soon it'll be all over and you'll be holding this perfect little person, with ten perfect, tiny fingers and ten perfect, tiny toes."

"What else?" Ingrid asked.

Lisa was running out of positives. "You'll get to wear your own clothes again?"

"Now that's something to look forward to. I'll be able to sleep on my back again." Ingrid cracked a small smile that transformed as quickly as it had appeared to a grimace. "I'm having another one." She breathed through it listening to Lisa's mantra. "Tell them again that I have to push. I can't stand it."

"But the nurse said she would call the doctor."

"Lisa—*please*!" The cords in her neck strained against her flushed skin. When she considered what was worse to endure—Ingrid's begging or the nurse's irritation with her nagging—she went back out to the nurse's station.

Being as apologetic as she could muster, Lisa said, "Um, I'm *really* sorry to bother you guys again, but she's saying she really has to push and can't stand it any longer." Lateefa was absent. The nurses exchanged a knowing glance before one of them reluctantly heaved herself up from her chair, her body offering up the sigh that she wasn't allowed to verbally express.

Ingrid's breath was shallow, her eyes squeezed tight, as she braced both hands on the bed. Lisa and the nurse stationed themselves on each side of Ingrid.

The nurse asked, "Okay, honey; how're you doing?"

"I'm trying to hold it in, but the pressure is so strong."

Lateefa arrived with the doctor, a young Asian man, whose presence seemed out of place in the company of all these women.

He murmured a hello to the staff and asked, "How's our patient?" to which the nurse responded, "She's nearly dilated and says she needs to push."

The doctor examined Ingrid. "Okay, I'm going to have you scoot down a little."

Ingrid looked at him like he was nuts, then sort of inched her mass forward to the edge of the bed.

"Please," he said, pointing his gaze at Lateefa and Lisa. "I'd like you to hold her legs." The other nurse raised the bed until Ingrid was crouched forward in a squatting-sitting position. "All right, Ingrid, when the next contraction comes, you'll be able to push."

Ingrid looked at Lisa with pleading eyes and whispered, "What about John?"

Yeah, no shit; what about John. His wife was about to give *birth* and she was his stand-in. Lisa looked at her watch. Twenty minutes had passed since he called. She said, "He'll be here any minute."

Everyone waited for the next contraction and for John's arrival. In that brief interlude, Lisa prayed any prayer that came into her head: *Hail Mary, full of grace ... Our Father, who art in heaven ... Come Lord Jesus be our guest ... Now I lay me down to sleep ...* and a spontaneous *Lord, make this all turn out all right.* Who was the patron saint of mothers? Would that be Mary? She was such an illiterate Catholic. Whichever saint applied to this situation: *Hear my prayer.*

Lateefa petted Ingrid's arm. The other nurse busied herself, putting the final touches on a tray of instruments and towels. She and the doctor exchanged soft, single words. A station for the baby was wheeled in. The pace of the beeps emitting from the machine Ingrid was hooked up to signaled the onset of another contraction.

Ready or not, this baby was coming.

Dr. Asian Guy said, "Okay, Ingrid; go ahead, but I need you to stop pushing when the contraction subsides."

Lisa held on to Ingrid's leg. As she bore down, Lisa felt this incredible strength emerge from her friend. Lisa pushed back on Ingrid's leg, giving her the support she needed. Ingrid's expression morphed from despair and exhaustion to determination. She grunted with effort instead of discharging the blood-curdling scream Lisa had expected. After the first push, Lisa exhaled. That was intense. Just a few more and they'd be out of here, right?

"Is the baby almost out?" Ingrid asked hopefully.

"Not yet. The baby is still working its way down the birth canal. But it's coming."

Another minute passed, then another contraction, and another push. No change. Another contraction, another push.

"How about now?" Ingrid asked. Lisa felt optimistic with her.

"Not yet," said the doctor, "but the baby has moved a little farther down."

"How many pushes will it take?" she asked, exasperated.

Immediately the image from that commercial of the owl licking the Tootsie Pop came to Lisa's mind. "How many licks does it take to get to the center of a Tootsie Pop? One ... two-whoo ... three. *Crunch!* Three."

"It's different with every woman. You're doing fine," he assured her.

Lateefa added sagely, "The first one paves the way." As if Ingrid could think about having another baby at a time like this.

Too curious to resist, Lisa discreetly peeked between Ingrid's spread legs. She didn't see anything other than the standard, yet very swollen, female equipment. The beeps picked up speed again and the team hunkered down for another contraction. This time Ingrid earned a "Good job" from the doctor.

They heard a squeak of tennis shoes against the hallway linoleum and in a flash, John skidded in, disheveled as hell, his eyes bugged out from lack of sleep, and his face scrubby with whiskers. He came around to Lisa's side of the bed, and taking Ingrid's entire head in his hands, he kissed it. Lisa looked away, not wanting to intrude on their intimate moment.

"I'm so sorry," he whispered.

Ingrid said, "I'm so glad you're here."

When John asked what he could do to help, Lisa gladly handed over his wife's leg and scooted out of there.

Once she hit the hallway, she felt pure relief pump through her veins. Although she'd been willing to be of aid, she didn't mind skipping out on the opportunity to witness the miracle of life.

John's brother Jim told her the story of their parents' arrival at the cabin. Bert and Milly had driven around all of the lakes they thought the guys would be fishing on. None of the boats on the lakes looked familiar and, not feeling bold enough to ask strangers for help, they settled on returning to the cabin and waiting it out. Meanwhile, the fish had stopped biting and the guys had enough for a meal, so they had decided to call it a day. At about six o'clock, they headed back to the cabin, looking forward to a night of beer and fresh fish grilled over a campfire.

While Jim told the story, noises from Ingrid's room filtered through. Some sounded painful, others encouraging.

Hardly twenty minutes passed when John came out, looking up and down the hallway. Jim and Lisa immediately made their way toward him. She waited with bated breath for the verdict.

"It's a boy."

They followed John into the delivery room. Ingrid was fixated on a swaddled bundle, her face radiating with joy. When John joined his wife, Lisa noticed a soft light outlining the huddled shape of the new family, as if they were *the* holy family. Ingrid's energy level seemed to have rebounded and she was a completely different person. She was a mommy.

Lisa herself was so hormonal, she expected to cry at any moment. She looked at the baby. He was sort of splotchy and purple, but yet so precious, so tiny. So new.

"He's beautiful," she said. Which he was, in an esoteric, meaning-of-life sense.

"Isn't he?"

"Have you named him yet?"

"Justin Gabriel."

"Hello there, Justin Gabriel," Lisa crooned, already enamored.

Chapter 27

"Jake, you should have seen it. Ingrid was in labor all day and she was crabby and in pain. And when it was over, she had this beautiful little person in her arms and she looked at me and said, 'Look, Lisa. It's a boy.'" She put her hand on her heart and turned to him. "Oh, I wish you could've been there."

It was Sunday night and she and Jake had just joined the steady progression of people walking on the boardwalk around Lake Calhoun. The last rays of sunlight sparkled across the lake. The evening was humid, but tempered by an occasional drift of cool breeze off the small lake. A few boats were anchored and quiet silhouettes of paddle surfers glided across the water.

She'd been bursting with the news of Ingrid's new baby and since Jake came over; it was all she could talk about. After recounting the unforgettable experience for a solid three minutes, she stopped to breathe. She ended her monologue and matched his pace, taking his hand with her nonbruised one.

"So you had a good weekend?" he eventually asked.

"Incredible," she said, the warmth of happiness still in her chest.

"And what about your friends?"

"What do you mean?"

"Weren't you getting together with some friends this weekend?"

At first she didn't understand, then remembered her concocted cover story.

"Oh. Right. No, they were cool about it."

"So, what exactly did you have planned?"

"Ah, well, you know, stuff." She paused. What had she told him before? "*Girl* stuff. Pedicures, shopping—things like that."

"Huh. And they didn't mind?"

"No." Jake had gone to the reunion. By the looks of it, she guessed it hadn't gone well. "How about you?"

"How about me what?"

"Your weekend. How was it?"

"Fine." Silence. "I went to my reunion."

"Right!" she faked. "How did that go? Was the incumbent re-elected?"

"No, but I was voted most likely to be married, with kids, living in the suburbs."

"With a dog," she added, encouraging their usual repartee.

He chuckled only slightly. "There *was* something that happened that was kind of weird."

"Oh?" she asked, waggling her eyebrows conspiratorially.

"Yeah. You see, I saw this girl—and I knew who she was—only I didn't understand why she was there. It turned out she was one of my classmates. Can you believe that—that I wouldn't recognize someone from my own class? I felt so stupid." Jake scoffed. "I mean, how can you know somebody now and not *know* them from before, even though you should?"

Foreboding bullied all of the joyful warmth out of her chest. She kept her eyes down.

"I was—shocked. It just wasn't possible. So when I got home, I looked through my yearbooks, and sure enough, there she was." He shook his head. "I couldn't believe it."

He paused, then said it again. "I couldn't believe it. I kept asking myself, 'How could *that* girl, from high school, be the same person I know today?'"

The question hung between them.

"Can I ask you something?"

"Sure," she said weakly, the sense of foreboding invading her stomach like a cancer.

Jake removed his hand from hers and crammed it into his shorts pocket. "Were you ever going to say anything?"

She was busted. Her mind went spinning, a mangled mess of beginnings to what she didn't know how to say to him.

"At the reunion, you see, there was a slideshow. You know, flashbacks to our senior year, and suddenly there you were—on the screen. The new you. The old you. *Both* of you."

"But—," she started to say, then it hit her. The photo. When she'd registered that day after the golf tournament, she had uploaded a photo of herself to the reunion website. It had been one from the gala. He would have recognized it immediately.

"And now I'm in a predicament," Jake continued. "I'm not sure if I should be mad at you for not saying anything, or be mad at myself for having been such an idiot. On the one hand, I suppose it's not your fault that I didn't remember, so you can't be held entirely accountable. But on the other hand, you would think that a friend—a good friend," and here, he stopped, turned toward Lisa, and locked his angry blue eyes on hers, "someone who *really* cared about me, would have said *something*."

"Jake, I can explain ..." Except she couldn't explain. All she could do was stand there with a brain full of words that created excuses, not explanations. Expecting to see fire shooting from his eye sockets, she saw instead an eerie calmness. And hurt. Lots of hurt.

He angled his head and prompted, "You were saying?"

Lisa looked out over the lake. In the span of these few minutes, the sun had surreptitiously slunk below the tree line. A small, wiry woman in her forties jogged by, pushing a three-wheeled stroller with a sleeping baby in it. A single streetlight flickered on. She started wringing her hands, consumed with anxiety and fear of saying the wrong thing.

"It's just that—and then—and you—but now ..."

Her words were pathetically senseless. She couldn't even come up with a simple confession to redeem herself and recover with some dignity. "I got used to being the way we were," she said in a small voice. "I didn't think it would matter."

"You didn't think it would matter? Are you fucking kidding me? You thought that *lying* to me wouldn't matter?"

She flinched on the word "fucking."

"Jake, I didn't lie to you. I just didn't know how to tell you. At first it *didn't* matter, because you didn't mean anything to me. But then I wanted to tell you and I tried to that day after the block party, but you started kissing me and begging me to go to the reunion with you. I didn't know what to do."

"That's bullshit. You had plenty of opportunities to tell me the truth, way before any of that happened. What really pisses me off is the fact that you didn't say anything at all—ever."

She looked at him skeptically. "Come on. If you *had* recognized me, do you really think that any of this would have happened between us?"

"I don't know. Maybe. I barely knew you in high school. But if *I* had recognized *you*, I would've said something, instead of stringing you along and then making you feel like a jackass."

"I didn't mean it like that."

"Then how did you mean it? Why was your picture in the slideshow, Lisa? Was it some kind of joke? Did you want to hurt me?"

"No!" Then she started to cry. Embarrassed by her tears, she stepped off the path and onto the grass. She turned away from the lake only to face a group of teenagers with skateboards, lazing on a picnic table, watching them. Searching her pockets, she found a wadded, slightly used tissue. She dabbed at her eyes and her nose and moved to a young maple tree that provided some small privacy behind its slim trunk.

She *had* meant to hurt Jake, just a little, so he would know how it felt. But that was before—before she'd fallen for him. Jake stood on the other side of the tree. He stared at her expectantly; his eyes still blue fires of anger. His brows furrowed, creating deep valleys of concern; his dimple had long since disappeared from the disappointment she had caused.

"I never, in a million years, could've imagined that I'd end up working with you and having feelings for you," she began. "You have to believe that. And I really meant to tell you. I was planning to go to the reunion to *surprise* you. I thought it might give you a laugh, or something—I don't know—and at the same time put it out there, because it is kind of funny, in an odd, twisted sort of way, isn't it?"

"How could you even think that I would find that funny?" He stepped away from her, exasperated, rubbing his hands back and forth over his head, his nostrils flaring, and his face crimson.

"Please, don't be mad at me," she begged.

He circled back to her. "You know, this is *exactly* why I'm still single—because women like you don't take me seriously."

"But I do, Jake, I swear. I didn't mean for it to happen this way."

"I don't even know who you are anymore," he said bitterly. "You know what else? I can't believe what a hypocrite you are. I felt so bad about what happened at the golf tournament. And I thought about what you said. Do you remember? You said, 'The truth is always simple.' In fact, I felt so bad *I* wrote Grant's speech for the block party, just to make sure that you and everyone else got credit for their work. And come to find out, you," and here he jabbed his finger at her, "*you* were the one not being truthful."

The accusation was like a cinder igniting her own dormant inferno. "That is not fair and *not* the same thing. In this situation between us and our past, it is not entirely my fault you didn't remember me or what you did. In high school, I was the victim, and I didn't have any choice about that."

"What do you mean, what I did?"

"You know what you did, so don't even bother denying it," she spit out angrily. The old hurt surfaced like a dull ache in her heart. Why, *why* did this still bother her? She was in love with Jake. She didn't harbor any ill will toward him. Did she?

"What the hell? I hardly remember you as a person, let alone anything I might have done to you."

"Just forget it." His words cut. It was her turn to be disappointed. Not only hadn't he recognized her, he didn't remember anything about her. She didn't want to talk about it anymore. She didn't want to talk about it at all. "Look, I'm sorry I didn't *reveal* myself to you, okay? I didn't think it mattered and that's all there is to the story."

"No. I won't forget it. How were you a victim? What on earth could I have possibly done to make you despise me so much that you felt the need to mess with me like this?"

Lisa anchored her eyes on the opposite shore of the lake, her mouth clamped shut, refusing to look at him. She was crying so hard that her eyes hurt and her nose was snotty. The soft tissue she'd used was saturated and falling apart. Her entire body was shaking. She didn't know if it was because she was sad, angry, or both.

After more long moments of torturous silence, Jake shook his head. "I should have known to expect this kind of reaction from you. It's what you do. Whenever I try to get close, to figure out what's really going on, you shut down. How are we supposed to have a relationship if you won't open up to me?"

Still, Lisa said nothing. She had done more damage than good. Any more words at this point would only make it worse, although she couldn't imagine how it *could* get any worse.

All this while, they'd been standing apart from one another. Lisa by the tree, her arms crossed tightly, trying to subside her body's shaking; Jake pacing back and forth, his hands on his hips.

Then Jake approached her, close enough that she could feel the heat radiating from his body, and rested one hand on the tree. With a calmer voice, he said, "Look, I have no idea what I could have possibly done to make you hate me so much that you couldn't find it in yourself to be honest—even after all these years. So, whatever I did, I'm sorry." And with that, he pushed himself off the tree, turned, and walked away.

He got as far as ten feet, then pivoted and came back.

"Wait a minute. I'm not the bad guy here. *You* lied to *me*. I can't believe I just apologized to you. I don't even know what I should be sorry for!"

She closed her eyes, too numb to do anything other than absorb his emotions. He was standing so close to her that she felt his breath. It would have been so easy to touch him. A light caress, something—anything to abate his fury. That's what he wanted. That's why he stood so close, waiting for her to respond. He wanted her to appease his anger. To understand. To make it better. But she couldn't do it. She just *couldn't*.

She heard him sigh and opened her eyes. His head hung low but when he looked up, she saw that all the rage had been spent. "You know what? We will forget it; like you said. It's over. You're not the woman I thought you were and you're obviously incapable of having a mature relationship." He took one small pause to breathe. "I'm so mad right now, I can't even stand to look at you."

And on that note, he walked away again, and this time—he didn't come back.

She sobbed all the way home. When she dragged her sorry ass into the apartment, she heard her phone ringing. Hoping against hope that it was Jake, she quickly saw that it was Angela.

"Hi. How's my girl?"

"Okay." Lisa sniffled. "How about you?"

"Other than the wedding details being slow and tedious—I'm fine. I'm trying to finalize the guest list and was wondering if Jake will be coming out with you."

At the mention of Jake's name, Lisa broke down all over again.

"What's wrong?"

Through convulsive sobs she said, "The reunion was this weekend—and I couldn't go because—because Ingrid—had her baby—and I had to be with her—because John wasn't—here and then Jake—he—saw a picture of—me—at the reunion—and now he hates me!" Her voice rose at the end and she bawled even harder.

"Did you try explaining what happened?"

"I did—but he was just so mad. Do you know what he said? He said—he said he was so mad he couldn't—he couldn't even look at me."

"Sometimes people say stuff like that when they're angry, but they don't really mean it."

"No, he meant it. He—hang on." She set the phone down to blow her nose. "He said it was over between us and then he walked away."

"Can you blame him for being upset?" she asked gently.

"No. But I thought he would at least try to understand."

"Give him some time to cool off. If you love each other, you'll get through it."

"I don't think so. If he says it's over, then it's really over. There's nothing I can do no matter how sorry I am about it."

"Maybe you feel that way now, but it could look different tomorrow," she persisted.

"Angela, would you please spare me your sappy love-conquers-all speech? I'm really not in the mood. Maybe in your world it works. But in the real world—just being in love doesn't solve every problem."

"Okay. I think maybe I should let you go and we can talk another time."

"I'm sorry, I don't mean to be bitchy. I'm just really, really sad."

"I know you are. And remember I *am* on your side."

"Thanks. Do you mind if we save the post-breakup analysis for another night? I don't think I'm up to it right now."

"Sure. I'll call you in a few days."

When Jake said all of those horrible things to her, it hadn't seemed real. But now repeating them to Angela, having his words come out of her mouth, she knew it was. She grabbed two rolls of toilet paper from the bathroom closet and went to bed.

. . . . .

"Where's Lisa?" Scott asked.

"She's not coming," Jake said. He watched Chad and Mark chatting while they stretched. It was Wednesday and they were getting ready for their weekly softball game. Nearly everyone on the team was there.

Scott took a practice swing of the bat. "That's a relief. She's a lousy right fielder."

"Yeah. I don't know what I was thinking."

Scott smirked. "I do."

Jake ignored his comment and called his players into a huddle, offering the team a few words of strategy and encouragement. If they won tonight, they would be playing in the regional tournament. Sports always gave him focus, a clear objective: to win.

Tim stepped up to the plate as the rest of the team took their seats in the dugout. The pitcher threw the first ball. Tim, for once, managed to hit a decent grounder and made it to first base. Next was Erica, the first woman in their line-up. She swung. Strike one. The next pitch came and she let it pass. On the third ball, she connected with a loud *crack!*—sending the other team scrambling. Tim hauled ass, making it all the way to third base. Erica stopped conservatively at first.

Chad was up next. The resemblance was obvious. Chad's hair was darker, but they had the same face shape. The same nose, lips, and chin. They even parted their hair on the same side. Chad took a few swings, none of which hit the ball. Finally he hit one high into the air, which was easily caught by the shortstop—the first out for their team. Jake didn't mind.

The next woman, Amber, was their secret weapon. She had played softball in college and on a national team. She walked up to the plate and hit that first ball with such ferocity that the other team had no hope of catching it. Tim ran easily across the home plate. Erica came in next, and Amber made it as far as third before the pitcher recovered the ball. Yes, what *was* Jake thinking putting Lisa on the team?

His team clobbered their opponents sixteen to four. They were headed to the regionals.

After the game, they shook hands with the other team and decided to celebrate with victory beers.

When Chad sat next to him, Jake was mad all over again. Under normal circumstances, he thought Chad was a decent guy. But now when he looked at him, all he saw was Lisa's accomplice. And Jake had thought Chad had been interested in her. Boy, he'd been off base. Way off.

Chad handed Jake a beer. "Hey, what's up with you? You seem so serious."

"I was just thinking about your sister." Jake eyeballed him, waiting for his reaction. Chad's blue eyes had a pinch of brown, whereas Lisa's were straight blue.

"So, the game's up, huh?" Chad asked. At least he made no pretenses.

"Yeah. You could say that."

"That probably explains why she's not here and why you benched me for most of the game. When did she tell you?"

"She didn't. I found out at the reunion."

"But she wasn't there."

"No," he said, sipping his beer. "Her picture was in the slideshow."

"Really? I missed that."

"Yeah, I know. Because if you'd seen it, you would have seen my reaction."

"Man, I am so sorry. Really, I am." Chad held his hand up as if to take an oath. "I swear I had nothing to do with it."

"Of course you did. All of the clever remarks between you two? She'd say something like 'dating Chad would be too close for comfort' and you would say, 'I'm just not into her. She feels like a *sister* to me.' How could you not be involved?"

"Jake, I have nothing but the highest respect for you. I told her to be straight up with you or else you would get mad and she wouldn't believe me. She thought that showing up at the reunion would somehow fix everything."

"What were you trying to accomplish by not telling me?"

"Look, this is all about Lisa and has absolutely nothing to do with me. All I know is that last fall when you started working together, she didn't want you to know who she was. I just tried to stay out of it."

Jake looked at him skeptically.

"I'm not bullshitting you. I mean it," Chad said.

"You don't know anything? She didn't tell you why?"

"I swear. In fact, I told her *more* than once to level with you. I thought it was really shitty of her to treat you that way. I *know* how much she likes you and I'm sure she thought she was doing the right thing."

Jake took another swallow, ruminating on his friend's words. "Well, that helps a little, but I'm still pretty pissed."

Chad stood up. "Would it help if I offered to let you beat me up? I'm willing to accept full responsibility for my actions. They were dishonorable and I shouldn't have been a part of it, even if it was for my sister."

Jake appreciated the gesture, and while punching him in the face probably would make him feel better, he shook Chad's hand instead. "I have to say, you're much better at apologies than your sister is."

At that point, Scott leaned in, catching the tail end of the conversation. "You have a sister?"

"Yeah," Jake said for Chad. "It's Lisa."

"No shit?" Scott pointed to Chad. "Now I get why you didn't go out with her."

"Shut up, Scott," said Jake.

"Oh, right; she's your woman now."

"I'm not seeing her anymore."

"So that's why you've been PMSing on me."

"I have not."

Scott was already halfway to shitfaced. He pointed his bottle at Jake and swayed. "Look at you! You've been acting all pussy whipped and you weren't even getting any!"

Right then and there, Jake decided to get a new roommate when their lease was up. "You know, Scott, if you only allowed yourself to get beyond the pussy, you might see that there's an actual person attached to it."

Compared to Scott, Chad wasn't a bad guy at all.

. . . . .

Her brother called, asking point blank, "What is wrong with you?"

"Hello to you, too," Lisa said.

"I saw Jake tonight and I almost had to get beat up because of you."

"But this has nothing to do with you."

"I know. That's what I told him. But he thought that I was in on your conspiracy. What did you do to him?"

"Nothing."

"Lisa, don't give me that crap. You said you were going to tell him at the reunion and then you didn't even show up."

"I was going to, but then Ingrid went into labor and I had to go to the hospital with her. Then we had this big fight and, basically, he broke up with me."

"I told you this would happen. You got exactly what you deserved."

Lisa flinched. "Is he still mad?"

"Mad? Let me put it to you this way: He found out that the woman he's in love with lied to him, and not from her, and then doesn't tell him why she did it. How do you think he's going to feel? After what you did, I'm surprised he didn't just pitch a ball at my head."

Love? Jake loved her? "Did he say that? That he was in love with me?"

"I told you, I'm staying out of it!"

"Okay, I'm sorry. I didn't mean to jeopardize your friendship."

"Listen. You better figure out what you do mean, because I can think of at least one person who you owe an explanation to. And from now on? I'm not keeping any more secrets for you; especially since now I know that it'll only come back to bite me in the ass."

"I said I was sorry."

"Yeah, you better be."

Like Chad, she, too, was wondering what was wrong with her.

She hadn't been able to give Jake a worthy explanation that night. She watched him walk away, and that was the end of it. She'd contemplated running after him, but the surreal sense of the confrontation had kept her glued to the spot. After having a few weeks to reflect and analyze, Lisa could admit that her pride, more than anything, was what had stopped her from lambasting him with a soul-baring confession. Maybe it sounded crass to choose to ally with pride instead of her feelings for Jake, but she felt she couldn't be blamed for acting on her sense of self-preservation.

After all, Lisa had never asked for this. The day she saw Jake in the elevator, all she had thought of was hiding. Before that, she'd been happy. She hadn't asked him to work with her, or fall in love with her, or take her to his high school reunion. He had brought that on himself. And for Lisa, *that* was the distinction between what she had done and what she had failed to do.

Striated layers of hurts accumulating over the years; that's what her heart was. Jake's genuinely good character had drilled through to her soft, tender core, where she held her hopes. And there a prospect of love had been unearthed, mined from a seemingly impenetrable substance.

Mostly she was mad at herself—mad for letting ten-year-old injuries to her ego get in the way of what she had in her life now. How could she so easily discard all that had happened between them? She'd been so busy judging Jake against her adolescent standards for him that she'd forgotten that he wasn't a Spiderman or Superman—a human with supernatural powers and a great costume—but was only human. How could she blame him for that? Being human, wasn't it possible he also had the ability to experience pain, rejection, and disappointment?

During the post-breakup deconstruction, Angela postulated that maybe Lisa was preparing herself subconsciously for their relationship to fail. Then she could reject him and thus obtain the revenge she had always wanted—for him to know how it felt to be hurt. But that didn't make sense. Since she'd gotten to know Jake, she had already come to terms with the fact that it had been unfair holding him to such a high standard. She had made him out to be a monster, when it seemed that the only monster that really existed had been the one in her mind. All of these years later, it had just been a bogeyman of her own making.

And how could she have stood there and said that crap about it not mattering? Of course it mattered. That's why she'd never said anything. And when finally confronted? Why hadn't she had her confession prepared? Why hadn't she bothered to come up with something to say when that fateful moment presented itself? Surely, she knew that if she wanted to be with Jake, she'd have to tell him sooner or later. Rehearsing would have been a big help. Was she so delusional that she believed herself exempt from her progressive lie? Had she spent so much time mooning that she'd just skipped to the good parts? The only truthful thing she said to him that night was that she had gotten used to the way they were—and that was what she didn't want to change.

The only remaining tainted sentiment was regret. The situation had exceeded ludicrous and there was no justifiable way to bring it back to any level of respectability.

Since that day, Lisa played their last conversation over and over in her mind at least ten times a day. What else could she have said? Or should have said? In each rerun, she worked out her words, scripting and rescripting, until she cobbled together a scene that ended with a little more dignity and a little less disaster. If she were to see him again, she thought she'd know what she might say. But it was too late for that. It had taken her too long to see what everyone else saw: that he was a good person and so well liked because he was, well, likable. And she thought she had worked through her "issues."

And yes, she had thought about calling him. Every moment she thought of him, she thought about calling him. Once, she actually wrote it on her agenda—*Call Jake*—and allocated it for the seven-thirty time slot on a Tuesday night. On that evening, however, she became conveniently engrossed in an impromptu project, which involved removing all items from the kitchen cupboards, washing the shelves, and then restocking the items according to a new categorization. She now had a can opener, pegged and outlined, hanging on the wall next to the canned goods. The pasta stood tall next to the cereal boxes. The items she never ate, yet that still managed to claim a spot on the shelves, were pushed to the front, lined up in order of expiration date.

She would have to schedule another time to call Jake.

Chapter 28

The wedding party lined up in the back of the church and waited for their cue. Angela had said it would be a small wedding, but from the looks of it, there had to have been 250 people. Lisa was paired with Julian's first groomsman, the cheerful Alberto/Roberto from her last visit. It turned out his name wasn't Alberto or Roberto. It was William. The organ struck the signaling chord and he offered his arm as they commenced their slow trek up to the altar.

Lisa pasted her best rendition of happy on her pursed lips, but she was far from happy. Of course she was happy for Angela, but as she passed rows and rows of unfamiliar faces, the persistent sadness in her heart pervaded even the joy she felt for her friend.

Angela had spent the very last night before marriage with her old roommate drinking water, eating fat-free frozen yogurt, and watching HBO, which happened to be featuring timeless teen classics. Together they sympathized with Molly Ringwald in *Sixteen*

Candles and sang along with Olivia and John in *Grease*. They reminisced about their college days and analyzed every past boyfriend, which inevitably brought them to the topic of Jake.

"Still haven't spoken to him?" Angela had asked.

Lisa hadn't, and thought that by that time it would be pointless to try. Angela said encouraging things like, *Have faith*, and *It'll work out*. Lisa gave vague answers like, *Let's not talk about it anymore* and *Let's focus on you, instead.*

Strained from lack of sleep, in addition to her emotional coma, Lisa was only too glad to be ushered mindlessly to the front of the church. Before parting ways, William squeezed her hand then winked at Julian, who winked back.

Julian stood with perfect posture, giving him a noble air. She liked the way he wore his black-brown hair a little longer than most men in their thirties. It was thick and wavy, and matched his warm eyes, which were reserved only for his bride.

Wagner's "Bridal Chorus" began and the congregation stood, facing expectantly toward the church's entrance. Angela, on her father's arm, appeared relaxed and regal in her elegance. To complement her simple dress, Angela's hairstyle was a complicated array of curls pinned with pearls and wispy tendrils. Her naturally curly blond hair had the perfect weight and consistency to hold it all together. There would be no worry of locks unfurling with bobby pins hanging on like fishing tackle.

Angela, her friend who never faltered in exuding kindness, walked toward her future with no worries of her past. When she reached Julian at the altar, Angela smiled at her groom and passed Lisa her bouquet of champagne tea roses. A stab of jealousy and longing hit her right where she held Angela's flowers.

During the ceremony, Lisa's mind intertwined the words spoken out loud with her own thoughts. What would it be like to be the bride standing at the altar? Who would her groom be? Did she have what it would take to be a wife? She thought about John and Ingrid and the tenderness she had witnessed between them. Could she ever have that with another person?

The night before, Lisa had dreamed of the ocean, of a world that was two parts blue: cheery sky paired with the Pacific's calming azure. She swam naked toward the horizon, the water's movement especially sensual and freeing over the parts of her body usually covered by a swimsuit. She swam until her lungs burned from the effort, far enough out to be alone. She stopped and treaded water, feeling liberated as the water flowed over her skin. Sunlight glinted off the watery surface, causing her to squint as she watched a cluster of children frolic in the water, while parents stood ankle deep, supervising. Runners stayed close to the water's edge, hugging the shore, as dog walkers moved in both directions. Groups of all shapes and shades had staked territories of blankets and towels in the sand.

Lisa spotted Jake standing apart from a group, near a volleyball net. He waved and she waved back. He beckoned her to come in and she wanted to. Conscious of her nakedness, she wondered where her clothes were. How could she get out of the water if she was nude? What if all those people saw her? What would they think? What would Jake think?

While agonizing over the decision, Lisa heard a *rap, rap, rap.* Then it came again. *Rap, rap, rap.* How could water rap? She realized she wasn't naked in the Pacific, but sweaty, despite the air conditioning, in a hotel room and someone was knocking on the door. She heard the knocking again, this time an impatient *thud, thud, thud,* as she got off the bed and opened the door. It had been Angela's mother in an emerald green velour tracksuit with no makeup, ready for pedicures, coffee, and muffins.

During the exchanging of the vows, it was Julian, not Angela, who teared up as he promised to have and to hold this woman until death did they part. She marveled at how a man could be so sensitive and so unafraid to show his love—in public, no less. Julian's tears reminded Lisa of vulnerability and she was grateful for his openness and willingness to share it. Jake was this kind of man.

Julian and Angela were pronounced married and the new husband and wife celebrated the Eucharist. The Catholic guests approached the altar. After Lisa's turn, she took her place in the line of bridesmaids and prayed that God would guide her in love the way he had successfully done for her friends.

Now that Angela was married, how long would it be before they would be expecting their first child? She'd already intimated that she and Julian were anxious to start a family. How many of her friends had children? The amount was no longer limited to the number of fingers on her hands. Now the question was: who *didn't* have children?

Ingrid was loving motherhood, with her only complaint having to wake up in the middle of the night. Holding baby Justin in her arms and feeling the strength in his tiny fists curled around her finger, Lisa couldn't help but be moved by the mystery of life. His head wasn't shaped so funny anymore and his skin had smoothed out to a nice pink, his face adorned with chubby red cheeks. What would Lisa be like as a mom? When Ingrid wasn't taking care of the baby, she was uploading the most recent pics of him on Facebook. She posted more pictures in a month than she had in the last year.

The organist gleefully banged out a wedding march. The ceremony was finished. Life moved on unfeelingly, unapologetically, whether Lisa was ready or not, and the wedding procession retreated to the back of the church.

After the wellwishing to the happy couple and a photo shoot of the wedding party, it was time for the reception. Maybe Angela wouldn't notice if she slipped away after the meal. Some alone time on the beach sounded like good medicine for her aching heart.

Standing at the church entrance, she felt a hot breeze on her face and looked through the propped doors. She saw a tall man standing alone, his eyes on the street, as if expecting someone.

"What are you doing here?" Lisa asked, stepping outside.

David Cibulka turned at the sound of her voice and smiled broadly. "Your email."

Since the park project, David and Lisa had been emailing regularly. She wouldn't call him a friend exactly, but that was what they had sort of become—or as much as one could be with a professional athlete living in California. Last week she'd lamented to David about her best friend getting married and having no date. She'd suggested that if his schedule accommodated, he would be welcome to come.

"But I was kidding."

"I know, but I didn't have anything going on and I thought it would be nice to surprise you." In one stride, he cleared three steps and was next to her. "You look beautiful."

She blushed. "What did you think of the wedding?"

"It's a wedding. Aren't they always nice?"

"I suppose so. But I loved this one the best. Did you see Julian cry?"

"Is that what he was doing? From the back it looked like he had something in his eye."

"I've never seen a man cry at a wedding before."

"I know," David shuddered mockingly. "Don't think we're all like that."

"Maybe if you were, I'd like you more," she kidded.

"In that case, I think I might need a hankie." He wiped away pretend tears.

"Cheer up; there's a party to go to." She hesitated. "That is, if you want to come."

"Sure." He looked up at the church. "Is it here?"

"No, it's at a place on the beach."

"Do you need a ride? My car is parked around the corner."

"Sure. Let me get my bag. There's a beach party afterwards, so bring a change of clothes for yourself."

She hurried to the changing room, a wash of gratitude flooding her. Maybe she could actually have a nice time now. At the minimum, with David by her side, she wouldn't have to worry about getting groped by some naughty uncle. Collecting her stuff, she caught sight of her reflection in the mirror. She stopped, stood up straight, and regarded herself. She had dark circles under her eyes that couldn't be masked by makeup, her eyes shadowed by her soul's sadness. She saw not a girl, but a woman—a woman grieving, but one who still harbored hope and clung to some small sense of determination. She said to the room, "I hope you know what you're doing."

"I can't get over this car," Lisa said, amazed with the luxury and technology packed into David's black BMW SUV. Flipping switches and pushing buttons, she asked, "How long can you stay?"

"I drove down, so I'm flexible."

"How far is it?"

"About seven or eight hours, depending on where you are." David smoothly changed lanes.

"Don't you have a game or practice?"

"It's July. There's not much going on." He looked over at her. "It's okay."

David smiled and turned up the volume on the radio. They drove the few miles to the beach in silence, listening to the music. She could feel her muscles give in to the soft, warm leather of her seat and closed her eyes. When the car stopped, they were in front of a long white stucco building lined with floor-to-ceiling windows facing the ocean. After the stuffy air of the church, the air conditioning of the club was a welcome relief. Tables were nearly filled with guests and the servers had food readied on trays. Lisa's single chair at the head table remained empty.

"David, I have to sit at the head table. I can ask Angela if you can sit with us."

"It's okay. I'll take a seat at the back and catch you later."

"Are you sure?"

"Yeah. This is their day." As he walked away, he pointed to her and said, "Save a dance for me."

He selected a table tucked into the back corner by the kitchen with what Lisa guessed were young Peruvian cousins. David said something and the boys laughed. Lisa wondered if he spoke Spanish or if the young men knew anything about hockey.

Angela whispered, "Who was that?"

"David Cibulka."

"Really! I thought you weren't bringing a date."

"I wasn't. He surprised me."

"That was sweet."

"Too sweet," Lisa said, lifting the long-stemmed glass of white wine from her setting and taking a large gulp. She pointed to the room. "Everything looks so—perfect."

"You really think so?" Angela surveyed the room then nodded toward the five-tiered white wedding cake covered with white sugar roses and intricate piping. "I don't even want to tell you how much we spent on the cake."

Angela suddenly took Lisa's hand, causing her wine to ripple. "Thank you for everything. I'm really sorry this has been more of working weekend instead of a vacation."

"This is your wedding! I'd much rather help you than lay on the beach."

"After the reception, you can lay on the beach for as long as you want." She added causally, "So, will the hockey player be sticking around?"

"We'll see."

"Don't you think it's interesting that he drove all the way down here just to be with you?"

Lisa didn't want to think about what Angela was suggesting. "Most women would jump at a chance with a man like that."

Angela looked at her levelly. "Yeah, but sometimes you can't help who you love."

She didn't want to think about that either. Julian joined them and kissed Angela on the cheek. A fork clinked on crystal, followed by a chorus of fork clinking prompting the wedded couple to kiss again.

Lunch was a delicious, drawn-out affair with more courses than it took to get her degree. There was a consommé, and a small taste of lox, followed by cheeses and fruits she'd only ever seen on the Food Network. Next was a salad with arugula, which tasted tough and bitter, but she chewed on nevertheless. The entree included chicken and lobster with a light white-wine sauce and small new potatoes roasted with parsley and garlic, followed by lemon sorbet. The meal concluded with coffee and small tea biscuits, with Angela and Julian's initials stamped into the chocolate.

It was time for the maid of honor, Lisa, and the best man, William, to give their congratulatory speeches. William insisted Lisa go first. She took a hearty swig of champagne and pulled a folded square of paper from her bra. She saw David gesture with his hands while the boys leaned forward in their chairs and laughed. Julian's father handed her a microphone. She cleared her throat. "Hello."

Her greeting had no effect on the crowd.

Julian's father clinked his dessert spoon on his wine glass. His English accented with Spanish influences, he boomed, "Welcome family and friends."

The response was immediate.

He continued, "We are very happy you could join us today to celebrate the marriage between our son, Julian, and this beautiful woman, Angela. And now, Angela's friend, Lisa, would like to say a few words." All eyes turned toward her. Julian's father nodded his permission for her to continue. She saw David in the back, looking solemn, his hands folded on the table.

"Thank you," she spoke into the microphone, her voice sounding amplified but soft. "Angela, you are my very best friend. No offense, Julian, but I was hoping my brother would catch her, so we could be sisters."

A few chuckles came forth, building her confidence. "But she found her soul mate in you. For weeks, I'd been racking my brain, trying to come up with something witty, yet endearing, to say as you begin your life journey together. Angela is usually the expert on love, but I thought I could come up with at least one inspiring message. I'm sorry to say, I came up with nothing. So, I turned to the next best thing: the Internet. And there I found something. Mother Teresa once said, 'I have found the paradox that if I love until it hurts, then there is no hurt, but only more love.'" She raised her glass. "To Angela and Julian."

Chapter 29

She made a mental note that, should she ever marry, a beach party was the way to round out a wedding. Lisa reclined on a patio lounge chair having changed into a violet summer dress—the one she'd bought especially for the reunion—and watched Angela and Julian twirl a following of toddlers on the dance floor. "This is the life."

"It's a nice party," David said, getting comfortable over on his own turf in plaid khaki boardshorts and an orange Billabong T-shirt.

"Yes it is," Lisa agreed. She stretched and exhaled luxuriously. For the first time since the blowout, she could let her worries go and just be.

"Nice speech, too."

"You think so?"

"Yeah."

"I wanted it to be sentimental, but not too heavy; funny but not corny. Angela and Julian are so in love. It only takes five minutes to see that they were meant for each other."

"They look very happy," he said.

She sensed him watching her. When she glanced over, his eyes had that lovey-dovey light about them. It was a look she recognized from a time or two previously. Maybe there was some truth to what Angela had suggested. A guy wouldn't drive eight hours just to help a buddy out, would he? She shifted her arm over her head. "Do you like living in California?"

"It has its good points, I guess," he said, moving easily with her topic shift.

"Like what?"

"Great food, great culture, always something going on. Not really different from Minneapolis, in that respect."

"Except for the weather. I could live in sunshine every day."

"Actually San Francisco can get pretty cold and foggy."

"Then why not get traded down to San Diego?"

He chuckled. "For starters, they don't have a hockey team."

"I suppose that would be necessary."

"I can tell you what I miss about Minnesota."

"What's that?"

"Four seasons. My family. Friends. Being with people who really know me."

"Ah. A sentimental fool, are you?" she teased.

"No. It's just nice to go back to things that are familiar once in a while." He looked out at the ocean, then back to her. "Would you like to take a walk?"

As they walked up and down the shore, he told her about his new volunteer projects in San Jose since Grant Park. She could see why David and Jake were friends. He was contemplative and cared about what his contribution was to the world. It made her concurrently enjoy David's company and miss Jake.

She asked, "Do you like your life?"

He raised his eyebrows in surprise. "Mostly." After a few steps he asked, "How about you?"

"Yeah, I guess." She wondered how much to share with him. With the wedding and now, walking on the beach, being with David, she could barely contain her emotions and thoughts. If he'd been Angela, she would have already spilled all of her doubts.

"Sometimes I wonder if I'm not missing something," Lisa ventured to admit. "Being a guy, do you ever feel the pressure that you should be married by now?"

"It's not pressure, exactly. Although I would say that sometimes I have a desire to be married, or at least be in a serious relationship, and sometimes it bothers me that I'm not."

She looked at his profile, while he kept his eyes on the shoreline. Maybe the wedding was having a similar effect on him. "Were you ever in a relationship that you thought might lead to marriage?"

"I had a girlfriend in college, but when I decided to play hockey professionally, she decided that wasn't something she wanted."

"Were you planning to propose to her?"

"I was considering it. I thought I would wait and see how it went in the NHL, you know, that maybe we could try living together or doing the long-distance thing if she wasn't ready to come out here."

"Are you still friends?"

"No. We were for a little while, but then we sort of drifted apart." David seemed lost in his own memories, then he sort of half-smiled. "It happens."

She heard the disappointment in his voice. "Do you have any regrets?"

"Do you mean breaking up or losing the contact?"

"Both."

"I suppose a few. I'd be lying if I said no. I don't regret that we didn't get married. I do wonder how she's doing, though—what she's done with her life and if she's married now, or has kids. She wasn't a bad person. What about you? Have you ever been close to marrying?"

"Not even close. Sometimes I think there must be something wrong with me."

"I don't think so."

"Only because you don't really know me." She could rattle off a list of her shortcomings, but settled on sharing the one that bothered her the most. "I have a much larger capacity to be cruel than I thought I did."

She watched his reaction for confirmation of her admission, but his face remained blank.

"Everyone has their bad side," he said. "Sometimes I think it's not about what you have in common, like the good stuff, but how you deal with each other's faults—that's what matters the most."

"I've never thought about it like that before. I tend to think that if I focus on the positives, the less desirable qualities will work themselves out."

David shook his head. "You can't ignore them. Say, for example, that I take a shower, and after my shower I leave the wet towel in a heap on the bedroom floor. If it bothers you, it's going to keep bothering you, no matter how much you like me."

Although the part about a wet, muscular hockey player didn't seem too bad, she wrinkled her nose. "You do that?"

"No, but you get my point." He nudged her with his elbow. "I have other bad habits."

She returned his nudge. "And what would they be?"

"If you really want to know, you'll have to find out on your own." His eyes were full of meaning and she felt a spark jump between them.

She had an impulse to reach for his hand, but resisted. She imagined it would feel large and rough, but comforting and warm. Had she known him better, or the circumstances been different, maybe she would have.

David spared her a reaction and spoke first. "All of this serious talk is depressing. I suggest we either go for a swim or go back to the party and have some fun with your friends."

On the dance floor, David and Lisa busted out some classic moves to ABBA and the "Chicken Dance." She showed him some salsa and merengue steps she'd learned from Julian's friend, William. When the pace slowed to a ballad sung in Spanish, David wordlessly put his arm around Lisa's waist, took her right hand, and pulled her closer to him.

Being in close proximity to a man again, especially one who was compassionate, intelligent, and incredibly good-looking—never mind famous—was unnerving. No one seemed to know who David was; or if they did, they kept it to themselves. She resisted the urge to make a joke, putting her attention instead on the melody of the song. After a few moments, her body relaxed; when it did, David shifted his grip, bringing them closer together. Rather than analyze it, she closed her eyes and rested her head on his chest. He wrapped his arm farther around her waist.

How long had it been since she'd enjoyed this kind of embrace? She had to laugh at herself when she recalled how she had tried convincing herself she had been in love with Tony. She hadn't loved him. She had wanted to be loved *by* him—to have a man want her. To be desired. She'd slid into the trap of being a pleaser. And what had it gotten her? Nothing. The time she had spent with Tony felt wasted, distant, and irrelevant.

But she had loved Jake. She hadn't said it to him, but she felt it through and through until it ached. He hadn't said it, either. But she surmised that only a man in love would have taken the news of their shared past so badly. She pushed those thoughts away. It hurt too much to think about him. She was no longer worthy of Jake's love. That was over. But David—David was here. He was real. This was her present.

The cadence of the song merged seamlessly into the next. Lisa inwardly thanked the deejay for prolonging the moment. David's arms around her secure and safe, they circled in time with the music.

His presence made her feel less criminal. This gave her hope. Despite what she'd done to Jake, maybe, just maybe, she was loveable after all.

When the song ended, they looked at each other. David had that look again. That meaningful look. She wasn't sure she wanted this to mean anything. She dropped her eyes first. Feeling attracted, guilty, yet noncommittal, she said, "How about a drink?"

The next day, David held her luggage while she checked in at the kiosk. With Julian and Angela already on a plane to Thailand, David had offered to take her to the airport. She had flashbacks of being with Tony at the airport on New Year's Day. What was it with her, athletes, and airports?

"It looks like I'm all set," she said, once she had her boarding pass in hand.

While he hadn't pressured her to declare any affection for him, David had kept close the rest of the previous night. After the dancing, they'd gone back out to the beach to enjoy a bonfire. When a blanket had been offered, they'd wrapped it around themselves, trapping the heat, creating a bit of emotional as well as physical warmth. He'd taken her hand in his. His fingers had been long and she'd felt calluses stretch across his palms. Jake's hands were wider, but shorter, and he had a funny bump on his middle finger.

She'd been standing on a precipice, teetering between David's evident desire and her guilt. If he had dared to kiss her, she would have let him. Through the course of the night, she'd tallied a list of what she would have been willing to do if he initiated anything.

She was in San Diego, far away from her life in Minneapolis. The distance gave her perspective and space to feel; maybe even gave her permission to explore something new. She was her own paradox, equal parts potential recklessness and resistance. David had probably sensed both, drawing his own lines around her hazy boundaries.

Looking at him now in a sensible place like the airport, preparing to return to her life, she was glad that nothing more had happened between them. Even though it was over with Jake, she needed time to figure out what she wanted. She loved California; maybe she would look for a job out here.

"Thank you for being my date," she said. "I had a really great time."

"It's not every day you lose your best friend to a husband. I'm glad I could help out."

"Julian is a great guy, so I'm trying not to think of it as a loss. But it wasn't just that. I really appreciated you driving all the way down here—to be with me. You reminded me that men can have a softer side, too." Her cheeks burned, like she'd revealed her innermost secrets.

She added, "Even hockey players."

"I like to think so, but don't tell anybody." He winked, then pulled her in for a hug.

She spied the clock above the United Airlines counter. It was time to say goodbye. David kissed her on the cheek and as she walked away he waved. She didn't say she would see him again, or promise to call because she couldn't offer any guarantees.

"Lisa."

She turned around. "Yes?"

"When you get home, talk to Jake. And if it doesn't work out, let me know."

Chapter 30

His words had knocked the wind out of her. They'd spent the last twenty-four hours together and not a single mention of Jake. Not a word. If she hadn't had to catch her plane, she would have marched back to him and demanded an explanation.

As she buckled herself in and peered out at the tarmac through the small window, her mind reeled with comebacks and questions, analyses and rationales.

He had known.

The question was what exactly did he know? What had Jake told him? They were good friends—probably best friends—and if Jake had felt compelled to say something to her brother, surely he would've shared it with David, someone he could really confide in. Was he suggesting that Jake was still interested in her? That she still had a chance? She didn't dare to hope, but there it was, the seed planted, already being watered by her wish to make things right with Jake if she could.

He'd also presented her a choice, an alternative to her melancholy. David was unquestionably attracted to her—enough to leave her hanging with a serious consideration. She couldn't deny she'd wondered once or twice, before Jake, what dating David would be like. And yesterday, the thought had occurred to her multiple times. The problem was when she thought of him, he always came in a pair—with Jake, the two inseparable. She only knew David because of Jake. Grant Park had been successful in part because of David, ergo because of Jake. Could she picture herself with Jake's friend? Didn't that violate some kind of guy code of honor? What about her own moral standards?

She squeezed her eyes shut, forcing herself to surgically separate the conjoined twins of her mind. Kind and considerate David. A man who made her feel safe and comfortable. A man who'd almost gotten married. A man who planned to resume a sensible life some day when he was finished with the NHL. She could picture him coaching Tiny Mites, toddlers on skates, gazing up at him with unadulterated affection. He was someone who knew what he wanted. Someone she didn't have a past with. A clean slate. She could love someone like that, couldn't she?

Who was she kidding? She'd only been play acting with him—a fantasy brought on by the woozy combination of the wedding, the beach, and masculine attention.

But it had meant something to him. David hadn't hid or denied anything. In return, she'd been an emotional slut, using David as a romantic rebound. Their short time together had been nice, but realistically more of a superficial flirtation to pump herself up than an honest invitation. A fresh variation of guilt riffed through her.

She shook her head. That wasn't entirely true, either. She did care for David; she just didn't know in what way. Even if Jake was out of the picture, his aura clouded any objective judgment. She wanted to smack herself. She wasn't returning to the mess that was her love life; she was in it.

Talk to Jake. If it doesn't work out, let me know.

After stewing for another half hour, she pulled out a book. She couldn't do anything about it now. Eventually she dozed, the storyline mixing with the events of the weekend. David moved in and out of her subconscious, Angela and Julian sliced into a tier of their wedding cake, and Lisa lay on the beach in seventy-degree solitude, the heat drying her skin from a swim instead of in a cramped plane with air blowing on her hard enough to dry out her sinuses.

The plane's descent woke her, the respite leaving her still sleep deprived, miserable, and unresolved. She'd had over three hours to process all that had occurred between her and David and was no closer to a solution than when she'd left. As soon as she debarked, she switched on her phone.

"Why did you say that—about Jake?" she asked, skipping the pleasantries.

David sighed. "Jake told me about what happened. I'm not going to deny that I have feelings for you, but he does, too."

She scoffed. "Jake and I were hardly dating two minutes before it was over."

"It's not that easy, Lisa."

"Are you saying that he wants me back?"

"I'm saying I've never seen him like this. He's still pretty upset by what happened between the two of you."

"Why is it so hard for him to accept the fact that we went to high school together and leave it at that?"

"Because that's not who he is."

He was right. It hadn't been fair or realistic to expect Jake to just accept her flimsy request to get over it. Despite herself, she mumbled, "It was just a stupid misunderstanding."

"Then tell him."

"And if I don't? Then what?"

David was silent. Then he said, "If something were to happen between you and me—if we started seeing each other—it would be hard for me if my girlfriend and best friend weren't on speaking terms."

There it was: the guy code of honor. "So you're asking me to talk to Jake to get what—his blessing?"

"Something like that."

"What if I still have feelings for Jake?"

"Then I have to live with that."

"Will it affect our friendship?"

"I hope not. From my side it won't. What about you?"

"Of course not. You must think I'm a loser after what happened with Jake."

"You have your reasons, Lisa."

"Are you going to tell him about this weekend?"

"Why not? There's nothing to hide."

She recalled his face and how relaxed he made her feel on the beach. It had only been yesterday and already felt so long ago. "You're a good person, David."

"Remember, I have my dark side, too. Don't give me too much credit."

"I'm too tired to think right now, but if I do talk to Jake, I'll let you know."

She hadn't seen or spoken to Jake in almost six weeks and now that he was sitting across from her at a Grant Park board meeting, she felt smothered in a blanket of guilt with an abundant fringe of anxiety. She'd only gone to the meeting as a favor to Ingrid, who had to present a report but couldn't attend. If he was surprised to see her, he didn't show it. For once, Jake wasn't his usual friendly self. He made no pretenses about busying himself with his work and made no acknowledgment of her arrival.

The meeting was torturously slow as they ticked through the agenda items. For Ingrid's sake, Lisa took notes, but was so distracted that she couldn't say what they were about. She looked at Jake squarely when he addressed the group and stole sideways glances when he didn't. Not once did they make eye contact. She read Ingrid's report as fast as she politely could, the words coming out of her mouth while her mind was piecing together options for an exit strategy. She wondered if Jake watched her while she read the report, if he saw how sorry she was, or if she looked as stoic as he did. She'd been praying for an opportunity to make things right with him, and here it was, but would she take it? What if he approached her? Or worse, what if he didn't?

After an hour and a half, the meeting adjourned. She dallied while collecting her things, watching for Jake's next move. Several members stood and chatted, including Jake.

Mrs. Chang approached her. "Lisa, I've been putting together some plans for showcasing the neighborhood's cultural diversity. Would you mind taking a look at them and letting me know what you think?" She handed her a set of stapled pages.

"Sure, I would love to."

"Thank you. Call me when you're done and we can meet for lunch."

"I will. Thank you." Lisa felt honored that Mrs. Chang would ask her for help and if it had been any other time, she would have looked through Mrs. Chang's papers right then and there. In her periphery she spotted Jake still talking with two board members, his hands in his pockets, relaxed, either oblivious or completely disinterested in her suffering. He threw his head back and laughed. Bastard. She was a wreck and he was laughing. Maybe David had it all wrong and Jake was just fine. He certainly looked it. She hastily put Mrs. Chang's proposal in her briefcase and gathered her purse. Jake's stuff remained sprawled across the conference table—a quality that vexed her sense of tidiness. At least David was right about that part: you can't love away someone's annoying habits. She was glad to be rid of tolerating Jake's sprawly nature and vowed to pay close attention to the next guy's irksome ways. She left the conference room with her head held high and just enough huff to hopefully let Jake know that she could be just fine, too.

She reached the elevator and pushed the triangle pointing down. There had been no *missed* opportunity—there had been *no* opportunity. Lisa had waited too long to rectify things with Jake and now—it was evident that he no longer cared. At all.

Seconds dragged to eternity before she heard the familiar ding and entered the elevator. As it closed, someone shouted, "Wait!"

A hand slid between the closing doors, causing them to open again. She looked up and locked eyes with Jake. A bolt of electric emotion zapped her. Beautiful, handsome, perfect—Jake. Whom she had to let go of.

"Sorry," he mumbled, as he stepped to the back and leaned against the mirrored wall.

"It's okay."

He slipped a pair of earbuds into his ears and trained his eyes on his shoes, the Italian ones she'd noticed during their first elevator encounter and had come to love. Lisa stared unabashedly at his reflection, his body pressed to his twin image. He'd gotten a haircut recently and she followed the pale edge of skin along his hairline. He wore a gray suit jacket with a white shirt, the top button undone, his red tie loosened. His back slightly slumped, curving into his strong shoulders. She wondered if the softball team had finished the season well and what he was into this month. Jake bobbed his head slightly to the song only he could hear. She saw his jaw clench and unclench, rippling almost imperceptibly under his skin. He looked tired. Her annoyance melted and the floodgates of her heart opened.

Pain was relative. That was what she had learned from Ingrid's labor. The pain she felt now, from hurting Jake, was so intensely and infinitely beyond anything she had ever felt for herself. This pain made her high school experiences, her breakup with Tony, any of her breakups with past boyfriends—any past experience, period—seem silly and trite. She couldn't compare it to losing a job or the loss of a friend. This was worse. Much worse, because she had caused it.

Looking at him—watching him avoiding her—she knew she couldn't justifiably call herself the victim, because this time it had been her fault. The guilt, the pain, and the shame pointed her to this one infallible conclusion.

Then all the garbage she'd been recycling inside herself over the years came pouring out.

"Our sophomore year, in geography class? I experienced this—embarrassing flatulence—while we were taking a test, and you laughed—you were there—and I was really hurt because you were Jake Hanson and you were supposed to be perfect, which meant you would never laugh at anyone because you were supposed to be too nice to ever do such a thing.

"But that's just stupid, and anyway, that's not what I wanted to tell you. I don't know why I'm even bothering to tell you this, but that's beside the point. The truth is, you've always trumped me. People. Everybody. That's what I was trying to tell you before. In high school, I started keeping track of all the times you got picked, or won something, or whatever, and you always got it. Always. Even if someone better than you deserved it, you got it. Just because you were you.

"And then Key Club. I was running for president, Jake. I was. Then you showed up on the last day and one-upped me with your typical one-upness.

"And then when you won the trip to Washington, D.C. and I didn't, I hated you, because I didn't think you deserved it and I really did. I worked so hard for that trip and then you just came in, took my notes, and did your, your—Jake thing—and won. I couldn't believe it. I even talked to the teacher and she was all like, well what could I do, it's Jake. I felt like you got it just because you were Jake Hanson and I was only Lisa Johnston, the girl who was constantly being mistaken for someone else. But you were in everything, Jake. You see? I was in nothing and when I tried to do something, *you* got it.

"After high school I just sort of forgot about it—well, no, I didn't forget—I just decided to move on with my life. High school was crap but I wasn't going to let it define me. I thought I'd done a pretty good job, too.

"But then you showed up in the elevator—this one probably. I realized that I hadn't gotten over it. It turned out that, all this time, there'd been this grudge buried deep down inside of me, not forgotten, but lying there like a big pile of fossilized shit.

"My life was fine before you showed up. I was happy; I knew what I was going for. Then there you were, back in my life, forcing me to face all of my high school issues when I would've been perfectly happy just keeping my shit to myself.

"And then after hating you some more, I got to know you—and then I began to actually like you. A lot. Then I really didn't want to tell you, because I was embarrassed and I know it's stupid to hate someone for ten years because they laughed when you farted or had boogers hanging out of your nose, because, hey, sometimes that's funny and Mrs. Nelson was right about what she said about you and why you got to go to D.C. and not me. Then I felt stupid for holding on to something so juvenile for so long, and I was hoping that we could skip over that part and move on. But still, I knew I had to say something, even if I was afraid you wouldn't forgive me when you found out, and that's how I came up with that stupid idea of surprising you at the reunion.

"I was hoping we'd be able to laugh about it and then Ingrid went into labor ... and ... and ... I messed it up anyway. And now you're mad at me because I didn't say anything and you feel like I betrayed you and I don't blame you for feeling that way and I know that if I could go back and fix it, I would, but I can't, so I'm sorry for that, too. I'm sorry for hating you. I'm sorry for not being honest with you. I'm sorry that I'm not with you and I miss you and now I'm babbling like an idiot, because I'm trying to tell you everything that I can think of and I'm terrified that if I forget something you'll think that I'm still lying to you, which I'm not."

Her chest hurt from spewing so much emotional baggage. She wasn't sure how much Jake heard, just that at some point, his eyes found hers in the elevator's reflection and stayed on them until she finished her flurried confession.

The bell dinged and the doors opened. The lobby was empty. Neither one of them moved. She cursed herself. Stupid girl. *Stupid, stupid girl.*

The doors closed and the elevator remained motionless. Jake pulled the earbuds from his ears and placed them in his pocket. He pushed himself off the back wall and moved closer until he was facing her. Another jolt of guilt, hope, and trepidation charged through her body.

He ran a hand through his dark brown hair before looking at her again, his eyes troubled clouds of blue. "Look, I'm sorry, but I hardly remember you or who you were then and I don't remember making jokes at your expense."

"I know. And you didn't."

"And Key Club? *Really?* You were mad about Key Club? If you'd wanted to be president so badly, you could've just told me."

She only had one straw left in her clutched hand. "What about the Washington, D.C. trip? You have to remember something about that."

"What about it? I earned that trip."

"No you didn't." Her ten-year-old indignation stomped its feet like a child in a temper tantrum. "Our group was a joke, so I did everything. Then on the day of the debate, *you* finally showed up to do your typical dog-and-pony show based on *my* work."

Jake's cloudy eyes flashed to storms. "I did my own research." He stepped back from her. "Why would you say that? Why would you think that?"

"You took my notes ... ," she began.

"Maybe I did; I don't remember. But if I had, it had only been to see if you had any new points to add."

"But if you had done the work, why didn't you share it with the team?"

"Because I didn't have time. I had baseball, a job, student council; I was finishing up scholarship applications. It was easier to just do the work than try to get the others to help. Besides, it wasn't a contest solely between you and me. It's not my fault that I was chosen and I certainly wasn't ... *plotting* against you. And that trip to Washington is what made me want to be a lawyer instead of a hockey player. I'm not going to be sorry for that."

Her entire paradigm had just shifted. Everything that she'd thought about Jake—*poof*. Hearing his logic was hard, even if she had already figured some of it out on her own. She'd expected him to deny her allegations, sure, but not to have a logical explanation—let alone a sound, rational explanation. If she felt stupid before, now she really felt like the prize idiot.

Jake said, "Is this what you think of me? Is that what you thought of me? Is that what this is about? This entire time you've been thinking that I'm what—some kind of jerk—who used you? God, Lisa. That's cruel. That is low—about as low as a person can go."

Her injured pride wanted so badly to say that he was wrong, that he didn't understand, but she knew in her heart that he was telling the truth and he had understood—perhaps better than she had.

"Is it possible that you took my actions out of context? That maybe you were so wrapped up in your own insecurities that you found it easier to use me as a scapegoat?"

It stung, but she agreed. "Do you hate me?" she asked, disgusted even more with herself for asking such a typical prize-idiot question.

"Hate isn't the word I would use to describe my feelings." His voice was thick and bitter. "The question is: do you still hate me?"

"No. Oh, God, no." She regretted having caved in to her impetuousness. She had meant to reconcile with Jake, not push him farther away. "I'm crazy about you, Jake, and I am so very sorry."

The elevator jumped to life and surged upward. Jake pushed the button closest to his hand, number five, and when the doors opened a few seconds later to the fifth floor, he pulled Lisa out with him.

He stayed close to her, his hand not leaving her arm. For a long time, he just—looked at her. She wanted to touch him, but was too afraid. She waited, still as a rabbit.

At last he opened his mouth, then closed it and looked away. If only she knew what he was thinking, she might know how to act. Then he looked at her again.

He said, "I've spent a lot of time thinking—trying to figure out what happened back then. You were such a quiet girl—I honestly couldn't think of anything that I could've done. I can only apologize for the past, but I promise you, that since I've known you now, I never meant to hurt you."

"I know," she whispered, tears of gratitude springing to her eyes.

"At the lake, I really wanted to give you the benefit of the doubt. I had no problem accepting that I hadn't recognized you and moving on. But when you couldn't be honest with me? And then to suggest that I did something to you and not tell me what it was?

"There was a time when I would've gone to the ends of the earth for you. But there also came a point when it wasn't worth it anymore. You crossed that line, Lisa. And once you cross that line, you can't go back. So, while I appreciate your explanation and your apology, it's too late."

"Jake, please."

With an almost painful tenderness, he said, "I can't be in a mature relationship with someone who behaves like a scorned schoolgirl."

He let go of her arm, walked to the exit, and took the stairs.

That was *not* what she had expected.

Chapter 31

Jake sat in his car, debating what to do next: cry about it or get drunk. Whichever one he chose, it was a lousy way to spend the rest of the night after telling the woman he loved that he couldn't be with her. No; he needed to stay clear headed and not do anything stupid. Besides, he had a lot to do the next day. Despite his success with Grant Park, Grant hadn't let up on pressure or expectations. Not that he'd expected it, but a breather would have been nice.

He turned the key in the ignition and started driving. Eventually he got out at Lake Harriet and stood at the place where he and Lisa had eaten ice cream and debated about who would become the next president. It was the place where he'd opened up to her—told her all those things about high school. He scoffed to think that he'd wanted to take her to his reunion. Their reunion. Now he was thankful she'd turned down his invitation. At least she'd had enough heart to spare him the embarrassment of looking like a chump.

His eyes had been opened. All of her weird behaviors—her evasiveness, standoffishness, and arguing—made sense now. What had attracted him to her—her confidence and strong will—had been motivated by her dislike of him, not the other way around. He'd grossly misread her.

Lisa had been the first woman he'd been attracted to in a long time, probably since Anna, who hadn't fawned over him or thrown herself mercilessly at him. She'd done the opposite. She'd given him plenty of reason not to be interested and had actually *discouraged* him.

But then there was this whole other part of their relationship, the post-coffee shop era when she'd been *nice* to him. She'd gone from ice queen on her moral soapbox to interesting and interested. Relaxed and funny. Open. All the runs, meals, games, movies—all the time they'd spent together. Hadn't that meant anything to her?

He didn't regret what he said to Lisa in the elevator. He'd had a good while to process it, and as hard as it was to say, he'd done the right thing. There was no point in rehashing it now.

It had been a failed experiment. At least it hadn't dragged out over four years like with Anna. Losing four years with a girl as a teenager was nothing, but at this age? He'd invested nearly a year into Lisa and he was almost thirty. The odds of finding a single, smart, beautiful woman with no kids and had a way of making him feel equal were getting smaller.

He looked up at the sky—clear and as beautiful as that night when he first kissed her. All he wanted was the pain to go away so he could go back to being a regular guy. Not talking about it anymore was probably the best therapy. If Jake and Lisa weren't meant to be together, then someone else was still out there. He just had to get out there and start looking. Again.

. . . . .

Angela was on her honeymoon, Ingrid had a baby, and Chad was mad at her. Tim? It was a stretch, but he could be a good listener and he knew Jake. She tried his cell phone. It rang four times before going to voicemail.Would *this* qualify as a good reason to call her parish priest? Somehow it still sounded too insignificant to bother him. She might have a broken heart, but it wasn't like she was actually *dying*. There was one name left on her list.

"Hey, Lisa," David said, sounding upbeat and pleasant. "I was just thinking about you."

"Oh? Why's that?"

"I TiVoed *Dancing with the Stars* and I'm watching it now. They say they're doing merengue, but it doesn't look anything like what you taught me."

"If you're busy, I can call back later."

"No, it's okay. I'm pretty bored, actually."

"How can celebrities be bored?"

"It's the off-season. I have a month or so to go before I head back to the office, so to speak. I've been thinking about going back to Minnesota to visit my parents, maybe do some sightseeing. How are you?"

"Oh, I've been better … ," she trailed off. She should've just written about it in her journal like a normal sad, single woman who's just been spurned instead of crying on the shoulder of his best friend. She despised herself for being so needy in spite of her efforts to be strong.

"You don't sound okay. Did something happen?"

"Well, you said to let you know if I spoke to Jake."

"Yeah?"

"And I finally did. Tonight. I hadn't planned on it, but we were both at this meeting."

"How did it go?"

"I apologized to him and tried my best to explain why I did what I did. And he, more or less, accepted my apology."

"Were you able to work it out?"

"Um …" Fresh tears perched on her lower lids, ready to plop onto her cheeks in fat droplets. "He said he still couldn't be with me, so when you look at it that way—yeah, you could say it was worked out."

"Are you okay with that?"

"I have to be." She felt three droplets splash onto her raw cheeks and brushed them away with her index finger.

"So … if you don't mind my asking, do you have an idea where that might leave us?"

"You and me?"

"Yeah."

She leaned back on her couch and exhaled. Leroy jumped into her lap. The cat looked into her eyes and touched the tip of his nose to hers. His small nose felt dry and cool. She petted him, grateful for the distraction and comfort.

"I don't know what to think," she said. "Right now I suppose it's best if we just stay friends. I'm really sorry to say that to you. You are so wonderful and it's not what I want to be saying, but—"

"I understand. You love Jake."

Emotion squeezed her heart, hearing his declaration. Yes, she did love Jake, even if she'd never told him. Not saying it didn't mean it wasn't true. "Even if he doesn't want me back, I can't just turn it off. And David, I want you to know that I really did think about what you said, because a part of me was attracted to you, too—"

"I understand," he said before she could say anything more. "And if it turns out that all you need is more time, that's okay."

"Thanks for being so nice about it."

"So, what happens now?"

She stroked Leroy's back and the cat began to purr. She sighed again, thankful that she had no more tears. She hated crying. It made her feel weak. "I guess we go on living. What more can we do? I messed up and I can live with that; it's just going to take me awhile. And you? You've got hockey and fans to attend to."

"Well, if you ever need another wedding date, you can call me."

"As long as it's not during hockey season, right?"

"That would make it easier. If I do decide to go to Minnesota, do you mind if I call you?"

"No, not at all."

"Good, then I'll book my flight. Keep August open."

All summer Lisa rode the bus. She had a group of strangers she considered her regulars—those people who rode the bus the same time she did and sat in her general vicinity. A sense of camaraderie had evolved. If one of her regulars was ever short a dime, or needed help carrying groceries, she hopped up in a second.

She rested her head against the window, watching cars and meditating on the now. She watched people board and exit and looked at those on the sidewalks. She studied the colors of their clothing and wondered what their personalities were like. Was the man wearing the houndstooth cap and tan trench coat, sitting across from her reading *The New Yorker*, on his way to the library or to a job?

Such mindlessness was a welcome reprieve from the thousands of thoughts of Jake that crowded her mind. When she stepped out of her life—with its own agenda, troubles, and circle of friends—she saw that the world kept turning at its normal speed. In this space, she could breathe. She was all right.

A reflection of a man in the window caught her attention. She sat up, searching for the face. It was Jake. She was half out of her seat, neck craned, looking for him. Her regulars eyed her warily but made no move. She spotted the man again. Her heart sank as she sat back down. It hadn't been Jake and it hadn't been the first time her mind had played tricks on her. Her favorite regular, the wizened Greek woman who always carried an antique paisley carpetbag with a large handle, asked, "You miss stop?"

"No." Lisa answered. She looked back to the man's reflection in the window. It had looked so much like him.

Since that fateful night in the elevator and Jake's rejection, Lisa had become his spook. She'd taken to haunting every place they'd ever been to together, hoping to bump into him. Her theory was that a serendipitous encounter would improve her chances of getting him back more than if she were to go straight to him and grovel. She'd started running their Lake Calhoun loop twice daily—once in the morning and again in the evening. A couple times a week, she sat for a few hours at the Serene Bean, the coffee shop where it all started. She'd rallied the guys on more than one occasion to go bar hopping, but still—no Jake. Showing up at his office would be one stick short of desperate and she was no Bridget Jones. But something was going to have to change soon, because the sadness was unbearable.

She had loved what she had with Jake. If David had made her feel safe and comfortable, Jake made her feel challenged and stimulated. With him all things were possible and this filled her with excitement.

A week after she spoke with David, he came to Minneapolis. They met for a morning run followed by breakfast. Despite being a professional athlete, he had to put out some effort to keep up with her. She was mildly pleased and let him think she believed him when he claimed he wasn't out of shape—just that running wasn't his sport.

Despite her feelings for Jake and the declaration to remain only friends, Lisa felt a tiny ping of regret for not giving David a chance. During his visit, they'd spent a lot of time together, not only running, but trying a variety of out-of-the-way restaurants and going to outdoor music events. He'd even been willing to tough it out at an art exhibit featuring blank canvases.

Whenever she felt maybe she could have a relationship with him after all, Jake's face slid into position over David's. After two weeks of pseudodating, she gave it up. As Angela reminded her, you can't help who you love.

When they hung out, neither of them said much about Jake. David was spending time with him, too, but she didn't want to know about it. She could only hope that he would put in a good word for her should her name come up.

When the bus stopped in front of the Basilica, she remembered it was the Assumption of Mary, and a holy day of obligation. The sign said Mass was at five thirty. She looked at her watch. Standing abruptly, she murmured a polite goodbye to her bus crew and leapt from the backdoor exit, feeling and hearing the whoosh of air as the door closed behind her.

After dipping her fingers into the holy water, she made a sign of the cross then slid into a back pew. She lowered the kneeler and closed her eyes. Several people toward the front were praying the Rosary and she fell into recitation with them. *Hail Mary, full of grace, the Lord is with Thee ...* She stayed with them through *Hail, Holy Queen.*

During the Mass, Lisa fixed her eyes on a smooth alabaster statue of Mary that had been placed near the altar. A small smile clung to Mary's lips. She thought about Mary's sacrifice, her suffering, her love, her reverence, and finally her veneration. In her heart, Lisa rested her head on Mary's shoulder and imagined Mary's arms wrapped around her, comforting her like a child. The Mass being so ingrained in her, much of what the priest said hadn't registered until he announced he was available for confession.

The confessional wasn't a partitioned closet with a divider and kneeler, but a small room with evening light shining in. A short painted statue of Mary dressed in blue robes holding baby Jesus stood next to an exceptionally prolific fern. A plain wooden cross hung on the wall. Father Daniel sat in a simple wooden arm chair, a bible in hand. A single candle flickered next to the matching empty chair across from him. When she sat opposite him, Father Daniel made the sign of the cross and said, "In the name of the Father, and of the Son, and of the Holy Spirit."

She crossed herself.

"When was your last confession?"

"Last Christmas."

"Okay. Begin when you're ready."

She liked Father Daniel. He was a newer priest in the parish. This was her first confession with him and she wondered if she should start out light or launch into the big sins most pressing on her conscience. She'd heard that Father Daniel had been in a satanic cult before turning to the priesthood. In light of this, perhaps what she had to confess was trivial.

"Well, the most obvious one is that I didn't go to confession at Easter and I didn't fast consistently or give anything up during Lent.

I've used the Lord's name in vain, and have been vain myself. I've had impure thoughts and haven't been honest with someone." She paused there.

"Can you tell me a little more about that?" Father Daniel prompted.

"I was malicious toward someone. I was vengeful and wanted to hurt him and his reputation. I considered him evil without sufficient reason and judged his character very badly."

"Is this a coworker or someone closer to you, like a friend or family member?"

"Both, in a way. I ran into this man a year ago—his name is Jake—and when I saw him, I recognized him immediately. But he didn't remember me, so I didn't say anything. And the reason was because I knew him in high school and didn't like him very much. Honestly, I hated him, so that's another sin, too."

"Did he harm you?"

"No, not in an abusive way. I mean not physically or sexually or anything like that. But I thought he wasn't very nice to me. But it turns out," and here Lisa sort of laughed, "he hardly knew who I was."

"And when were you in high school?"

"Ten years ago."

"I see. And how did you meet this man—Jake?—again?"

"At work. We worked on a project together. Grant Park? Maybe you know about it?"

"Yes, I remember reading about it in the papers."

"Right. Anyway, I wasn't very nice to him and was very judgmental. But over time, it got a little better until this incident where Jake was given credit for the work that we all had done, and I got angry. I was vain, because I wanted the recognition and I was vengeful because I made some inappropriate comments in front of both of our bosses. Ironically, during all of this I fell in love with him, and after the project was over, we started dating. And during this entire time our past never came up."

"And he didn't remember you?"

"I meant to tell him at our ten-year reunion, which was in June, but then a friend of mine needed me to go to the hospital with her. He found out who I was at the reunion. He was so angry. He said that I had lied to him. And he was right."

Rehashing all that had happened, in the presence of a priest, made her tear up. Father Daniel pushed a box of tissues into her reach and waited for her to resume. He reminded Lisa of the nurse Lateefa.

"I eventually apologized, but it took me six weeks and it was too late."

"So, there isn't a romantic relationship between you anymore?"

"There isn't even a friendship between us anymore."

When Father Daniel sensed she was finished, he said, "Well, first I want to tell you that we all struggle with honesty. It can be especially hard when it's embarrassing and even more so when we learn that our perceptions are unfounded. Secondly, Jesus does forgive us. He knows our struggles and he's compassionate, especially concerning issues of the heart."

She nodded her agreement. "What should I do?"

"You've already apologized to him. Now you'll have to decide if it's truly over."

"Do you think I should contact him again?"

"Have you spoken to him since the breakup?"

"No."

Father Daniel said, "I think it's okay to make one more attempt at reconciliation. But understand that reconciliation may not mean dating Jake again, or marriage. It may mean moving on. But at least you would be at peace with it. And place it in the hands of God. His will be done."

"Pray about it?" she asked for clarification.

"Absolutely."

Chapter 32

The doorbell rang, which was weird, because Jake hadn't ordered any pizza.

He opened the door and saw a middle-aged man with a bowling-ball belly and a mesh Vikings baseball cap holding a large vase of flowers.

The man thrust the vase toward Jake. "I have a delivery. Sign here please."

Jake nearly missed the hand-off and tried pushing the pen back into the man's hands. The guy gripped his clipboard and took a step back.

Jake said, "I'm sorry, but I think you have the wrong apartment."

Squinting at his slip of paper, the delivery guy said, "Are you Jake Hanson?"

"Yes."

He pointed to the flowers. "Then those are for you."

Jake signed the paper, returned the pen, and closed the door. He set the vase on the kitchen table and regarded the flowers. There were a dozen white roses, two of which had already started blooming. The vase was heavily etched glass. A square yellow envelope about three inches tall was tucked into a plastic forklike thing among the flowers. It was *weird*. The closest he'd ever come to receiving flowers had been in the form of a boutonniere. He hoped he hadn't incurred a stalker.

After checking the vase for an explosive device, he opened the envelope. Inside was a card with a cover that read "Thinking of You." He opened the card and a piece of folded paper slipped out. As he unfolded the letter and looked at its contents, his curiosity dissolved into a mixture of dismay and heartache.

Dear Jake,

I would like to be able to say I'm sorry until you believe me, but I know you've heard it enough and my saying it now would probably only strengthen your resolve to have nothing more to do with me.

But I'm going to take the chance anyway and tell you again how truly, truly sorry I am. I never thought that I had it in me to behave so badly. I feel ashamed and disappointed that I didn't offer you the same respect and integrity you have always shown me.

You had every right to call me a silly schoolgirl. Rather than respect you as the man you are today, I chose to judge you against the boy I imagined you to be back then. I know I can't expect you to forgive me for that. I'm still in love with you, Jake, and I don't expect that to change, either.

I've been running a lot lately and decided to sign up for the Twin Cities Marathon. I'd like to have a training partner, and if you feel so inclined, you're welcome to join me. We can meet at the usual spot on Lake Calhoun. I know you're really busy, so if you need a few minutes, I can wait.

Lisa

He looked at the attached schedule. Her next run was the following morning at five thirty. That was way too early. He saw that she had some after-work runs, and on her rest day she'd scheduled walking. She had something planned for every single day.

He was so glad Scott didn't live with him anymore. He'd never let up that a girl had sent him flowers.

. . . . .

The first day after Lisa sent the flowers, she was two parts optimistic, one part pessimistic that he'd show up. He didn't. Not on the second day, or the third day, either. Each day, she waited for fifteen minutes. And each day she had a different excuse for his absence. The first morning was too early. The second day, he was working late; the third was too long of a distance. So on the evening of the fourth day, she was hopeful, because it was a walking day. In fact, she was so confident that she waited for twenty-five minutes. He didn't show.

At her confession, Father Daniel had given her the penance of praying the Rosary; then she recited the Act of Contrition and was absolved of her sins. When she thanked him, he said, "You are always welcome. You don't have to wait for confession." Rather than take it as an admonition, she felt encouraged.

That very day, she returned to the sanctuary, prayed the Rosary, then prayed some more, and continued to pray in earnest for a few days after that. Then she woke up and, with her whole being, knew what to do. She would attempt reconciliation.

As a symbol of forgiveness and new beginnings, she had sent Jake a dozen white roses. If he didn't accept them, then she could begin the process of acceptance and take with her the lessons she'd learned in knowing him and what had happened between them. The one blessing in Jake dumping her was for the first time she was able to see that men could love. And men could be hurt.

. . . . .

Dreamt about you in the early morning, time between dreams and conscious thought …

The lyrics drifted out of the stereo speakers.

Dave walked in, heard the music, took one look at the kitchen table, and asked, "What is going on here?"

"What?" Jake knew what he was getting at, but still didn't want to talk about it. "I'm fine."

"Jake. Depressing music and flowers? You're *not* fine."

"They're from Lisa."

"She sent you flowers? When?"

"About a week ago."

"They look good. You must be taking care of them."

"Just changed the water a few times." He offered Dave a glass of water, then pulled out some maps and a notebook, and sat down at the kitchen table.

"Why would she send you flowers?"

"She's doing a marathon and asked me to train with her. So, about this camping trip. Where do you want to go?"

"Why would she send flowers to ask you that?"

"She didn't. She sent the flowers to apologize. She wants to get back together. I think five days in the Boundary Waters would be good. I'll borrow my parents' canoe and we can portage into some really remote areas. Have you ever been to Rainy Lake?"

"And you don't?"

He kept his eyes on the map, feigning indifference. "No, Dave, I don't. On second thought, maybe we should get a cabin and a fishing boat. It would be miserable to camp if it rains."

"Have you even seen her lately?"

Irritated, Jake looked up from the map. "No, I haven't. Now are you here to talk about this damn trip or do you want to cross-examine me some more?"

"Honestly, I think you could use some more cross-examination."

"I get enough of it at work. I don't need it; especially from you."

"Fine." Dave placed his index finger on the map and traced a path. "We can drive up to Ely and enter the Boundary Waters from this point here. Do you want to go into Canada?"

"We could. What kind of gear do you have?"

"Haven't you punished her long enough?"

"I've never heard of that kind of gear before."

"Jake, I'm serious. What does she have to do for you to forgive her?"

He leaned back in his chair. "Nothing. Because I don't care anymore."

"Look, we've been friends a long time and I've seen you with a lot of women. In all of those years, I've never seen you act this way before. That tells me only one thing: you still love her."

"I've already made my decision, Dave. It doesn't matter anymore."

"I think it's the *wrong* decision. She's not perfect Jake, and neither are you. She's pleading her case and I think you should at least hear her out before you have her tried and convicted."

"I already did that."

Dave shook his head. "Either you're really stupid or really arrogant to have that kind of attitude. I've gotten to know her well enough to say—with confidence—that you'd be crazy to give up a woman like that."

"Well, then don't let me stand in your way. She's all yours." Jake stood and walked over to the sink, his back to Dave.

"Are you listening to what I'm telling you?"

He turned around and looked at him angrily. "What's that, Dave? That you're interested in her?"

"Yes, I was," he admitted, without blinking. "But she's chosen you."

"She told you that?"

"Yes."

. . . . .

She took to calling it Solo Saturday because it appeared, again, that she would be by herself. Maybe by next week it would become a term of endearment. She bent over to tie her shoe, the morning sun just starting to warm the day, then glanced at her watch. Nine thirty. Stupid flowers.

She stood up, closed her eyes, and did some deep breathing, windmilling her arms in circles. When she opened her eyes, she saw him.

When Jake approached, the only word she knew how to say was hi, and even that came out like an exhale of wind instead of a real word.

"Hi," he answered.

"Thanks for coming."

"Sorry, I'm late."

"Better late than never," she kidded, not sure whether it was safer to be funny or serious. "Are you ready?"

"Yeah."

She felt his presence next to her as they quickly fell into their old familiar pace. Neither of them spoke and she hadn't expected him to want to. His breathing, his pace, felt both challenging and comfortable. When he pushed her, he made her a better runner. He made her a better person.

"Do you want to go around one more time?" she asked when they returned to their starting point. Her legs felt alive and energetic, her lungs strong. Just a few more minutes with him would be a gift.

"Sure."

This time around, she felt glad. Grateful. Her legs moving in a world of their own, she focused on the peace she felt in her heart. Father Daniel had said it might happen.

When they finished, he asked, "See you tomorrow?"

"Okay."

He looked at her, and she thought he might say something else.

"Bye," he said. He gave a small wave and turned to go.

She watched him walk away from her again. She watched him going farther and farther away. She couldn't move. The fear of losing him again had her petrified. What if he didn't come back tomorrow? Tears of helplessness sprang to her eyes. He was so far away. Her mind shrieked, *Come back! Come back!*

Just then a golden retriever knocked into her, breaking her free from her paralysis. She bolted.

"Jake!" He didn't hear her. She pushed her tired body to run harder. She called again, "Jake! Jake!"

At the street corner, he looked back, then took a step toward her just as she crashed into him, throwing her arms around his neck.

He wrapped his arms around her, his strength nearly crushing her, and lifted her off the ground.

"I'm so sorry, I'm so sorry, I'm so sorry," she blubbered, her wet cheeks chafing against his scratchy stubble. She held on to him, fearful of letting go.

He held her, his arms not stiff, but warm—his embrace safe. She smelled his scent. Everything about him felt *right*. Through her hair he said, "Lisa, I forgive you."

She squeezed him even tighter around the neck, then pulled her head back to look into his eyes.

Then she kissed him.

And he kissed her back.

Acknowledgments

This is the part of the book where I get to gush my thanks to everyone waving from the stands as my book goes out into the world and makes its own way. To the Wise Ink team: Amy Quale, Jennifer Manion, Jessie Sayward Bright, Tiffany Laschinger, and Molly Miller. Thanks, Amy, for believing in Elevator Girl and for the kick in the pants to not let fear stand in the way of my dream. (And a special thank you to Bev Bachel for introducing me to the talented Amy Quale!)

A stack of thanks to the people who reviewed and contributed to earlier drafts: Sonya Anselmo, Bev Bachel, Laurel Baxter, Fr. Don Braukmann, Chet Carlson, Cheryl Christiansen, Jennifer Dahlgren, Cathy Fiorello, Sergio Garcia, Jeanette Granger, Maud Greenhoe, Deidre Hahn, Solveig Harren, Jennifer Hilligoss, Tereza Hruba, Paula Keller, Renata Kingsbury, Trish Klein, Kelsey Koster, Kirby Koster, Lynnette Labelle, Kathy Lainez, Ann Marie Lamser, Dorrie

Lamser, Jan Lamser, Barb Larson, Bridget Lindner, Pat McKeever, Martie Monsrud, Janell Pelland, Lori Schaible, Heidi Schaum, Ron Schmidt, Lea Soltis, Ley Soltis, Kathy Thiele, Caryl Turnow, Michele Thomson, Fr. Paul Vota, and Linnette Werner.

A huge heap of thanks to Ann Marie Lamser for being my constant go-to gal; to my writing partner, Cathy Fiorello; my book club; and to all the men, especially Chet Carlson, who read my book and told me when the guy parts sounded too girly.

A ginormous pile of thanks to all of my crowdfunding supporters for pitching in their pennies to help me publish and to Pubslush for lots of tweets and virtual rah-rahs.

And finally, a mountain range of thanks to my family—my husband for holding down the fort, and our children who endured many, many (many) hours of rewrites, edits, proofs, and cereal for dinner. (Just kidding. I fed everyone. Really. Mostly.)